CW01500643

Praise for
THE FERTILE CRESCENT

———

"...gripping and emotionally charged... Wall's portrayal of Laurent is both raw and relatable. As Laurent navigates the murky waters of a struggling restaurant partnership with Wilson Turner, we are drawn into the tension-filled world of a chef on the edge."

–Charnjit Gill, author of *Pray Tell*

"It's a portrait of creative drive tested to its limit, set against the vibrancy and hardship of a modern New Orleans trying to reclaim its culinary soul.

Author Chadwick Wall has a superb sense of detail and culinary knowledge to bring this story to life. His smooth prose simmers with sensory detail, capturing the chaos and beauty of culinary artistry in post-Katrina New Orleans, giving readers a unique glimpse into a world few would otherwise experience. This is a real character-focused tale where Laurent's inner emotional journey is paramount, and I was invested in the stirring, slow-burn narrative thanks to its emotional depth and cultural resonance. We're right on Laurent Ladnier's shoulder through some really important decisions and evocative challenges that the plot throws at him. This nuanced and unforgettable protagonist has a lot of internal battles that are as compelling as the external ones of the story. Overall, I recommend The Fertile Crescent as a feast of a story that explores ambition and grief with raw honesty and smooth literary grace."

–K. C. Finn, Readers' Favorite

"Whoever has been affected by New Orleans, the Crescent City—especially whoever fully appreciates its food and its music—will want to read this novel written by Chadwick Wall, a native of the city. It is the story of a great chef finding his way in this urban culture of a "whimsical, hedonic spirit" that is unique among American cities. The obstacles that Laurent Ladnier has to overcome—from horrendous potholes through homicidal violence—are true to New Orleans, but also true are its glories that help fashion this innovative fusion chef: the international flavors both of its people and its food, its superlative jazz, and the intense loyalty that it evokes in so many of its citizens."

    – **Jo Ann Kiser**, author of *A Young Woman from the Provinces,*
Sunday People, and *Guitar Player*

THE FERTILE
CRESCENT

THE FERTILE CRESCENT

a novel

CHADWICK WALL

atmosphere press

for my mother Sandra and for the city of New Orleans and its people—living, dead, and those to come

CHAPTER 1

Rosacea splotched his swollen cheeks, his wrinkled forehead, and was so heavy on his pointy, ski-jump nose that it appeared crimson. Dark half-moons sagged under his warm yet bloodshot eyes. My new acquaintance also seemed excessively hungover, his large and heavyset frame sagging in his chair. Surely this New Orleans Falstaff, somewhere in his mid-fifties, had slept too little, and indulged himself far too much, and for too long.

That Saturday night, we sat at the bar in Buffa's, on the border of the French Quarter and the Marigny. The boudin balls, Shrimp Creole, Redfish Beurre Blanc, and several drinks, along with the instant rapport I enjoyed with Wilson Turner, rounded off another fraught day in my kitchen. Food, drink, a kindred spirit: It was my frequent escape—if for a moment—from my reality as a stressed, overworked chef.

We were talking shop, culinary things.

"My foot traffic is down," Wilson said, his eyes watery and drooping under his shaggy yet helmet-like hairdo, one reminiscent of Eric Burdon's or that of some other figure from the British Invasion. He looked wounded, even crushed, as his broad shoulders slumped. "My regulars are falling away, eating elsewhere. I heard chatter around town—some said my quality's suffered, that my kitchen's mailing it in. Suffice it to say, something's gotta change."

I remembered dining in Wilson's restaurant, The Cayenne Club, about five months before—and several times about a decade prior. The chatter did ring true; there was a marked decline. But I would reveal nothing, unless he asked.

"I know that feeling," I said.

I considered my own situation, just as dismal as Wilson's, perhaps worse. Mere months away from turning forty, and those memories had half-faded: my awards at NOCCA, the city's professional arts conservatory, where I'd been seen as a prodigy. My two interviews on local television before graduation, culinary school, and my six months in western Europe as a *stagiaire*, or apprentice, in restaurant kitchens. It was just so very long ago.

I had surrendered it all: my dream since before culinary school of a move to New York City or San Francisco to cut my teeth in top restaurants, before I launched my concept of what I called true world fusion. I'd postponed it for a year, then another, for nearly two decades, all to support my widowed mother, grandmother, and a drug-addicted aunt. And to be present when they needed me. While lulling myself into near complacency with food and drink. Where had it taken me? Running the kitchen of a popular and well-paying but unimaginative Cajun-Creole establishment, Café Bonhomie, owned by a tyrant of a man. Abasing myself.

Wilson's candor—and without me even inquiring—I did find quite moving, even endearing.

"This is on top of being a widower," he said. "I lost Katie years ago. Now I still have my daughter, who lives out west. Won't have much to do with me. But Katie, she was my everything, and I'll never love again. Or try to."

"I'm sorry, Wilson," I said.

"Now I guess I'm resolved to engorge myself, make nonstop love to the plate," Wilson said. "Eat and drink myself to death. I don't care."

He smiled, a weak grin, his gaze limping along the length of the bartop. "Despite all that, Laurent, I still want one more shot at glory in this food scene. Before the curtain draws. Just don't know how to go about that. I'm lacking ideas."

And confidence, I could tell. We shared more, lingering, until I paid my bill and said my goodbye: not a wave and nod, but a spontaneous hug for this deeply wounded soul who one hour before had been a stranger. My new friend was surprised, but I could feel his appreciation.

"We'll talk soon," I said. "Have another foodie adventure."

I had to get back to my apartment, see my girlfriend Noelle, and sleep. Ahead loomed a very big day, even a monumental one. And I could not share the details with Wilson. I could feel it still calling me. My old vision, since I was fifteen—at last, mere months before turning forty, I would chase it. It would begin the next day with a well-planned experiment in my kitchen: a handful of eccentric specials, unapproved by the owner Gerard Lonsdale, an idea he would surely deny.

I could wait no longer for my opening. The occasion I had planned for weeks. Nowhere else could I test my innovations on a large group of diners except in the restaurant where I worked as chef, and Sunday was our best day of the week, and Gerard was still out of town. He had left his cocky son Patterson—twenty-three and recently graduated from Vanderbilt with a history degree and befuddled as to his next move—behind to supervise. And that voice within me swore many times that hot-tempered Gerard would not approve when he caught word. So I opted for asking for forgiveness over permission. Along with our normal Sunday brunch fare, my line would plate unlikely creations for the daily specials: duck and andouille sausage gumbo with notable Asian influences, and an Indian and East Asian version of an old Creole dish, chicken fricassée. How many customers would order them? What would their feedback be? How would Patterson, and later Gerard, react? Even if Gerard grew irate, would I lose my position?

Entering the Armstrong Lofts, I was reminded that sleep would not come just yet. It was a Saturday night, after all. For the thousandth time, I imagined a college dormitory. The top floor of the building was not loud but lively, with many of its studio apartment doors ajar as chatter and music spilled out.

Now to visit Noelle. Though we lived on the same floor, my jazz singer girlfriend and I maintained separate apartments there, just as when we met. A studio for one was small enough as it was.

Her door was open, too, just a crack. I passed down the corridor, holding the rose I'd kept for a few hours on my car's console. I could barely discern the music within: It was her own.

Inside, Noelle Doucet sat at her desk, scrawling in her large Moleskine notebook. I knew that notebook: She was writing new songs. Mostly of love, but many of ambition, of a zest for living, and of new beginnings. Dressed in black stockings and a black velvet skirt, a white long-sleeved shirt with a purple scarf encircling her neck, she had done her dark brown hair into waves, as if to go to a fine dinner, or even dancing. Truly, she was beautiful.

"Baby," I said. "You're listening to your second album. What are you thinking about?"

She looked up, her blue-gray eyes regarding me with skepticism. My Noelle, with her feline aura, shrewd and worldly-wise past her twenty-six years. I approached, extending the single red rose as I kissed her on the mouth. But something had changed. I felt the slightest turning away of her face as our lips connected, but her lips and neck yielded a half a second later.

I hoped she was not cross with me again. Our union had revealed cracks as of late: We had begun to have arguments, mostly over my extreme work schedule, and even the time spent practicing new dishes in my apartment kitchenette. Noelle admitted she had changed her mind and did not want to have children for many years. She had even admitted a dissatisfaction with New Orleans, and a temptation to move to Los Angeles to advance her musical career. Three weeks before, we barely averted a breakup.

"Just thinking about what I could have and should have done differently on this song," she said. "I'm like you: I want perfection in my art."

"Very true," I said.

"Laurent, I thought you were going to start getting off early. Spend time together on a weekend night for once. Now it's past ten."

"What we want and what I have the freedom to do are two different things, my love."

"I taste wine on you. And whiskey. Drink with me, Laurent. Not your kitchen staff. Or strangers."

I chuckled, trying to mask my discomfort.

"Then again, Laurent, you really should stop drinking altogether. At least take a pause."

I sensed we were nearing rocky shoals again. Rather, we were already there. But I needed sleep for what was coming the next morning.

"Noelle, I—I've got to turn in. I promise I'll see you tomorrow afternoon. You know we close early on Sundays."

"If you didn't, I wouldn't see you much 'til Tuesday morning, damn it. Can you take this whole Sunday off? Just this once?"

The idea was impossible, but still delicious. To wander from restaurant to restaurant, this time seated with Noelle in the dining room, hoping for a peak food experience. Hell, even to spend some of the day in bed with Noelle, making love and then sleeping off the stress from the kitchen and my financial woes. Despite me cheffing at the Bonhomie, I was not at the helm of my own establishment, as a chef-owner. Had I missed the train to greatness, somewhere years back, some golden opportunity of a great restaurant job? The trials of being a chef with vast promise and even no spouse or children, yet so many familial obligations.

"Noelle, I can't take tomorrow off. We only close on Tuesdays. And Sunday afternoon."

She sighed. "I'm not sure how it's looking for us, Laurent Ladnier. Fine, get your sleep. But we need to do something special tomorrow afternoon and night. Make it up to me. To us."

"It'll be fantastic, babe," I said, vowing inside to take her somewhere memorable.

"Hmmph," she said as she at last took the rose. I kissed her once more and went for the door.

"Thanks for the rose. Good luck with your big fusion surprise thing, or whatever."

***

There it is again, I thought as I stirred awake: that same dream of the outstretched arms of the live oaks moving above me. Or rather, it was I who moved below their branches. Ever so slowly at first, then faster and faster. In my nostrils, stronger and stronger, swam those scents of cayenne, cardamom, and lemongrass. Then a flash of light signaled the exhilarating part—I was soaring eastward over the rooftops of my city. The Warehouse District, the French Quarter, the Marigny and the Bywater, then swooping north and west over St. Claude, the Tremé and Mid-City, and on to the Garden District. Was it a dream or a fantasy? What was its meaning? I did not know. But it was the tenth, perhaps even the twentieth time—that very same dream.

My phone's alarm sounded. I sat up in bed, blinking my eyes open in the cool stillness, on that morning I had waited for: eight AM on Sunday, January 5, 2014. I looked down at my phone as my heart picked up pace. A few hours remained before the restaurant opened for brunch service. I normally arrived hours earlier, but it had taken me longer to nod off. As I wiped my cheeks with my hands and as the last traces of sleep left me, I recalled the dream before the dream. Once again, I had been preparing a new dish in my sleep. This time with rabbit, andouille sausage, chocolate, cayenne. Wait, chocolate? Yes, raw cacao powder. Must have been the culinary student from Puebla, Mexico, I chatted with days ago. I grabbed my ballpoint pen and pocket Moleskine journal from the bedside table and scrawled the ingredients and cooking directions before they were lost forever. If only I could test this one out in my restaurant. Well—Gerard's restaurant.

Ah, another morning at the Armstrong Artist Lofts. Rent would be five days overdue tomorrow, as I had paid my Aunt LaFaye's medical bill. My friend Ben Hesser, a Tulane music alum from New York and Noelle's bandmate, was playing his trumpet again. His high-spirited jazz, as exuberant as his personality, this time at just past eight in the morning.

I chuckled. I did not mind. In fact, I loved it. The Armstrong Lofts—there was nothing like it anywhere in the city.

Dawn wove through the half-open blinds, illuminating my studio apartment's exposed brick wall with the softest light. I stood, stretching my aching limbs, and staggered to the coffee machine, smashing its button. My ears caught a mechanical tapping down the hall. It was my novelist friend Jim Scoresby, at his 1920s Underwood typewriter. Jim discovered me the year before while writing a food article, then later introduced me to the Lofts. No doubt Jim was now brainstorming or outlining his next novel. How quirky that he drafted his fiction on his laptop, but typed notes and outlines on his Underwood. All this bohemian penthouse floor lacked was a filmmaker, a dancer, and a sculptor spinning a pottery wheel, and then all the arts would be represented.

I passed my tall and densely packed bookcase and stood peering out of the window.

The day had arrived, and I was far more apprehensive than I'd anticipated. I felt squeezed, as if between four enclosing walls. Paying my rent here in the Lofts, while ensuring my father's mother and sister did not lose their house in the Irish Channel, their health insurance, meds, or food. Getting payments here and there to my mother out in Mid-City. Then came today—the day I might lose my chef job if either my project failed or infuriated my hot-tempered boss, who was traveling. And then with no job, it would be weeks before I could make any of those payments.

But it was my watershed moment, and I must adhere to my plan. I must do it for my family, for both families. For those living and dead, my father's French family and my mother's Irish one.

My mission set to begin, both in the attempt and the victory, would honor my father, a failed chef, who perished nearly twenty-seven years before—after years of personal struggles—in a mysterious work incident.

Yet I was my mother's son, her dead ringer, something relatives always mentioned. Several friends also revealed this over the years. And much of what I fought for I did for her. I would disregard that often she shook her head, uttering some cutting remark, dismissing my ambitions.

I would even do it for her Uptown family, the Crowleys. The family that rejected my father when he returned from his tour in Vietnam, in a spiral from heroin. And shunned his mother, sister, and my mother and me for many years after his death. So many from that side still let me know through various means that I was, but was not, of their clan. That I would always be an outsider, more of a distant cousin than a beloved scion. And so I remained a restless wanderer, moving back and forth like a wraith, into and out of both communities, bereft of any true home except in the kitchens where I worked.

As I poured out my coffee, I recalled the key impetus behind me pursuing my dreams at last. Fear that I would, like my father, utterly fail as a visionary chef by age forty.

I grabbed a protein bar from the counter. As I chewed, the irony and incongruity of this act were not lost on me. But I was one of countless chefs who cooked so much at work they often chose to avoid it at home.

I should shower. But that was done last night, before bed.

But there was my shave. Upon entering the bathroom, I recalled my toothpaste had run its course. I could not ask Noelle. She might be sleeping. Or she would comment on my experiment at Gerard's that day being a reckless move. There was one neighbor who would have toothpaste and would not be perturbed.

Yes—Jim. My most whimsical and indulgent friend, a gourmand and bon vivant enamored with restaurants and watering holes as much as myself. I headed down the hall, paused before the door, and knocked.

The typing ceased. Seconds passed. The door opened, and a mixed scent of sandalwood incense, jars of pipe tobacco, and stale beer and wine hit my nostrils. The hungover, sleep-deprived eyes met mine.

"Chef Laurent Ladnier, native N'awlins sensation," Jim said with subdued cheer in his wrinkled white linen shirt punctuated with a single red wine stain on its breast pocket.

"James Scoresby! Writing the great New Orleans novel?"

"Let us hope," Jim said as my eyes caught the gray at his temples amidst his otherwise sandy-blond hair. Despite this, he was two years younger than me, with a face that looked even younger.

"Get some good sleep, Laurent?"

"Not quite. Trouble you for some toothpaste?"

"Come in, bud," Jim said, and opened the door wider.

I stepped inside as Jim headed for his bathroom. My gaze swung across the tall bookshelves, stuffed full of hardbacks of mostly fiction, with some exceptions.

The scent of stale beer and wine grew a bit stronger, overpowering the scent of the pipe tobacco. It reminded me of Jim's dark side. The blackouts, the segments of missing memories from the night before, the shame suffered by a man haunted by so many tragedies and regrets. Behind that jocular exterior hid a grave melancholy. Alcohol was his elixir, the elixir of so many artists, the age-old perilous balm of the spirit. We were alike in so many ways.

Jim returned and placed the toothpaste in my hand.

"Thanks, Jim. So what are you writing this morning?"

He sat before his typewriter, lifted the top portion of its page, and cleared his throat.

"'What a wondrous curiosity New Orleans is, where two opposing forces coexist in equal measure. One will find life at its most vibrant and festive. Yet is it not just as haunted? Reminders of death, murder, and the tragedies of its past are everywhere. It's as jubilant as it is dangerous, gothic, and macabre. No American city is more dead, nor more alive, more at risk of annihilation by nature, while still celebrating, day after day. Despite its economic stagnation and poverty, what city is more creative, for its small population? New Orleans is the fertile crescent, that name once given to the land shadowing the Nile that birthed much civilization. More original music, fine cuisine, architecture, and literature have been born in this crescent-shaped city than in cities far larger.'"

"Beautiful, Jim," I said, "and well put. You're a legend."

"The tone's a bit elevated," he said. "That's my default. But it's part of a very rough draft. So I suppose today's the day. You'll finally test your avant-garde dreams in a restaurant. Albeit on a conservative set of New Orleans customers."

I felt the blood rush to my face. Testing my innovations on the public was a necessity, but at that point I had no other choice than to attempt this in the establishment where I worked. And conservative diners they were.

And wait—Jim had always been supportive. Now my isolation felt absolute. Had he spoken to Noelle, or started doubting me? I had no time to inquire, or debate.

"Today is right," I said. "Can't weasel out because I bought special ingredients for this, and otherwise they'd spoil. Well, I've really got to get going. I'll be getting there late."

CHAPTER 2

T he kitchen thundered with shouts and the sharp ring-
ing of the bell signifying dishes were "put up," ready
for delivery. It wasn't even peak brunchtime and the
line was buzzing, with each station firing on overdrive.

I still loved it. The art of the kitchen lived strong within
me, dwelling in every cell. Nature had passed this to me from
my chef father, but above all, from Mémère, my grandmother
who first trained me as a child. This passion for the kitchen
had melded with my own quirky spirit to produce a love of
preparing unique, even completely original dishes. Original to
the point of the eccentric, while still delicious. I loved this
form of cooking more than decent sleep, financial security,
even my own health.

"Laurent?" a voice called to my right. It was my Vietnamese
American sauté cook, saucier, and lifelong friend, Derek Pham,
spinning on his clubfoot toward the lone figure that always
drew him out of his introversion. Excitement illuminated his
face, like that of an eager child. "Any feedback on our new
plats du jour?"

"Not yet," I mumbled. Anticipation already gnawed at me.

But it was my time. Come what may. So many of my
C-school classmates had gone on to pursue their own dreams
as chefs of renowned restaurants, preparing all manner of cuisines. By now I felt late to the dance—but not irrevocably late.

Long minutes passed, longer as they went. Those glances
from my one true supporter came with greater frequency as
we prepared the orders. Pham, the only one on the kitchen

line who revealed curiosity, in a culinary sense. The only one who had supported each recent brainchild. Water chestnuts, hoisin, and sriracha in duck and andouille sausage gumbo. Red curry, soy sauce, and other South Asian and East Asian ingredients introduced to that old Creole dish, chicken fricassée. The rest of our line seemed bewildered, even amused, but I paid them no mind. And luckily no cook, waiter, or hostess had blown my cover yet to Gerard by calling him on his vacation or notifying his son.

Patterson Lonsdale had arrived late that morning but cloistered himself in his father's office, hypnotized for hours before its desktop computer.

The line continued at its feverish pace, each station preparing its portion of meals. I had bribed all except Pham with a promise of a kitchen party the next week, to keep silent about my experiment.

Along with Pham, I had enlisted my tall and slender, almost gaunt sous chef, Minnesota Brady, to help me prepare the specials. I had ordered the rest of the line to prepare orders from our established menu.

After plating with haste another order of Chicken Curry Fricassée, I slowed my pace. I tenderly applied the garnish, feeling as if I were applying socks onto my infant child. Just taking in the vermilion of the curry sauce made my soul leap. I released a joyous whoop as I seized my squeeze bottle of thick balsamic glaze and autographed the rim of the plate with an LL. Tears obscured my vision. Truly thus far, it was one of the most thrilling days of my life. My old dream still lived and breathed inside me, a dream I sensed I could still will into reality.

I heard Pham whoop in turn, but when I raised my eyes, a smirk tinged the edge of Minnesota's mouth, joining the trace of condescension in his light blue-eyed glance my way. Minnesota was probably back to his old idiosyncrasy: grinding his teeth, the sound masked this time by the growing volume in the kitchen. He pulled the bill of his baseball cap even lower, as if to hide his face, then resumed his hectic pace with the specials.

The gesture was only fitting. I never felt that I could trust my thirty-six-year-old sous. Besides being caught in two lies, Minnesota had admitted to both a worsening cocaine habit—enabled by some family money—and feeling stagnant in his position as sous in his last two kitchens.

Well after the peak of the lunch hour, I had already received five deliveries of gratifying feedback from my servers. Customers enjoyed the specials, after all: I had autographed only my specials and most of those plates returning to the dishwasher were either picked clean, or close to it. I whistled in delight.

I found Pham at his station amidst a victory dance and laughed. Along with the spikes atop his head dyed blond, he looked like a jubilant but rebellious teenager. Then came that pompous voice, off to the side. I turned and looked past Minnesota at the two figures beside the garde manger station. Gerard's son. The waiter Frank stood beside Patterson like a bodyguard.

"Laurent Ladnier," Patterson droned, his cobalt eyes drooping and eyebrows raised in his perpetual expression of bored arrogance. Though his hair was cropped rather short on the sides and back, his bangs of black curls hung down onto his forehead, just north of his eyebrows, completing the image of some aristocratic youth being kept from his daily nap. "What were you thinking with those specials? Why didn't you get approval for those?"

Because I did not care for an immediate rejection, I thought with an inner laugh.

"We now have quite a complaint on the floor, Laurent," Patterson said. "Let's address it. Come with, guy."

Come with? And now I am his young boy. Pompous brat.

That warm, calming light suffused the dining room, as if

from gas lamps, the one feature I fancied in this side of the place. The side I never enjoyed, in all my time at the Café Bonhomie. For the back of the house—the kitchen—was the only world I knew.

As I crossed the half-full dining room at Patterson's heels, sweat broke free on the nape of my neck. I felt myself simmering at medium-high heat.

The child's punishment is underway, I thought. Not the fate I'd anticipated that morning. Not merely a disobedient child bound for a spanking—I felt like a once-proud soldier taken prisoner, bound for a public lashing.

I nodded and waved at the many diners who looked my way. A few smiled with affection, some staring with curiosity and amusement, both perhaps resulting from my flushed face—or was it because of those odd new specials?

Their table swung into view. There were four of them, a gathering that would make a local reporter come sprinting: Senator Jay Broussard, Congressman Hugh Guidry, the investor and socialite Wade Connaughton, and another figure I recognized, staring at me with a flustered expression. Luc Breton, my old NOCCA classmate and ex-friend, regarded by so many as the most polarizing, and mercurial, chef in New Orleans.

"Gentlemen," Patterson said. "I told you I'd bring our bold chef, Laurent Ladnier. Now you can give him your impressions of your lunch, in person." Patterson glanced at me with a strained expression, tweaking with disappointment and urgency, like a father adamant that his son learns a harsh lesson.

"Well, now," said the senator in his dark blue pinstripe suit. "We have some mixed opinions here. I ordered a cup of the gumbo, and I did have the fricassée. I was quite shocked by your spin on both. Not quite used to that. But the more I tasted them—the more I became quite impressed. Love how you autographed the plate, too."

"Why, thank you, Senator," I said, feeling the tension

loosen within my belly like an unwinding coil.

"So what statement are you trying to go for with the—pan-Asian gumbo and fricassée?" Breton said, with rapid blinks and his arms crossing his chest. Something about the man, with his jaw-length shaggy blond hair, his squinting light blue eyes, and his aquiline, broken nose, his tanned face accented by a five-day beard stubble, reminded me of a retired European soccer star-turned-coach. Cementing this image, Breton seemed oddly lean, unlike most chefs, perhaps from the cocaine several in the industry told me he loved.

"Were you just nerding out on it?" he said. "Or experimenting, in some—culinary expedition?"

A closer glance revealed what I'd missed: Breton had pulled his chair a foot from the table and turned it, facing me as if he awaited my arrival. I felt a chill as I imagined him as my shadowy doppelganger: After all, he sported a navy-blue peacoat as I often did, and instead of a red handkerchief, he had twirled a crimson scarf about his neck. Was he mocking me?

"What I intended when I created it," I said, "was to produce something pioneering in terms of Creole and Cajun cookery. There are currently 1,429 restaurants in this city and the majority serve gumbo, and they serve Creole dishes like étouffée and fricassée and there are just the slightest, unimaginative, ordinary differences between most of them. That's boring, de rigueur and old hat. I'm trying to deliver something people haven't tasted in New Orleans. That may sound odd or at least very bold on the menu, but on the palate, it tastes like heaven. Did you at least enjoy the—"

"Absolutely not," Breton shot back. "That's why I ordered your more traditional trout amandine with corn macque choux. I couldn't finish your fricassée."

"Chef Breton, I'm sorry you did not like the special," I lied.

It was clear the man was either narrow-minded, or envious and petty toward a culinary rival, or both. Or—was there a chance I had missed the mark with that dish?

"You didn't like the trout amandine either, did you?" I said.

Breton hesitated, smirking.

"But we do get a lot of call for that trout amandine," I said.

"It was fair," Breton said with a bored sigh. "I won't lie. But the amandine was the same dish I could eat at many other places across town. Simple to prepare, easily plated. And the macque choux? Sautéed corn and diced bell pepper, onions? Neither original, nor difficult to make."

"You're speaking about a dish from our standard menu. That is what I'm trying to present an alternative to," I said. "From the ordinary, endless, sacrosanct tradition in New Orleans. Rich traditions, even unparalleled ones. But there can be monotony."

I heard Patterson *hmmph* beside me.

"As for me, you broke my heart, son," Congressman Guidry said in a gentle baritone. Somewhere in his late seventies and with a calm, affectionate smile, this man in the gray tweed blazer seemed the grandfatherly elder of the table. "When I read the menu, I couldn't believe a man would do that to two of our great South Louisiana staples. I wasn't going to order them, but Senator Broussard here encouraged me. And so my curiosity took over. Now wouldn't you know—I'm in love with that fricassée. And I had a cup of that gumbo. Marvelous stuff."

The heat in my ears vanished and I said, "Aw, why thank you, Congressman, glad to hear. And you, Mr. Connaughton?"

"Simply magnificent, Laurent," Connaughton said as I observed his brown camel hair sport coat, hunter green turtleneck, round-lensed tortoise shell eyeglasses, and small mid-century leather band wristwatch. Though fully salt and pepper, his hair was much like Jim's: short on the sides and back, yet tousled and seemingly windswept on top. "I had your fricassée. You outdid yourself and I've eaten in almost every restaurant in this city. I applaud you following your vision. Don't listen to Mr. Cantankerous. Ol' Luc's just green with jealousy."

Connaughton looked over at Breton and laughed. My, he was so different from his friend. I'd seen them together with their wives in the *Times-Picayune*'s society section and in *St. Charles Living*. I smiled back at Connaughton as I felt the wound to my pride smarting less. I could see why so many found him charming.

"I am glad some of you gentlemen liked it," Patterson said. "But I can see one of you absolutely didn't, and one was put off by the ingredients or description. Rest assured we will be only serving our menu of traditional Cajun and Creole dishes going forward. My father will agree, when he finds out."

Patterson uttered the last line while glaring into my eyes. Then he jerked his head toward the table. "Gentlemen. Suffice it to say I have something that will prove to be a bit of an olive branch, at least to Chef Breton. A digestif for each of you, on the house. And desserts. Your server will bring out menus."

Patterson bowed his head, lips pursed, and with a jerk of his head signaled for me to follow.

I pushed my legs into motion, and made sure my chin remained poised high, though it seemed as if some odd force strained to pull it downward toward my clogs.

Once inside the kitchen, he turned. "Look, we all know how good you are. Still, from now on, you will only prepare what my father approves on the menu. *Capisce?*"

I gave a slight nod.

"Understand, Laurent?"

"I don't, but I will comply, from here on out."

"Then I will help you to understand. Our customers, Laurent, especially our regulars, come here for our usual, traditional offerings. Not for something with any fusion spin. And tourists that come through our door—they're not on the hunt for some Asian-Cajun or Asian-Creole oddball, bizarro concoction. Understand your clientele, Laurent. And respect their preferences."

I glanced beside me. The entire line was staring, listening. For a moment, I caught myself wanting to duck and hide beneath the metal kitchen counter at my side.

I should explain myself at once, before Patterson called his father.

"We should speak in the office, Patterson. About one thing. Not here on the line."

Patterson sighed. "Just tell me here, Laurent. Divulge."

I paused, wondering if I should unleash my private thoughts, or hold off. I glanced behind me. My line was still watching. I felt my face redden as I turned back to Patterson.

"Patterson, when I interviewed here, your father told me this venue serves New American cuisine, along with Cajun-Creole cuisine and Creole Italian dishes. Well, Creole Italian was a pioneering cuisine accepted as mainstream in New Orleans generations ago. I won't even get into how Creole cuisine itself was fusion. East Asian influences are now part of New American cuisine. So understandably, I wanted to produce new conceptions of what food can be. I explored, and I kept just having illuminations. And today I forged my own creation. Chicken Curry Fricassée—so, Creole—but done with an East Asian spin. Chicken and andouille sausage gumbo—so, Cajun—with an East Asian twist, too. What atrocity have I committed?"

"Fair enough, Laurent," Patterson said. "But it's 2014. The public here isn't prepared for it. It might be many, many years before—"

"Really, Patterson? Of the four VIPs at that table, all loved it except for Luc Breton. Come on, now. You know he's the biggest hater on the New Orleans food scene. He could've found it the best meal of his life, and he would have openly condemned it the same. He hates all chefs here. Especially an upstart. Don't be fooled: He hates your father, too."

But I could not expect young Patterson to know what I knew of Breton. Truly, Patterson had scant knowledge of our city's food scene. He was not privy to my teen years as Breton's friend at NOCCA, trouncing him in competitions until the hotheaded Breton aligned himself forevermore as my enemy. Patterson was oblivious to the many firsthand accounts of Luc Breton I'd heard since from chefs, cooks, food writers, and my own observations when dining in Lacassine.

"Laurent, listen. I respect your creativity. I even commend you for it. Okay? I said it. But even so, veer from my father's menu again, or fail to clear one of your newfangled specials with him, and we'll have to immediately part ways with you."

Patterson's eyes enlarged as if he hoped to sear the words into me. Then he turned and whisked himself from the kitchen and down the hall toward his father's office.

Heat surged up my neck and into my face. The eyes of my entire crew were still fixed onto me. Pham looked crestfallen. He blinked his morose eyes at me a moment, then lowered them toward his own Croc clogs.

It stung, discerning this disappointment in my closest friend, who had struggled along with me through our careers, even sleeping on each other's couches between jobs. The one soul whose belief in my abilities in the kitchen was immeasurable.

Minnesota's narrowed eyes were riveted onto mine, the face angled somewhat downward, the eyebrows raised. It was a look of pity, laced with an acknowledgment that his head chef had carried out something strange and inappropriate.

Lucio, Sarah, and Jeansonne nodded as their eyes met my own. I noted the pity within: They had witnessed their chef get dressed down in front of the entire line.

Steps sounded behind me. Ellie, the waitress on table eleven.

"Hey, Chef. Order on eleven—four desserts, four digestifs."

"I've got the desserts," Sarah said.

"Let me see that dupe," Jeansonne said, stepping forward, snatching the yellow paper. "I'll make the drinks."

As brunch service wound down to its close, I longed for the cool January air of the outside break area and headed for the door. I was standing there alone, gazing at the moon—still hung in the early afternoon's azure sky—and feeling the wet slick of sweat on my back when the door creaked open behind me. Minnesota. My sous chef had removed his baseball cap, as if in mourning, releasing those flowing blond bangs. The wild Viking youth, who had voyaged far into the humid marshlands of the frontier. What did Minnesota want? Was he sent by Patterson?

"Rough day, Cap'n," Minnesota said. "I know."

"Oh my, was it," I said. "My day in the lowermost region of hell."

"I love the way you phrase things sometimes, Chef," Minnesota said. "You're a smart one for sure. Hey, I did say you might not wanna test hardcore fusion at Gerard's."

Minnesota pulled something from his back pants pocket. *Not again.*

"Now you don't want to be the second one his son catches in rebellion," I said, though I knew Gerard dabbled in it, too. "Told you never to bring that in here."

"Come on, Monsieur Escoffier," Minnesota said with a wry grin. "Time to let loose a bit."

Minnesota opened the tiny plastic bag and unfolded a small pocketknife. He shoveled a tiny mound of white powder onto the blade, lifted it to his nostril, and snorted.

"You know you want some," he said. "Could use a little bump in your life right about now."

I imagined it: A rush of energy, a sudden sensation of false power and confidence might help me forget the explosion I had just caused in our restaurant.

My gaze fell toward my scuffed clogs as Minnesota snorted more of the cocaine, then released a long sigh of satisfaction.

I recalled my first cousin Champy, lost to the drug game when I was thirteen. A dealer and a lover of that pale demon, the cousin who for much of my boyhood seemed like an older brother. Forever lost to the rock, Big Champy. My eyes started to well up. And then I saw the face of his mother, my Aunt LaFaye, the Ladnier family's albatross. Aunt LaFaye, who became pregnant with Champy at age sixteen. Aunt LaFaye, my father's much younger sister, now fifty-nine, who had wrestled with the same sinister trap of that white poison, off and on throughout the years.

Hold steady, I thought. Proceed at an even keel. Make no such moves—at least for them.

"No thanks, Minnesota. You just don't know. I just can't do it."

"No big deal, brother. I respect it. Just wantin' to have a good time with you."

"I will ask you for one thing," I said, even though I knew I shouldn't, as it might affect my palate. "One of your cigs. That, Minnesota, I can do."

Minnesota closed the bag with his other hand and returned it with the pocketknife to his back pocket. He reached into his kitchen whites, fished out two Camels from his pack, and handed one over. He lit mine with his Zippo, then placed the other cigarette between his lips and lit it.

"Now you're in business," he said.

I exhaled the smoke as I gazed into the clear blue sky. Gerard did not have me bound by golden handcuffs, but I'd grown so comfortable at Café Bonhomie for the good pay, which was far better than most kitchens in the city.

But my time for some kind of endgame had arrived. Gerard and his restaurant were stifling my creativity, my dreams. There was but one more experiment I should launch, in my last days there. A catering job of my latest dishes. I would purchase the ingredients, but must use Gerard's trays, pans, and kitchen, on a Sunday evening when the restaurant had been closed for many hours. This project would be completely clandestine, save for one person. I would approach Pham and give him the option to participate. Though I knew he would accept.

Yes, that was it: Wade Connaughton would be the first I'd approach. I'd read of his dinner parties in *St. Charles Living*, and I had seen the photos. And it was clear he liked my specials.

I glanced at Minnesota. He puffed his cigarette in silence, staring also into the sky, his other hand on his hip.

Gerard would uncover my catering project, no doubt, after the fact, and would be enraged. He most likely would fire me. My greatest worry was not that it might prove hard to get hired in a good New Orleans restaurant after that. It was the financial toll it would take in the interim.

I should visit my grandmother that afternoon, before I took Noelle out. I wanted to ask my grandmother and my aunt again about that one person who kept appearing in my thoughts, more and more, as I approached my fortieth birthday, looming a few months off. My father, once locally celebrated to a degree, before this food scene and profession had crushed him, not long before he lost his life.

I felt someone watching me. Minnesota was holding his cigarette a few inches from his face, his light blue eyes narrowed and studying me with keen curiosity.

CHAPTER 3

I t was near four in the afternoon when I rolled up to that Irish Channel shotgun house on Annunciation Street, and I could see her lights on within. My grandmother, Madeleine Montreuil Ladnier, known to me by that old French term for Grandma, Mémère. Who viewed me as her favorite in the whole family, something we all knew she'd never admit. The one she loved so much, the one she prayed over whenever he left her house, as a boy.

She probably would notice I looked spent. Almost haggard. Yet she had warned me for so many years a chef's life was no stroll in the park. She'd lived it. As had my granddaddy, or Pépère.

Someone was peering through the blinds when I ascended the few steps to the front porch. Before I could knock, the door opened. Dressed in one of the florid and embroidered duster robes she always wore around the house, Mémère smiled as her warm, light brown eyes lowered to one of Pépère's old cooking handkerchiefs tied around my neck. The ones I had started to wear as a boy.

"Aw, Mémère, great to see you," I said, stepping within and embracing her. Even Mémère's snow-white chin-length bob smelled like gumbo.

"You make my day so much better, Laurent."

"Mémère, you've got something simmering on that stove. And I know what it is."

"My gumbo you love. Come in quick, baby," she told me. "Last three days, your aunt's been up to no good. Come see."

"Well, now," I said, following her. "Did we expect any change?"

My Aunt LaFaye Adams was reclining on the couch, eyes closed, her dyed-blonde hair disheveled as a rat's nest. Mémère had dressed her in one of her own duster robes, but a plain white one. I grasped the irony: It resembled a hospital patient's gown.

Another morning, strung out from another long, wild night at her friend's house playing cards. No way it was just alcohol. I knew better from so many years of witnessing her struggles, habits. It was hopeless. But this time, Aunt LaFaye and Mémère were almost flat broke. No more money for Aunt LaFaye's rehab. And this time Mémère had hidden everything Aunt LaFaye could steal. Buried cash and cards in double-bagged Ziploc sacks in the dirt under the house. Mémère would refuse for three straight days to let her leave, while she recovered. And if Aunt LaFaye fought her on it, my grandmother would call me.

"Auntie?" I said. "You did it again, didn't you?"

"Why y'all gotta both be after me?" she said, her eyes still shut as she wiped the palms of her hands down over her wrinkled cheeks. Fresh burns from the pipe punctuated her lips. "Gangin' up on me. You just don't know how hard it is. It never ends. Only thing can cure it is dyin'. You want that?"

At the sofa's edge, I stared down at my dead father's only sibling. Named by Pépère after his grandfather, Jean Fayard. The crosshatch of wrinkles on her cheeks, forehead, and around her eyes seemed to have grown deeper. All at once I felt the rush of pity and love, frustration and disappointment as I shook my head and bent down and held her. That smell of dried sweat, perfume, cigarette smoke, and liquor met my nostrils. I recalled that first time, fifteen years before, that I'd put her in my car and whisked her into rehab. I had been so full of hope, but after several attempts through the years, I expected nothing.

"Auntie," I said, "if you'd just do what Mémère tells you to, the cycle would end."

Aunt LaFaye turned her head away, inhaling hard through her nostrils as if she were snorting a line of cocaine.

The sound evoked a scene long since passed. It was a sunny but breezy late spring morning in 1987, and I had just turned thirteen. The end of the good years. Champy, my father, and I were in the street, throwing a football in front of Mémère's Irish Channel house. Even Big Bobby Adams—Champy's father and Aunt LaFaye's husband—was in the game. Mémère and Pépère sat in their front porch rockers, watching us, along with my mother and Aunt LaFaye.

It was the last time I could remember that we were all together.

My father and I comprised one team. Champy and Big Bobby were on the other, and they were ahead by seven. I was faster, but Champy was older and taller, and I couldn't block him well. But within fifteen minutes, Dad and I had pulled even at fourteen points due to my speed and Dad's still-solid throwing arm, as an ex-Redemptorist High quarterback.

Champy snapped the ball and Big Bobby fell back, but when he found Champy and tossed the ball, Dad slapped it down.

"Hoo-ah!" Dad yelled—perhaps a remnant from his Army days. Big Bobby cursed, then apologized and looked over at the seated row of four spectators.

Dad and I made that last touchdown. I scrambled and then sprinted free and looked for his pass. He tossed as fast as he could without breaking my hand, it seemed. I grabbed the ball and clutched it to my chest like it was a bag of gold. Disbelief came over me as Champy arrived a moment too late.

"Short round, you clinched it," he said, smiling. Champy ran his hand roughly through the waves atop my head, with both affection and frustration.

We heard the rap music thundering down the street, then the shiny 1960s-era Buick rolling near, and we stepped out of the road. We all recognized that car. Our whole side of the neighborhood did.

The sensation of danger crashed onto me like a wave as Dad pushed me behind him. Pépère stood with a scowl. I peered past Dad's hip at the tinted windows as the engine revved. Yet it wasn't like in the movies, where the four tinted windows came down, revealing blinged-out gangsters. The deeply tinted windows remained up the entire time. None of us knew who sat inside, except my cousin.

The car lurched forward, then hurtled onward as we all stood with unease, looking at Champy.

"You need to start steerin' clear of those folks, nephew," Dad said. "You hear?"

"Yeah, you heard him," Big Bobby joined in. "Will be the death of you. And maybe us."

Within a year, almost as if from a curse: Champy was found shot dead in the Hoffman Triangle, on a street notorious for crack deals. Along with her drinking habit, Aunt LaFaye delved into coke, then buried herself in it, out of sheer grief. She got Big Bobby hooked on it, and soon he abandoned her and vanished, forever. Months later, after years of so many personal setbacks and wrestling with the bottle and worse, Dad fell to his death into the Mississippi while working with his crew on the Crescent City Connection bridge. Mom moved with me to Mid-City. A massive heart attack claimed Pépère, from the sheer loss of it all. Aunt LaFaye moved in with Mémère and became her daily struggle.

All of this because of that damned white powder.

I shook my head, then walked toward the kitchen.

"Mémère, let's see if we can get some of that gumbo into my aunt."

I lowered my face right above the pot as I pulled off the lid and stirred with her wooden spatula. I heard myself moan.

The smell of Mémère's gumbo conjured up that memory that often calmed my worries: those Réveillon dinners that she so excelled at preparing. That old New Orleans tradition from the French, conceived in the early 1800s, that almost disappeared in the 1940s but enjoyed a revival in the 1990s. Mémère would serve the Réveillon feast after we had returned from Midnight Mass. When she was sober, Aunt LaFaye was even a spirited participant in the kitchen for those.

"You know, Mémère," I said, "this gumbo was the first meal I ever had that was entirely perfect. That spurred me on to dream of becoming a chef. Remember?"

"Oh I haven't forgotten," she said. "You wanted to eat one bowl after another, even as a little boy. Then you asked to help make it. Remember what you wanted to do with that gumbo from almost day one?"

I smiled. I knew. One of the first times I'd helped, I wanted to add new ingredients from the pantry and the spice cabinet. Then at the grocery I'd asked Mémère to buy all these bold new ingredients, some she had never heard of despite her decades as a cook. Sometimes she would let me design and cook the whole pot. I always swore her original was perfect, but I still wanted to branch out on my own. My defining trait had set in, even then.

My grandmother once told me she knew I was destined for interesting things when I ate at her place or at a relative's or in some restaurant, and I'd take out a pen and scrawl on a napkin, envelope, paper tablecloth, or whatever was lying around. I would guess all the ingredients in whatever dish I tasted, and if she had made it, she would confirm. I was almost never wrong.

"Mémère, yesterday in my kitchen I tried to channel my love for innovating. Owner's son hit the ceiling. Even though most of our customers who had my specials gave good feedback."

"I love ya, baby," Mémère said. "But like I told you, New Orleans is not the easiest place for that. Usually only tourists and the young people will be open to it. Least at the beginning."

I didn't reply, but stood there, my arms folded, gazing back at my aunt now snoring on the couch.

"But—Laurent, if that's what's in your heart, if that's what your heart's calling you over and over to do, above all—you should chase it. Because it won't be going away, otherwise."

"It's what's been burning inside me for so long," I said. "My greatest urge, in cooking. My strongest instinct. And a dream I can never extinguish, or even bury. You know I always come to you. You made me who I am, taught me the kitchen—kitchen arts—from the time I was five, six."

"Then you gotta pursue it, grandson," she said with a laugh, despite her serious eyes. "Though we can't predict how people here will react."

Relief cooled my hot brow, almost like an ocean breeze. I felt she had given me her blessing, after all. But one thing remained worth mentioning.

"What worries me," I said, bringing my eyes down to my shoes, "is I've gotta keep the money coming in. For you, and Aunt LaFaye. And some for Mom."

"I appreciate all you do, Laurent."

"Thanks, Mémère. I love you," I said and started toward her, as her face beamed and her arms outstretched for my embrace.

I held her tight, resting my cheek on her head.

"Before I forget, I have something for you," she said, and broke free and grabbed something from her kitchen table.

She held the royal blue handkerchief, folded into a square, toward me. "Here's another one to add to your collection. Take care of this because this is my last one. This was your Pépère's."

"Aw, thank you so much," I said, blinking away tears, placing it inside the breast pocket of my peacoat.

"Wear it, and keep remembering your grandaddy," Mémère said, placing her hands onto my head as if blessing me. It brought back all the times she prayed over me as a boy.

"Always," I said.

"Grandson, know who you remind me of? So much. The resemblance—it's unmistakable."

"My Pépère?"

"No, your daddy. I'm seeing and hearing it again, right now."

Flattering it was, but also startling. I remembered the dashing man who for some years charmed the New Orleans food scene, not long before he fell to a watery death.

"Are you sure about that?" I said. "I look and sound nothing like the man. And I still remember him, you know."

"All right, then."

"But thanks for the compliment, Mémère. God, I miss him."

"You're sure not the only one. Twenty-seven years gone."

My eyes caught one of his framed pictures, and I walked into the hallway. Mémère followed. I turned on the light, leaning toward the frame.

"Where did he go? Where do they all go?" The words trickled from my lips in a mumble. "I've always wondered if we'll see him again. And if he's watching us."

Dead, cold silence ensued as I walked back into the kitchen, my grandmother turning and joining me. I lowered myself into a chair at the kitchen table and paused.

"Mémère, there's something about him I wanted to ask. I've been thinking of him a lot lately. The closer I get to his age when he died."

I would not reveal that recurring thought: If I failed in my top dream as a chef, and then cut my life short—at least through my own habits—I might meet an end like my father's.

"Laurent, he fell off the GNO Bridge while doing some repairs with his crew. Well, your generation calls the bridge the Crescent City Connection. Anyway, we'll never know what truly happened. The details. Is that what you were going to ask about?"

"Not completely. But that was part of it. It just never got resolved: suicide or accident."

"It had to be an accident, Laurent. Don't disturb the dead. Let Claude rest in peace. He didn't want to die."

I recalled that rumor I'd heard, and wondered if it had merit, that Dad longed to escape his family. The burden, the stress from supporting several of us, while the demons of his past—combat in Vietnam, humiliation from his professional and financial failures Uptown—sapped his energy.

"The rumor that he tried to take his life months before—that never happened, right?"

"Grandson, that's an urban legend in your mother Mary Anne's family. No, he did not."

"Myths, assumptions," LaFaye said from the couch. She could hear us.

"Aunt LaFaye?" I stood and walked over to her. She did not raise her head, nor open her eyes. "You think clearly for being so hungover. Tell me."

"Laurent, you remember that guy on the crew your father told me and your mother about? Guy named Rodney. Rodney Reynolds."

"Of course I remember, Aunt LaFaye."

"Guy was so jealous of your dad. Police questioned him and the whole crew after, twice. Rodney and this other guy on the crew said your dad didn't make a sound as he fell. But a couple other men said they heard his scream, clearly. Rodney swore Claude took his own life."

"But Dad had to unhook his harness, right? Investigation found nothing had snapped, nothing was compromised."

"Right," Aunt LaFaye said. "That's part of the mystery, nephew. No suicide note. Claude was unsecured, somehow, and he fell like a rock. And not from the base, one hundred and seventy feet up, where the cars drive across. He fell from near the top, near the frickin' crest. One of the steel beams in the trusses up there. About three hundred sixty-five feet down and hit the water. Coroner said it broke his back and fractured so many of his bones, instantly. Had to have been knocked clean out. He didn't feel anything past that. They found him days later. Downstream, in St. Bernard Parish."

"And as much as he drank," my grandmother said, "and as much as he messed with pills and worse, his toxicology report came back squeaky clean. He had nothin' in him."

"Truly," I said with a sigh, "a mystery."

"One day we'll know the answers," Mémère said.

But I would at last try to find those answers. Though the police had closed the case decades ago. Before leaving to meet Noelle at the Lofts, I'd look for Reynolds in Mémère's phone book—and call him in the next few days.

"Answers? Ha, only in the next life," Aunt LaFaye said.

"I do think Dad took his life," I said. "But there being no suicide note, I want to try to confirm why. Somehow."

"Proof? Good luck, nephew," Aunt LaFaye said. "Mama, can you give me some o' that gumbo? Head's killin' me."

Aunt LaFaye's eyes opened at last, and I was reminded of that bottomless depth of dejection within, an expression that after decades never seemed to abate. She rose with an almost glacial motion from the couch and shuffled into the kitchen. I imagined her emerging from a cemetery crypt, then treading away. I followed.

"Nephew?" she said, turning her head and then bloodshot eyes my way. "Now, what's this about you tryin' out strange concoctions in that restaurant?"

I shook my head, forcing a smile as I pulled out a kitchen table chair for her. She must eat, and I must leave for the Lofts, for Noelle.

CHAPTER 4

I parked in the gravel and shells against the levee and our group—Jim, Ben, Pham, Noelle, and I—crossed Barracks Street toward the two-centuries-old corner building housing one of my favorite venues in the city. I could discern something magical in the air—something beautiful was about to happen. After all, it was Bacchanal, of all places.

I squeezed Noelle's arm and she raised her eyebrows, smiling at me with delight under that broadbrimmed felt pink hat, her firehouse-red feathery boa looped around her neck. I had kept my word to her, to take her out that Sunday evening and night, and she had surprised me—but had not disappointed me—by inviting the others. I just wanted her happy.

We approached that square old Creole building, its façade that classic French Colonial mixture of gray stucco and, in places, exposed red brick, punctuated by a single sign of dark, weathered, and unpainted wood bearing its name.

"This is quite the wine spot," I said. "Been here before?"

"A few times," Noelle said. "Ha, remember how much wine we had that first night together at the Corporation Bar?"

"Now, you know I rarely drink," I said as we stepped inside. I looked askance at her with a smile.

"Sure, mister. When you do, you really fall in," she said, squeezing my arm.

Shame burned in my face. Somewhere deep inside, I knew she was right. It was one of the main impediments that had slowed my rise.

I could hear Jim, Pham, and Ben lingering just a few steps

behind. Jim was recounting his many great times in the place.

Once inside, my author friend clapped his hands together and then held them outward toward the walls of wine bottles and refrigerators of cheese. His widening eyes illuminated his face by some odd sort of enchantment, even possession, as if he was the first archeologist inside of a pharaoh's treasure-filled tomb. Here was an adventurer enthralled, standing before his new frontier—and I'm not sure the cheese was much of a factor.

"Ah, heaven. Simply heaven," Jim said. "Let's indulge in a little Bacchanalia, shall we? Of the low-key variety. Y'all go grab a table. I'll score some wine and cheese in here and bring 'em out."

"I'll help him bring it out," Pham said.

"Thanks, gents," I said. "I'll order the small dishes out back."

I passed the cluster of young hipsters at the counter, one sporting a gray top hat with a dark blue scarf encircling his neck, and squeezed Noelle's hand as we led Ben down the short corridor into the cool air of the rear yard.

Memories from the days before intruded on my mind, but once again I pushed them out. Patterson humiliating me for my experiment, and so many close to me—Mémère, Aunt LaFaye, Noelle, Jim—relaying their doubts of my plans. But Bacchanal was built around forgetting the worries of the week. And Noelle would help.

"Ohhh, I love this place," Noelle said. "I love the courtyard sooo much more in the winter."

"I'll second that. Winter version for me," Ben said. "I didn't leave New York and move down here for the summer weather, that's for sure."

"Noelle will keep us all warm with her hotness," I said. "She's just radiating heat."

She flashed a bright smile and winked.

Patrons sat warming themselves beside heat lamps pushed

close against the tables, watching the stage beyond. Bebop, Latin Jazz, and New Orleans jazz acts usually performed, but that afternoon a funk rock quartet topped the stage.

I spotted an open table at the far-left edge of the patio and pointed.

"That one over there, my beautiful songstress," I said, heading toward it. I pulled out a chair for Noelle and we sat. Ben lowered himself into his chair and, a moment later, Jim and Pham appeared on the far side of the patio.

Jim neared us like a giddy child, a paper bag in hand and a bottle of red under each arm. Pham held the cluster of glasses in a cardboard wine bottle carrier.

"Now the party will commence," Jim said as he set the bottles on the table and opened the bag. Jim uncorked one bottle, and then the other. Appearing behind Jim was a thirtysomething white man with red-lensed sunglasses upon his aquiline nose, a longish puff of curly blond hair, and Mardi Gras beads around his neck. He slapped his hands onto Jim's shoulders. Jim spun and gave the man a warm handshake.

"Russell! Mr. Russell Ledoux!" Jim said. "I present to y'all the illustrious and uber-cool manager of this fine establishment."

The man smiled and waved. "Welcome, Jim and crew! Told myself I need to come say hi to all y'all. Hope you enjoy what I put together today."

"We love this place, Russell!" Noelle said.

"Well, Noelle Doucet, I love your latest album," Russell said. "Great to see ya here. Yep, this is an amazing place, awright. I'm hopin' it's here for generations."

"Oh, I forgot to introduce you to my friends here, Russell," Jim said. "You know our superstar, Noelle. Here at my left is Mr. Ben Hesser, my good pal and jazz sensation. And he's Noelle's right arm."

Ben blushed, and for a moment, lowered his gaze and head of light copper curls, thinning despite his twenty-six years.

"And now for the chefs," Jim said. "Here on my right is

Pham, sauté cook at Café Bonhomie in the Warehouse District. Pham's the only one at the table who doesn't live with me in the Armstrong Lofts down on Constance Street. Sitting at the head over there is Pham's chef, my good pal Laurent Ladnier. I'd venture to put my wager on it; you're looking at a culinary genius there. A true alchemist. Really, he grew up a prodigy and—"

"Actually, wait—I know Laurent," Russell said, smiling and pointing. "You're almost a regular. You *really* love your food and wine."

I suppose that is what others remembered. As I arranged the glasses before us, my voice sounded subdued in my ears, "That's yours truly."

"Yep," Jim said. "There's more talent around this table than at a Pulitzer award ceremony."

"I think so," Russell said in a voice hoarse, I imagined, from cigarettes and booze as he withdrew to greet another table. "Nice seein' y'all. You better have the time of ya life, baby."

A true New Orleans character. Just the type that helped me keep loving my home city, again and again.

I drew in a profound breath. I wasn't fully free, but maybe as free as I'd ever be. Still no children yet, though I wanted them. As much as I loved my family and New Orleans, it was technically possible that I could leave for a few years. I could return to Europe, but this time bring Noelle. Backpack again until I found a restaurateur to win over with a display of my skills. I could venture instead into Asia this time. We could start in Shanghai and make our way down to Vietnam. I could line-cook in hotels while Noelle bartended, and we could eat our way down to Saigon—or Ho Chi Minh City, the home city of Ong Ngoai, my father's close friend still in New Orleans East.

Exciting fantasy, and perhaps possibility, but it was not the time. I had explored Europe enough to soak up much inspiration and influences, with enough time as an apprentice. Asia would be ideal but not now. My one surviving grandparent was older, and I wanted to be there for her, and to help her, Aunt LaFaye, and Mom with bills, property taxes. Just as much, I longed to triumph in their midst. Not them reading about my enchanted life in New York or London—I envisioned them eating in my own innovative restaurant in our hometown and seeing me cook again on WWL-TV. Mémère was like a theatergoer, seated and watching the performance of her long, often painful life draw to a curtain close. She lost her son before his time, her grieving husband fell dead in her presence, and her daughter destroyed her own life and survived only as a zombie. I so longed to give Mémère one of the most exciting interludes of her life. A time to rejoice, of jubilation—and not a mere passing moment—near the end of her eighty-three years.

And then there was Noelle. As troubled as our union had grown lately, I had not lost her.

As the others conversed, Noelle and I sat in silence, sipping our wine, observing the band. Russell wandered through the courtyard, lighting the tiki torches. Someone turned on the strings of lights over the garden patio. That Bacchanal magic was almost complete. Later that night, the Brazilian jazz group, a mainstay of the venue, would take the stage.

"So what should we do about food?" Noelle said, leaning over the table as she held her sides, allowing her porcelain upper chest to move forward into view. "This delicious cheese is just making me hungrier."

"I'll take care of that," I said, rising. "My turn. I'll order some dishes for the table."

The group sounded their assent, and I wound my way through the tables to the window of the outdoor kitchen.

The smell of crepes hit me, then some divine aroma of stewed meat. I glanced past the empty counter and scanned the day's menu scrawled on the chalkboard beyond.

"What am I smelling?" I called out into the kitchen.

"Would that be the beef bourguignon? I smell wine and beef."

"Hey, I cooked that one," a young man's voice said. "You can already taste it through your nose, huh?"

"Almost, but I'll be having it soon," I said.

The young man turned from the stove and approached. It was the square-jawed Hispanic man I'd seen cooking there. A definite talent. Lean and well-muscled, he seemed a few years before thirty, with his sleek brown hair shorn into a fashionable undercut.

"I'll take an order of that beef bourguignon and two of your lemon and sugar crepes," I said. "An order of your pad thai, too. Then I'll take some of your mushroom quiche there."

"I like it, I like it," he said, scrawling in his pocket steno pad, then tearing out the page. "One minute." He walked into the kitchen and handed it to one of two figures near the stove.

When he reappeared, I handed him my credit card, which he swiped.

"Hey," he said, pointing at me with confidence. "You're Lawrence Laneer? The chef on WWL years back?"

There it was again. He was one of several I had encountered in the city who recalled that interview but otherwise knew little or nothing of my work.

"Good memory. But the name's Laurent *Ladnier*," I said, smiling at his transformation of my father's Alsatian surname. "That story ran when I won an alumni award from NOCCA."

He handed me my card and the receipt. As I signed it, he said, "You know, I've watched all the WWL recordings on chefs, cooking shows. Always lookin' to improve."

The young man scrawled something else on his pocket steno pad. He looked behind him to ensure his crew wasn't watching, drew closer and handed me the paper, then shook my hand.

"Mr. Laurent, Ramón Aguirre. I cooked your beef bourguignon, and that pad thai. Baked that quiche too. If you love 'em, shoot me a call. Always wanted to work for a top kitchen.

Guessing you probably got one now," he whispered with a wink.

My stomach dropped. But I looked harder—the eyes were sincere.

"It's a kitchen. My line's a bit full up," I said. "But I just might call you."

"One second," Ramón said and vanished once more into the kitchen. A minute later he reappeared with a tray of plastic utensils wrapped in paper napkins, and paper plates topped with steaming food. I grabbed some extra paper plates at the stack in the window, thanked him, and headed out across the patio.

Yet even if I liked Ramón, and his skills checked out, I could not poach from the likes of Russell Ledoux and Bacchanal's kindly founder, Chris Rudge. Only if Ramón had already quit by the interview.

My eyes swam through the tables of patrons, some bobbing their heads to the music. The band, complete with sax, synth, and bass guitar, had struck up a faster, livelier rendition of the Meters' funk classic, "They All Ask'd for You."

I found our table, about thirty feet ahead. Rather, the flash of that red boa found me. Noelle was on her feet as she faced the stage, her hips swaying to the rhythm, her arms held aloft. As I neared, I smiled. Her eyes were closed in bliss, the boa framing each side of her ample bosom. She was just so *fun*. I paused in my walk, my eyes feasting upon the arresting image. As clear as day, I felt it: I always wanted her at my side. That desire seemed in that moment like some mighty hunger that could hardly be abated. But I must always gratify her and demonstrate my devotion. Our union would not simply take care of itself.

As the daylight faded toward dusk, we headed to our vehicles, then, to crown the evening, we reconvened at a place few New Orleanians ever sought out, or even entered. On the opposite western end of the city from Bacchanal, but still on the northern side of the river. These long early-twentieth-century brick warehouses up against the Mississippi, at the far southern rim of Uptown. Most of the buildings were abandoned, and looked it. They always brought to my mind the abandoned factories and warehouses of some Rust Belt city. Crumbling brick edifices graffitied and populated by no life-forms save rats and ivy, some with a few trees even growing through them.

Perhaps we would lose most of those buildings before they could be reborn as apartment and condo complexes, malls, and food courts. But I believed at least one of them would be saved—the one featuring the fundraiser art show that night.

We parked in the crowded lot against one of its graffiti-coated walls. Noelle, Ben, Jim, Pham, and I crossed the asphalt pavement as I eyed the weeds sprouting through its cracks. The soaring wall loomed above us, a monument to a time when New Orleans, like Detroit and Buffalo, was a major industrial and commercial player. It looked more like a monument to urban decay than anything. But when we handed our tickets to the doorman and breezed inside, I was taken aback by the vitality within. Across the vast swept concrete floor stood scores of attendees, many examining the paintings, photos, and sculptures displayed along the well-lit inside walls as jazz played on some unseen stereo.

We strolled along those walls, examining the art illuminated by battery-powered lamps.

"Are y'all thinking what I'm thinking?" Jim said, turning our way.

"Probably," Pham said, smiling. "Beside all of this art being quite—aggressively priced?"

"Exactly," Jim said. "Most of these guys are early thirties and younger. Several years younger than you and Laurent and me. They're commanding those prices and aren't yet well-known. Fifteen hundred dollars, twenty-one hundred dollars, hell, I've seen four grand for an oil or acrylic painting. Two grand for a large black-and-white photo. From local artists I've never seen before."

Noelle said, "Maybe the prices are higher 'cause some of the proceeds go to saving this building."

"Good point," Jim said. "But I saw these inflated prices at the Riverwalk Art Fest, few months back. And a gallery event for different artists on Magazine two weeks ago. Neither involved a charity. Perhaps at some point, this became the new normal."

I stood there in silence, swiveling my gaze across the building at the exhibitors along the opposite wall. Men and women, of different races, in starkly varied types of dress, but a majority in their twenties and early thirties. Whether or not Jim was correct, these artists had followed the clarion call within their souls. And the public was on the other end of this, devouring their art.

Had I missed the chance to embark on my own voyage? When would my moment arrive? Or rather, when would I seize my moment?

As I swept my eyes from Noelle past Ben and Jim to Pham, it came to me. Just how I would do it. A restaurant offering an amalgam of East Asian, South Asian, and traditional south Louisiana cuisine, with some Middle Eastern, namely Persian strains. I glanced at Ben—yes, New York—I would mix in some of the better American trends. Who could I approach with my business proposition? Who had the least to lose?

My first try would be with Wilson, that bighearted, hard-living owner of the Cayenne Club, the run-of-the-mill Warehouse District Cajun and Creole spot. A once-proud ship now sinking ever so slowly beneath the waves, a venue in sore need of reinvention. By our conversation the night before at Buffa's, my new friend grasped this full well. And in true New Orleans spirit, I would lobby Wilson to have a section, a corner in the dining room for musical performers. It could also be a great means to get Noelle and Ben more exposure, to locals and tourists alike.

I recalled Wilson's words and body language. I saw and heard a broken man. Yet through all his barstool venting, his midriff bloated and face reddened by years of drink, I sensed he'd be open to a change. He had almost nothing to lose. But he might have so much to give.

Yes, Wilson Turner. The very axle upon which my life could turn.

A second idea surfaced: I'd forgotten to call Connaughton and suggest I cater the next one of his storied cocktail and dinner parties. This I would do back at my apartment.

My leisurely evening and night transformed into a pressure-cooker of anxiety as the anticipation gnawed at me. At last, I crossed the threshold of the Lofts.

"Be right back, will meet you in your place," I said to Noelle. "Have to make a quick call. Business."

I wanted to not wait for her reaction, but I at least owed her a moment of reassurance. Our eyes connected and I nodded once, biting my lip.

Her eyes grew larger, her lips parting as her shoulders and face fell.

"Just a few minutes," I said. I could not wait for our elevator and thundered up the three flights of stairs to my studio apartment. I was fortunate to find Connaughton's landline number online.

"Hello?" a man's voice answered.

"Hello, is Mr. Wade Connaughton available?"

"May I ask who is calling?" the man said. It did sound like the man himself.

"This is Laurent from the Café Bonhomie."

"Hello, Laurent? All okay?" Connaughton said with an uneasy laugh.

"Absolutely," I said. "But it would be even better if you let me cater your next dinner party at your beautiful home. It's why I'm calling on a Sunday night."

"I see. Go on."

"I've read about your soirées in the *Picayune*. And in *New Orleans* magazine and *St. Charles Living*. It's the stuff of legend, and I just know the food will be a hit. Surely your circle has the—worldliness, sophistication to receive it well. They're pretty open-minded, right?"

"Well—at least I would prefer to think so."

"What do you think, Mr. Connaughton? Could we do one Sunday evening, or night?"

"Wade, Laurent. Actually, I was about to line one up for next weekend. I was thinking just hors d'oeuvres and cocktails, but we can convert it into a sit-down dinner party, after some libations. Could you be ready here this coming Sunday at five sharp with the food? Enough for seventeen?"

Perfect. Hours after the Bonhomie closed after Sunday brunch, Pham and I could prepare the food.

"I sure can."

"Very well. Let's chat tomorrow about what you'll be catering. Looking forward to it."

"Thank you for this great opportunity, Wade. You won't regret it."

Next, I had to call Wilson. I would offer him a demo in his kitchen of a couple of my dishes. Then I recalled Noelle's falling expression and shoulders as I swore I'd return in mere minutes. We were at risk, after all. I resolved to call Wilson tomorrow morning and headed out of my apartment and down the hall toward hers.

Then came this overwhelming feeling that if I did not call Wilson at once and pitch my proposal, my opportunity would pass.

My intuition had proven correct enough times—I turned and reentered my apartment. Wilson answered in two seconds.

"Laurent Ladnier?" Wilson said.

"How'd you know it was me?" I said. "Guess we exchanged

digits last night at Buffa's."

"Of course. What's new, Chef Ladnier?"

"You've got a few hours off tomorrow between your lunch and dinner services. Right?"

"Cayenne Club's closed tomorrow. Why do you ask?"

"I remember something you said, Wilson. About your kitchen line, and your restaurant."

"We covered a lot," Wilson said.

"You admitted your foot traffic had declined. You were even losing regulars. That some said your kitchen wasn't even trying. Isn't all I just described the current situation?"

Wilson paused. "Regrettably, it is."

"Between your two services tomorrow, let me do a cooking demo for you."

"You want to work here? In The Cayenne Club? For me?"

"Possibly. I certainly can't work any longer for Gerard. You and I have a great rapport."

"We do."

"Even a friendship," I said.

"Sure, I'd agree, but—Laurent, I hope I'm not pissing away a great opportunity, but you're over-qualified for my kitchen. What it's become."

"What it's become," I said, "is something I can turn around for you."

"Why this cooking demo? I've eaten in the Bonhomie. I know you're *more* than—"

"Just let me cook you three dishes. I'll bring the ingredients. I'll explain why later."

"Can you come tomorrow?"

"I can. Between our lunch and dinner service at Bonhomie."

"Cruise by here at two forty-five PM sharp, then," Wilson said.

"Will do. You'll love this. You'll see."

"All right," Wilson said, laughing. "Bye now."

What a Sunday night. I had the catering offer and then

the green-lighted cooking demonstration. As a rising wave of excitement buoyed me upward, I remembered Noelle.

I locked my door as fast as I could and jogged down the hall to her apartment.

I knocked, then tried the knob. Her door was locked. I pulled my cell from my pocket and called. Her phone was off.

CHAPTER 5

Frazzled by my utter lack of sleep due to excitement, nerves, and my humiliation by Gerard's son, and yet rallied by both Wade's offer and thoughts of the cooks in my family—Dad, Mémère, Pépère—I parked against the curb of the Warehouse District's St. Joseph Street. I tried to forget rent was still overdue. Damned nerves. I moved in a brisk walk, my satchel of kitchen knives and bags of groceries in my arms. It was my moment. I did not know what would befall me on the other end of it, but I felt strong and, as I massaged the handkerchief about my neck, proud.

Before me loomed the three-floor building of white-painted brick, a fortress I longed to conquer, then defend. The Cayenne Club had occupied the entire first floor for almost two decades. Wilson lived on the third floor, he'd told me. As if standing guard.

I found the front door locked. I knocked, and Wilson appeared, unlocking the door and clasping an affectionate hand onto my shoulder.

"Right through there, Laurent," Wilson said, "into the conveniently empty kitchen." I set down my load on one of its stainless-steel counters and brought in my remaining bags of groceries.

I could not in good conscience use anything from Gerard's walk-in, freezers, or cupboards. Even spices, or salt. I'd sourced everything from two grocery stores, just after I'd broken free from lunch service.

Wilson showed me around his kitchen, his walk-in, his dry

pantry, and all through his smaller refrigerators and freezers, his ovens and broiler, sparing no detail.

"All right, I'll be in my study," he said, his shoulders slouched. His button-down long-sleeved shirt was tucked in as his paunch hung just over his belt. "While you make magic happen in your study here. Right?"

I said, "I think you'll be surprised, but pleased."

"Surprised?" he said, an eyebrow raised.

"You'll see."

"The suspense builds. Come get me when everything's done. Accounting work's calling."

"Fun," I said.

Wilson chuckled and departed the kitchen. His steps on the hardwood floor sounded farther and farther away.

I noticed the radio on the counter against the wall and turned it on.

I paused. "Take Me Home," by Phil Collins. One of my father's favorite singers, and songs. Released two years before Dad's death. What was Dad trying to tell me? Was he watching? I smiled and plunged into my work.

Sixty minutes later, my cooking demonstration was complete, and I awaited Wilson's judgment.

I stared across the table as Wilson sampled each of the three dishes. My Chicken Curry Fricassée with Indian and East Asian influences. The Szechuan Shrimp Creole and Lo Mein. Then my favorite of the three: the Crawfish and Sea Urchin Momos. As he forked the food into his mouth, pausing, breathing, and then chewing in silence, I prayed, trying to ignore the sweat dripping down my chest and back within my kitchen whites.

In my heart, I felt some restaurateur would welcome my idea. But I wanted it to be Wilson.

Please, God. Please, Dad and Pépère, let Wilson be won over.

But my insomnia and another week of long days and

nights in Café Bonhomie's kitchen made it hard to hold my gaze steady. I was running on coffee and cortisol, and Wilson knew it.

I prayed Wilson would decide within seconds. Watching him chew and swallow, from dish to dish, wasn't torture, but something not far off. Wilson cleared his throat.

"Stunningly delicious, Laurent. Never had anything quite like this."

I grinned as I felt much of the worry flowing out of me. I was almost there.

"So, Laurent, what do you propose? And by the way, I can tell you're needin' lotsa sleep. Almost none of my chefs *ever* looked as worn as you right now."

I knew he was probably right. But my, the irony. Perhaps because I was dead sober, Wilson appeared even more worn down by life than when I had encountered him at Buffa's two nights before. The forehead wrinkles, the rosacea across the cheeks and so intense on the Nixon-esque nose that it seemed of a crimson hue—they were there as before. But the half-moons drooping under his eyes were even darker, to the point where they had assumed a dark gray shade. Gravity seemed to pull his jowls down even further.

"You know as well as I do that most restaurants, like most magazines and startups, fail," I said, unleashing my gaze to let it crawl up the drab walls of the empty dining room. At least it was faded paint and not aging, peeling wallpaper.

"Don't let that happen with this place. Wilson, bring me aboard as your chef. We'll remake the Cayenne Club into a *boîte*. A small restaurant with live music. We'll rename it. And I'll replace your current team. For sous I've got a very qualified cook I've worked with for years. The others I can sniff out through interviews, cooking demos."

My stomach constricted at my words. That was always my least favorite role as a chef. Firing someone, or recommending their termination.

"I'll admit," Wilson said. "I was already considering replacing my entire kitchen staff. Except for Osvaldo, my dishwasher and night porter."

"I can understand why. Wilson, just give me authority over hiring. And let me change up that menu. Some of your old mainstays we should preserve, but I can add many quite original dishes. I've tested some out before at Café Bonhomie. Got a great reception."

"Why would you want to leave that place, by the way? You said you don't get along so well anymore with Gerard Lonsdale."

I hesitated. I had to navigate this well, and touch on it gingerly.

"Of course, this entire conversation never took place. Gerard would only let me cook what he's always had on his menu. Never what I introduce, my experiments and my specials. Even though people love them. There's no room to grow. It's now clear it'll be just filler for my résumé. And he often talks to me and my line like trash. I'll leave it at that."

"So, you're looking for a place where you'd be head chef and innovation would be the focal point of the menu?"

"Yes. So with all due respect, I'm going to realize my dream, with either you or another owner. But we would go well together."

"I do think we'd get along well," he said.

I could see he was intrigued. I even detected a sliver of affirmation and acceptance in his eyes.

"Wilson, you need a game-changer. A complete reshuffling of the deck. Hell, even a new name for this venue. Otherwise, this place will tank inside a year. Already sinking, with all due respect. You know it, too, sir."

Inside I grimaced at my own words, those I forced out of my mouth to prove my point. But his eyes signaled confirmation.

"The good news," I continued, "is that with me running

the kitchen, I can have your place hopping in a few weeks. Give me two months, three months tops, and I'll make it the hottest new restaurant on the scene. I want people to have peak food experiences here. Sublime sensations with food, sensations previously unknown to them. And that can have as much to do with the customer's immediate surroundings, even music, as much as the food. So we can redesign the place, plan some playlists, even get some live music in here."

Wilson remained immersed in thought, his steepled hands pressed against his pursed lips. My sale was not yet complete.

"I like your ideas," he said. "But why fusion over what's proven successful in New Orleans?"

I felt a tinge of annoyance. But it was that same question any restaurateur would ask.

"And be just another of the hundred established Cajun-Creole or Creole restaurants in this city? That uses way too much butter on its line, rather than sesame oil? No thanks. We need to be on the bleeding edge here for where food is going in the country. And that's different cuisines coalescing on each plate. We will set the trend here. Tourists and the younger crowd will be more open to it, but that's just how it starts."

I paused, searching for his reaction. His eyes rose to the ceiling, where they seemed to crawl across the white plaster in deep contemplation. I grinned, realizing we shared that mannerism.

"See, Wilson," I said, "most cuisines have cultural mixture already built into them. Take Indian cuisine. Vindaloo or *vindalho* curry's based on the Portuguese dish *carne de vinha d'alhos*. Look at Viet cuisine. Pho has mung bean sprouts—very Asian, right? But its rice noodles are vermicelli, from the French colonists. Look at the pâté and the quasi-French bread on banh mi sandwiches. Look at pho bo. It's less than a century old, and it's an adaptation of France's *pot-au-feu*, with its beef, carrots, and potatoes. And you know a lot of Cajun and Creole and Creole Italian cuisine was innovative, mere generations ago. Lots of African and Native American influence, too."

Wilson remained silent, his eyes still wandering along the ceiling.

"A form of fusion's been done successfully here before," I said. "Richard Hughes and Chin Ling did it first in 1990, at The Pelican Club, in the Quarter. Don't know if you've tried Café Minh in Mid-City. Minh Bui started cooking at Commander's Palace, and he and his wife started Café Minh in 2007. It was the first real fusion restaurant of Viet, Cajun, Creole, and French. One of my favorite places to eat. Not too well-known. Elegant and delicious stuff—Viet food to eat mostly with a fork and knife. But nowhere as daring in its ingredients and preparation as what I'll do. Mine also combines more cuisines. Right now, fusion to that degree is alien to New Orleans."

I paused, then said, "Who's your fishmonger? What purveyor do you use for your seafood?"

"Frechou Food Distributors, out of Gretna," he said, lowering his eyes to meet mine. "For four years now. I get everything from them."

I hated being so critical. But in that moment, I had to be.

"Do you really think you get good product there? I've eaten here a few months back. Your vegetables were fine, but your seafood wasn't as fresh as I had here many years before. We would use American Seafood, and its manager Wayne Hess, like many of the culinary bigwigs here."

"Hmm," was all Wilson said. But I could see the gears moving behind those bloodshot eyes.

"We want primo ingredients," I said. "I've got this dogma of freshness and high quality. I avoid using anything frozen. But we can still swing this while keeping our food costs as no more than thirty-four, thirty-five percent. I estimate labor will be about twenty-nine percent. I can have this place running at a sweet sixteen percent profit margin. Thirteen at the least. I did it for Gerard."

Silence was his only reply.

"We can start out with a *prix fixe* menu, at least for lunch service," I said. "That way we can guarantee a known amount of profit per meal."

"Not a bad idea," Wilson said.

"I learned that a few restaurants ago," I said. "Customers were ordering just a main and no dessert and often no app. They were leaving after spending only some of what they could. You've got a smallish shop, so you'll have the same overhead and the same amount of staff to pay."

"I like what you said too about the distributors, Laurent. And the next-level ingredients."

"And there's another distributor I can rope in," I said. "We can talk about them another time. They can pull in pheasant from Scotland. Squab from farms in California. Some great fillets of sole from Holland, and France. Ducks come from Indiana farms. Big rabbits from Arkansas farms. Pompano and frogs' legs from Florida. They get all their four-pound free-range chickens from Amish co-ops in Pennsylvania and they're top notch."

"Nice," he said. "Anyway, tell me more about Laurent."

"Ha, deal. Wilson, now you know *Gambit* ran that feature article on me, when I was graduating culinary school. And WWL ran a story on me too, a few years back. NOCCA gave me an alumni award for my cooking. But thus far, I haven't yet cheffed in the venue I'd envisioned."

That last line turned my stomach, just a bit.

"Wilson, once people know there's a new establishment here, new menu, new decor, pumping out dishes this city's never seen, this place will get a lot of fresh new attention. And I know so much about cooking because I've made so many mistakes, two decades of them. But I learned from them. Learned from them at this French white-linen tablecloth place Uptown when I was fifteen. Learned in those two years at an Indian place, a year as sous chef in an upmarket Chinese restaurant, three years at an Italian spot, over fifteen years at Cajun-Creole restaurants. And, of course, over a year as chef at the Bonhomie."

I paused, searching his face. The oddest, most inscrutable Mona Lisa smile played upon his lips.

"All I need is to be that authority in the kitchen and over the menu, and a salary of just four thousand a month. At least for the first three months while I make the place really pop."

More silence. Hold your tongue and wait, Laurent. What was the old sales mantra? After the sales pitch is made, he who speaks first loses.

After half a minute, Wilson cleared his throat, slowly, and stood.

"Laurent, give me today to think it over. I got your number. I'm torn because so many things I've tried haven't worked. And I've been burned so many times. This restaurant business can make you jaded. And with each year, more jaded. You know this. But I'll shoot you a call sometime today or tomorrow. My promise to you."

"Wilson, whatever you decide," I said, rising to my feet, "friends, either way."

I slapped my palm into his outstretched hand and squeezed. His face studied mine with a pleasant, calm expression. It would be hard to predict Wilson's decision.

Out in the street, a cold breeze was blowing. I'd forgotten about the cold front rolling in. Gumbo weather. I started my car and zipped off toward the Lofts. I was missing Noelle. Joy brimmed within me, and I took heart she issued that demand for another overdue date and less lonely nights at bars after work. I would find another special venue for us, beyond Bacchanal.

Noelle was the enduring summer day in my life. This new partnership with Wilson could form or might never manifest after a refused offer. But Noelle—after the arguments, the near-breakup mere weeks before, and her revelation of a potential relocation to Los Angeles—she remained in my life, and she was marvelous. Noelle—the one person who helped me to love living, adventuring, and the spontaneous—almost as much as I loved cooking.

As I trudged up the stairwell and emerged onto the fourth floor, Ben was locking his door. Noelle stood at his side, her hands on her hips, casting a pensive glance at her feet.

"There was an incident, a few blocks away," Ben said. "Not common in this hood. But the painter, Mark—he got held up and robbed."

"Mark's okay," Noelle said, "but—you know."

"Oh no," I said. "Life in New Orleans."

My phone buzzed in my pocket. I glanced at the screen.

"Sorry, I've got to take this," I said. "Big update coming."

Wilson's voice was soft, but resolute. "I just can't, Laurent. It's too big a risk. I've never offered any menu like this. My customers haven't tasted anything like—"

"Your customers are leaving you," I said, "because they're dissatisfied with your Cajun and Creole dishes. You and I agreed on that. Wilson, in a couple months you won't have enough covers to keep the lights on. You know this yourself."

I felt desperation rising within me like fiery clouds from an explosion.

"Wilson, my menu would be too big a risk? It's too big a risk to keep offering the same experience and expecting a different result. Here's my offer. I'll co-chef at The Cayenne Club for free for one day. Your current chef can lead your kitchen on your current menu, and I'll prepare mine, which will be your specials. I'll even shop for the ingredients. You won't have to use your vendors."

Silence. Five seconds, then two, three more. I swore I could hear my heartbeat racing in my ears.

"You know, Laurent, that is—that is an interesting—a fun little idea."

I sensed a breakthrough, along with a coolness on my forehead.

"What's to lose? We'll offer my specials at a low rate. A blue-plate special, but something novel. You keep the proceeds. You don't even need to reimburse me for the ingredients."

"Done. When?"

Tears began to cloud my vision. Could this be real?

I cleared my throat and said, "Which day has the highest traffic? A weekday, right? Fridays?"

"Exactly, Fridays. CBD worker bees celebrating their last workday of the week."

"Not this Friday, but the next it is, deal?"

"Yes. Yes, deal."

"I appreciate your trust and vision, Wilson. Greatness awaits us."

"Greatness, Laurent? Let's look over your specials menu this Wednesday. I need all the ingredients stored in my walk-in by next Thursday evening."

"You won't regret it, Wilson. You'll see."

CHAPTER 6

I had this odd, even foreboding feeling—something was off—when I parallel-parked Noelle's van that Sunday afternoon against the curb on Prytania Street. This sensation only grew as Pham and I carried the first covered trays of food between the square columns, through the open black cast-iron gate, and then along the brick walkway between the two large magnolias to the mansion just beyond.

That sense of unease and even danger clashed with what I saw before me: a bright edifice, not imposing but charming, that reflected the sunny warmth of its owner.

My eyes crawled up and across its magnificent façade, noting its jutting first- and second-floor galleries, its slate roof darkened by time and patches of dark green moss and lichen.

Before I could ring the bell, the door opened, revealing a beaming Wade Connaughton. Once again, that benevolent aura contrasting with my ill feeling. For the occasion, he had donned a seersucker suit.

Wade nodded and said, "Chef Ladnier. I've already told my party about you. Trying to get you some more exposure Uptown."

"Very thoughtful of you, Wade," I said. Exposure—it was so true that catering allows a chef to test-run his creations before launching a restaurant. And to build a local groundswell of fans. The food I prepared that afternoon for the soirée was among my most unique. It did align with my vision. But would it be appreciated by the guests?

"My pleasure. Now y'all come in. Let's put these in the kitchen."

"We do have more in the van, of course," I said as I followed Wade's trail down the foyer, with Pham a few steps behind me. Chattering and laughter sounded ahead. As we swung left into the living room, I saw the party had begun.

There were just under twenty of them, well-dressed and sitting upon couches and standing around, chatting there and toward the rear of the long parlor as they looked through the French windows onto the back patio. Most seemed north of fifty, cradling martinis, cocktails, and glasses of wine. Many turned and stared and a few of them gestured with closed eyes, smiles, and raised chins that they enjoyed the aromas wafting from the covered trays. I spotted Erik Brauer, owner of the Armstrong Lofts and amateur boxer, regaling with animated expressions and gestures a laughing young beauty.

"Gents, just place those on the stovetop, over there," Wade said, entering the kitchen area and motioning toward the stove, situated under a tall stone hood descending from the ceiling.

Pham and I set down the large, covered trays and headed out of the kitchen and up the foyer toward the front door. After shutting the door behind us, we walked in silence toward the van.

We returned to the kitchen each with a tray, and then made a third trip, then a fourth. When Pham and I placed the last two trays on the stovetop, Wade pulled the covers back, inhaling deeply and releasing a loud moan in delight.

"There he is," I heard Erik say. He was pointing at me, his ruggedly handsome features broadening into a roguish grin. I grimaced inside, praying he would not reveal I had been days late a few times on my rent. "As for cooking, Ladnier won't disappoint. That I can assure you."

"Now that smells beautiful and I know it will taste even better," another voice said. I craned my neck to peer at the figure in the tan suit midway across the parlor. It was Tom Fitzmorris, the local food critic. Small worlds indeed, both Uptown and the New Orleans food scene.

"Why thanks, Mr. Fitzmorris," I said. "I remember you appreciate my work."

"Sure do, Laurent," he said. "Your star will rise fast. Wade told me you were catering."

"Laurent, now you and your friend join me over here," Wade said. "Want to introduce y'all."

Pham and I followed him to the edge of the group, which turned our way, then fell silent.

"Honored guests," Wade said, "meet a great local talent who prepared tonight's fare. Laurent Ladnier, chef over at Café Bonhomie. Gerard Lonsdale's place. Laurent's cooking up some cutting-edge stuff over there. Y'all go pay this gentleman a visit!"

As several of the guests clapped, I recalled none knew of my upcoming test at The Cayenne Club. God willing, I thought, I'd soon give Gerard my two weeks' notice. I still believed in that gesture, and I could not leave Café Bonhomie flailing on its back.

I looked closer. Most of them were amiable, nodding and smiling. Some were inquisitive, and a few seemed skeptical. I could feel it: Some sensed I might be the son of Claude Ladnier.

Sure enough, one guest, an older man in a seersucker suit, said, "Hey, are you any relation to Claude Ladnier?"

"He was my father," I said, the words sounding in my ears like the saddest melody.

A few older guests gawked as if I were some unexpected curiosity. I looked back down at my feet, feeling the heat build in my cheeks and on my forehead.

No doubt Dad's memory endured in some circles of older Uptowners. The charming but troubled chef who wed a daughter of the Uptown Crowley family. A groundbreaking talent who triumphed, then failed for years, then abandoned the food scene. Some still held him in a sort of respect. But they did not miss him as I did. I thought of Jim. How easy and fortunate he had it with his close friendship with his father, an oilman, engineer, and geologist.

It was then that I heard a familiar voice, albeit a dreaded one.

"Making a second try at glory, Laurent?" the voice said. I searched the room, squinting with annoyance. I had prepared myself that Luc Breton could be there.

"It's no *try*, Mr. Breton," I said, hearing my own words in my ears as a sneer. "It's a direct hit into the pleasure centers of your brain. Maybe this time you'll admit it."

The well-liquored swell of partygoers oohed with surprise and delight, a few laughing at what sounded like Breton's expense. I sensed there were a few in the audience who weren't exactly part of his fan club. He stared back at me with fury, his nostrils flaring.

"Come on, Luc," Wade said. "You promised to be nice. Or I wouldn't have invited you."

Breton's ire seemed to give way to embarrassment as with ruddy cheeks he glanced at the other guests.

"And now who is this young man with you, Laurent?" Wade said in a friendly tone.

"This is Pham," I said. "My great saucier at Café Bonhomie. Great supporter, I should add."

"Nice. Folks, y'all remember Laurent and Pham," Wade said, "when you're hungry."

I made sure to find Breton again in the crowd. My glare was met with a smirk, coupled with a momentary vanquished expression in the eyes. I gave him the broad, toothy smile he deserved, and a lift of the chin. What a bully he was. Yet I knew that moment wasn't the end of it.

Wade cleared his throat and said, "Laurent, Pham, why don't y'all join me on a tour of my humble abode? Many of my guests are relatively new friends and haven't yet seen it."

I looked back at Pham. "Sure, Wade—let's go, Pham."

"Let us begin at the beginning," Wade said. "Retrace our steps to the front porch. Bring your libations!"

Pham and I joined the cluster filing out of the parlor and

into the foyer. I grinned, imagining how Pham and I looked in our polyester kitchen whites, plodding in our clogs amidst the train of perfumed women in dresses and men in sport coats, tweed, and pants of wool and corduroy.

As Wade held the front door ajar, the group fanned out onto the lower front gallery. A car slowed, its driver watching the partygoers in their finery.

"So," Wade said, with a light clap of his hands. "Y'all know I'm a passionate lover of architecture. And especially what we have here Uptown, whether it's Greek Revival, Federalist, Italianate, late Victorian, Richardsonian Romanesque, you name it. So, pardon me as I geek out. Here you have a Greek Revival edifice constructed in 1850, the year when the economy here was at its zenith. The first owner was Dalton Keys, actually from New York, who'd built a fortune here. Keys planted these two magnolias, laid this brick pathway, and put in the cast-iron fence and pilasters. This wood you're standing on, along with these seven fluted wooden Ionic and Corinthian columns spanning the width of the porch, that's all original to the house. All cypress, as it withstands humidity so well. Those windows, of course, clearly aren't the original blown glass. Now, let's step inside back into the warm air."

Wade disappeared into the house, and we followed.

"This entrance foyer has this antique Regency console table to the side. Those large Cuban mahogany sliding doors at the end of the hall, they open to the central hall." He slid them open and led us inside. He pointed upward. It seemed as if I was gazing upward inside a medieval cathedral.

"This remarkable spiral staircase," Wade said, "it's an architectural marvel. Defies gravity."

"And nice balustrade," a man said.

"Absolutely, Tim," Wade said. "The rail's walnut, and the balusters and steps all pure mahogany. Note that grand stained-glass dome above. Allows this soft light to seep through that I just love so much. All while you stand here on a marble floor."

Whistles and excited chatter ensued.

"One lovely feature," Wade said, "there are fourteen-foot-tall ceilings throughout the house. I should add this home's two features I love most are hidden. The first? There's a twelve-inch space between the eighteen-inch inner and outer walls. Makes the house cooler in summer, warmer in winter. Some older Uptown homes have these. You could only imagine the things we found hidden in that space. Now for my second favorite feature. Only my friends see this."

Laughter arose among a few guests.

"It's not a bizarre bondage room," Wade said. "It's elegant, on a grand scale. Follow me."

I did, into the most awe-inspiring room I had ever seen in New Orleans.

"Behold one of three original ballrooms still in existence in the Garden District. In those days, installing this in your home was quite a feat. I plan to finally host a party in this room. It's almost sixty feet long, almost thirty-five feet wide. Anyway, that piano was built in 1861 as a gift for Prince Albert of England, though he died before it could be shipped. And those are various antiques on those tables against the wall. Those gilt-framed French mirrors come from this one riverboat; I forget the name. This floor's just gleaming, and you can see the boards are arranged on a diagonal formation. That's imported French oak."

"Look at those chandeliers," a lady said.

"Those are twin grand crystal chandeliers, Margie," Wade said, "Baccarat chandeliers, hanging from those striking white ceiling medallions. And that's a gilded archway dividing the ceiling of this opulent room. Archway's flanked by those two fluted Corinthian columns. The windows are floor to ceiling, and unlike in the double parlor, they are heavily draped. We want this room dark and cool for some great dancing. Now, what feature haven't I pointed out that leaps out at you?"

"That piano," a man said, "that's a Steinway?"

"Correct, Ron, but that's not what I'm referring to," Wade said.

"Wade, is that real gold?" a woman said, pointing across the room at the opposite wall.

"It is, Sue. Those sconces and moldings on these walls are indeed of twenty-four-karat gold. Just like in the Van Benthuysen-Elms Mansion on St. Charles, known then as Nayades Street. We're the only houses in New Orleans with that feature. A bit of a security risk, of course. There's enough gilt on the ceilings and walls that this ballroom was known as the Gold Room."

Steinways, gilt walls and ceilings? Floors of marble and French oak? The Garden District was a different world. But I never saw anything close to this in those years when Dad had us living in an apartment Uptown. No matter—I would trade ownership of the Garden District, all of Uptown, and even all of New Orleans for my father to be alive again, and healthy.

In my peripheral vision, Breton extended a finger upward.

"Bathroom break for me," he said in a half-whisper. He turned and departed, smiling.

"Now, this feature only elevates the opulence of this room," Wade continued, and though I found this all intriguing, and impressive, that feeling of impending danger returned. But was it mere anxiety, social awkwardness? These feelings had often steered me from mishaps in the past, and I had learned to trust them.

I trained my eyes on our host. His lips were moving but I hardly caught a word. Pham was following along with the entire group. But I couldn't. After ten more seconds, as Wade's back faced us while he gestured at the gilt sconces, I yielded to that feeling, turned, and zipped out of the room.

Yes, the kitchen. I must retrace my steps and get to the food. That feeling of danger surged, and I launched into a jog through the central hall, past the grand winding staircase and, just inside the entrance foyer, I hooked right.

Breton was leaning over one of my trays. The aluminum foil was bent back, and he thrust a hand deep into the pocket of his slacks. I tiptoed his way as fast as my feet could bear and, as Breton's hand pulled a small glass bottle from his pocket, I slapped it from his hand. The bottle landed on the brick floor and rolled. With all my might, I gave Breton's back a shove.

I lunged and picked up the bottle. Not just Tabasco. Tabasco Habanero.

"Is this an assault?" Breton said in a mocking tone.

"I caught you," I said. "Now I'll expose you."

"Whatever you say," Breton said.

"Why, Breton? Is it insecurity? Jealousy? What other chef in this city would do this?" I said, my voice filling the room. I heard alarmed voices, then brisk steps scurrying up the hall toward us.

Wade rounded the corner, with Pham just behind, then Erik and a handful of the other guests. Wade's cheeks and brow were flushed red. Erik's eyes narrowed at me in an annoyed stare.

"Wade," I said. "I had a strong feeling this serpent wasn't heading to any bathroom. Look at what I just prevented."

Wade's eyes shifted to Breton, then to the open tray, then to the Tabasco bottle in my hand.

"What in the hell's going on here? Luc?" Wade said.

But Breton said nothing. That diseased mind was working behind the darting eyes.

"That's not mine," he said. "It came from inside his pocket. I saw him pull it out and—"

"Then Luc," Wade said. "Why are you in here? You know my bathroom's way down there."

"Breton was trying to sabotage me. Starting with this tray. Loading it up with this." I extended the bottle upright and label facing outward toward Wade, Pham, and the group.

"Don't lie to me, Luc," Wade said as gasps erupted just behind him through the sliding doors. "You can't lie to me, man. Is Laurent right?"

"Don't look at me, Wade," Breton said. "Look at him. He's behind this."

"Why would he sabotage his own delivery?" Wade said with a laugh. "When I'm showcasing his cooking for my guests? Luc, kindly remove yourself from my property. We'll talk later."

I glanced at Breton's expression, full of flushed disgrace, even to the point of watery eyes.

"Yeah," Luc said. "We'll talk later. I can explain."

A volley of laughter erupted from the guests as Luc brushed past them, into the hall.

"Can you at least tell us," a man blurted out, "if you're a Tabasco man or a Crystal Hot Sauce guy?"

Many in the group laughed. I could hear the front door open, then shut.

"I'm sorry, Laurent," Wade said. "I'm so sorry. Please accept my apologies."

"No worries," I said, "I'm confounded a man of your caliber associates with—that person."

"A childhood friend," Wade said. "I guess I'm sentimental. And I helped him get his start with his first restaurant."

"The contrast between you and Breton is jarring," I said. "I bet you're a great friend to have, though. Oh, isn't it that time you wanted me to kick off dinner?"

Wade checked his wristwatch and nodded, then turned to the group.

"Guests, our tour's concluded, at least for now. Let's enjoy dinner. The dining room tables are already set. Please be seated; you'll be served there."

"Thank you, Wade," I said.

"Thank you. Looking forward to it," he said and headed into the dining room.

Pham drew up alongside me, his eyes widening with shock at Breton's antics. And then his face lightened into a grin.

We plated the food and assisted Wade's two servers in bringing it into the dining room. Seated at the head of the stunningly long table, Wade presided over the chattering guests. After everyone was served, Pham and I stood against the wall, observing. They were wading into the Crawfish and Sea Urchin Momos, the Massaman Curry Shrimp, and Ginger Miso Grits, smiling, eyebrows lifted as they chewed. Their enjoyment was undeniable.

"Ladies and gentlemen, what do you think?" I said, lifting my voice to be heard throughout the room.

The next minute was one of my happiest in years. Their words wafted back to me like the most welcome summer breeze.

Marvelous...amazing stuff...uni and crawfish and crawfish fat but now I'm a believer...I didn't think I'd enjoy this, but I really do...

Then came my favorite: *complex, but rewarding...can I get the recipe?*

Some wanted second helpings, half an hour later. Apart from getting those, Pham and I stayed in the kitchen. When the two servers had brought in all the dirty plates, and served the digestifs of port and sherry, Wade appeared in the kitchen.

"Well done, Laurent, Pham. I knew you'd be a hit," he said, shaking our hands and handing me the envelope of cash. "For the ingredients. With a little extra for y'all."

"Thanks, Wade. I'm so happy," I said.

"Let's do this again soon. Laurent, you'd asked me to let you know when to wrap up. You could start packing up your trays and things."

"We'll do that now, Wade," Pham said. "Thanks again for this opportunity."

Pham and I shook his hand once more and headed with the first of the trays out of the front door, onto the porch, and then down the brick pathway to the van.

It was confirmed: My second public experiment was successful.

Yet as I walked, that feeling remained: danger, though Breton had vanished. Perhaps it was just that I was Uptown again. What my father once felt he had graduated to and attained. Once my mother's domain, the world from which they had long ago been exiled.

I recalled Mémère's words: *I told your dad many times he'd always be a stranger in a strange land Uptown. That he was an Irish Channel boy, through and through. No sense pretending.*

CHAPTER 7

That entire following morning and early afternoon, tension built closer and closer to a white heat within the walls of my temples, sending beads of sweat down my brow into my handkerchief, now tied as a bandanna around my head. I was a walking aneurysm, ready to burst. For it was taking every molecule of my being not to storm out of Monday lunch service at the Café Bonhomie, or, even worse, to lay out Gerard with my fist once and for all.

The heckling commenced the week before, soon after Gerard had learned from his son of my experiment on our customers. The first day, Gerard forced me to clean the dishes with Pham, and the kitchen floor with the porter after lunch and dinner service. But each day since had been almost as grueling. Gerard's jabs would persist throughout the lunch hour and showed no signs of stopping. Whenever Gerard passed the cramped kitchen, as compact as the galley in some old submarine, he would shout a snide joke or some new nickname in our direction, meant for Pham and me. To diminish us, no doubt, in the eyes of our crew.

And here he was again. Those loud footsteps of his leather wingtips, signaling the approach of what I knew to be approximately two hundred and eighty-five pounds of lard and ego.

"We gotta learn all we can from Mr. Genius now," Gerard said, his perpetually pinched facial expression reflecting the sourness within his soul. "All secrets to the mysteries of cookery. Our proven menu wasn't enough for him. Professor Ladnier's been dreaming of greener pastures."

That was a milder one. I would just clench my jaw and bear it. Maybe it was about to end, after all. Could it really continue indefinitely? But this was another form of torture: so I was Professor Ladnier, dreaming of greener pastures. Had Gerard somehow discovered my proposal to Wilson? Did he or did he not know?

A chill crept up the nape of my neck. Gerard couldn't have learned of my overture to Wilson from my ever-loyal Pham. Wilson would not have said anything. Perhaps it was all in my head. Gerard didn't seem to know—yet.

I paused, then focused on preparing and stirring the roux for forty-five minutes to my preferred dark brown. At the Bonhomie, this was the one cooking task I wanted to always manage myself. I then turned the roux over to Minnesota, who prepared the chicken and andouille sausage gumbo, while I made the rounds, checking on my string of line cooks. For the next several hours, they snuck looks at me, as our boss continued to inject even more drama into our day. No doubt they watched to see if I would crack. Or shoot back some defiant, mighty retort to our mutual bully, so they could feel both entertained and avenged.

"I know it's a pain to listen to," Minnesota said, drawing up near to my right ear. "But after your experiment while Gerard was away, I can't believe he didn't fire you, boss. Anyway, my days here are numbered. Gotta break out of the Angola State Penitentiary." He said the last words with an exaggerated Southern accent.

"Yeah, Laurent," my line cook Charles said, walking up beside Minnesota. "You helped float the Bonhomie another year. But you get no respect. Guy shoulda trusted your instinct on those new dishes."

"I thank you guys, truly," I said, hearing the words soft, almost mournful, in my ears. "It just wasn't meant to be. Gerard, the die-hard traditionalist. Opposed to anything new or experimental, or involving any risk. And then, of course, there's me."

"Yeah, then there's you," Minnesota said. Somewhere in those words, I detected a sneer. "Wish you'd just tell us what you're thinkin'. You stayin' put, or goin' somewhere else?"

"Maybe, maybe not," I said.

I would not disclose the truth, that I was trying to hold out at the Bonhomie until Wilson accepted my proposal, or, if not, until some other restaurateur did. For my bills could not wait, and I could not deny Gerard paid me above the industry average for New Orleans. Yet nothing like that highest echelon of chefs in the city. But *they* paid *themselves*. Paul Prudhomme, Emeril Lagasse, John Besh, Susan Spicer. Donald Link.

A lull had come to my kitchen, free of Gerard's taunts, when I heard his voice near the pass-through.

"Laurent Ladnier! What's this about you and Pham catering a dinner party last night Uptown, using my chaffers and pans?"

There it was. We'd been found out, somehow. I suppose it was merely a matter of time. Still, I felt stark naked in front of my whole line.

Gerard burst into the kitchen, moving toward me like a crashing wave, and stopped within inches of my face right there at my *mise-en-place*. His eyes narrowed, full of fury, and his breath stunk of halitosis and whiskey. I found myself holding my breath, feeling on the verge of passing out from both revulsion and nerves.

"I warned you after my son told me of your sneaky move with those specials. And now this. I can trust you 'bout as much as a pickpocket out on Bourbon. You, Ladnier, are fired. Get your gear and clear out of here!"

It was Gerard at his most tyrannical. Then he swept his stare toward Pham at my left.

"And you, too, Spike. Yeah, you, Pham. You picked your side. Out, now!"

Pham stood in silence with his hands on his hips, a grim expression on his face as he stared down at the floor. Then he headed to the locker room for his clothes, his pace slowed only by his clubfoot.

Now that my torment had met its end, nothing remained but shock, and fear. Rent statements and bills would rush toward me and well up around me like a deluge.

"Minnesota, take over as chef for the time being," Gerard said. "We'll talk after service."

A large part of me was happy for my sous. But had he known of my impending firing, and his ascendance? I still could not trust him.

I gathered my father's mid-1980s stainless steel Hoffritz knife set, clutched it to my chest, and headed out of the kitchen toward the locker room. I tore off my cap, untied my apron, and threw both along with my polyester whites into the hamper. As I changed into my street clothes and shoes, Pham nodded with sad eyes.

"I'm sorry, brother," I said. "You did this for me, to stick with me. Was it worth it, for you?"

Pham's eyes brightened as his face morphed into a mischievous smile. "It was," he said. "Let's talk later. There's gotta be a better place for you. And me."

Some of my tension dissipated. Yes, Pham had risked his hide on my two test runs. He would be part of my new concept. As sous.

I headed out through the kitchen with my knife set. Pham followed, a few steps behind.

"Now, crew, back to work," Gerard droned amidst the line and its workstations. "The blind have been leadin' the blind in here."

So, this was how my time at the Bonhomie would end. And I had planned to hold my tongue on my way out the door. Too bad the whiskey and cocaine had regained control of Gerard. Even so, at one point a man must accept responsibility for his actions, and words.

"The blind leading the blind? So that means you're the blind leader?" I said at last, feeling myself explode inside. "Gerard, you're blind, all right."

Gerard stopped in his latest sweep past us and stood, looking my way, straight through the kitchen. His face was nothing but pure hatred, indignation. And unmistakable aggression.

Laurent, you've already crossed the Rubicon, I thought. Or, like Cortés, you've burned your ships in their moorings. No turning back. Might as well proceed with bravado.

"Blind, that is, to any sense of artistic individuality or adventure," I said. "Or setting a trend others will follow. Instead, you always follow the most established trend in the city. Like a sheep."

Pham grinned. I loved that rebellion in him, a dissidence against the right things, and his originality. As if he were made to be my sidekick on my mission.

"Excuse me?" Gerard half said, half gasped. Then he uttered a louder, full-throated "What?"

I said, "You think I'm fine with you storming past us every twenty minutes insulting me? Jabbing me while I'm here working for you?"

"You'll be replaced, all right," Gerard said. "Won't be easy, but won't be too hard. You aren't the genius many take you for. You're not the next Eric Ripert. You're a good chef, but back when you were celebrated, you were also a trumped-up, over-hyped poor kid from the Irish Channel. Bleedin' heart journalists loved to oversell you. But after all these years you showed you got noth—"

"Shut your trap, you bloated loser," I said, hoping to forget his latest searing words, or at least to stop their flow. It was the most painful insult I'd ever endured.

Gerard started to yell invectives, but I vied to shout louder.

"Keep your tired, clichéd menu, Gerard. Perfect for

unsuspecting tourists. Yeah, and burnt-out, unimaginative corporate types. Fine, replace me with Minnesota here. He does have the right stuff. Deserves to be a chef somewhere, anyway. I'm making my exit. You made me."

As I clenched my jaw and marched with Pham past our line toward the kitchen exit, I detected both amusement and respect in their faces. But it was the amusement that irked me.

"Get out is right," Gerard said, with a sudden, strange calmness. "Before I have these guys throw you out."

"Sure," I shot back as I continued my march. "Won't happen. Only Breton's kitchen crew hates him more than the line here hates you."

When I pushed the metal bar to open the door, a cold breeze greeted me, reminding me that I was being exiled from the warm security—but emotional violence—of the Bonhomie's kitchen. Sunlight streamed upon my face like a promise of something new, something extraordinary. Again I heard Gerard's mouth, and I spun and screamed, "*Au revoir*, blind bastard! Look me up in four months. Do a simple Internet search. And eat your heart out!"

"Won't happen. I'll blackball you," I heard Gerard say with confidence. "No owner will keep you on board for more than a month, after I get the vendors to cut y'all off."

"You wish you had that pull. All lies," I said, hoping I was right. Yet I knew I could be wrong, and I felt the dread descending on me.

The door retracted shut behind us with its mechanical hiss, as if from some agitated viper. Such a bitter and ugly ending for my time at Café Bonhomie. Ha, the irony of the place's name.

"Well, it's been decided for us," Pham said with a weary laugh. "No more suspense. Or wondering when we'll leave."

"Right," I said. "Guess we won't be showing up for dinner service. I'll call you later, though."

"I'll be around," Pham said as he unlocked his car.

I trudged toward mine, parked down the street, but all I saw as I gazed before me was my grandmother's face. And my mother's, and that of my aunt. Staring at me as if in shock.

Opening my car door, I remembered the specials I'd tested out in the Bonhomie, and at Wade's dinner party with Gerard's equipment. A wave of nausea ripped through me, and I drew in a deep breath. I had entered a new universe. Indeed, I had never risked so much due to artistic ambition.

As I started my engine, I realized my proper destination. Not taking a much-needed nap, not dallying with Noelle, not numbing my wounds and worries at some bar, or embarking on another solitary foodie adventure. I must, at once, practice cooking those specials in my studio apartment kitchenette. The Friday showdown was less than four days away. I had to win over Wilson, and his Cayenne Club. Mémère's groceries, meds, and insurance, and that oft-depleted bail fund for my aunt could not wait. And neither could my looming rent payment, due in a few weeks. Perhaps at that time, if luck was on my side, Wilson could grant me a draw on future salary. If not, I might meet my ruin right at the start.

CHAPTER 8

That Friday morning, I arrived early to The Cayenne
Club, well before six. I felt ready. After all, I had cooked
for three days straight in my apartment, constantly
setting my alarm, ensuring my timing and quality was on
point. At first Noelle was crestfallen at my job loss, unamused
by my kitchenette cooking binge, but she had loved the series
of candlelit meals. And I'd promised that if Wilson hired me,
I'd celebrate with her at a new level.

At that hour, I found but two souls there: Wilson and
Osvaldo Torres, the swarthy fifty-something dishwasher and
night porter built like an ox and given to long stretches of
silence. I asked to see the ingredients for my specials, for in
the end, Wilson would not let me bring them or pay for them.
Still wary after Breton's attempted sabotage at Wade's party, I
straightaway checked the ingredients in both the pantry and
the walk-in to ensure Wilson's line had not attempted the
same, especially with the meat. Wilson reminded me he had
the meat delivered after closing the night before, after which
only he and Osvaldo had access to the restaurant.

Osvaldo, Wilson had assured me, was the only trust-
worthy person in his employ, and that was also my read. There
was a reason Wilson entrusted the man with the keys for so
many years. Wilson joked Osvaldo never made mistakes and
couldn't even if he tried, from managing inventory, empty-
ing the grease trap every six weeks, to keeping the walk-in,
kitchen floor, dining room, flatware, plates, and glassware as
immaculate and tidy as his slicked-back, jet-black hair.

I sniffed the various cuts of chicken, beef, and pork quite hard, several times, up to my nostrils. Fresh as could be. All the other ingredients checked out, too. Soon the line began to trickle into the kitchen, each new arrival eyeing me with irritation and deep suspicion. I nodded and smiled at each, but almost none returned the gesture.

I turned and resumed chopping shallots and yellow onions at my *mise-en-place*, whistling to hide my sense of awkwardness.

Soon someone behind me cleared his throat, and I turned around. Wilson.

"This is my friend Laurent I told y'all about," he said to the line, pointing his thumb sideways in my direction. "He's trying to start a catering business. And it's a fusion catering business. He and I are conducting a test today—our specials will be quite original. All prepared by Laurent."

A volley of grumbling, laughter, and muffled expletives erupted from the line.

"Be nice to my guest," Wilson said. "I got things to attend to in my office. Give 'em hell today, crew. Make our customers happy."

And with that, Wilson disappeared around the corner.

"You're gonna cater with fusion?" the broiler cook said, his hands on his hips and eyebrows raised perhaps as high as they could go. "You expect folks in New Orleans to pay you to eat that?"

"I sure do," I said, feeling my temper simmer as I took in his grinning face. "Wait and see the reaction out on the floor, why don't you?"

"All right, let's see it," the broiler cook said as he weaved his hand before him with an arrogant flourish.

"This is how you treat Wilson's guest for the day?" I said. "Who he's trying to help out?"

"You mean help out by making you the new chef," said another line cook, smirking over his shoulder as he chopped a link of andouille.

"Yeah," said the square-shouldered chef, also smirking, his large eyes narrowing to the point of appearing asleep. Completely bald and somewhere in his late fifties, he had the look of a once-athletic man whose brawn had mostly slipped into corpulence. "We know that's really what Wilson's considerin'. An experiment for a day? Please. But I'm not so sure you'll replace me. I'm Cal Bourgeois and I'm stayin' as chef here."

"What makes you think I'm auditioning for chef here?" I said, opting for a lie. Wilson wouldn't want them to know. "Seems like I'd be preparing Creole, Cajun."

I hesitated, hating the thought of delivering any criticism before my experiment. Yet they were setting upon me like a pack of wolves. The smirks, narrowed eyes, and shaking heads throughout the kitchen just intensified it. Not one of them had risen to my defense, anyway. Even Osvaldo, whose silent glances revealed a subtle desire for me to challenge the others.

I remembered what Wilson disclosed when I first pitched my concept. He was considering the replacement of his entire kitchen staff, minus Osvaldo. Wilson sure had good instincts there.

"Everyone here with a hand in the food," I said, "y'all should be downright ashamed. I ate here a few times through the years. And a few months back. Wilson gave you all a chance here and you let him down. Your quality keeps dipping and dipping but despite the complaints and lost customers, you don't even try to save his establishment. You're cooking dishes you know full well are so ordinary for New Orleans. But you don't even cook them decently."

"Go to hell, man," Cal shot back. "Who are you to say that? Why haven't we heard of you?"

That riposte cut through to my heart, like some red-hot blade pulled from a fire.

"That's actually a good question," I said. "I know the answer, and it's a complex one. But you'll hear lots of good buzz about me in three, four months."

The line burst into laughter. I shook my head, then returned to rearranging my *mise-en-place*. What if I was mistaken? What if I failed and sunk at last into obscurity? And what if no one, including Wilson, would hire me?

The tension and discomfort made minutes seem like hours. Relief came at last only when the orders started to flow in, the waiters clipping the yellow dupes onto the pass's wheel. The line grew quite busy, and I along with it.

Perhaps the worker bees were feeling adventurous that Friday, as the sous called out more specials from those dupes than I had anticipated. Or perhaps the wait staff merely followed Wilson's order he'd sworn he would issue, to steer customers toward the cheap lunch specials. Now working at fever pitch over my pans on one of the stovetops, I could at times feel the eyes of the line hot on the back of my head.

There was no deluge of specials ordered in that lunch service. But it sure was quite a few dishes for one cook to prepare alone, those three and a half hours. For most of service, I maintained the tally in my head, then when I got into the weeds for a bit, I lost count. It totaled somewhere between sixteen and nineteen.

I could not recall ever feeling so fatigued. And harried, and scared. I wanted to win over Wilson, but nearly as much, I just wanted the verdict to come soon.

At last the dupes slowed, then trickled in, then ceased altogether. As I dabbed my face dry, I realized my polyester whites were nearly drenched in sweat.

"How in the hell did you get so many orders?" growled someone behind me. I turned, and this time, Cal stood a mere three feet from me. "I know this crowd, okay? Few if any of 'em have tasted fusion. Wilson must have had every server pushing that hipster crap today, and pushing it hard. Or giving one hell of a discount on that weird trash."

I felt my temper flare as my spine grew further upright, my eyes locking onto his. But some large blue blur was not far behind, in my peripheral vision.

"Yo, Fifty Cal," someone on the line called out. "Hey Cal, turn around, man."

Wilson's hands were on his hips, his face a picture of barely restrained fury.

"Weird trash, Cal says," Wilson said. "This is how you treat my guest, and friend?"

"Well, I just..." Cal said, shrugging his shoulders, his hands held open.

"I've had quite a time out on that floor, today," Wilson said, shaking his head, as he walked farther into the kitchen. "The things I heard." He brought his eyes up toward mine, several feet away. "Laurent, they been talking trash to you today?"

I looked at the line, then back at Wilson. I felt my eyebrows rise, my mouth form a smile.

"I take that as a yes?" Wilson said.

"Of course," I said. "Just about all day. Except for Osvaldo."

"Everyone except Osvaldo clean your damn *mise* and get outta here. Out. I'm pissed. I want you all outta here in ten minutes. I need you back at the usual time, though, to prepare for dinner service. Laurent, follow me to my office. We gotta talk."

I felt my spirit collapse within me. I had failed, after all. In my only shot. I'd burned Gerard, then oversold my abilities. Now I'd be lucky to land any cheffing gig in the city. Where now—across the lake in St. Tammany Parish? Thirty miles north? I thought of my grandmother, mother, and aunt. I saw their faces as tears welled in my eyes. Truly, I had failed them. I wiped my wet face with my clammy palms.

Defeat, even annihilation, closed in on me. I remembered my father all those years ago. How he had fought mightily for years, yet submitted at last to the void, the unknown. How he left the restaurant industry forever while getting lost in booze and heroin, then renounced and vanquished them, then surrendered again to them, and, not long after, fell to his death.

With a towel, I dried my sweaty hands, then forced my feet to follow Wilson across the kitchen. Cal was not smirking this time but hitting me with a broad, toothy smile, his eyebrows raised in amusement.

"Good luck, pal. Ya gonna need it."

I could not bring myself to retort. Instead, I swung out of the kitchen and past the dining room. One of the waiters grinned—it seemed like a mocking smile. I hastened down the hall after Wilson, nearing him as he veered into his office. If I was to be struck down, I wanted it to be swift, then for me to leave as soon as possible.

"Shut the door behind you," Wilson muttered, hooking around his desk. He crashed into his padded leather chair. He piled his hands onto his head, like some surrendering soldier.

Silence. Three seconds, then seconds more. I dreaded his next words. If only I could hold my breath, and wait for his judgment, but I could almost hear my heart race.

"Laurent, what do you think happened, man?" he half said, half sighed. "Just curious."

"Clearly, you're ticked. Frustrated. Full of regret."

"I am," Wilson said. "All of that. Absolutely."

He leaned across the table with a glowering face, his eyes drooping with a hint of anger. I understood, feeling strange new anger toward myself, and my ambitions. In that moment, I thought, my ambitions had emerged from what I had denied for so long: my own arrogance.

"I talked to every table on that floor, Laurent. Did quite an audit of my clientele. Those who ate the specials, those who ordered from the main menu. I asked them for unadulterated, fearless opinions. Holding nothing back. And I was shocked. It was stunning."

My stomach sank even further, as far as it could go. I was on the verge of telling him to hasten to explain. Then I could wait no more. I had to bring this humiliation to an immediate end. After Breton, and Gerard, rejection by Wilson might destroy any remnant of my pride.

"Stunning?" I said, feeling my lips quivering.

Wilson stared, then continued, "Now I did like your dishes when I tried them. But these people—they liked them even more."

What? Could it be? What a great delivery, Wilson. My spirit surged within me, like a swimmer launching off from his block.

"Laurent, I mean—not a one of them said anything negative besides some of the descriptions on the specials menu sounded odd. And that they hadn't expected such combinations. These people aren't like my weekend crowd. We'd discussed this. They're a little more diverse in age, ethnic background. Some are tourists, but most are breaking for lunch from their jobs in the CBD. They're closer to what our crowd would be if we launch your concept. And yeah, I said I have deep regret. That I kept these bums so long in my kitchen. And that I didn't find you sooner, somehow."

I choked back tears. "I was thinking—you'd give me—some kind of rejection."

"And how the line treated you," Wilson said. "After I told them you were my guest. And my pal. Shows you how they disrespect me. It's a pattern here. Good riddance. But I can only afford to lay them off when we've got commits. Well-vetted ones."

"I've never been more disrespected by a line in my life," I said. "Frankly."

"How much do you need to be my chef? With you redesigning the menu? You choose the new line. But I approve. How much do you need, pay-wise?"

"Sixty thousand a year. With a reworking of my salary six months from my start date."

Wilson's massive paw broke free from the other side of the desk, palm upward as it extended toward me. His face was beaming.

I slapped my hand into his in a firm shake. "I'm with you, Wilson."

"Beautiful. Laurent, like I said, I wish I could call everyone on my line, tell 'em I'm mailing their last checks. But let's write up some online ads for the open positions. Except Osvaldo, of course. He stays—he's got to."

"I agree, keep him."

"He's like family and I can trust him. You can, too. Besides, he never had his hands in the food. He refuses to leave until every glass and plate's washed, dried, stowed away. Only after the counters and floors are gleaming."

"Glad there's one salvageable," I said.

"Laurent, the others failed me for so long. They knew this. Just phoning it in for the paycheck. Now you and I can start fresh and build a new crew."

"Deal," I said. "If I can bring that cook aboard that I've worked alongside for years. The one I'd mentioned, Pham. He's like a brother to me."

"Sold, Laurent."

"For now, I'll need a line of four. Pham and the other three. Each earning thirty-six hundred a month except Pham, who gets four thousand. Deal?"

"Sure, Laurent, but they've gotta work six days a week. Sunday's the sixth day but we can close after brunch."

"Perfect."

"So why didn't you chase your dreams earlier? You're thirty-seven, thirty-eight?"

"Turning forty this spring. Didn't have the guts to pursue it until this year."

I recalled the impetus behind my shift: that growing fear of following my father's example.

"So," Wilson said, "can you just put in your two weeks?"

"Don't worry about the two weeks," I said, then laughed. "Let's just say I know Gerard, and he'll understand."

CHAPTER 9

O nce I reached the Lofts from The Cayenne Club, I suggested to Noelle an Uptown excursion, first dinner at Upperline, then accompanying her on her set at the legendary Maple Leaf Bar. It was not a Tuesday night, when the Maple Leaf hosted the Rebirth Brass Band. But it was a Friday night, and the music and atmosphere were nearly as exhilarating. A local blues rock band I'd never seen had the crowd packed up to the stage.

After a half-hour over drinks at the dimly lit dive, the blues band finished and the crowd dispersed into the back patio and flowed into our bar area. Noelle and I crossed into the even darker adjoining music hall. Ben and the others in Noelle's band had arrived in the van and had brought in their instruments on stage, where they stood amidst sound checks. People started to trickle back into the hall, drinks in hand. I smiled and waved at Ben, then smiled at Noelle.

"Wish me luck, babe," Noelle said. She pecked me on the mouth and embraced me, then turned and ascended the stage.

My next hour passed as if in some enchanting, fantastical dream. For that is how it always was for me, watching Noelle perform. My eyes and ears disappeared inside her to where I saw and heard nothing else, just this beautiful spirit in flesh form towering over me and the surrounding crowd, sharing her essence with us.

Was I not so fortunate to be hers? I had forgotten that over time. And each performance I experienced reminded me of how she had captivated me in our first encounter.

So much of what I loved in life, Noelle exuded: art, beauty, ambition, humor, adventure, the richness of the senses, spontaneity.

My heart smiled when she launched into my favorite of her songs as the last in her set. "Singing Through Sleet," the one about the rare sleet storm in New Orleans and the lovers running for cover under the balcony on Magazine Street. While the narrator sings as they run and then while waiting under the balcony for the sleet to pass. Being lighthearted and optimistic and taking joy in the moment, namely an uncommon moment—so much like Noelle herself.

After her set, I wanted us to enjoy the Maple Leaf's back patio, but I knew from experience we would keep getting interrupted by adoring fans from the crowd. We said goodbye to Ben and the band, crossed the music hall through the thick crowd of revelers, into the raucous barroom, and out of the door.

"Another brilliant performance, babe. Let's head to Oak," I said, once outside. "Just a block away and so much quieter."

And it was against the white marble bar of that place that my Friday night began to unravel.

"I forgot to ask," I said, "you come across that royal blue handkerchief? It's my favorite one from my grandparents. I don't know when I last wore it, but it was in the last few days."

"You look distraught, even crushed, Laurent. I wish you would miss me like that, when I'm away."

"How do you know I don't?" I said, smiling.

Noelle sipped her Cosmopolitan, paused, and then unleashed hell. "Seriously, Laurent, your handkerchief's not in my place. I clean really well. And I clean every other day. I'll look in my car, though."

"Fine," I said. "No problem."

"Laurent, so—you and I have talked about this, but I've been feeling L.A. calling more lately. Even more than last month. It's not just that I've grown bored. I've done it all here, over and over, all through the city, and I feel like I've reached its limits. And I don't feel as inspired as before. Am I making sense?"

Each one of her words felt like the jab of a needle into my soul.

"Noelle? This doesn't sound like the Noelle I first knew," was all I could say.

"Laurent, please, hon. Being young and living in New Orleans is about people getting fat, sweating to death, and getting drunk. Going from hangover to inebriation to hangover. While, every day, risking being murdered, or at least robbed. And I struggle with this sometimes."

I couldn't stifle the laugh erupting from within me. "Noelle, you've listed most of the negatives. You know the positives. What about those?"

"The positives outweigh the negatives? New Orleans was great for me at a certain time, growing up. Then getting started in my career. But now I—I'm already twenty-six and I'm at a crucial—"

"Juncture, pivotal point?"

"Yeah. Yes."

"If you're saying this having just played one of the most New Orleanian of New Orleans places," I said, "you got a big problem with this city."

"Look, I love the Maple Leaf. I've got another set there next week. I even love the owner, Hank. But that doesn't change what I'm saying."

"Noelle, are you breaking up with me?" My question was met with a momentary widening of her eyes, locked onto mine.

"No, Laurent."

"Then, does being in this relationship make you feel trapped, Noelle? We've talked about it before, settling down here and one day starting a family—"

"Agh, Laurent, that kids subject again. You always bring it up. I know it's been on your mind the last few months. Mr. Procreator Gladiator."

She was hitting me again with that amusing nickname she'd coined.

"Noelle, I've been thinking more of kids. I'm thirty-nine, remember?"

"Sometimes I think you want us to have kids so you can forge the nuclear family you didn't have, for long."

"Not true, Noelle." But was she correct?

"I didn't have much of an immediate family either. So don't sweat it, Laurent. I told you my dad never made any time for me. One reason I keep telling you to stop disregarding me. Backburnering me."

My heart dropped, as did my eyes, toward the bartop. That old sense of failure returned, imbuing my every cell.

"I'm sorry, Noelle."

"Yeah. Well, sorry it cursed me, Laurent, with being attracted for years to emotionally unavailable men. And men who don't make enough time for me."

Seconds passed. She smirked, awaiting my reply. Shame enveloped me. I had devoted that night to her—but perhaps I did not love and value her to the extent she deserved.

I remembered that first encounter with Wilson weeks before, that night at Buffa's. His words of adoration for his dead wife: *But Katie, she was my everything, and I'll never love again. Or try to.*

"Anyway, having children is light-years from my mind, Laurent. Plus, neither of us is financially stable. Now you got fired, then hired, and you're rebuilding from scratch."

That last line cut the deepest. Many seconds passed, and I could not reply, but merely sipped my Manhattan. Accumulating at the white marble bar were men in sport coats, and women sipping wine and French 75s. I ran my eyes across the white walls, white ceiling, and white columns of that establishment, opposite in style from the Maple Leaf, wishing the brightness and elegance of the place would lighten the moment. I longed to return to my place and shut myself inside, alone.

"But Noelle, I landed that great new chef job today, remember?"

Yet it was as if I had said nothing.

"And I hate saying this, babe," she said, as I winced inside. "You've got to make some hard changes before you ever become a dad. Get more sleep, drink a lot less, sure. But you work early, and late, and on weekends. And through holidays. You've been married to your kitchen staff, hon. And instead of children, you got the food you prepare."

"Noelle, you've been dating a chef," I said. "This is a given. And I'm straight edge compared to many chefs. Alcohol and caffeine, and here and there a little nicotine and that's all it ever is with me. And I've gotten a day off per week, Noelle. And half of each Sunday, right?"

"Now Laurent, come on. You say it's only alcohol and caffeine, and that's truthful. But how much alcohol? You always blame you helping your family as the reason your career hasn't advanced further. That's there. But the *main* reason? Your drinking and hangovers, your spending on food and drinks all over the city? Saps your energy, concentration. And money. Self-sabotage."

I was stunned into silence. I knew there was truth to some of it.

"And about me ditching New Orleans," she said, "maybe this is just a phase. I've been thinking of New Orleans being limiting, but I'm just sharing how I feel. That's part of any relationship. A healthy one."

"Noelle, I'm hoping it's a phase." After all, Noelle was not exactly predictable, even to me.

My eyes scoured the white marble bartop for the next subject. Noelle making that move to California? My stomach burned. I could no longer discuss it—not on a night out, over drinks.

"So, a question," I said. "Are you and Ben working on a new album?"

She looked relieved, probably thankful to move on to a lighter subject.

"Absolutely, and I really like it. But I keep having Ben and the guys redo the tracks with me. Like you, chasing glory and greatness. To be at the top of my form. If I listen and feel I could've done better, I go for a do-over."

"Fantastic," I said. "And singing gigs? Besides this one tonight?"

"Sure, I've got some news," Noelle said, her eyes illuminating with an inner light. "This attorney saw me perform on Decatur at the Palm Court Jazz Café. You know, near the French Market?"

"I know that spot."

"Months later, at Three Muses on Frenchman, I see him again. He introduces himself after, to me and Ben. Said he could get me in as a singer at his favorite bar, that upscale, romantic jazz club and restaurant on Conti, The Bombay Club. The one decorated like an English manor. He also said he could get me a slot singing at Loa. You know, that sleek, trendy yuppie lounge downtown, with the candlelight on the walls? Even said he had a party Uptown he wanted me singing at. Guy wasn't lying. It all came to fruition. Just in the last few weeks."

Her smile broadened to the point of being radiant.

"I guess while I was in my own world, in the kitchen."

"Yes, babe. How'd it go with your restaurant?"

"Exciting things are happening," I said. "I really like my new venue's owner. He'll give me almost free rein with the menu. Even reworking the decor, once his current staff leaves. And we launch with my concept. Over the next few days, I'm interviewing and testing my new kitchen line. Our soft opening should be coming soon."

"Look at you," she said. "I'm there, if I'm not performing that night. So—fusion cuisine. In—New Orleans."

Once again, I felt knocked down by someone so close to me. Perhaps I would one day join them, and at last give up on myself.

"No one believes in the mission. Except me, Pham, and the owner, Wilson," I said. "Everyone's gotta be a naysayer. Even you, Mom, and Mémère. And Jim for a bit, before he recovered."

"Laurent, we both grew up here. You know how people are about their Creole food. And their Cajun food. They probably aren't ready for it, not in 2014. This isn't New York, San Francisco. It's not Austin."

"I suppose you're just waiting to see how I perform," I said. "But you doubt me, overall."

She sighed, but said nothing.

I leaned forward, thankful I had already paid my tab, and spoke into her ear. "As for me, I'm calling it a night. Let's head out, Noelle."

As I stood, I caught her astonished expression. She slowly rose, as if with reluctance.

An odd silence overcame her, persisting even until we sat inside my car. I started the ignition and turned toward her, just as her voice reemerged.

"Laurent, it's not that I've doubted you, and your talents. I doubt this eating public, if that's a term. But I don't doubt you, Laurent. And I don't doubt our love."

Second by second, her eyes lifted until they came level with mine.

"Laurent, I haven't said this enough, but—you know that I really do love you."

Surprise must have flashed in my eyes, for she laughed at my expression, her eyes darting from one part of my face to another.

And then, as if annoyed, with a slow blink she sighed, shaking her head.

Noelle was a hard one to read and even harder to predict, I thought yet again, as a smile started to play at the side of her mouth.

CHAPTER 10

I t was two nights later, and hours after The Cayenne Club had closed after Sunday brunch service. Wilson's old kitchen line had departed, and then Osvaldo, after cleanup. One kitchen candidate left and the next remained across the dining room from me, standing at the hostess's podium. They were all so different from each other. And this new candidate was most intriguing.

"Ready?" I called.

The candidate nodded his head of longish, combed-back auburn locks, descending from a brown velvet beret. He was a large-framed, portly man, but not quite as heavy as Wilson. He approached with his chin high, almost with an air of haughty imperiousness. Until I saw his blue eyes, warm even to the point of tenderness. Here was a dandy, complete with a brown suit, brown vest, and red bow tie. Patent leather dress shoes encased his feet. The style even seemed vaguely Victorian. Was this a twenty-first century Oscar Wilde? All he needed was a cane.

He was going for our opening for *pâtissier*. And he looked the part—plumper than the rest, but not to the extent that would keep him from being an effective player on the line.

I extended a hand, which he shook with a surprisingly firm grip. "Mr. Ladnier?" he said.

"That would be me."

"I'm Roosevelt Flannagan," he said. "Many call me Rosie, or Rose."

"A pleasure. Have a seat," I said as I sank into my chair.

"So—would you be willing to work in this attire? Just kidding." Glancing down at his résumé, I said, "So why are you looking to leave The Barrington?"

"It's a hotel job. Hotels pay higher than most restaurants, as you know. Provide the best benefits. But it's not advancing my career. I'm taking higher pay over building my résumé—and being able to try my hand at new things and show off my talents. I never want to see another steam kettle or butcher station again. Or see our waiters breaking down a buffet."

"I can appreciate that," I said.

"I want to join a new place that doesn't skimp on creativity," he said. "Where creativity is actually the focal point."

"Sounds like you're quoting me, Roosevelt."

He laughed, then said, "Glad you feel the same. And I'd love a restaurant that isn't just transient, with so many tourist diners. Or the well-heeled Uptown geriatric types that used to flock to Cayenne Club, geezers wanting the same worn-out spread of dishes."

It was uncanny, I mused, how his views matched mine. It was a comfort to find this kindred spirit. What if I could find more of such people?

"I'd love to work at a place that innovates," Roosevelt said, "and that's intimate, that feels like a private dinner party. And the menu doesn't need to be super-elevated. The line doesn't need to mount its sauces with foie gras, or garnish dishes with black truffles."

"I often share those same sentiments. So Roosevelt, what's your philosophy on cooking? And making desserts?"

"I always hope to get those people who don't have a sweet tooth to be so wowed they wonder if my dessert was even better than the entrée or apps. I want them to get as close as possible to having an amazing orgasm, but with their taste buds, by eating."

I stifled a laugh.

"And I want eating my dessert to become a great memory," he said. "I've read customers tend to remember the apps and dessert the most, if they have a three-course meal."

"True," I said. "Interesting how that is."

"So, I think this place would be good for me," he said. "And I like fostering a little friendly rivalry in the kitchen, as to what feedback's more positive—the desserts, apps, or entrées."

"I love it. I like you, Roosevelt. You and I share a lot of the same philosophies. What's your favorite thing to prepare? Your specialty."

"For dessert, my raspberry soufflé. And my blueberry one is a close second."

"Nice," I said. "But because this isn't a French restaurant, in place of raspberries, what are your thoughts on substituting lychees and kiwis? Japanese plums?"

"Sounds exciting," Roosevelt said.

"Where do you want to be in a decade, when it comes to food? Your dream?"

"To own my own *pâtisserie*. Where I make at least most of the product."

"Nice, Roosevelt. If I hire you as our pastry cook, would you be good with thirty-six hundred a month, for the time being? And a six-day work week?"

"I am," he said. "I'm ready to make the move. The leap."

"Just what I wanted to hear," I said.

Was there any essential question left to pose? This was a veteran of hotel kitchens. I didn't need to ask if he was willing to come in very early, like most *pâtissiers*.

"Roosevelt, I'll call you in the next couple of days to schedule a cooking demonstration. We do have a few more interviews." Yet I sensed Roosevelt would clinch it.

The next visitor in that chair was also intriguing, yet edgy.

"Etienne Babineaux," I said, scanning his résumé. "Excellent name. You hail from Breaux Bridge?"

"I do. Full-blooded Cajun, down to the cookin' fingers." He held up both hands. Half of his left index finger was missing, and his forearms were covered with bad tattoos and more than a few burn scars. His dark eyes squinting at mine were granite-hard, untrusting and topping a web of wrinkles, and his cheeks were ruddy. Too much sun or good times, hard to say which. Porcupine spikes of dark brown hair ascended from his head, with mere stubble on the sides. I imagined his rebel Acadian ancestors, refusing to take the oath to their British conqueror, King George III, instead choosing the surrender of all belongings and then deportation to parts unknown.

"I was a line stud by age eighteen, peeling fifty pounds of shrimp in one clip. And I can really sling some food," he said, his striking chin jutting outward and slightly upward like the curved end of a cudgel. "I'm hoping you got an opening for sous. And if not, that I can move into that role *very* soon."

My, quite an ambitious one. First things first, Etienne.

"I brought my sous chef aboard from my last kitchen," I said. "But we can talk about a sauté cook role, or an alternating sous chef role soon. But first, there's an interview process here."

I chuckled, then cleared my throat.

"So, looks like you've been a broiler man at Temps Perdu for two years. Nice place for steaks. And both Cajun and Creole. You were at a Cantonese spot before that, for three years. I like that, both southern Louisiana regional and East Asian. That's what I'm ideally looking for."

"That's great to hear," he said.

"So Etienne—what form of cooking would you hope to do if we brought you aboard? You saw my ad, that my menu will be 'world fusion, with south Louisiana influences.'"

"Cajun and Gulf Coast cooking but not necessarily all handcuffed to that. I fancy surprisin' the diner. Something they've never quite seen before and certainly never tasted before, but on the surface, it might look like it started out as something they remember."

"I think I follow. So how important is originality to you in cooking? Or is it more important to get something well-known right, to render it in a correct fashion?"

"Originality's important. Near the top."

"Near the top?" I said. "I like that."

"But I also want people to leave feeling completely satis-fied," Etienne said. "And so wowed they tell five people, ten people."

"Nice. Good answer, Etienne. Have you found any original Cajun dishes here in N'awlins?"

"More traditional than original. But I've found a couple guys do it damn good."

"So, like Donald Link?"

"Yep. Donald Link is popular, of course. But he's also the real thing. My go-to chef for Cajun food whenever I'm here in N'awlins. Link's an actual Cajun."

"What about Lacassine, Luc Breton's place Uptown? Been there? What's your read on that?"

"His use of cheese and offcuts is elevated. His stuff isn't upper echelon, or authentic. But it's respectable for Cajun cooking done outside of Cajun country. You couldn't pay me to work for Luc Breton, though. I'm not into masochism."

I laughed. "Etienne, what do you like to cook on your off-time, at home?"

"I love doing charcuterie. Making boudin, too. I've thrown a few *cochon d'lait* parties for friends. And you'll like this: I like making pho. With brisket, rare beef, ham hock. But I've thrown some tasso in there, and a touch of cayenne. Acadianed it up a little."

"Ha, fusion. Music to my ears," I said, feeling that comfort-ing warmth, as from a thick woolen coat in winter. Another kindred spirit had arrived.

"I know my pho's quirky," Etienne said. "But New Orleans chefs tend to cook in quirky ways. Right?"

"I'd agree with that," I said. "Not as much original, as quirky."

Interesting—Etienne already called himself a chef. And he cooked fusion pho. If he checked out, I'd have to keep an eye on this one. He didn't just want a job; he just might want *my* job.

"So many of us are quirky, idiosyncratic, but a chef must have a point of view," I said. "Like a writer must attain a certain unique voice. I like that you can cook pho. It's really catching on here, too. Perhaps because Viet cuisine is delicious but light."

"Love that Viet food," Etienne said.

"It's just what NOLA needs," I said, "an alternative to so many heavenly, but heavy dishes."

"Lord knows we got the heavy part down pat," he said.

"Let me think about it, Etienne. I'll shoot you a call or email either way. But I'll probably be calling you today or tomorrow to schedule the next stage of the interview. A cooking demonstration. Each candidate for my line does this. If you pass, and I think you will, are you good with thirty-six hundred a month, for pay? On a six-days-a-week schedule?"

"For now, sure. For the near future at least."

I nodded and we rose in tandem, our hands clapping together in a handshake bordering on painful, from his powerful grip. I also noted a slight limp as Etienne crossed the floor toward the front door. No doubt some rich tale hid behind that detail. Etienne Babineaux, a character indeed.

I knew it in my gut, hours before I was to invite them to demonstrate their cooking skills, that Roosevelt and Etienne would get an offer. And of course, the ever-loyal Pham, whose powers I would never test. That made four in the kitchen, including myself. Chef, sous, sauté, pastry. I envisioned one more. Two more Wilson could not afford, at least not now. I could spread Roosevelt out to other tasks when he was idle, when there were no desserts needed—he would be the *tournant*, the rounds chef. What we needed was a *garde manger* to handle the cold apps, salads, vegetables, and help with the fish.

The door opened and a man filled up the frame. He was red-haired, his face speckled with freckles.

"I'm Matt Diggs," he said. "Laurent?"

I recalled his name from the phone call that morning. The line cook at that breakfast joint in Mid-City, Mama Knows, or Mama Knows Cooking.

"Yes, sir. Welcome," I said, and offered him a seat. But I could see it in his gaze. Telling me he didn't care for me—without saying a word.

He sat in silence. "Y'all still got a line cook spot open?"

"We do," I said, hearing the words upbeat and almost lilting in my throat as I strained to mask my unease. "Say, Matt, I didn't get a résumé from you yet."

"Well, me as a line cook at Mama Knows, that's my first cookin' job ever. But I do it so good. Anything Southern I can whip up lightnin' fast. And there's a lot I can cook when it comes to Cajun and Creole. And I can also do yakamein. Not many people know how."

"That's true, Matt. Not many do. What do you think about putting new spins, new riffs on soul food, Cajun, Creole? As in, with Asian influences? Middle Eastern and Indian influences? What if we were to do smothered chicken, but say, with an original sauce, partly African peanut sauce?"

He met my query with an almost irritable stare, which three seconds later morphed into laughter. "I'm not sure. Then it wouldn't be soul food. Or Cajun, Creole, or anything even close to bein' Luzianna."

"Fair enough, I hear you," I said. "What do you like to cook, Matt? Your favorite dishes? And what are your strengths?"

He was silent for a good while. "Mac and cheese. Chicken and andouille jambalaya. Gumbo. Shrimp Creole. Meatloaf. Collards. That's my specialty and what I like cookin' up."

"So, if I call you later to see if you can cook a dish for the owner and me, are you game?"

"Hell yeah, I'm game," he said. "Does a bird fly?"

The masculine energy coming off him brought to mind Etienne, but here was something else. An odd rivalry, a condescension, and an almost bristly dislike. I couldn't see him on my side in the heat of battle, on the line during peak dinner hour. And that opposition to my style of cooking. This line cook belonged in a far more traditional kitchen, not mine. Unless I reconsidered.

"I might give you a call later, when I'm scheduling follow-ups."

"Sounds good. I'll be waitin'," he said, then shook my hand and left.

The next arrival was unexpected, but not unfamiliar.

"I remember you," I said with a smile. "The star of Bacchanal's outdoor kitchen."

"I try," he said, now across the table from me as I rose to my feet. He extended a hand. "Ramón Aguirre. You didn't call that number I'd left you." He laughed. Then he said, "But I found your ad. Mind if I sit?"

"Of course," I said, shaking his hand. "Apologies, Ramón, for my lost manners. Good to see you again. So which position are you applying for?"

"The sous chef spot. I think I have the chops for that. I can show you what I've got, again, if you'd like. But I'd like to cook in your outfit, period. Remember, I saw your WWL special. Knew what I was looking at."

"Thanks, my friend. You still over at Bacchanal?"

"I am," he said. "Looking to make a move. But the right move."

"How is it working for Chris Rudge? And with Russell Ledoux?"

"Great people as you might expect," he said. "You know them?"

"Russell's tight with my good friend Jim. And Russell became a friend of mine. And Chris as well. He's admired in the city for good reason."

"Oh, damn. Please don't tell 'em you found me looking."

"I promise I won't, Ramón. You've got my word on that.

And my word means something. But full disclosure: It's against my code to peel off talent from a friend's kitchen. I can entertain you maybe coming aboard, but it would have to be when you were no longer working there."

"Seriously? Well, I could have lied."

"No, not that, Ramón. I'm sure you'll agree if you think about it. Just come see me when you've already jumped ship. I already suspect you'll pass the cooking demo."

Ramón rose, biting his upper lip, his lower jaw protruding in an image of frustrated regret. He shook my hand again.

"Laurent, I respect a man with a code. And a chef who respects other chefs, and his friends."

"Thank you, Ramón," I said. "Maybe we'll see each other soon."

He nodded, crossed the dining room, and disappeared out the door.

Wilson said behind me, "I would have interviewed him and vetted him. But I respect your thinking. Maybe I should think like that again—I thought that way, when I was younger. Anyway, I'm hitting the bathroom."

"Well, a chef," I turned and said as Wilson approached the rear hallway, "a business owner, really a leader of any type will suffer a bit in adhering to one's own code, and scruples. But there are certain lines I don't want to cross."

Something moved outside the window as I sensed an odd lump in my throat. It was Minnesota, of all visitors at this hour. He was heading toward the door.

"Certain lines we don't want to cross, like this one," I mumbled as the door opened.

"Minnesota, haven't seen you in a while," I said.

"Likewise," he said as he closed the door and stood, surveying the dining room with his gaze. "Wanted to see your new venue. Heard through the grapevine you'd settled on this spot."

"Settled, huh? Well, the New Orleans food scene is pretty—"

"Smaller than it seems? Interlinked?" he said with a wolf-ish grin.

"Well said, Minnesota. At least you didn't say 'incestu-ous' like everyone else. Come take a seat. How's the old spot? Emperor Gerard and our old kitchen pals? I at least miss my crew. Not so sure about Gerard."

"I understand. We miss you. And I know what you mean about Gerard. I've been sweating it out. White-knucklin' it, under his tyranny. He's gotten worse, if you can believe that."

"I can," I said.

"And you're missed, as I was saying. But I never would have become chef if you hadn't left."

"I guess you're right," I said, studying his narrowed eyes. He was hiding something behind them. Then again, he wasn't hiding it. He had just revealed it, in a sense, with his last words. No doubt he was grateful for my departure.

"So, fusion? Pan-Asian and Cajun-Creole fusion is what you'll be doing here?" he said.

"Absolutely. You got a taste of my menu, the rough genesis of it, at Gerard's spot."

"Just throwing this out there, Laurent. So if I bail, would there be any place for me here?"

There it was. He just had to ask. For whatever true motive he had for his visit, that question must have eaten at him.

"But we now have the entire team we need, Minnesota."

"You got Pham on board here as sous, right?"

"Yes, of course."

"But what if you lost your sous chef? Or I outcooked him?"

"Minnesota, you know Pham's not going anywhere."

"Hypothetically. If you lost any member of your line, would you ever consider hiring me?"

I paused. And pondered. That was enough for him.

"So, it's my little habit," he whispered. "Isn't it? It must be."

I glanced across the dining room toward the rear hallway. Wilson still had not returned.

"Minnesota, you know that's against my code. Maybe herb, but no hard drug *habits*. If I'm running the kitchen."

Minnesota's eager expression transformed into something stunned, then wounded. "I knew it. But you ran Gerard's, and you always fought alongside me in the trenches. You knew my vices. You knew your line like the back of your hand."

"I wouldn't have let you go then. You were at Bonhomie before I came. And I did cover for you, several times."

"L, I second-degree burned myself and kept working at your side when we were short-staffed two heads."

"But Minnesota, this environment's different. We're building a different culture."

"You've got to be kidding me, Laurent. You don't know how clean your new hires are."

"You're the one who had to ask. And kept probing, digging. Look, why go down in rank? You finally became a chef. Build that résumé."

"I'm bouncin'," he said, the hurt and astonishment in his face morphing into fury and disgust. "Off to my drudgery. Toxic as it is, yes, at least I'm still the new chef. Best of luck, Ladnier. Fusion, in New Orleans? World cuisine, huh? Shoulda hightailed it to Austin. Or L.A., Denver. Or Asheville. Whatever."

He rose from his seat and sighed, shaking his head. I thought to speak, to interrupt his plodding toward the door, but decided to hold my tongue. It would not help the situation and could only enflame it. I stared down at the table, as if I was waiting for him to fade away.

The door started to close, almost tenderly. Then a loud slam ensued. I looked up and he was gone. Just like Minnesota. Two armies always warred within his soul, one of gentleness and kindness, and one of darkness and fury.

Minnesota's parting insult lingered in my ears. What if he was right about my chosen city for my concept?

It was as uncomfortable as I could ever imagine, those last few minutes. If only my final moments with my old sous chef had transpired that last day in Gerard's kitchen, weeks before. But it was not my fortune, and it seemed to be part of a recent pattern. Whatever governed the universe seemed to want me to endure the most uncomfortable situation possible, in so many facets of my life. Was I being tortured out of whimsy? No, I did not believe in that sort of deity. Was I being prepared for choppier waters?

I slouched in my chair. Maybe I'd catch a break and some good news would find me and pull me from the morass I felt myself sinking into. Rejecting Minnesota—that was not what I wanted to define this crucial day in the life of my fledgling enterprise.

Wilson reappeared, heading for the kitchen at my back, likely to line up our second pot of coffee. It had been a long day already.

I joined him in the kitchen. My encounter with Minnesota left me feeling oily from his presence. Yet I still felt guilt over-all—must have been my Catholic upbringing. But truly, was I responsible for a figure from my past I could not trust? One I could not depend on? Who had rolled his eyes a few times before at my inventions?

Soon I found myself pouring yet another cup, and I sipped over and over as if I needed it for survival. Wilson winked at me, smiling. We waited another minute, then fifteen. I was pouring myself another cup when the front door opened. A slender white woman of delicate build, and no more than thirty, stepped across the empty dining room with hesitation. Encircling her neck a few times was an orange scarf.

"Laurent?" she called as I entered the dining room.

"I am. Would you be Brooke Durer?"

"Hi there. That's me." As I approached, she blushed.

"Take a seat there, if you would. Coffee?"

"No thank you."

She was beaming, her chapped but beautiful lips parting in a broad smile, revealing crooked but white teeth. We sat at the four-top, facing each other. My nostrils caught an unexpected but pleasant scent: sage and eucalyptus.

"So, you're applying for the line cook position?"

"Actually, sous chef would be ideal. If not, sauté cook."

"The sous position is taken, to be honest," I said, remembering Pham. Then I recalled Etienne. "And possibly the sauté cook spot, but we shall see about that one."

"Oh," she said.

"Would you also consider a *tournant*, a rounds cook role?" I said. "Or a spot as *garde manger*?"

"If there's a path for me soon into sous. Or even a sauté cook role, you bet. I'm really looking for a place that fits me, my personality. A team I gel with."

"If I have you in here to cook alongside about four others, are you up for it? In a demonstration?"

"Of course."

"So, you're over at Indian Summer. One of my favorite spots in town. What's your favorite thing to cook in a restaurant kitchen?"

"Thai and Indian. I love cooking goat vindaloo, chicken tikka masala. Dosas, and aloo gobi. And western Indian cuisine, like Goan stuff, with seafood and curry."

"Delicious. Do you cook any Creole, or Cajun dishes?" I said.

"Rarely, to be honest. But I believe I do it well."

"What do you tend to cook at home?" I said.

"Indian and Thai, but usually vegetarian."

"Great," I said. "What do you think about this: combining curries and say, coconut lemongrass sauce or ginger with Cajun or Creole cooking? Or with traditional Southern dishes?"

She laughed, her hazel eyes sparkling within an expression

of softness, of gentleness. That trait might serve as a good counterbalance to Etienne.

Yet in those eyes I sensed something else: attraction, and keen interest. But that was probably just my imagination.

"That sounds like a lot of fun," she said. "I'm down with breaking new ground. Otherwise, you get bored eventually. Right?"

"I like your perspective," I said. "Some cooks, chefs lose sight that cooking's above all meant to be enjoyable. Otherwise, why put ourselves through the stress and chaos? And those long hours? So, Brooke, tell me your philosophy of cooking."

"Cooking can be a spiritual art. When done right, cooking might be the most sensual form of all the spiritual arts. When performed badly, or unimaginatively, it just fulfills a function. Filling up your tank for the workday. That's cooking with the soul removed from it."

"I couldn't agree more," I said.

"And I think, Laurent, we should cook with love. With a spirit of love. You can be the most sophisticated chef, full of knowledge and technique. But if you don't give every meal and ingredient that love, you won't give the customer their best possible experience."

"I feel like I'm speaking through you, Brooke," I said and chuckled.

"Have you read Jacob Hardy's *Spirits in Your Kitchen*?" she said. "It's become like my scripture. That not only humans have spirit and energy. Animals do, and plant life has it. A certain remnant of an animal remains in the meat. Something remains in every vegetable, too, and eating it can influence who you are. Thoughts, behavior. And that a chef can evoke the essence, the spirit of an animal or plant through its presentation on the plate. Paying homage to it. Amazing stuff."

"I haven't heard of that book, Brooke," I said. "I'll look into that."

Many chefs would deem her a little too transcendental,

in interviews. Perhaps she was just more candid in mine. Regardless—I liked it.

"So why cooking, Brooke, as a profession? Lots of easier ways to make a buck, right? You stand all day, you lift so much, you cut the hell out of your hands and burn them, too. You sweat all day and inhale smoke. Like some mill in Victorian England. Or smelting steel in a plant."

"Laurent, I can't imagine doing anything else. I need to be cooking for at least part of my job. It calms me down, gives me peace. And I wanted to since I was maybe—ten? I love that feeling of accomplishment at the end of dinner service, the camaraderie and fun with the rest of the line. And that desire to improve the next day. I'd have to be pulled kicking and screaming off the line. This is my thing, my vocation."

"Wonderful. What's your ultimate dream in our profession, Brooke?"

"I'd love to own my own restaurant one day. Organic, vegetarian and maybe even vegan. With a yoga and meditation center and classes. And a small lending library and a bookstore inside."

"Splendid, Brooke. Not many of those in this town. I'd be one of your first customers."

"Why, thank you," she said. "Another reason you might consider hiring me: I'm a Level Two Sommelier."

"As in, you passed your exam and got your Advanced Sommelier Certificate?" I said.

"Exactly. I was tested on terroir, winemaking styles, the major viticultural regions. But the Big Kahuna awaits. I'll take that master's exam probably sometime later this year, or next. I have a passion for wine. I can direct your wine program, unless someone here's more qualified."

"No one at that level, Brooke. Superb."

She did cook at an excellent Indian restaurant, which would prove an asset on our team. And I loved that she was a Level Two Sommelier and interested in innovating in the kitchen. But her general attitude seemed an equal strength.

"Brooke, I'll be calling you soon to schedule that demonstration. If you pass it, are you good with thirty-six hundred a month, for pay? On a six-days-a-week schedule?"

"I am."

When I walked Brooke to the door, she made pleasantries and I replied but did not hear her words, or my own. I might as well have been an automaton; I was so entranced by one sudden insight. As she continued out the door and into the street, I turned the lock and smiled. I knew I had it. If their cooking demos checked out, I had my beginning team of four, and I was the fifth. If their cooking proved to be what I thought it was, I had my squad. I had my tribe.

CHAPTER 11

Noelle really brought out a lot of the romantic in me, and she had admitted something a few times. She loved how I often stretched the boundaries of both my imagination and her expectation, all to deliver some beautiful surprise. Like the single tulip shaped from edible candied chocolate I placed one winter night for her in my car's cupholder. And this must be another surprise, she likely thought, as I turned down St. Joseph Street and parked in front of my restaurant.

My thoughts reverted to Aunt LaFaye. How I wished she, too, would at last find love, after losing Big Bobby so many years before. Mémère had called earlier that evening to reveal that Aunt LaFaye was not upset, but she had wandered off drunk the night before and had not returned. But she had vanished before, every few months, for a day and night. It was that red double shotgun house Mémère and Aunt LaFaye had called the House of the Rising Sun—that was where my aunt would end up, before she would find her way home each time. Inside that house, she would descend into inebriation or, at other times, a drugged state. And as Mémère had whispered to me before, there was a man—and at times men—present. I forced the thoughts from my mind.

"Noelle, I've got something inside you'll like," I said, eager to introduce her to my new world, and the beginning of my dream being realized. I longed to give her a spectacular night, and for her to gain complete faith in my dream, and abilities. "Your night's just begun, babe."

She loved when I spoke like that. Keeping the spirit of mystery alive whenever we were together, teasing her imagination with some imminent revelation.

"The sign's missing," she noted. I looked up and remembered. The old cypress Cayenne Club sign above the door was gone, a discolored rectangle on the bricks in its place.

Inside, the air was warm, even cozy. The decor she knew from her occasional Cayenne Club lunches through the years was no more.

"You see this new decor?" I said. "A welcome change—I'd always found it cheesy and full of Cajun cliches."

"I agree," she said, smiling. "I remember it."

I was glad Wilson could not hear our comments from his third-floor apartment.

Noelle took in the Japanese folding wall, the large Moroccan lamp hanging in the corner, the framed Chinese calligraphy on the walls, and the Thai Buddha seated in another corner. Then the small elephant sculpture with an embroidered Indian saddle in another.

"Yes, interesting what you're doing here, L."

"You like?" I said as I locked the door behind us. "Definitely unique in this food scene."

I led her through the bare wooden tables to the four-top draped with white linen and set with cutlery. In its center stood a vase nearly overflowing with red long-stemmed roses.

"Oh wow," she said, pointing.

"Those are for you," I said with a smile.

"This is so thoughtful," she said.

"It means so much to me that you're here," I said. "Right before it's reborn. Just interviewed my candidates a few days ago. They're doing their cooking demos tomorrow night. I should have my new line this week."

"Exciting," she said.

"Maybe I'll work with them a long while," I said. "Kitchen

staff and floor staff both. One day this place just might have dynastic employees."

"What's that?"

"Mainly waiters, sometimes cooks that work in the same role as their parents and grandparents before them, at the same restaurant. You see this in Antoine's, Galatoire's."

Her nostrils were flaring. She no doubt caught that aroma from the kitchen—but it must have seemed a vastly unfamiliar scent. Not quite Chinese food, nor a Thanksgiving turkey feast, but perhaps something in between.

We threaded our way through the tables into the short hallway and service area, where I paused and adjusted the stereo. That immediately recognizable smoky baritone of Louis Armstrong filled every space and crevice around us. Even better, it was his interpretation of "*La Vie En Rose*."

"How fitting, Laurent," she said as I chuckled, motioning with a sideways jerk of my head to follow.

"And what is that heavenly smell?" she said.

"A mystery treat, ready-made for you right before I picked you up. Just need to plate it all up for us. But that's a bit later."

I reached into a kitchen cupboard and removed a bottle, then set a corkscrew and two wineglasses onto the stainless-steel counter.

"Something I hid away for the occasion," I said, uncorking the bottle. Pinot noir, a reprieve from her rotation of Shirley Temples, Cosmopolitans, and champagne. Noelle stared in silence at the crimson waterfall descending into the glasses.

Like the lyrics to the song around us, perhaps Noelle felt as if she was at that moment viewing her now-merry, magical world through a rose-colored or pink lens.

"Here's to another enchanting evening together," I said, raising my glass in a toast. "And may this beautiful woman enjoy the adventure I have in store for her, and appreciate its meaning."

Her eyes twinkled as she met my gaze with a broad smile.

"Now you've really piqued my interest, Mr. Ladnier. You've got tonight all planned out."

I smiled, then tasted and savored my wine. She followed suit.

"I'm liking this red-brown Mexican tile in your kitchen," she said.

"Nice touch, right?" I said. "And Wilson's got two great floor model combi ovens from back in the day when The Cayenne Club did high-volume business. Those ovens were overkill for more than a decade. But they'll be fitting, soon."

"It's so cute how you get thrilled by your kitchen," she said.

"I love it, Noelle," I said, closing my eyes and inhaling as if breathing in her perfume. "Just being here in the kitchen. Even when I'm alone here. Food is my religion. My kitchen is my church, my refuge. Inside here, I'm at my most confident. Even that smell of minced garlic cooking with shallots or yellow onions in butter or oil—it makes me feel more alive."

There was that other scent, I thought. A close second. Oyster juice, heavy cream, and white wine.

After a few sips, she said, "Besides being mysterious, and complex, you're pretty eccentric. You know that, right?"

I felt shy, even embarrassed. My gaze sank to the floor. Then my eyes rose to meet hers. "I know this, and you've known this. We've been together over a year, Noelle."

She seemed taken aback at my words, my grin, and my now-confident stare. Her gaze wavered and she took in my shoulders atop my slender frame, and the red bandana knotted around my neck. She knew I loved those talismans from my grandparents. I'd never found my royal blue one, but I had at least a few others.

"True," she said, smiling.

"So, I guess I shouldn't tell you I've fantasized of swimming in a pool of warm tonkotsu broth? And other times a pool of Korma curry?"

She laughed and shook her head. "You probably fantasized about covering me with that curry, am I right?"

"Just perhaps," I said, smiling. "Yes, I am eccentric. But I'm still going to enjoy you later tonight, anyway."

"That's rich, Mr. Ladnier. And bold."

"Not as bold as the surprise I have in store for you."

"Ah, Laurent—you keep talking like you're going to either murder me or show me some hot new car you've bought me with your new salary."

"Those are the only two possibilities?" I said.

"You cooked for me," she said. "That's the surprise. It was my first guess."

"That's not all, my lady," I said. "It's only that—I might sing for you."

"Silly Laurent. Always joking, like your friend Jim."

Releasing a quiet laugh, I set my glass down on the metal counter. "Keep enjoying your wine. I'm adjusting something in the dining room. Then I'll get our dinner—arranged."

I shot her a sly smile as I headed into the dining room. After adjusting the lighting knob on the wall, I moved the vase of roses to another table. Back in the kitchen, I passed her and headed about ten feet down the kitchen line, where I snagged a pair of mitts off the counter and opened the oven. Out came the two broad Le Creuset pots, which I set on the stovetop, then removed the lids.

I told her, "I've had my little concoction here waiting for us, set on warm."

"So this is it," she said. "And I know I'll be experiencing your own style."

"Absolutely. You've had it many times at the Lofts," I said. "But not this dish. Recent invention."

I grabbed two plates off the top shelf of the range and set them on the counter.

"Now you've got the face of a gleeful child playing in a sandbox for the first time," she said, as I ladled out some of the contents onto the two plates.

"Laurent, will you finally tell me what it is?"

I said, "Smoked quail, poached quail eggs, and turkey hash in duck confit with bok choy, Chinese broccoli, and water chestnuts, in ginger, za'atar, and garlic miso reduction. The American South meets the Far East and the Levant. One uncommon mix. Like all my quirks, I suppose."

"A dish as unique as you, my king," she said, topping off her wine, and then mine.

"Now that was a beautiful thing to say," I said. "You're the unique one."

"You know, you're the only man I trust," she said. "Besides my dear friend Ben."

"Another beautiful thing to say, my love," I said. "Let's sit down. Can you grab the wineglasses? I'll bring the plates."

We took the plates and glasses through the kitchen and service area.

"Ohhh, love the lighting, L. Great touch."

"Thanks, though it's a work in progress," I said as she led the way into the dining room.

We placed the dishes and glasses onto the table settings.

"And so is this dish," I said, "a work in progress."

"Looks like a stunner," she said, sitting and running her eyes across its elegant presentation. On her visits to Los Angeles and New York, she might have seen such minimalistic portions and such a geometric arrangement on a plate, but surely never in New Orleans. Or that combination of ingredients. Now to get her impression on the taste.

"Can't wait to bite into it, Laurent. But first, a couple snaps to mark the occasion."

She pulled her smartphone from her purse and took some photos of me, then her dish.

"I totally understand," I said. "I indulge more than anyone out there in ogling food. Thousands of pics in my phone of plated dishes."

"I'm not used to seeing this. I like it."

I said, "I'm enamored with the smaller portions you see in Japanese cuisine, and in much of Europe. That idea in French cooking of leaving the customer just slightly hungry after the meal, that's a good thing. And it's great for longevity, health. But that idea's rarely well-received on our shores. In New Orleans we're used to leaving the table feeling like our ribs are starting to come apart, stretching from the load."

"So true," she said.

"I want to push back against that. But not vehemently," I said. "Smaller portions, just not *too* small. And I feel like a great presentation on the plate, geometry and all, helps the brain in forming a distinct memory. It also sets expectations that the meal at hand will be different, and a cut above. Just my theories."

"I love that," she said, and sipped her wine. "You're a real philosopher of the kitchen, L."

"Ha. Something like that."

Noelle speared the largest cuplike dollop of the quail egg-turkey-quail mixture and brought it into her mouth before the runny yolk dripped away.

But what if she didn't care for it? I chased the thought from my mind.

She savored her mouthful, breathing through her nose, before she began chewing.

"Thoughts?" I said, though I could see she was already floored.

She made no reply but scooped another portion of the mixture into her mouth, this time from one of the smaller dollops atop her plate. I did the same. The wave crashed against my taste buds in the most magnificent way: that smoke from the quail's gamey flesh, the richness and creamy texture of the poached quail egg, the turkey so moist that it almost seemed injected with something, it was all there dancing with abandon on the tongue.

"Outrageously delicious, Laurent. And complex. So many layers and facets to what I'm putting in my mouth here. This is really the most amazing thing I can remember eating."

I could feel my heart pick up pace with her last words.

"Here or in L.A., and all your other stomping grounds?"

"Anywhere. Ha, I'm glad the portions are on the conservative side. Hide the leftovers, mister."

I smiled, then howled with laughter. Whether it was real or not, I felt my heart fluttering again. My night, and I believed hers, was becoming better by the minute.

"It's not that rich of a dish, though," I said. "I'm leaving you some for your fridge, my queen."

"You've got to be kiddin' me, Laurent. I'm so used to you eating yours and what I can't finish. Then going for more."

"The best chefs are sensualists who are given to wretched excess," I said. "Good one, from Joyce Goldstein."

All she could do was smile. "I've never met anyone like you. My wretched sensualist of the kitchen."

I unleashed a mischievous laugh, then sipped my wine.

"Anyway, you see the marriage of the East with the West, right there on the plate. In this one, China meets south Louisiana."

"Yep, look at those water chestnuts and the bok choy," she said.

I pointed to my plate with my fork and said, "The garlic is universal. But that sauce—oyster soy sauce, as thick as syrup, is very Chinese, like the ginger. The use of poached quail eggs, also hard to come by. I used the turkey, too, to offset the gaminess of the quail. Turkey and quail, so American. It's my spin on a Thanksgiving or Christmas Day meal, in a sense."

"It's astonishing," she said.

"The irony, though, is that for the last couple of centuries, this city avidly created a lot of never-before-seen dishes. Being a little freewheeling. Taking some liberties, with unlikely combinations, but in a more established, conservative manner than my full-on fusion."

"I'm following," she said.

"Remember the Crawfish Alfredo we had at Jacques-Imo's a month back? That dish was once New Orleans' hottest creation. Creole meets Sicilian. Antoine's invented Eggs Sardou in the mid-nineteen century. Those dishes aren't new today, but they aren't incredibly old. At Jacques-Imo's, remember that other dish was this union of soft-shell crabs and fricassée and béarnaise sauce, so that's N'awlins Creole, then it's fused with andouille sausage and dirty rice—which are of course Cajun. By now it's—established, mainstream. Almost no one would know it was once bold."

"So you're taking it one big step further, right?" she said. "You're mixing cultures, cuisines that are even more different? Like China meets South Louisiana."

"Exactly, Noelle. And it carries risk. Many Westerners think coriander tastes like soap. And many don't care for lemongrass and fish sauce. On the other side, many older Asians don't prefer fish cooked in butter and cream. Many don't eat cheese. But still, I forged ahead, and now East meets West meets the Near East. Meets Africa, to an extent. I'll be weaving more of that into the mix in the future. That's where okra came into Creole cuisine—Africa."

"Never knew that," she said.

"Honestly, Noelle," I said, and drew in a deep breath, "my inspiration came from my travels and that I've tried to just eat *everything*. But a lot of it's from my really—unique—heritage. Not a racial or ethnic heritage. More like the way I inherited from my family an obsession with all kinds of food. And I was truly blessed to have that heritage. Food was my escape from my life. Because I was never accepted by either community here, my mother's Uptowners, or people in the Irish Channel, where my dad grew up. Bullied and disregarded by many on both sides since I was five. And my innovations?

Folks in the Channel, many in Mid-City where we moved, they think they're bizarre."

"Really?" she said.

"Yep. That I'm doing bizarre things with Creole cuisine. People in the Village De L'Est, you know, Little Vietnam, even think it's an insult. Doing Vietnamese with pork in place of beef."

"Insult?"

"Of course. Some in the Village De L'Est take such offense to this. Like pho with beef only is a sacred cow that must be worshipped, and any deviation with new ingredients is an actual insult to their culture. And Viets do use pork meatloaf in pho. That's what *cha lua* is all about."

Her eyes enlarged, focused down onto her plate.

"Noelle, some have told Pham, and me, that someone along the line persuaded me to push barbecued pulled pork and smoked pork ribs and other ingredients into a perfectly fine bowl of pho. Then there's my fusing Vietnamese with Cajun and Creole and Chinese and Indian, Persian. Many older Vietnamese, mainly in my parents' generation, they think it's an insult to their culture, and so strange."

"You've never mentioned all of this," she said.

"And that's not all," I continued. "Many older Uptowners see me as the son of my father: a failed, tragic legend who lived and operated for some years in their neighborhood. Not as my own person. And the family in Little Vietnam, Village De L'Est that was close to my dad—that my dad sponsored in the seventies—they know of my creations. Some of them see me as a kind of thief."

That was heavy. I could tell I had her there.

"So, who accepts you?" she said.

"You do. And Jim and Pham and Ben. The artists and the eccentrics here. It's enough for me. But it's still painful. Every visit to the Irish Channel, Uptown, my mom's in Mid-City, and then out in the Village De L'Est reminds me. I'm glad I can call the Warehouse District home."

"Me too," she said, sipping her wine as she reached over and squeezed my hand.

"Anyway, so glad you liked my creation there," I said. "Ha, see why I've been chained to my kitchenette lately, practicing? And fanatically bent on this wild mission?"

"I do," she said. "That I do."

My night was a success after all, on all fronts. I plowed through my serving, though I could see her pacing herself. Her long gazes at me, even staring, caused her to pause in her meal again and again. I could sense it for sure, without hesitation: Noelle loved me. And she was thinking about us.

The meal was done, my belly eighty percent full, when the music stopped. Satchmo had gone silent.

"One moment," I said, rising. "Got another surprise."

I walked to the stereo and put in the CD. In less than a minute, Noelle would not believe her ears. *Dark Harbor*, her first recorded LP, released when she was eighteen. A limited release, maybe one hundred copies, and it was so very difficult to acquire one. It wasn't sold online, or in much circulation at that point. Perhaps she hoped it had been forgotten, buried.

I selected the third track, "Second Line Surprise." The one that captured her spirit. The exuberant song about the charismatic woman on a dinner date in a packed New Orleans restaurant, where she leads the diners on an impromptu second line procession around the dining room.

The music flooded the room as I approached our table. Noelle rose to meet me.

"Laurent, how in the world did you find—"

But then she saw I was about to kiss her, and she reached her arms around my upper back, and I pushed my lips against hers in a kiss so passionate it bordered on violent. She brought her hands up to the back of my head and pulled me harder against her, as if I could come even closer.

I scooped my arms under her and lifted her off the ground.

Cradling her against me, I walked her several steps across the dining room. What a perfect metaphor for that moment: being utterly caught up and swept off her feet by an underestimated but potent outside force. She had closed her eyes, enjoying the moment.

I lowered Noelle downward, her back placed onto the spread of thick blankets, and she turned to her side and saw I had laid her down on the stage. Again, how fitting. Noelle, making out on stage—a stage I'd had created solely for music.

Blankets—this yet was another part of my plan. Like playing Satchmo and Noelle's first LP.

In a violent frenzy, Noelle tore off her green velvet dress—I recalled it was a delicate vintage 1940s piece she'd bought while we'd been shopping along Magazine Street one day, at Miss Claudia's. I unbuttoned my shirt as fast as I could, then slid off my jeans. My final gesture was pulling my trademark handkerchief from around my neck.

I fell toward her but caught myself with the palms of my hands planted on either side of her. She placed a hand on each side of my face, pulled me down closer, and kissed me hard on the mouth. With each second, our passion waxed with intensity.

Euphoria coursed through my every cell. It was one of the most unique nights of my life, this private dinner date with my lover and friend, an interlude from our busy lives when she was delighted by my admiration for her art, while she was charmed and thrilled by my own. When she at last fathomed my obsession with my vision. If only more of those days with Noelle had been like that, when she seemed to fully believe in my artistry as I fully believed in hers.

CHAPTER 12

The next day, across the chopping island, they eyed me with uneasy faces, their backs to the stovetops: Brooke, Etienne, and Roosevelt. Pham and Wilson stood off to the side, beside the walk-in fridge. Each cook was dressed in a white polyester uniform from their latest restaurant's kitchen.

"This is it, folks," I said. "I'm assigning you each one dish to prepare. Roosevelt is doing a dessert, of course, and as this dessert requires more time to prepare, he's already gotten started. Brooke and Etienne, you'll find all the ingredients you'll need in either this walk-in locker here, in the pantry, or in the rear storage room. All ingredients are labeled. As I did here for Roosevelt, I am giving each of you the list of your ingredients, where each ingredient is, and a brief description of what I want you individually to prepare. Your assignment might reflect what you like to prepare, but with a twist. Maybe even with a major twist. Are you still up for the challenge? No matter how different your dish may be from your typical style?"

A flurry of hums, mumbling, and exclamations of assent burst from the trio.

"I think each of you has little to no fear," I said. "A great sign. We will see if you make the cut. I'm rooting for you." I walked around the island and passed the candidates their lists.

"Now look at your list for a few moments," I said. "I'll wait."

Brooke giggled. Then an expletive and chuckle escaped from Etienne, who stared down at the page in his hands. I could see his ensuing laughter ripple through his body. Like the others, Etienne was not used to my odd marriage of Cajun and Creole cuisines with Indian and East Asian.

"Spend the next ten minutes getting your ingredients and arranging them at your station. Don't stampede each other. When that clock strikes eleven, I'll give you the good word to start. And just remember, I saw something in each one of you that brought you to the second round. I see strong potential in each of you to join my crew. I smell talent in front of me. Show me and Mr. Wilson Turner here your best effort, please. We will both be sampling your gustatory delights."

Etienne nodded, staring at me with a keen squint. "Thank ya, podnuh."

"No, thank *you*," I said, then added in a louder pitch, "Just determine what your assigned dish wants to be."

"Wants to be?" Etienne said.

"Yes—I've given you the recipe thus far. But now you choose what direction you take. For example, do you want to go lighter? Or should you add some duck fat or chicken fat and make it richer and more comforting? Try to determine that early on. And don't forget, as Brooke here reminded me the other day, and it's so simple—don't forget to have fun."

My eyes found her. Breaking through her nervous expression was a beaming smile, and then a wink my way.

"Now go for those ingredients!" I shouted as Brooke and Etienne launched toward the pantry and walk-in.

I turned to Wilson. He stared back with this expression, one not fascinating, but fascinated. Perhaps he found me quite intriguing, or odd, but likely both. Whatever it was, he seemed devoid of the strain I'd seen him manifesting days ago.

Minutes passed. Soon it was sixty seconds until eleven.

"Sixty seconds 'til go-time!" I shouted across the kitchen. I turned back to the wall clock, saying a prayer inside for my three candidates.

"Get set—let's go!" I yelled. "Get those hands dirty! Let

your plates speak for themselves! Let 'em sing!"

As their workstations came alive, I turned back to Wilson.

"Let's discuss further revamping this dining room, shall we?" I said, motioning toward the dining room. "Can we walk?"

"Sure," Wilson said. "You've mentioned some additional ideas. Let's get down to details."

"Yes," I said. "I envision an interior that reflects our menu. Mostly regional southern Louisiana cuisine, but rendered in original interpretations. South Asian, East Asian, North African and Middle Eastern influences. So this decor should get people talking. Spark and fuel conversations about this place, its food, what makes it unique. What do you think?"

"I like it, Laurent. But nothing too outrageous, right? What do you have in mind?"

"The jewel of this room is that large exposed wooden beam up there. And those over there."

"Agreed. This one is sinker cypress," Wilson said. "The others are just cypress."

"We shouldn't add anything on top of the exposed brick walls. We're lucky to have them."

"I concur," he said.

"But we should add small items to what we've currently brought into here," I said. "Integrate them throughout to give the room a more exotic air. While keeping what I've arranged here, like the Moorish lantern hanging from the ceiling in that corner. The Japanese folding curtain over there. The elephant lamp over on that marble-top round table near the entrance. It's unique and our Uptowners should appreciate it. Many of these are imported from India."

"Conversation pieces. That don't overwhelm the room," said Wilson.

"Precisely. They just punctuate it, here and there. Spice it up. Over there, we could have a table topped with a pirogue. An oar, a crab cage, a couple conical straw Vietnamese hats."

"Right on, Laurent."

"Wilson, we should have a common symbol that keeps appearing throughout the place. Just as Brennan's has those great rooster statues everywhere, some being quite colorful. That's perfect for a restaurant specializing in brunch, being a symbol of morning. Maybe we can have a globe appear throughout. We produce an amalgam of cuisines from across the world, right?"

"Great idea, actually, Laurent."

"And wouldn't you agree that we should rename this place?" I said. "It's a rebirth, after all. Delta, we could call it. For both our Mississippi Delta here and the Mekong Delta in Vietnam. Or better yet, Café Mundi. A world café, as this is world cuisine. Or we could dub the place Crescent, for our city. Just that one word."

"I like those options, Laurent. But Crescent resonates with me, as a name. We'll talk further."

"Shall we go peek on the motley crew in there?" I said. "Ensure no one's killed anybody? Or already quit?"

When we walked up, we could see the frenzy buzzing in the kitchen. Pham watched as Etienne and Brooke zipped back and forth, agile on their feet, from their positions to other stations they appeared to have colonized. Roosevelt stood, fixed at his station, but his arms shooting around as if on fast-forward. Just at that moment, it hit my nostrils—the confluence of perhaps ten of the richest aromas, some of them my favorites. Sautéed garlic and onions, andouille sausage, curry, crawfish fat, duck. Smelled in isolation, each scent could transport me to a different memory. Or a far-off place I always longed to see—as curry whisked me away each time to India and Thailand and the heart of China with its countless cuisines. Baked duck ushered me at once to the French countryside I'd seen in my youth. Crawfish fat brought me to that Irish Channel kitchen decades ago, as Mémère or Pépère stirred the étouffée. Andouille sausage brought me to a house I once visited in Acadia, supported by wooden stilts in the marsh, its interior walls fully rustic, of rough-hewn, dark wood.

The trio creating this blend of aromas was working with such vigor and haste. Each contender wanted it—a spot on my cooking team. I could see the desire, the striving in each of them. And I did not want to turn any of them away; my instinct the day before was that each was well-qualified and could at least learn my style. But it would come down to the quality of the dish. And if it was prepared when I called time.

I checked my watch. Forty-five minutes in. The final sprint.

"Team," I shouted. "You each have fifteen more minutes. To finish your creation, and get it plated."

I turned and headed for the dining room, but then decided to turn back and watch them alongside Pham in their last minutes. How did they all get along, after all? Quite well, it seemed. No arguments or screaming. Etienne did roll his eyes and release some sort of impatient growl, but nothing more.

Roosevelt was delivering that marvelous final touch on his dessert: using the small butane kitchen torch to flambé its top layer. Just in time.

As the candidates plated the food, I cleared my throat.

"Excellent, team! Good timing. You now have three minutes. I will be seated along with Wilson in the dining room. Bring out your plates when I call time."

While I crossed the dining room floor toward Wilson, I felt both a giddy anticipation, and a touch of trepidation. I could hardly wait another minute to taste each creation. But what if someone failed? I would hate turning that cook away, but do it I must.

I sat at the small table, across from Wilson. He had poured water out for each of us, and set the table with a linen tablecloth, flatware, and napkins, with the exception of plates. Those remained in the hands of the three cooks arranging themselves in a line, about eight feet to my side.

"Why don't you go first?" I said, glancing at Brooke. Her

face was the picture of serenity. Was there a drop of anxiety or doubt within her? Brooke stepped forward with excited steps and placed a plate before me, then another before Wilson. She returned to the line, observing us through eyelids drawn down in relaxation, but not quite with fatigue.

I placed my fork into the Szechuan Shrimp Creole and Lo Mein. One attempt in my original goal to establish a Creole Szechuan cuisine, like a bold few once created Creole Italian. But would this prove a success by my latest culinary foot soldier? I heaped a decent amount onto my fork and brought it into my mouth.

As expected, a delight. My Level Two Sommelier was safe. I looked up at Wilson. He was chewing with a thumbs-up. I moved my plate to the side and turned to Brooke.

"Could use a bit more heat, Brooke, and that would make it almost perfect. Right now it's still excellent."

I turned to Pham, whose face glowed with excitement. Like me, he could envision our line taking shape. And he knew I would never test him in this way. This was for newcomers, fresh candidates. I knew his capabilities well and had eaten his dishes hundreds of times. Above all, he was perhaps my most loyal friend, sacrificing his latest job for me.

"And now for Monsieur Etienne," I said, grinning. "Your day of reckoning has come."

"I've had more stressful, believe me," he said, and stepped forward. He placed the plate before Wilson, and then before me, just the slightest bit too heavily. Odd. I could feel that rebel energy through so many intimations.

Etienne stepped back into the line and watched Wilson and me like a soldier standing at ease, his arms connected behind his back, his chest puffed out and chin raised. I brought a spoonful of his duck and andouille sausage gumbo—with water chestnuts, hoisin, and sriracha—just below my nostrils and inhaled. Heavenly. Better than I could remember mine smelling. I tasted it slowly, chewing even slower, breathing out of my nose with closed eyes.

Could it be? It could not. No—but it was. This wild-eyed Cajun had, quite possibly, beaten me at my own creation. But I would not admit it, and especially not to Etienne. I was their chef, after all. Any doubts I would have trouble with his cooking skills vanished. It was his pride and edge I must ensure to keep in check.

I took another spoonful and inhaled, then closed my eyes. I chewed, rolled the gumbo around from inside one cheek to the other, paused in thought—then swallowed. Indeed, he had bested me.

"So—Etienne," I said, opening my eyes. He watched with narrowed eyes and a roguish lop-sided grin. "All I could have hoped for. Good work!"

He nodded, and winked once.

"Wilson?" I said. But Wilson had already tasted the dish and was gazing at me with eyebrows raised.

"You don't even have to ask. Amazing, Laurent. And Etienne, I'm keeping you on our team if I gotta feed you lunch and dinner daily for free."

"Whooh!" I shouted.

At last, Etienne smiled, and he took a bow.

"Glad to hop aboard!" he said. "And hey, 'stead of feedin' me every day, how 'bout you just replace those two old-ass combi ovens in there?"

"We lack the capital for that right now, Etienne," I said. "They've got at least a year of life left in 'em. Priorities."

"If you say so," Etienne droned.

"Now, for dessert," I said. "The best meals all end with dessert, right? Roosevelt, you're up."

Roosevelt appeared wracked with terror as he held the two plates before him, each bearing a ramekin and spoon. His eyes were larger than I'd seen. His lips slightly parted, he was breathing out of his mouth as if to prevent fainting. The forehead and cheeks looked blanched and not simply damp—he was sweating with ferocity. Good thing diners wouldn't see Roosevelt's deluge of perspiration in the kitchen, if he passed the test.

"It's okay, Roosevelt," I said. "I know you'll do well. Come bring that over here. Can't wait."

Roosevelt inched forward in his polyester kitchen whites, at first with hesitation. And then with slow strides.

"Don't trip or fall over, bud," Wilson said.

I extended my hands from where I sat, and Roosevelt placed one plate in my hand. Then he handed one to Wilson. Roosevelt stood there between us, clasping his hands to his chin, his eyes bulging as they watched me.

"Kheer Brûlée," I announced to Wilson. "Indian rice pudding, using whole milk and ghee, meets the egg-and-heavy-cream-rich crème brûlée of France," I said to Wilson. "Served with a caramelized top layer and a honey-covered kumquat slice on top. Almond, pistachio, and walnut fragments inside, along with crushed cardamom pods and a dash of saffron strands, nutmeg, and rose water. India meets France meets—with that kumquat, Louisiana."

Wilson hummed with interest, and I could hear the cooks chattering. Surely no one save Pham had heard of my creation. Or any of them, for those were all my recipes, that night.

"Rosie, you could always do some hard sauce on top," Wilson said, but his face revealed he was not jesting. "Or a kiss of brandy, then flambé it after."

"Wilson, that's so very Wilson," I said and laughed.

"Scratch that idea of mine," Wilson said. "Roosevelt, glad you're not operating the blowtorch out here, with these nerves I'm seeing."

I moved aside the honey-covered kumquat slice and tapped the hardened top layer with the edge of my spoon, taking in those high and sharp sounds. Then I plunged the spoon into the top layer and into the pudding. I inhaled, then shoveled it into my mouth. I chewed, breathing out of my nose several times, straining to fathom every layer of what I was tasting. More golden raisins and more pistachio, almond, and walnut fragments than my version. Less crushed cardamom pods, thus less fragrant and floral notes. Less saffron strands and rose water, but more nutmeg than my version. And perhaps almost as good. Roosevelt had hit the mark.

"Celestial. Masterful, Roosevelt!" I stood up. "Wilson?"

He chewed as Roosevelt and Pham stood to his side, watching with riveted eyes.

Another thumbs-up from Wilson, and with eyes closed in bliss.

"Lady, and gentlemen," I said, turning to nod at Brooke and the rest of the line. "We have our team. You each made it. I'm offering you each the same monthly amount I quoted you in your interview. Pham is our sous. But I can offer Etienne the sauté cook spot, while doubling as the rounds cook, at least for now. A vital position. Brooke as *garde manger*, Roosevelt as our *pâtissier*. Here you'll build speed. Accrue a larger arsenal of skills. Improve on your techniques. Interpret the orders of your chef easier. Deepen your own identity as part of a line and in time, perhaps as a chef, when we open a second venue. And as your ally I'll support you if you want to grow into that role. So—are you in?"

With gusto, each cook yelled in affirmation. Except Etienne, who nodded once.

"Beautiful," I said. "Now I'll need everyone here no later than seven-thirty AM each morning we're open. But you'll get to work a split shift."

"Yes, Chef," many of them said.

"Give yourselves a round of applause," I said, and joined everyone in clapping. Wilson had disappeared around the corner to his office, and when he returned, the cooks were surprised to see him wheel out the rolling table topped with the bottle of champagne on ice, alongside six flutes. Wilson set the flutes on the table nearest to me and handed me the bottle. In a frenzy I tore off the blue foil atop the cork and popped it as the others howled with delight. The champagne fizzed and overflowed. I pressed my thumb onto the bottle's opening, then pointed it, laughing as I sprayed Wilson and then our cheering new kitchen line.

Exultation and relief vibrated through my every molecule. I was yet another step closer.

CHAPTER 13

———

Later that Sunday night, I opened the door for Jim, though I found myself struggling to move across the room to the door. Fatigue, partly. Desire for solitary time. And something else: worry over so many comments from others, like Minnesota, doubting my plans. It was remarkable how rapidly I could segue from a sense of triumphant exhilaration, and confidence as a chef, to near-paralyzing self-doubt over my craft. Even in the span of a few hours. But I had answered his texts. Though he'd briefly doubted my vision weeks before, Jim had regained his old self and resumed being so supportive.

"Hey, Jim," I mumbled. "Come on in, take a seat. Talk to me."

"What are you working on there?" he said, gesturing to the ballpoint pen and my black pocket Moleskine journal still in my hands.

"Designing my new menu," I said, and gestured to a thick volume beside me. "And doing a little studying."

"Of what?" he said.

"This is an exploration of molecular gastronomy," I said.

"Now that sounds interesting," he said. "First I've heard of that term."

"It refers," I said, "to the part of food science that explores chemical and physical changes food undergoes during its preparation. Affecting, of course, its taste. That most crucial outcome in a restaurant, right?"

Jim walked past me a few strides and stopped at my bookcase, staring up at its top shelf as if hungry to peruse its contents. I'd reread them so many times. Escoffier's *Le Guide Culinaire*. James Beard's *The Theory and Practice of Good Cooking*. Madeleine Kamman's *The Making of A Cook*. The two-volume *Larousse Gastronomique* 2010 edition. *The Joy of Cooking* by Rombauer and Becker. Waverly Root's *Gastronomy in America*. Julia Childs' two-volume *Mastering the Art of French Cooking*. Barbara Tropp's *China Moon Cookbook*. And Apicius' *Cuisine in Ten Books*, the first known cookbook, dating from the 300s in Rome. Its recipes for sauces were followed to some degree until 1955, in France.

"Like my selection on that top shelf?" I said, pocketing my journal.

"Most of it's clearly dated. Well, older," he said, "but timeless. Classics by the greats."

"Those books aren't just for inspiration," I said. "Seeing certain ingredients together over and over reinforce certain things. Seeing an exciting technique and ingredient in one cuisine and then a few in another often compels me to fuse them together within one dish. You know, Ong Ngoai, my father's close pal who became somewhat of a grandfather to me as a boy—he says I have what the Vietnamese call *tran hieu hoc*. The love of learning."

"Patently obvious," Jim said, grinning.

"Anyway, Jim, what's new with you?"

"Nothing much, just heading out to meet an old Boston friend who just arrived in town. But wanted to stop in first. Hadn't seen you in a few days. How's your new restaurant?"

"Everything's going right. Interviewed and hired my new staff, and the soft opening's set. But my grandmother hasn't seen Aunt LaFaye in two entire days."

"But your aunt's done this before."

"True, Jim. For one day and one night. But not for two days and two nights."

"But it's her general behavior, her pattern. Has your family filed a miss—"

"Yep, Mémère filed a missing person report yesterday. But this is the N.O.P.D. we're talking about. On top of this—anxiety about Crescent is eating me alive. What if I was overconfident in my concept and the public here? That it's a grand delusion? What if Crescent's an abject failure?"

"Why would it be? Let's examine the evidence," Jim said, facing me with his fingers steepled before him. He resembled a defense attorney during a trial, poised to set out on an argument.

"So most who tried your specials that day in Gerard's loved it. Same with Connaughton's dinner party. Wilson really liked them. As did most of his customers that day in The Cayenne Club. So why the self-doubt?"

"Because every last person's got to hit me with their opinion of true world fusion in New Orleans. That it's a risky bet. That this isn't the market."

"To hell with 'em," he said. "Chart and pursue your own course."

"But Jim, you know Mémère, Noelle, and most of my old Bonhomie crew told me this? Even you told me it's probably a risky idea here."

"Risky to some degree, but it doesn't mean it can't be successful. It's usually tough in the beginning and sometimes along the way for trailblazers. And Laurent, you're a trailblazer."

"It might've hurt most when even Noelle proved to be a naysayer, I've got to say."

"How's it going with her?" he said.

"I took her out for drinks, and to dinner a few times. We had an amazing date and talk the other night. She loved the new dish I cooked. But before that, last Friday at the Maple Leaf, she joined the local chorus of skeptics. I felt sick in my soul. And her words keep haunting me."

"But Laurent, you wowed Noelle after that with your cooking, right? Anyway, glad you answered my texts."

"You're a steadfast friend, Jim."

"And you're a great pal, Laurent. Let me share a bit about my own experience as an artist with friends and the public. It should help."

Jim started to pace back and forth across the room. "I stand astounded even today at how people I loved, and grew up with, reacted to my success. See, everyone who knew me from a boy of eight knew of my—authorly aspirations. That whatever I'd do for employment, writing was my calling and purpose. I built my youth and my higher education around it. Guess how many of my family and close friends from those years read even one of my three novels?"

"Very few?"

"Correct. And respectable awards didn't matter. Some never touched my work but always asked how sales were—a very American reaction."

"The money thing," I said. "Always."

"And one of my best childhood friends, Tom, lives out in California. One of my very closest friends for almost three decades. A voracious reader. Never read one of my three novels."

"Passive aggression?" I said. "Or just a disregarding?"

"That's unknown. And he could be very good with some things. Calling to meet up during holidays. Showing up at my family's funerals. But Laurent, the last couple of years he'd text me links to short stories from *The New Yorker*, and from the literary journal *McSweeney's*, then add, 'This is amazing!' Or text me out of the blue, asking if I think he should return to reading Faulkner."

"That's rough," I said. "And odd."

"This all cut me, Laurent, deep into my core. And though it didn't stop me, it slowed my progress and output. Certainly made me drink a lot more. Hell, it's also what made me start drinking again, after several years' hiatus. I halfway wanted to die. Alcohol numbed much of it, for several hours here and there."

"That's hard to hear," I said. "Truly."

"What I should have done, Laurent, was pay no heed. And just kept plying my craft. Creating, and enjoying the act of creation. You should too. Pay no mind to these people's reactions. Even your granny's. Even Noelle's. But those two will love it if you become wealthy, or even well-to-do, from your artistic gambit. As frankly, they stand to benefit. And your peers? Some will want you to succeed. But some will want you to fail, or to just be mediocre. Because they're insecure as to their own standing, and if you were mediocre, it would comfort them. It's the hard truth. So, ignore everyone. Press on. You must trust me in this: You have culinary genius, Laurent."

"No one tells me these things," I said, feeling relief wash over me like cool water.

"Laurent, aside from your creativity in the kitchen, that you love so many different cuisines, and aside from your grit and drive—what's your true gift and advantage? As a chef?"

"My ability to withstand criticism?" I said, grinning. "Of the constructive variety, that is?"

"Close. It's your humility," Jim said, then laughed. "Joking."

Jim was right to joke. I was arrogant, after all. I felt a tinge of shame.

"It's your relentless imagination, Laurent, itself the source of your originality. This is my well-founded theory. You're not content to forge a few never-before-seen creations. You're always searching for new combinations you can produce from an endless variety of ingredients. And fusing rare cuisines that have been rarely combined. Introducing ingredients not yet mainstream in kitchens here or in other parts of the country."

"Thank you, Jim," I said. "You know me well."

"And Laurent, from what I know, the greatest chefs are always keen to learn. Even established chefs, many still take new classes. Or enroll in programs. Many will shadow another chef for a day, or a few days. Not so with writers. I know many writers who publish their first book, and never again partake in another writing class, or join a writers' critique group. They think *they* should only be *teaching*. With other writers learning at their feet. Boneheaded move. They really miss out."

"Wow, Jim. That's kind of you. I'd have to say you're on target. And I know you're not one of those writers you mentioned."

"Know what most people in this country worship, Laurent? Wealth and status, both tied in there with power. Really, that impresses people more than talent or even greatness in an author or chef. Money over fame or recognition. People in a sense aren't worth impressing. You must follow your north star, if you're an artist. And that—entails fashioning the greatest art you can. *'L'art pour l'art.'* Art for art's sake."

"That's beautiful," I said. "And, I suppose, all very true."

I felt my confidence expanding by the second, rising from its crouch.

"Does all that help?" Jim said.

"Absolutely, Jim."

My phone buzzed in my pocket.

It could not be. But it was. I'd memorized the number. It was Rodney Reynolds, his landline listed in Mémère's phone book, and online. My heart raced as the phone vibrated in my palm.

"Jim, hugely important call, one second while—"

"All good," he said, letting himself out. "Goin' to pick up my pal. Look for you later, amigo."

When the door shut, I drew in a deep breath and answered the phone.

"Hello?" I said, pretending I did not recognize the number.

"Laurent Ladnier? This is Rodney Reynolds, returning your call, bub. You sure leave some looong answerin' machine messages."

I halfway had to force myself to laugh. Though I knew he was right, this was my father's old rival, perhaps at one time his enemy.

"Yes, Mr. Reynolds, I've heard that before. Thanks so much for calling me back. Do you have some time in the next week to meet up, grab a coffee or something? As I mentioned, I want to learn more about my father. I was only thirteen when he passed."

"Are you a drinking man, Ladnier?"

I felt my face redden. "A—a bit of one, yes."

"How 'bout tonight? Meet me at my neighborhood watering hole. Markey's Bar, in an hour. Know the place?"

"On Louisa Street, in the Bywater?"

"That would be the one."

"I'm there," I said. "See you then."

How could it have been so easy? Even so, a pit had formed deep in my gut. What might I uncover that night?

I sped over there, knowing I'd arrive quite early. But I'd stake out some spot, perhaps a quiet one at the end of the bar. I could start in early, order a drink, and quell my nerves a bit.

And that is just what I did. I hardly recall the drive over, as if I was locked in some trance, revisiting those last days with my father in the autumn of 1987. When he was not working on the GNO Bridge or lying hungover or strung out in bed, Dad was treating me to the cinema, throwing football with me in the street, and bicycling with me in Audubon Park. He did this at least partially, as Mom told me Dad had confided in her, to take my thoughts away from Champy's murder, months before. I often wondered if that whirlwind of quality father-son time was meant as a final goodbye, before he made his early exit from this world.

Markey's was not as full as I had seen it other nights. Perhaps because it was a Wednesday and there was some big event that night in the Quarter. I sipped my beer and recalled that day I rode the gondola with my parents 320 feet above the Mississippi River, during the 1984 World's Fair. I was but ten years old.

"We're so high up we can almost become part of the sky,"

Dad had said while looking through the window at the river far below.

"Daddy, what would it be like to fall from way up here?" I said, shuddering at the view.

"Don't ask," Dad said in a half-whisper. "Don't even think of it."

To think that three years later, he fell into that very river from an even greater height. I was finishing my first beer at my perch at the end of the bar when the door opened.

It had to be him. About two inches north of six feet, with the upper body and arms of some retired baseball player. And under the mostly gray mop of hair, there was the scowl and beady, smirking eyes of someone who would not be easy to manage, much less trust. In some old Western flick, he would have been cast as an old horse thief.

"Mr. Reynolds?" I said with a wave.

"Hiya, Laurent. Just call me Rodney, guy."

He approached and extended his hand. The strength of his grip rivaled Etienne's.

The bartender appeared, and Rodney ordered a bottle of Dixie beer.

Rodney paused, and, turning back to me with a smirk, said, "Now I bet people filled your head with all sorts of tripe. Like I'm your dad's so-called murderer. I never killed an animal, much less a man. But I'll admit, Claude and I did clash a lot. He sure could be a real royal pain in the ass."

As he laughed, I felt something flare up inside me, searing hot as a fireball. I almost wanted to swing at him. I knew I should have insisted on us getting coffee, and not alcohol.

"But I felt he was such a pain, well, just because I was cocky back then. For what we did, I was ambitious. I wanted to be the manager. I backtalked here and there. There were two different times we got into a brawl. Team stayed back, let us punch it out. He really could've canned me a few times. I was in favor of that stupid-ass war we'd both fought in—I always said we were trying to contain Communism—and he was firmly against us being over there. Even though it had been over for more than a decade. But he'd voice some of those hippie ideas from that time and it would just really grind my gears."

"Why and how do you think he died?"

"Honest opinion?"

"Of course," I said.

"Your dad had to have taken his own life. The investigators even proved his cord and straps weren't frayed. Clips were fine, too. That he had to have been at first fully secured with his harness. But released it while suspended. Like he intended to fall out. Like he'd planned it."

"We've always wondered," I said. "No one in my family ever broaches the subject, except me. I've had so many questions. But there never are any answers. There was no suicide note. There were no goodbyes."

"Oh yeah, speakin' of. Know another thing that leads me to believe it was suicide?"

"What's that?" I said, even more intrigued, but guarded, still unsure if I could believe him.

"The hug. Your dad came up to me, evenin' before he died, at the end of the workday. Gives me a hug. He'd never done that."

"Really?"

"We'd just gotten down from the GNO. The bridge. Told me I was a better man than people realized. Under my crusty, spiky shell."

Rodney laughed, then continued, "Then your dad said it was a good thing after all that we were on the same team."

Could I believe this? Should I?

"And I'm so glad Claude did that because it was like his goodbye. I think that's what he intended. Looking back, I remember his eyes looked different, a little misty. Like he got when he talked about his tour of duty."

I looked harder and it seemed his own eyes had become

the same. Rodney was either truthful, or one skilled actor.

"Is it true you wanted to be team lead, and you took his spot immediately after his death?"

"That's true. Look, Ladnier, I didn't kill your old man. Didn't mess with his cord, monkey with his harness, nothin'. Cops, investigators found nothin' on me. Because there is nothin' on me."

"I don't think he was murdered, Mr. Reynolds. Rodney."

"You know after your dad fell, I had nightmares for months?"

"Why do you think that was?"

"I wish there was something I could have said, or done. For this good man who overlooked my faults. My attitude. I already knew Claude felt like he was stuck, in life. I know he had suffered a lot of losses, hard times. Someone on the team mentioned he'd..."

His pause unnerved me. "What is it?" I said. "That he had—"

"That he failed a few times at running his own restaurants. Like two or three times. That he went broke. And that the war screwed him up bad. Really bad. That he tried to drown himself in booze and even got into the harder stuff, got lost in it, a couple times."

"Heard they found his blood squeaky clean?" I said. "The toxicology report. No booze, no weed, and nothing hard. This has always puzzled my family. I mean, was he trying to make a reversal?"

"No, goes along with my theory, son. I think he wanted to be clear-headed when he did it."

"Lucid? To make sure he was making the right decision?"

"Yes, sad to say. I'm thinking that's what happened. Claude felt stuck. Trapped. Like he'd always be spinning his wheels, goin' nowhere."

"I've wondered. And that, like you said, he felt he suffered so many defeats. But even more, that he was embarrassing us, his family."

"But in reality, Laurent, there was a lot to be proud of. Claude was a good man. Remember the hug and his words. He didn't have to do that. I think he was going to miss his team."

"I'm so glad you told me that," I said. "That does help me."

"Somethin' else leads me to think it was suicide, son. The point on the bridge where he fell."

"I've thought the same. From almost the highest point, you mean?"

"Kind of. I think he wanted to fall from a very high point on the bridge. So it would knock him unconscious on impact. And he'd just drown. But he didn't plummet from the highest point, from the peak. Why do you think that is?"

"I've made the same observation. Though I'm not sure Dad intended it."

"So, what is it?"

"Because Dad didn't want to split himself open on one of the platforms directly under those peaks. At the water level, where the two huge pillars are holding the bridge up. In the center of the river."

"Bingo, young Ladnier. I think Claude wanted to check out in a way that was painless. Fall might've been scary to him, or maybe not. Then he hits the water. Immediately knocked out and slips under the waves. Wakes up in the next world. But if he'd fallen from the absolute peak, he would've split himself open on the foundation, that platform in the water. Might've just lay there, dyin' a horrible death."

"Yes, I've thought of this. Standing under the bridge on the West Bank side, in that tall grass, near the trees. Not many people notice that the two columns under the center of each span don't just go into the water. They go down to those plat-forms. One under each span."

"We helped lay those foundations, your dad and I. We knew 'em well."

Much of it made sense. Like me, Rodney believed it was suicide, and for the same reasons.

"Anyway, Mr. Ladnier, I gotta get back to my wife. We're watching the grandkids. Just remember, don't let anybody judge Claude. Everyone always wants to judge. And we'll see him again. One day." He slapped a hand onto my upper chest, but I could not form the words.

Rodney fished a twenty from his wallet and tossed it onto the counter.

"Maybe you and I'll meet again, one of these days," I forced myself to say. "Thank you for meeting me, Rodney."

Though I liked him, there was something about the eyes. Still shifty, even wily. The eyes I'd seen when he first entered Markey's. I could see why my father might have mistrusted him at times.

Dad, be with me now, I prayed as Rodney winked, shook my hand, and walked across the bar and out the door. *Help me somehow confirm the truth, at last.*

CHAPTER 14

t noon on the following day, as Wilson and I were outfitting the dining room, I could not push the frenzy of thoughts from my head. I had ceased dwelling on my father and Rodney Reynolds. My worries about Crescent had abated. But Aunt LaFaye was still missing.

Mémère's call came as I ambled into my kitchen's walk-in. Her voice trembled as she implored me to search for my aunt. It had been years since I had heard her voice like that, I thought, as I rushed into Wilson's office.

"Should we delay the soft open by one day?" Wilson said, his eyes widening. Classic Wilson. "Laurent, how do you know you'll find her?"

"No delays. She will be found," I said, hearing my voice resolute in my ears, acting the part in every syllable. "One way or another. I've gotta leave for a bit."

Before Wilson could ask me if I was sure, I ran out of the restaurant and to my car.

Even more added stress and new chaos as the soft opening approached, I thought, as I sped westward. But my aunt was my father's only sibling. She babysat me as a boy, bought me gifts on each big day, from my birthdays to holidays to my First Communion. She brightened my dark moments for years with her humor. And she was part of us. Part of the shrinking remnant of our family. Yet in several hours, she would be missing nearly three whole days.

After parking, I unlocked my grandmother's front door and entered. Through the open kitchen door, I could see

Mémère chopping batonnets of celery. Normally I would stay at her side, helping her. But not today. I must be there for Mémère by searching for Aunt LaFaye. Her endless spiral and her refusal to reform herself, and to complete any stint in rehab—it was maddening, and after many attempts to get her clean, I had almost relinquished all hope. Even so, I could not detach myself. And I must find her.

"Hey Mémère," I said in a soft voice as not to startle her. She turned and I smiled.

"Hey sweetie," she said, her face striking me with its grave expression. "Wish you could take a seat here by me. While I get this soup ready. It is soup weather out."

I crossed the kitchen's linoleum floor and slid into one of the chairs.

"Mémère, you know how much I love your meals. Wish I could, but I can't sit idly and enjoy one while she's out there in grave danger. Tied to some bed. About to be stabbed to death."

"Or dyin' in some ditch," Mémère said.

"Two whole nights, Mémère. And in several hours it'll be nightfall, so three whole days. It's eating at me hard. She's never been gone this long."

"I know it. She's been gettin' worse and worse, Laurent. Crack's eatin' her alive, mind and body and soul. Heck, she might be dead by now. We know this in our bones."

"Where does she go—lately—when she disappears like this? Other than that red double shotgun house?"

"She never tells."

"She could've gotten a ride with someone. Mémère, your keys, let's get 'em. The tank's almost empty in my car and we don't have time for me to fill up. I need to look for her now. We can't just be passive and wait for a near miracle. With each night, it gets more dire. Hell, she might be out of her mind. In a stupor, wandering the streets. You never know."

"Follow me, baby," Mémère said. She led the way out of the kitchen in her nightgown, across the living room, and down the short corridor to her bedroom.

"Now, you know she's got no wheels, and I hide my keys really well. Even you prob'ly would never find 'em. They're under a floorboard under my bed. You can save my ol' knees and practice findin' the location. They're under the short board there under the suitcase. It's killin' me, hidin' 'em there. When I return from the grocery. Or from St. Mary's Assumption."

I lowered myself onto my knees, then my side, and reached under the bed. I moved the case aside and pulled up the loose board with the fingernails of my right hand. I could feel a few things under there, but my fingers settled on the keys.

"Now if you could put the board and case back," she said. I did so and slid further from the bed and rose to my knees, then my feet.

"How in heaven do you do manage this, Mémère?"

"Now, baby, I'm still tough as nails. Spanked your behind and your daddy's both. And your grampa when he'd done wrong."

We both laughed.

"Mémère, I guess you're right."

"Now you got more than half a tank. And a few hours of daylight left."

"Gonna give it all I got. Can't guarantee anything. Auntie's a real pain but we owe her this much. Plus, you know we love her."

"Bless you, Laurent," Mémère said as she let me out of the front door. "Bless you, baby boy."

I loved when she called me that.

"Mémère, I'll be back by nightfall. Or a little past."

As I proceeded in a slow roll down the neighborhood streets, I could tell Mémère's transmission wasn't long from going out. If only it could survive this one evening. And I took heart that the Irish Channel, like many but not all New Orleans neighborhoods, was laid out in a grid formation. Still, I kept glancing at my phone's GPS map to ensure I did not miss one street.

Would I spot Aunt LaFaye stumbling down a sidewalk? Or standing among others in an impromptu porch party? Or in the passenger's seat of a car as its engine idled, doing God knows what with or to the driver? I did not know. Chances were dismal that I'd see her at all.

At least Mémère had called the police and filed yet another missing person report. But then again—would anything come of it? Had they even gone to look for her? I should expect nothing. New Orleans was still a cultural gem, but by now rotten through, all the way from City Hall to much of the police department, even to the sewerage and water board.

Just on the cusp of giving up, I found myself mumbling, from both desperation and earnest humility, an old prayer to myself. The one my father used to say, the Prayer to Saint Michael the Archangel. Inscribed on the one prayer card he'd given to me. Yet I could only remember a section of the verse. And then, I paused. It was coming back, almost as if I could see that dog-eared yellowed prayer card I had lost two decades before. I whispered the words:

> "'St. Michael the Archangel,
>   defend us in battle.
> Be our defense against the wickedness and snares of the Devil.
>   May God rebuke him, we humbly pray,
>   and do thou,
>   O Prince of the heavenly hosts,
>   by the power of God,
>   thrust into hell Satan,
>   and all the evil spirits,
>   who prowl about the world
> seeking the ruin of souls. Amen.'"

It was almost as if my father were reciting the prayer to me from the beyond, from some unseen realm. But if so, what was his purpose? Did he desire that I at last turn to God? Did this memory signal that his sister was still alive, but in grave danger, encircled by evil spirits or dangerous people that hunted her?

Something pushed another memory into my mind: There was that one house I had heard Aunt LaFaye and Mémère both mention. The one many blocks north of the Irish Channel, even north of St. Charles, where the Lower Garden District bordered Central City. That double shotgun house with a red façade. My aunt had joked that it was the House of the Rising Sun and that she still visited friends there. That when she was younger, her times there had been her most exciting.

I cut short my canvassing of the Irish Channel streets and headed north, forcing myself to a rolling stop at each stop sign. It was odd—the streets were barren of activity, neither cars nor pedestrians. Almost as if a storm were approaching. Yet the sky was a uniformly cloudy light gray, missing any sign of a thunderhead.

At last, on the edge of Central City, I remembered what the mayor had said. It was the most incarcerated neighborhood in the most incarcerated city in the most incarcerated state in the most incarcerated nation in the world.

I was sweating through my shirt, despite the chill, as I sped past the parked rusting old clunkers, decrepit commercial vans, and hoopties accented with various degrees of bling.

A jolt rocked my entire body, and what seemed like Mémère's car itself. Was I shot? No, just a pothole, but a deep one. One of thousands around the city it seemed would never get filled. *Please,* I prayed, *don't let my tires blow now, and here.*

I parked against the curb just across the red double shotgun house, fittingly as red-faced as an alcoholic or drug addict. Just my good or ill fortune: The only sign of activity I had encountered in many minutes was this house. As I locked Mémère's car and headed up the walkway to the front porch, I neared the racing, almost violent rhythm of some metal tune blaring just inside the door and windows. Would they even hear my knocking? And what if there was no doorbell? This really could be my last night on Earth, with a door yanked open and a gunshot to my face.

I thought of my Aunt LaFaye. The version from the nineties, before the light of her soul had been blurred, the sparkling luster of her character marred by thousands of inhalations of what became her greatest love and her greatest enemy. The one who drove me to get cherry snowballs and ice cream cones, the one who saved me one day, running across the playground when an older, larger boy pushed me down and stepped on my chest, a boy she grabbed hard by the back of the shirt. Now it was my turn to repay her.

What if I was shot? Or a blade swung my way? Jim was right—I should not keep delaying that conceal and carry license class. What did I have to lose by doing so? Now I might lose everything. And then Mémère would be just about there, too.

I thought of Crescent, my greatest dream on the cusp of being realized, a dream that would perish that day with my likely demise. All my struggles, the decades of very early mornings and long days and late nights in kitchens, the stress, the insults, stitches, first and second-degree burns, had culminated at last in the promise of launching my concept's soft opening the following day. Yet in mere days I might lay in a casket.

I thought of Noelle, how I loved her but might never get to enjoy a future with her, nor say farewell. And yet—I had thought of my new restaurant before Noelle, and the shame hit. Perhaps she was right about me.

I formed a fist, drew in a deep breath, and knocked four times on the faded, peeling black paint of the door. And waited. No reply, just the thundering, angry cacophony of the song. But what did I expect, for them to be playing Noelle and Ben's latest? I inhaled deeply through my mouth. I spotted the doorbell, almost obscured by a black metal letterbox. I drew in another breath, then another.

Hurry up, Laurent, do it for your Aunt LaFaye, I thought.

I pressed the button. One seconds, two seconds, three seconds—and the music ceased. Another moment, perhaps five seconds. Steps approaching on wooden floorboards. I became aware of my violent heartbeat and reminded myself to breathe.

The door creaked open, just for a second, then jerked open wide. He was a tall, broad-shouldered white man in his early fifties with long, straight, greasy black hair, dressed in a stained white tank top. He drew closer, then stood looking down at me with very bloodshot eyes, an unforgettably irritated expression across his face.

"Hi there," I said, feeling a rush of confidence. I loved Aunt LaFaye too much to hesitate. "Don't mean to bother you, sir. Is this your house?"

"What's it to you?" he said in a half-growl. "It ain't for sale. You better be deliverin' a pizza. Or just axin' for directions."

"Sort of, sir. I'm just looking for family. For a sweet aunt who's done so much for me in my life. LaFaye Adams. They call her Shugah. She'd told me this was her favorite place to hang out. But she's been missing almost three days and nights. My family's going crazy, you can imagine."

As I stood there, I felt so vulnerable, at the mercy of anything, everything. Like a mere gust of wind could knock me over.

"We all know Shug, son. I won't tell you what all she's done inside this door. Over the years. Mainly when she was younger. Wilder than a tiger."

With every ounce of strength in my being, I forced my anger to remain hidden, to not reveal itself in the slightest. I even forced myself to release a joke.

"You might be right, on that," I said, raising my eyebrows in emphasis, but feeling guilt once the words left my lips.

The man paused, smiling as if his heart was at last softening, half in pity and half in amusement by what he saw and heard. He was missing an eye tooth.

"Shug came here yesterday. Was here all last night. And ovanight. Prob'ly got a holt o' some cash so she been makin' her rounds, enjoyin' the rock. Bein' away from her mama again."

He released a loud laugh, all hoarseness and emphysema.

"Left outta here 'round—hmm—eleven, eleven-thirty this mornin'."

My heart leapt in my chest. So she was alive, that recently.

The man continued, "Said she needed to go get some breakfast before she had to head back home. You better believe Shug was still high as a kite you cut loose. That's Shug, all right."

"Thank you so much, sir," I said. "Breakfast. Wonder if she meant that diner a few blocks from here. What's the name—the Reg Flag Diner?"

"Might be. She sure likes that place. Hope you find her. Shug is good people, whole lotta fun. And generous. Well, gotta run."

"Thank—"

The door shut.

As I headed down the porch steps and down the walkway, the metal song resumed behind me.

Generous, the man had said. What did he mean? Turning tricks for all within, for dope or booze? Or lending money to the man, or paying him to crash there? Did I truly want to know?

I locked myself inside the car. I couldn't save my father. But I would fight like hell to save his sister. Both attacked by that sick love for substances. The same curse that could end my dreams, just as it had helped delay them. As I started the engine, my phone buzzed in my pocket.

Wilson's voice in my ear was pure anxiety.

"Laurent, sure we shouldn't postpone this soft opening a day? A few days? Have you found—"

"Almost. But Wilson, no delays, please. Can't lose our

momentum. I'll be there before the crack of dawn tomorrow. No matter what happens here. Please stop worrying."

"All right, Laurent," Wilson said, at last sounding like he was acquiescing.

I rolled north. Yes, that is exactly what I should do. Proceed slowly. I scanned the sidewalks on either side of me like a ravenous eagle. While scanning the shotgun houses, camel-back shotgun houses, double shotgun houses, Creole cottages, street after street. Nothing. I swung east onto South Claiborne Avenue, and ensured I scoured each foot of the sidewalks. Homeless lingered in the wide, grassy median between east-bound and westbound sides of the thoroughfare. Several tarps, and many tents. I slowed—a body was laid out on the sidewalk ahead to my right.

An older Black man, a bottle clutched against his side, sleeping off some stupor.

Not far ahead, I passed a middle-aged white woman with a shaven head and missing teeth talking to herself as she carried a sack of something over her shoulder. Not the schizophrenic I had delivered kitchen leftovers to months before. I knew there were far more under Route 90 just a minute's drive east. Often arguing with themselves, gesticulating wildly in the air around them as they stood or walked. A hell of insanity I thanked the Creator, or whatever was up there, that neither I nor even Aunt LaFaye had suffered. About a quarter of a mile from the diner, I spotted a bulky form lying prostrate just beside the curb to my right, on the sidewalk. I slowed—a navy-blue peacoat. Like my older one I'd gifted Aunt LaFaye. It had to be her. I turned on the hazard lights and pulled up along-side the figure, still discernable in the ebbing twilight, shut off the engine, unlocked the doors, and bolted from the car.

I could see it was a female, belly-down in her stained blue jeans, and recognized at once the scuffed old black sneakers. The pallid right hand, covered with the crust of dried blood, lay beside her body. The shoulder-length blonde hair was unkempt and fanned out as if she had been blown onto the pavement with great force, the face buried under her left arm, as if in a defensive posture. My heart was sprinting, but my entire soul held its breath.

"Aunt LaFaye?" I whispered, then decided to shout. "Aunt LaFaye!"

I grabbed her left shoulder and pulled upward, hoping to turn her over. The body revolved in a limp motion in my arms as she came to rest on her back. Beneath the dried blood that had cascaded from the nostrils and all down the scratched jaw, I could make out her face—the near female version of my dead father's, the face that had rushed onto that playground two decades before to scoop me in the nick of time from danger.

She looked dead—was she gone? The full tragedy of it loomed above me like a towering assailant, poised to strike me with the most vicious blow.

"Aunt LaFaye! Come back," I shouted. "Open your—"

Her left eye opened, then her right. Tears clouded my vision.

"But—but—Laurent?" she mouthed the words from cracked lips covered with dried blood.

"Yes, Auntie," I said as I wept, "I'm bringing you home. This hell is ending tonight. No more searching for things in that evil rock."

Somehow, this time, I would ensure her time in rehab was completed, and successful. I would find a way. I gripped under her armpits, drew in a deep breath, and tugged upward. She released a piercing shriek.

"What? What, what is it? Does it hurt?" I stammered.

"Musta broke ribs," she said in a moan. "I remember flyin'. Car musta hit me. Hold your arm steady. I'm pullin' myself up."

I gripped her hand and she grimaced, then pushed with all of her might as she rose onto one leg, then two. "Legs are killin' me. But my ribs are burnin'. Shootin' pain, that left side."

I helped her into the passenger's seat of the car. She

shrieked again as her back and bottom contacted the seat.

"Ah, you're so bruised, Auntie," I said. "We'll get you feeling better tonight."

I shut her in, ran around the car, and we sped off, then swung in a U-turn west on South Claiborne.

I called Mémère. Her answer was instantaneous.

"Laurent?"

"I've got our LaFaye," I said. "Must have been hit by a car. Broken ribs, at the least."

"God bless you, Laurent," Mémère said, weeping into the phone. "You did it! But I never doubted you, grandson."

I could feel her gleeful smile through the phone.

"Your transmission's about to go out, by the way," I said. "It's got a little life left in it. Enough to get us to the hospital. I think."

"I'll pray. Waitin' up for you," said Mémère. "Or y'all, if the hospital lets her go."

Just as I hung up another jolt shook me and what seemed like the entire car. My aunt yelped in pain. Were we shot? No, just another pothole, another deep one.

"Frickin' New Orleans!" I shouted, furious. Aunt LaFaye laughed. I turned to see her smiling, shaking her head with her eyes closed. I found myself laughing, an involuntary reflex.

"Ah, this place," I said. "Please, God. Don't give us a blow-out now."

Aunt LaFaye was watching me. "I love you, Laurent. I'm sorry. I'm so sorry." She began to weep with shame.

I knew that feeling well. And, surely, my father had, before me.

I swung left off South Claiborne and headed south on Napoleon Avenue until I pulled up alongside the emergency room entrance of Ochsner Baptist Hospital.

I opened her door and eased her—despite her groaning—out of the seat and onto her feet. Withdrawals, dehydration, and missing sleep were written all over her sagging form as my arm shot across her upper back and held her shoulder tight. We took long pauses in our near stumble to the sliding doors. I exhaled with triumph as the warm air greeted us and a nurse came running.

Somehow, at that moment, I became aware of it. I could feel it. From some unknown vantage point, my father was watching us, and had not been a mere spectator.

Death had spared us. I was allowed to live, at least for the soft opening of Crescent. As the nurse hurried toward us, I found myself grinning. In that moment, I felt I could do anything.

CHAPTER 15

I t had finally arrived: the night of the soft opening, regardless of my poor sleep from several hours spent in the hospital with Aunt LaFaye the night before, then driving her later back to Mémère's house. And another hour of lost sleep, worrying about Aunt LaFaye's three broken ribs and nearly broken nose, trying to forget she had no health insurance. Crescent must succeed, or else.

As dinner service neared, I felt like hell incarnate, and that nervous tension Jim quelled had made its return. But that sensation of adrenaline and power while speeding my aunt to the hospital the afternoon before came to my own rescue when our doors opened at seven, and guests began to trickle in. Tourists who happened to be passing by, I took most of them to be, several underdressed and with clothing celebrating faraway sports teams, many holding paper and plastic retail bags. A few customers were older, sans shopping bags or Mardi Gras beads, and though I had never seen them before, they gave off the more restrained air of locals. And at last, Wilson pointed out one, then two regulars. And then a handful of them, their heads swiveling around in a frenzy, eyeing the bold changes to the decor. My heart leapt with excitement, and I headed back into my kitchen.

Twenty minutes in, the real sighting occurred. I had just exited the kitchen and stood in the service area, scanning the tabletops before me. Noelle sat in a royal blue dress at the far end of the dining room, just under the Moorish lantern, sipping her glass of champagne and eyeing all that was transpiring in my kitchen. No doubt she'd requested that seat: the optimal view into the back of the house. And seated under something she knew was my decorative addition.

As we made eye contact, Noelle smiled. There was something new in her gaze: a new respect, a greater desire. She had seemed different that morning after I had told her how I had rescued Aunt LaFaye, who was still recuperating in bed at Mémère's.

Noelle must have uncovered the date of the soft opening from calling Pham, or Wilson. For that morning I would not tell her the exact date, though she had asked. I wanted to work out any blemishes or rough spots before she attended the grand opening. My line's first night in battle, its baptism by fire, might prove a victory. But it would still be bloody. I hoped I would not struggle, or meet embarrassment, there before Noelle.

Wilson approached the service area from the dining room floor. He had crisscrossed that hardwood floor countless times that day, even after doors opened, fretting about how the evening would go, fixing his eyes on each server and cook's movements but saying little, just bothering himself into a discernible sweat.

I had urged him to quell his nerves, to even let me mix him a cocktail—all to no avail. His hands held no drink; he alternated between hiding them in his pockets as he walked, or wringing them together before him. In the last few hours, he had wiped the lens of his eyeglasses, over and over, in a compulsive fit. Just witnessing his nerves in action was making mine worse.

Maurice the server appeared at the pass-through, clipping onto the wheel the yellow dupe from the latest order he'd taken, then darted back into the dining room. My kitchen was not overwhelmed, but already under strain. It became apparent within the first thirty minutes: I should have hired one more line cook. But it was fine, I told myself—this is the purpose of soft launches.

"Laurent," Wilson said, pointing at the dupes clipped onto the wheel, "these orders are really piling up."

"Fatter turnout than we expected," Pham said, looking up from his feverish work at his *mise-en-place*.

"Indeed," Wilson said. "There's no line, at least. But I bet there's one on grand opening night."

"No doubt," I said, inspecting the next dupe, and turned to my crew. "All right folks, let's press on the gas pedal! Show ourselves what we're made of! Now, fire one étouffée, one fricassée, and two bowls of the duck gumbo. Then for the apps: one crawfish and sea urchin momo, one alligator with Creole hoisin. Fire, team!"

"Yes, Chef!" Brooke and Pham said in unison. Just not Roosevelt and Etienne. Roosevelt dashed back and forth, as swiftly as his rotund frame allowed, his brow dripping like a downspout in a drizzle. I discerned a heat rash where his neck disappeared into his polyester whites.

"Roosevelt," I said, "I'm gonna need you to wear a cap or headband next time, as hot as it is in here. You're wetter than wet. And set aside one of your side towels to keep drying off."

"Yes, Chef," he said.

I turned and my eyes found Etienne. Not once had he participated in that tradition so widespread in the industry: each cook responding to the head chef's command by addressing him by his title.

"Etienne, everything going well over there?" I said. He looked like he was simmering inside.

"Keeping the engine going, man. We're slammed silly. We're in the weeds already, and we ain't even at capacity for covers. I'm thinking we'll need one more hire, if this is even close to a normal night."

"I'm starting to think the same," I said. "Let's see how tonight shakes out. You're doing great. Just keep chugging."

"Ha, I'll be chugging all right, after I get off tonight," he said. "Abita Turbodog."

"Look at it that way," I said. "It'll make the first sip that much better."

"You got that right," he said. "Assuming we ain't all in the hospital at Rosie's bedside." Etienne turned to Roosevelt. "Don't ya have any heart attack on us, Rose."

"Trying not to," Roosevelt said, shaking his head, as he lined up another Kheer Brûlée.

"And stop sneakin' food," Etienne said. "Tastin' the dessert ingredients. We all saw you."

"Now, Roosevelt," I said, "as *pâtissier* I want you to taste your product at times, but don't snack on the actual ingred—"

"Table three just walked out," Maurice said near the top of his voice, right at my back. "The regulars. They said they'd call Wilson later."

"What?" I said, feeling the news burn deep in my gut like the thrust of a fist. "But why?"

"They didn't like what they saw on the menu. Any of it."

I felt the eyes of my line on me. Shaking my head, I plunged into sautéing shrimp. The others resumed working their stations in a fever pitch. After all, there was no time remaining to stand there in shock.

Those will be the first casualties, I thought, among the old-timer Cayenne Club regulars. The hardline devotees of traditional southern Louisiana cuisine. It was inevitable. But some would hang on. And perhaps prove to be ardent fans of the venue's new incarnation. At least that was my hope.

But no more than ten minutes later, Maurice's next words shattered my reverie. Not shouted again in the pass, but this time just inside the kitchen, as he first warned our line of his entry.

"Corner! Corner! Hey, Chef. Table eleven just left. Cancel the order, if you can."

I spun around, sensing my poise begin to collapse in upon itself.

"Why in the hell?" I said. "We're getting killed!"

"They said they couldn't wait any longer," Maurice said.

"I suppose we really are that slow," I said, feeling another jab deep in my gut.

"We are," Etienne said. "But we're fast for the circumstances. You heard my advice earlier."

His big head, and its endless advice. Somewhere inside me, I growled.

"You might have noticed I'm the chef, Etienne," I said. "I don't need your advice. I saw it at the outset. It's clear as day we need one more. But we lack the funds. Unless I convince Wilson."

Etienne grunted and shook his head as he pulled a Pyrex dish from the oven. I recalled how I at times disliked that part of myself—when I slipped into that candid, humble, gentle management style, a newfangled trend. Not the way the greats did it, decades and centuries ago. It yielded too many openings for the Etiennes and Minnesota Bradys of the kitchen to openly criticize. I often tolerated things I should not, suppressing my frustration until I would at last bristle, even pop on my line cooks. And once again I would feel shame.

"Wagyu meatballs are eighty-sixed!" Pham shouted. "Maurice, tell the rest of the floor staff."

I realized too late—I should have ordered far more supply. Along with budgeting with Wilson, somehow, for one more hire.

Minutes later, I crossed from the kitchen into the service area, peeking once more into the dining room. Noelle had departed. Along with a full one-third of the dining room, which had been completely full only twenty, thirty minutes before. The empty tables were unbussed.

Maurice approached on his way to the kitchen, and he turned my way. I softly said, "What the hell happened? One-third of the floor's gone?"

"Yessir, kaput," Maurice said.

"What's the feedback?" I said. "Just couldn't wait any longer?"

"Absolutely," he said, lowering his chin in a grim nod, then darted toward the kitchen.

What a night, I thought as I followed him, feeling on the verge of screaming in fury and frustration. Crescent was like a small but powerful ship plowing through the waves, springing random leaks that must be plugged, with fires erupting in various compartments that we had to extinguish, sometimes several at once.

Though I had doubted it was possible, I quickened my pace even further, making my rounds from station to station as the line's *tournant*, assisting each cook where I could, suppressing my desire to ask Wilson to join our line. I feared that would make me look incompetent in his eyes.

When closing time passed and the last customers departed, I bolted into the service area and crossed the dining room. I locked the door and leaned my back against it, exhaling loudly.

"How humiliating," I said. "At least it's over. There must be changes. We know this."

"This was a start," Roosevelt said as the line approached. "Messy, but our start."

"Emphasis on the messy," Etienne said. "We got a looong way to go and we gotta get there fast. Not sure if we can by your grand opening."

He pronounced *grand* with a tinge of mockery.

"Ah, Peter," I said with a sigh. "Ye of little faith. Where's Wilson?"

"He's in his office," Maurice said. "Trying to forget what he's seen."

"Tonight's atrocities," Etienne said with a devilish laugh. "And humiliations."

I crossed the dining room, nodding once at my four cooks, who watched me with intent eyes, their faces damp and long with fatigue. As I neared Wilson's office door, sounds inside of flatware scratching a plate reached my ears. Wilson was surely still a nervous catastrophe, wolfing down his meal in his go-to compulsion. Drawing in a deep breath, I rapped three times on the old wood.

"Come in," I heard Wilson say with food in his mouth. I turned the knob.

Wilson looked up from his plate of dirty rice and fried chicken, his face red and damp. He swallowed, his eyes bulging for a moment. Was it rage? Or was he in a state of fright over the last few hours?

I discerned a hint of humor in his eyes as he watched me while picking the last flesh off a drumstick with his front teeth, then chewed as he tossed the bone across the room and into the trashcan at my side.

"Sorry, couldn't stand to be in there any longer," he said, still with food in his mouth. I waited until he finished chewing and swallowed.

"I guess you're not in the mood to dine on my fusion," I said, unable to resist the joke, and stepped forward and lowered myself into the chair facing him, across the desk.

"Popeye's, from last night," he said with a weary smile. "Glad you're in a joking mood."

"I'm sorry."

"Laurent, I just lost the one positive remnant from my old business. I lost a few regulars tonight. Many, actually. Ticked mainly with the slow service. But I lost newcomers, too. I spoke with them all. Some were tourists. And some were locals, but not regulars."

"I suppose you regret it," I said. "And I understand. You know, casting your lot with some upstart—experimental fusion chef."

Wilson fell silent. He seemed to be staring into his lap.

This was becoming torturous. An unwelcome thought entered my mind: an image of me jumping from the Crescent City Connection to my own death.

"Laurent, I placed my bet on you. I gave up my declining business, my failed old menu, and I knew I'd lose some of my regulars. I trusted your assessment. You said hire three besides Pham. Now I might have lost almost all my regulars. See how many bailed? Even before placing orders?"

"I—I'm so sorry, Wilson."

"And no, I don't regret my move, Laurent. You are my best chance. You are also my last chance, and I believe in you. I tasted your dishes, several of them. And I didn't just forget that positive reaction on the floor when you tested your specials."

I felt some of the weight lift off me, leaving me sitting there with tears welling in my eyes. They could be salvaged, this relationship and project. All was not lost, at least, not yet.

"And Laurent, from the feedback I gathered, people did not walk out today from any food quality issue. But we're needing to make some big fixes come grand opening."

"Agreed," I said. "We lost some regulars, but we made some new fans. Learned of some things I need to tweak, too. About ten things."

"Like?" he said.

"Wilson," I said. "First of all, it's clear—I was overconfident in myself and the other four on my line. That we could take all the load. We're needing one more hire. As in—tomorrow."

"Clearly," he said. "At first, I thought: Just kill me, why don't y'all? Need, or want? Now it's obvious we need one more if we don't want a repeat. We could use two, but we at least need one."

"Absolutely, Wilson."

"But hire one more? You and I may need to lower our pay. Temporarily. Free up funds."

In my mind I saw Mémère, Mom, and Aunt LaFaye. And then my aunt's medical bills.

"Hopefully there's another way," I said.

"And we really need two new ovens, Laurent. You see how old they are. One, or both, might go out any day."

"They've got more life in them," I said. "We need to wait

on those. But the money we can scrape together we need to put toward that new hire."

"Well, I do have some cash I can pump into this," Wilson said. "I can hire one more head. At that same thirty-six hundred a month. And with the rest I can either buy the ovens or put it toward advertising, marketing for the next year, maybe two. I'd go with the ovens because—"

"Put it toward advertising, marketing," I said, the words shooting from my lips before I could contemplate the issue. Deep inside, I was seeing myself cooking on WWL-TV.

"You've been a stellar chef, Laurent. But you haven't run a restaurant. What happens if one of those two ovens dies?"

"They've got at least a year of life in them. Ad spend is crucial for a bold venture like ours, and in New Orleans."

Wilson glared down at his desk, as if frustrated that I'd disregarded his concern. Then his face relaxed. Something in his eyes seemed to show he had acquiesced.

"Anyway, there is a bit of good news," I said, an idea taking form in my imagination. "Since we've lost some regulars, we should make new fans fast. Guess the most efficient route."

"Oh?" Wilson said, reaching for a rocks glass. He poured himself a single of bourbon.

"We find a situation," I said, slapping my hands together. "An environment, an event, rather. Advantageous to us. Where we can showcase this restaurant to critics and the public alike. Where Breton cannot be an exhibitor. But Emeril, Link, and Besh will be participating, and that's great."

"Okay," Wilson said. "I think I'm tracking."

"Remember that annual Warehouse District Restaurant Festival? Emeril, Link, and Besh now have venues in this neighborhood. They'll have their own tents and lend the event great cred, and foot traffic. And you know them; they're supportive. So why not us? We'll join them in cooking, in our own tent. But Breton's the odd man out. He's got no restaurant in the Warehouse District. WWL-TV, the *Times-Picayune*, *New Orleans*

Magazine—they always have their people there. This will give us some nice exposure."

"Hey, great idea," Wilson said, nodding with a smile. "I'd forgotten about that one."

"It'll be grand. We hit it from the fusion angle," I said. "The competition will be stiff. Donald Link brings the Cajun big guns. He's riding high from just opening Pêche. And John Besh and Emeril Lagasse? That's star power. Bet we'll see the best restaurants in the Warehouse District."

"I've participated in that festival," Wilson said in a sub-dued voice, looking down into his lap. "A decade ago. Haven't had the stones to do it since. Cayenne Club, we couldn't quite get there. We weren't what we were in those years. But we'd better hurry and register with the director. Not sure who that is these days. I remember the paperwork. But it'll be great. Not too close to Mardi Gras."

"For sure," I said.

"I'll make the calls tomorrow morning," Wilson said, sip-ping his bourbon. "Congrats on a winning idea. And thank you for your work tonight, and thus far. Tonight was our first time on the battlefield together. A messy night, even a defeat, but we'll learn from this. Just one thing I need from you. Place ads again for that remaining spot on the line."

"I'll do it tonight," I said, then stood and walked toward the door. "Thank you, Wilson. Now I'll check on our crew."

Emerging from the mists of my memory was a face from my teen years at NOCCA, that of a good friend I'd lost touch with: JaJuan Phillips. All those years, over twenty of them, had passed since we last spoke. I simply had never felt proud enough of my standing in my career to reach out. But through the rumor mill, I heard he was working in our classmate Luc Breton's kitchen. I would look up JaJuan's parents and call their landline in the morning. They would remember me.

I had crossed the Rubicon with Gerard. And now I would do the same with Luc Breton.

CHAPTER 16

I hadn't laid eyes on him since graduation week at NOCCA, back in the early '90s, but those eyes remained the same. Laughing eyes, eyes that always seemed to harbor some inner humor in almost every situation. My hope was that at our latest NOCCA class reunions, I wasn't a running joke.

JaJuan and I sat at a two-top near that corner of the dining room farthest from the kitchen, but near the empty stage.

While the line snuck looks our way, I focused on his words.

"I know I'd be good for this place 'cause I'm ready to branch out," JaJuan said. "Made my bones in different kitchens, and now I'm lookin' to change up NOLA cookin' somehow, like with what you're doing here. And to enjoy myself in what we cook. And to not have a cruel tyrant always kickin' us with his words."

"I liked you when I knew you, and I am liking you right now," I told him. "If I can trust you as I did at eighteen."

"I'm sorry?" he said.

"I don't want to offend you in any way, JaJuan. But you are fresh from our old classmate's kitchen, at Lacassine, after all."

"Laurent, *you* called *me*."

"I know, true. Sorry. Luc wants to sabotage me any which way he can. He's done this twice before. I caught him trying to pour habanero sauce into the trays of food I'd just catered to Wade Connaughton's party. Wade even kicked him out in front of the guests."

"That don't surprise me, Laurent. He hates all chefs here. Maybe some more than others."

"Plus," I said, "at least right now, Luc can pay you more at Lacassine than we can, JaJuan. And he'd probably give you a raise, if you spied for him."

"I agree," he said. "But what does money matter if he runs me through the wringer, every day? Talks to me like a field slave. He mocks me in front of the whole line. Does it to others, too."

"That's not hard for me to imagine," I said.

"The nicest he will ever be is when he yells, 'Now get back to work, crew, before I cut off your sacks and julienne your balls for the next order! Or stick the tines of my serving fork in your asses! This is no union house here. Work!'"

JaJuan paused, as if contemplating the release of some secret. "Luc, he'll fall into the bottle even in the kitchen, and lotsa people know he got this other side where he numbs himself with coke. Gets even more mean. Yesterday Luc gets hot at a line cook, grabs the powerwasher from our dishwasher Shawn, and sprays down the guy. Who walks off the line in the middle of the rush. And last week, that bastuhd Luc told me, 'It's no wonder you couldn't smell the sauce was spoiled with that broad nose of yours.'"

That account of Breton's cruel joke reached in and sliced deep into my heart.

I studied JaJuan's eyes and recalled he was one of the few neighborhood boys in our part of Mid-City who never bullied me in the slightest for my diminutive size. And he always tried to intervene when he saw me under attack or being threatened. Just that mild manner and always with a harmless, ready joke. In those years, he was borderline lanky, but tall and broad-shouldered, and the larger boys respected him.

A long-forgotten memory surfaced: JaJuan's father had helped Mom and me build our backyard fence one weekend. For free, and the Phillips weren't even our friends yet.

The added risk was there, risk I didn't need to take on. No matter, for I knew at that moment JaJuan had won me over enough to offer him a shot at a cooking demo. I had to pay him back anyway. Did recompense have an expiration date?

"Three things," I said. "You have to pass the cooking demo. I'm sure you will. Then start within a few days, at the latest. Because we have our grand opening drawing near. And you've got to be good with thirty-six hundred a month, until we get more dough rolling in. And working six days a week. But the crew has a family dinner together every evening. And a late lunch after Sunday brunch ends. And we'll comp you a second meal some days, too."

"I'll do it. So, I just gotta cook a meal for you?"

"Of course, JaJuan. How about now? You'll carry an advantage—because I'm starving enough to devour my own dirty clogs right off my feet."

He clapped his hands once and produced that goofy laugh I remembered, guffawing while his head swayed like a tree in a gale. To my ears, an Eddie Murphy-esque laugh. I could see this was his winning quality: He was delightful to hear and see. His joy made you joyful.

"I can't even imagine what assignment you'll give him," said Wilson, appearing at my side.

Across the ceiling beam I ran my eyes, searching for something completely novel. I had it.

"It's an odd one, I'll warn you. You've surely never prepared this. I've got the ingredients all here in our walk-in. Bear with me while I write out the ingredients and instructions."

I could feel the eyes of my kitchen crew on me. And in that momentary silence, they were listening.

I scribbled the recipe with its ingredients, relevant measurements, and instructions into my notebook, then ripped out the page and handed it to JaJuan.

"Haha, whoa! Fried Alligator and Oysters Hoisin, with Jambalaya Hunan!" JaJuan shouted, flashing his exuberant smile. If his tenure in my kitchen lasted, he would enjoy himself. And most probably help us do the same. But again—could I trust him?

If his cooking skills hit the mark, I would have to.

Wilson laughed, and I shot him a quizzical glance.

"Why do you laugh, Wilson?" I said.

"I just never thought I'd hear those two words. Jambalaya Hunan," he said.

"I suspect we'll be hearing those words a lot in the coming years, within these walls," I said. "Prepared right, it can be the food of the gods."

I led JaJuan into the kitchen. "Use my station here. It's fully stocked. Stay here and I'll bring out your ingredients."

I selected the ingredients from the walk-in, feeling its chill down my sweaty back, and brought them out to the station. I pointed out the pans on the stovetop nearby, and the clean cutlery in my *mise-en-place*.

"Best of luck, JaJuan," I said. "I'm going off to discuss something with Wilson, but I might check on you later. When it's cooked and prepared, he and I want to taste it over here. Etienne will get you plates and cutlery."

Etienne's eyes widened and narrowed, and I noted his insecurity, just as I had anticipated.

"I'll give you forty-five minutes for this one. Actually, sixty minutes, as it's really almost two dishes," I said. "If you're finished before I call time, hit that bell there. Clock starts now."

I headed out into the dining room toward Wilson, stopping just outside the kitchen to turn down the thermostat a bit. Chatter, laughter—I could already hear JaJuan had my kitchen in stitches.

I felt my phone buzz in my pocket. A text, from Noelle.

"On that baby talk subject, Laurent, might as well tell you Aunt Flo's a few days late for her visit."

Stunned, I texted her back: "Really?"

Shock and terror yielded to hope, as I again envisioned fatherhood.

"It's happened before though," was her response. "You know my cycle can get irregular. Don't worry too much. Or get too happy."

"Please go buy some pregnancy tests at Walgreens," I texted back.

"I know the drill, L," was her reply.

"Just please," I texted, "could you take those tests the day after the grand opening? In a few days. I need to focus."

"Almost sure I know the result, but deal," she wrote.

I took a deep breath and seated myself at table three beside Wilson. I was inspecting the inventory sheet and a bill from one of our distributors—all with an eye on my wristwatch—when someone slammed a hand down onto the bell with a confident slap. JaJuan sauntered into the dining room, a full plate in each hand, his face beaming.

He placed one plate before me and one before Wilson. A smiling Brooke set a fork and knife down for each of us.

"I want Wilson to enjoy some, too," JaJuan said. "Even if it's just a bite or two. See what the hullabaloo in the kitchen's about. They each had a bite or two, or more, from another plate."

"Wow. It was pretty popular among our line," Brooke said. "The rest of the food's gone."

"Oh yes," Roosevelt said. "This gentleman's got some serious cooking chops."

"Let's sample it," I said, cutting a piece of the fried alligator and a piece of fried oyster, dragging them through the hoisin sauce, and beginning to chew, breathing through my nose and straining to capture the taste on my tongue. I swallowed, with enthusiasm, then shoveled a heap of the Jambalaya Hunan into my mouth. Traditional jambalaya was surely something JaJuan had prepared often at Lacassine, and it showed. He already had that stout foundation.

"Delightful. Even marvelous," I said, "both the main and the side. So—Wilson?"

"Oh...oh...oh..." Wilson said in a moan, his eyes closed, as if he was enjoying something intimate and amorous.

"Get a room!" I said and laughed. "So, I take that as a yay, not a nay?"

"Yay," he said with food still in his mouth. "Yay!"

"I concur. Welcome to our pirate's crew," I said, reaching out as JaJuan shook my hand with both of his.

I felt a bit less shaken by the fallout from the soft opening.

"JaJuan Phillips," I said. "A time will come soon when people eat at this place just to see you, my man. *And* to eat your cooking."

JaJuan leaped and clapped his hands once, then joined the rest of the line at the edge of the kitchen.

I smiled at my clapping culinary foot soldiers, and spotted Etienne, his face teetering on the edge of joy and jealousy.

CHAPTER 17

W hen the day dawned, I was already stirring inside my apartment, making myself ready. The Warehouse District Food Festival was upon us. My nerves were abuzz, but nowhere near like the morning of the soft opening. It was almost like a vacation day had arrived, and Wilson and I would soon be putting our boat out onto the lake. As much as I aimed to succeed at this event, and ensure Crescent had salvaged its flagging reputation, our participation did seem, in true New Orleans spirit, like partaking in a celebration. Ben's Uncle Morrie would be attending, down from New York. Surely at some point that day I'd be encountering the restaurateur and his foodie spirit. No doubt he'd heard of me from his nephew.

I recalled Ben explaining how his father and uncle had hammered him to quit marijuana, and to get his tattoos removed. Even more, since he would not renounce bohemia, join the bourgeoisie and enter the corporate world, they urged him to jettison his musical career to pursue a PhD in music, and join academia in the northeast, first as a teacher's assistant. From Ben's accounts, Morrie sounded like a demanding, somewhat imposing, but loving uncle.

Another memory surfaced: that late night in the Corporation Bar almost a year before, when Ben relayed how Morrie's life had been seared by tragedy, how it softened him, made him often sentimental about all sorts of random things, rendered him unable to work for almost a year, propelled him through a rotation of grief counselors and psychologists, and imbued him with a deeper interest in his nephew. Morrie had one child, Edward, a wildly successful stock trader who fell to his death from the balcony of his high-rise apartment. But Morrie never believed it was suicide, that instead it was a Mob hit. Edward had clients who were "made men" and he most likely knew too much about something. Soon after, Morrie saw his brother's son—so different from Edward—as his own.

The thought moved me: Morrie, like me, had suffered from a mysterious and tragic death in his father-son relationship, even a fall from a great height.

I steeped two bags of oolong tea in my big glass mug and, once it cooled a bit, drank deep. My eyes brushed past my still-unrolled yoga mat on the floor. Not this morning. It was not the time to quell nerves, but to get caffeinated and act, to do all in my power that day to repair and grow our reputation. I threw on my clothes and within minutes was driving eastward to Crescent.

Wilson and Roosevelt were the only ones who had beaten me there. As expected, their nerves were already well-frayed. Roosevelt buzzed about his station as if on fast-forward, putting finishing touches on the desserts. The rest of the line arrived in quick succession, and as Etienne helped Wilson arrange the tablecloth and paper plates, bowls and plastic utensils onto our table in our street tent near Crescent's front door, I helped the others prepare the four different mains and get it all into the large metal trays and storage bins to bring to our outpost. Roosevelt placed his desserts in the walk-in fridge, cooling them until the last minute. I tapped Pham with ensuring the line brought the containers out to the tent, before I joined Wilson out on the street.

Dappled by soft sunlight, Julia Street, Fulton Street, and St. Joseph Street had come alive, now three pedestrian thoroughfares lined with two opposing rows of tents, a few police positioned for security, and a WWL-TV news van parked nearby. Police had closed a section of each of the three streets to traffic, and only morning walkers and joggers coursed through, here and there.

Wilson and I readied the wine and champagne. I prayed my idea would go off very well—with each highly discounted five-dollar plate featuring samples of that day's four dishes, I would provide one free plastic cup of French red wine, white wine, or champagne. Not our good stuff, of course, but decent bottles. By day's end, even if all our food was sold out, Crescent would come out at a slight loss, dollarwise, and only slight because I had purchased all of the drinks as a lagniappe for customers. But as I had convinced Wilson: Our exposure would be far greater with the free drinks. I knew my city, after all.

And sure enough, though the start was syrupy slow, the attendees began to arrive, more by the minute, purchasing their tickets at the nearby tent and stopping at ours soon after. A familiar face peeked out from the blurred masses. Ben, with Noelle at his side. Beside them walked an elegant sixty-something couple I did not recognize: a short, stocky man with a slightly taller, quite slender woman with long, reddish-blonde wavy hair and finely chiseled features. I broke off from my line and walked out to meet the group.

"Chef Laurent Ladnier," Ben said, as Noelle gave me a wink. I waved as I approached, then studied their older companions. "Meet my Uncle Morrie, and Aunt Greta, in for a few days."

Dressed in a brown cashmere sport coat and green corduroy pants, and crowned by a puff of whitish-gray curls, Morrie studied me with his dark brown eyes, his face brightening into a pleasant, even content grin, his lips still shut. I imagined the face of an introverted but charismatic professor, loving toward his students, while missing nothing.

Our right hands clasped in a firm but warm handshake. I turned and gave Greta's hand a light shake. She gave me an even warmer smile, her kind eyes crinkling. I smiled, noting that she wore pants of some kind of purple. A wheat-colored shawl draped with grace over her shoulders.

"We've heard much about you," Morrie said, pulling my eyes toward him. "I'm always on the hunt for great cuisine. And talent. I own a few restaurants in the Big Apple, as my nephew probably told you. But I still make sure to spend a few days in New Orleans. Annually. It's one of my playgrounds."

"And Laurent, I'm a strict vegan," Greta said. "But I accompany Morrie as he eats his way through the city. He's happy as can be. A true pleasure to be around on these trips. Where else can you enjoy a two-hour, world-class breakfast? And not just at Brennan's."

"That's great," I said. "It's always a great time."

"Uncle Morrie and Aunt Greta used to make every Jazz Fest," Ben said. "But it got just too hot for them. Now they come in late winter or early spring, every year."

"Smart," I said. "In spring you also get crawfish season. Soft-shell crab season, great time for oysters, too. I hope you enjoy our food. The first true world fusion restaurant of its kind here. Sorry that we have nothing vegan today. I'll work on that."

I smiled at Greta, who gave a dismissive wave and a gentle laugh.

"True world fusion," Morrie said. "I like the sound of that, young man. Bold move in this food scene, these days. As I'm sure you already know."

"I've heard this a time or two," I said and laughed. Morrie elected a cup of red and I made sure to give him a small serving of each dish.

Morrie took one bite of the Massaman Curry Shrimp and Ginger Miso Grits, then sampled the Jambalaya Vindaloo, his eyes closed. Then came the Chengdu Duck and Andouille Gumbo. Then what I'd named La Noelle, the concoction I'd served her in our dinner in Crescent far past closing. Smoked quail, poached quail eggs, and turkey hash in duck confit with bok choy, Chinese broccoli, and water chestnuts, in a ginger, za'atar, and garlic miso reduction. Morrie concluded with a bite of the Kheer Brûlée. His moaning morphed into faint, lip-closed laughter.

Had I won him over? Or was he mocking me? I waited, my eyes darting from Morrie to Wilson, then Pham, to JaJuan, to Brooke and Roosevelt, then Etienne, all standing about fifteen feet away, then back to Morrie.

"Well. My, kid. This is simply marvelous. Haven't quite tasted anything of the sort before. Both delicious, and original. As Benjy had said, and that's what piqued my interest. My favorite nephew can still be a schlemiel and gets into all kinds of trouble. Rarely listens to his father and me. But besides being musically gifted, he's right about certain things."

"Thanks so much, Morrie," I said. "There's nothing like this in New York City? Surely there must be something."

"Oh, there's innovation. But south Louisiana regional fused with South Asian and East Asian? Not that I've seen."

He reached into his shirt's breast pocket and produced a card. I looked at Wilson and my team. They were occupied by a few of the event staffers who had stopped by.

"We should keep in touch," Morrie said, placing it in my hand. "Another city holds a lot of opportunity for you. How old are you, by the way?"

"Thirty-nine," I said.

Ben watched with a broad grin. "He's been cooking since about age seven. Attended NOCCA for high school, as a culinary student. That's the New Orleans Center for Creative Arts. And then he attended the New Orleans Culinary Academy. Laurent's got this crazy taste memory, as it's apparently called."

"I know that term," Morrie said. "He can call up in his own mind a taste he experienced ten years ago of a certain type of dish or ingredient. Yes?"

"That's it," Ben said.

I could feel my face flush. My kind friend Ben, always so supportive.

"Apart from my travels and classes, I've learned so much in New Orleans," I said. "First at this French white-linen table-cloth place Uptown when I was fifteen. Picked up so many of the classical techniques, making great stocks. And plate presentations, all of that. I've worked two years in the kitchen of an Indian place, a year as sous chef in an upmarket Chinese restaurant. Several years at Italian restaurants, then over fifteen years in Cajun-Creole kitchens before I was chef for over a year at another Cajun-Creole spot. And for the size of the city, for 1,440 restaurants here in 2014, it's just a wonderful food scene."

"Wonderful it is," Morrie said. "And the only American city that counts its restaurants, every week."

"Oh yes. But," I said, "I uncovered one thing lacking here. To me, it was plain as day."

"Besides certain cuisines being absent at this point," Morrie said. "Filipino, Russian. Nigerian, others. But with your idea, you are right on."

"My concept's also a way I can introduce those cuisines to NOLA. In a kaleidoscope, a symphony of flavors exploding on your tongue."

"Well phrased," Morrie said. "And I feel the explosion."

"I impose my will upon the ingredients, to produce the dish I envisioned," I said. "I always aim to keep evolving. I know many chefs will poach my menus, concepts, maybe even my cooks and waiters. You know how chefs, restaurants are. So I've got to keep progressing, stay ahead of the pack. Then own a restaurant by age fifty."

"That last part's tricky," Morrie said. "You gotta make sure you not only love cookery, but that you're willing to be another chef-owner. Managing the back of the house, while wrestling with payroll, finances, lawsuits, banks, unions, all that dreck. But I like your plan."

"Why, thanks, Morrie."

"Best of luck at the festival, Laurent," he said, shaking my hand. "I might see you soon."

Morrie and Greta turned and proceeded in their brisk Big Apple gait down the street, Ben in tow. Noelle lingered a moment.

"He likes you, babe," she said. "New York City isn't such a bad opportunity."

I paused, feeling as if my heart had stopped. Was she so willing to give me up to a far-off city? So she could move to Los Angeles? I wouldn't address this in front of Ben.

"Not at all, Noelle," I said. "New York City was also one of my original ambitions. Cheffing up there, too, while pursuing my own vision."

I felt guilty saying this, and flirting with this opportunity, all while wearing the polyester whites of Crescent—Wilson's last stand.

"Maybe many years from now, Noelle," I said, then eyed Wilson and the others, who were still speaking with the staffers about fifteen feet away.

As Noelle and Ben walked on, a flash of red emerged in our periphery. It was almost like sighting a prowling wolf pack. Clad in a red button-down shirt, Luc Breton strolled past my tent with a sly stare and wink in my direction, a beautiful brunette woman at his side. Wade and Erik Brauer followed a few steps behind, smiling my way as they passed.

I glanced over and realized JaJuan stood beside Brooke, also in Crescent's polyester kitchen whites, and Wilson. Breton's eyes had to have spotted his old cook. Yet those eyes had registered no surprise.

Fifteen minutes later, Pham, JaJuan, and I were replenishing the champagne and wine. Brooke, Roosevelt, and Etienne stood idle, but ready, behind the covered food trays. Wilson was inside using the bathroom.

"We should have worn toques on our heads," I said, hoping my joke would relieve my stress. "To make more of a statement."

I turned my head, and not even five feet away, Breton stood with his hands on his hips, smirking. The beautiful brunette woman, Wade, and Erik were gone. Breton held one index finger upward before him, as if on the cusp of revealing some observation, or anecdote.

He stared not at me, but at one of the others to my side.

"JaJuan Phillips," Breton said. "With your new boss, our classmate at NOCCA, too. That's quite a bold move, Ladnier, confiscating my line cooks. As good as mine are, I always knew they were peon idiots. That they'd leave me in a flash. They didn't stay on out of loyalty, that's for sure."

"Loyalty to an abuser?" I said.

"You can have him, Ladnier," Breton said. "How's this for poetry? JaJuan had this ridiculous, cheery lightness in his spirit that annoyed me, that frankly I wished I could destroy. Stamp out for good."

"Wish all you want," JaJuan said. "Our place is 'bout to go the moon."

"There you go thinking again, JaJuan. Your new chef knows nothing," Breton said. "Wet-behind-the-ears know-it-all. Punchin' way above his head, with his new concept. I've had his little 'experiments' at Bonhomie. They were such misfires that Gerard's son almost killed him in front of me. One reason this guy probably got canned. And that owner of Cayenne Club—"

Breton paused, and laughed. "Yeah, Wilson. He's one strange bird. Belongs in a circus show. A walking bundle of nerves, all right. He's not cut out for a risky venture like that. I give him two, three months tops before he reverts to that boring old menu mainly for CBD stiffs on their lunch break. Maybe even goes back to the old name."

As if from a mighty flame, my spirit retracted within me. Breton couldn't be right. Or could he? It could come to pass, after all.

"I admit, Ladnier, I can see why Wilson made this little

gambit," Breton said. "Cayenne Club was on the decline. Even the regulars weren't enough. Less diners stopping in and rents going up all over the city."

"You and your theories," JaJuan said.

"People in the know here, in the industry," Breton said, "they're aware the kitchen at Cayenne Club was infamous for having some pretty old kitchen equipment. And that it was dirty as hell."

"Yeah?" I said. "Then how did it never fail inspection?"

"Seriously? This is New Orleans, man," Breton shot back. "There are more corrupt restaurant inspectors here than you can shake a stick at. Anyway, Wilson didn't have much to lose. Lots of 'save for well done' in there, if you know what I mean. Hell, his fish tasted like menhaden."

"What in the hell's that?" Etienne said. Despite his directness, his respect for Breton was all there in his eyes. I wondered if Etienne was envisioning himself as Breton's sous.

"Menhaden? Yeah. The very small, oily fish that goes into cat food," Breton said. "Inedible."

The amplifiers a few hundred feet away released a piercing screech, and then a voice tore through the air. "Ah, sorry for that horrible sound. And now—we've tallied up the ballots. Are y'all ready for our winners here at the New Orleans Warehouse District Food Festival?"

My galloping heart, under strain from Breton's mockery, broke into a sprint. I could not leave this next moment empty-handed. Especially feet away from Breton's smirking face.

"Coming in third," said the announcer, "the bronze medal goes to Donald Link for Cochon. The silver medal goes to Laurent Ladnier at Crescent. And—Crescent wins Best New Warehouse District Restaurant. The gold medal goes to— Donald Link again, for his other venue, the brand new Pêche!"

Could it be? Had I misheard? I looked at my line for confirmation. They cheered with upraised arms, elation lighting up their faces. Etienne was releasing that devilish laugh, and

JaJuan was howling with delight.

My confidence, flowing out of me since the soft opening and trickling out here and there since, rushed back into me like some brisk mountain stream in reverse.

Are you watching, Dad? And Pépère? I thought.

"Insanity. Give me a taste," Breton said to us, haughty but nervous, snapping me from my drifting thoughts. "I'll be the judge of that, Ladnier."

"I can't," I said as I shook my head, feeling my whole face broaden into a wide smile. "Looks like we're sold out. But I am in a good mood, however. So I'll let you lick the tray."

His eyes revealed all: He so wanted to swing at me, but wouldn't. At least not here.

"Gold, silver, and bronze winners," the voice boomed, "please make your way to the stage."

I stared deep into his eyes, still smiling. I was relishing the moment, letting seconds pile onto seconds as if I'd never leave, and at last broke away and walked out of the tent into the sunlight.

CHAPTER 18

It was one of those magnificent New Orleans nights when late winter blends into early spring. The air was temperate; you could even walk outside without any film of sweat forming on your skin in the first minute. The six-month summer had not yet smothered us, and hurricane season was several months away. Grand opening night had come, and despite the excitement, my stress was peaking. Mémère's transmission expiring at last, and having to pay that bill, or buy some jalopy, was enough.

But that was just the tip of it. By that night's reservation list, we would have at least 139 covers, in a four-hour service period. And there would be VIPs: critics, food journalists, and some big names I recognized from around town.

As our opening at six o'clock neared, I sipped one bottle of cold Abita beer, then another, both offered by Wilson's equally clammy hand. It was no use. It was as if I'd found myself on a battlefield after a skirmish, and the enemy had amassed in the near distance, yet in far greater numbers than before. And no matter how trained my force was for its first major clash, there might be resounding victory, but there would surely be blood.

"We should both take a few deep breaths and think about how great this will go," I said as I accompanied him toward the front windows. "Wilson, let's win this, tonight. Let's do it for Katie."

I regretted my attempt at inspiration as his eyes flooded with tears and the sides of his mouth drooped in a wince.

His overwhelming true love for her was my favorite trait of Wilson's.

Grand opening night would also be for my Noelle. The soft opening I had dedicated to my family.

The Venetian blinds were still shut, but I lifted one with my finger. A line had formed outside the locked front door. Mémère, Jim, and Ben stood on the sidewalk, and my mother beside my father's eighty-something widower friend, Ong Ngoai, with his son Uncle Minh and his wife Aunt Tu, and their daughter Mai. Where was Noelle? I clutched the handkerchief around my neck, then headed back into the kitchen.

"Are we ready for service, or what?" I said, though I could see we were.

My crew seemed not as rattled. Perhaps they were feeding off JaJuan, who was singing some song at his station and looking cheery. I could feel my nerves loosen a bit just watching him. I tugged again at my neckerchief and cleared my throat.

"Lady and gents," I said. "Eight minutes to six. I've checked and confirmed twenty times: We've got all we need. Let's show that room all we've got in us. Remember, I saw each of you has got it. Stand and deliver."

"Yes, Chef!" the volley of replies landed around me. Once again, no lips moving with Etienne.

I stepped from the kitchen into the service area to observe. About twenty feet inside the door, our wait staff stood at the ready, their faces revealing both nerves and eagerness to welcome customers. Wilson unlocked and opened the door and, along with the hostess, greeted the train of customers as they filed in. Into my mind I forced the image, and then held it there, of my grandmother and grandfather Ladnier teaching me to prepare gumbo. My nerves loosened further, and I drew in a deep breath.

Within minutes, the servers began to filter in with their dupes, and I read them out to the line. Minutes crawled by like centipedes, but no impediment emerged, just us churning away at our own brisk pace.

"Bring back that singing, JaJuan," I said. "It's our lucky charm."

"I'm not a fan of that," Etienne said. "His voice and that attitude. Can't be upbeat all the time, man. Gotta have a reason."

"But it's our grand opening," I said, shaking my head at Etienne.

JaJuan said, "I tell you what my unlucky charm was, back at Lacassine. Breton's so intense he got a branding tattoo. A burn tattoo, man. Guess who else I noticed got one?"

He turned and nodded at a smirking Etienne.

Interesting—my line's new addition was ribbing our jealous kitchen bully.

Brooke eyed me with an indescribable expression. Like she wanted me to hear this about Etienne, but there was something more. Just barely, that look of attraction, at which I felt both flattery and unease.

"Brooke teed us up well tonight with the new wine list," I said to the line. "Can't wait to see the reaction."

"That's if ol' Wilson doesn't get into the supply and drain it dry," Etienne said.

"Chef, complaint on eleven," said Harold, the older waiter, appearing in the pass-through. "Guess who."

"Breton?" I said. "If so, he must have placed a reservation under a different name. I'd read the whole reservation list."

"Yes, Chef. Turns out he used a different name. Sounds like a girl's: Marie-Antoine Carême."

I couldn't help but chuckle at the prank. But what an egomaniac, using the name of one of the founding fathers of classical French cuisine, and undeniably the world's first celebrity chef.

But I had prepared for this. I sensed Breton would come that night to witness the crowd we drew. If he crossed my red line, his expulsion would be humiliating—to him.

I said, "What's his complaint, Harold?"

"Says the hoisin sauce smells," Harold droned. "He even used the words 'noxious stench.'"

"Apologize, even though we don't mean it. Tell him that's our only hoisin, that he'll have to order another dish. Tell him I'm an absolute stickler for quality, for freshness. I'll taste everything that we make in the kitchen, before it goes out. Everything. I tasted that hoisin just hours ago."

"Yes, Chef," Harold said and departed. Pham was staring at me.

"Guess we gotta be prepared to throw him out," Pham said.

"Agreed, brother," I said. "He'll have to cut it out now, before we get more covers."

Harold, Maurice, and the other servers zipped in and out with more orders.

Not long after, Harold reappeared just inside the kitchen's edge, rolling his eyes.

"Luc Breton is such a liar," he said. "Claims his replacement order's inedible."

"That's it," I said, tossing my cloth onto the counter. "Go get Wilson. Bring him. I'm heading over there."

I crossed the dining room, waving at a table of smiling diners. I must look relaxed, mask my rage. I mused as I walked that Luc Breton always drew such a strong reaction from me. Why was that? I had it: An accomplished and celebrated chef was hurling the harsh criticism and insults my way. And delivered with such conviction. Or did I also fear I was assuming his traits, such as arrogance? Perhaps both.

At table three, Mémère sat with my mother, Ong Ngoai, Uncle Minh, and Aunt Tu. I waved but was unable to feel the gratitude they deserved. My thoughts had traveled elsewhere, as my blood was so piqued.

Once my eyes found him, I felt my teeth clench.

Wilson and Harold stood at his table. Breton watched me approach with a defiant smirk.

"Laurent Ladnier," Breton said in a snarl. "The old Cayenne Club remade into a fusion spot. But truth is stranger than fiction. Had to see it for myself."

"Get going, Breton," Wilson said. "Before you're thrown out by about four of us. You'll be the first person landing on our out list."

The smirk vanished. The face morphed into one of unease: The mouth grew tight and twitched at one side, the eyes widened.

I sucked on my own tongue, struggling not to laugh at Breton's metamorphosis.

"You came just to cause trouble," I said, shaking my head.

Breton turned to me. "You think I'm the only arrogant one here, Ladnier? Do you have the courage to be simple? To have the guts to place three or four ingredients on a plate and have them just stand up on their own? It requires skill, you know, to make simple ingredients taste amazing."

"Laurent?" Wilson said, without removing his stare from Breton's face. "Laurent, do we need to bring in some more muscle from the kitchen? To toss him out in front of all these people?"

"Fine, I'm out," Breton said, rising to his feet, his face flushed pink and mottled red. "You people couldn't even honor my minor request. Well, I've got something in store for you."

He smiled, but in his eyes burned a conflagration of pure malice and hatred. I hadn't seen someone look at me like that in many, many years.

"Another foiled hot sauce trick?" I said.

"Ha!" Someone laughed nearby. Breton, Wilson and I turned. Reclining in his seersucker blazer at a two-top across from Ben, Jim was grinning ear-to-ear at our problem customer. "*Au revoir*," Jim said with a wave.

Breton hissed, rose, and faked a stroll across the room and out the door.

I winked at Jim, then returned with Wilson to the kitchen. I felt nauseated, yet relief lightened the weight on my spirit. I had won, if only for the moment.

"Interesting development," Wilson muttered.

"But was it really unexpected?" I said, then resolved to focus on our foremost goal. "Tell me about the feedback on the floor."

"Very positive, Laurent," he said. "Far more than at the soft opening. We've got into somethin' good, my man."

My eyes grew wet at his words. We had almost taken the hill.

Two hours later, just as the kitchen was set to close, I reappeared in the service area. The floor was still brimming with diners. The victory was mine. Or, rather, ours.

A splash of canary-yellow caught my eyes, off in the corner. She sat alone at table thirteen, grinning and staring right into me with a very engaged expression. Those eyes again. Vigilant, and hungry. Eyes of desire, and something else I could not describe. But I wished it was pride in me. Was Noelle proud of what I had just achieved? And had I shown I valued her?

Was she carrying our baby? That would change everything. We would know very soon.

CHAPTER 19

Lunch service had waned and gone out in Crescent like a flickering candle's flame. Wilson and I stood with our backs to the kitchen, surveying the empty, unbussed dining room tables like two generals scanning the battlefield after their victory was well-past declared. The grand opening the night before, along with our post-festival publicity, seemed to have worked in our favor. Crescent had seen its best midday turnout yet.

"By the way," I said, pulling my smartphone from my pocket. I scanned through our first set of Yelp reviews. "Wanted to show you something. Some glowing Yelp reviews. We're at a 4.4 average. But that one-star review by an 'L.B.' is harsh. Even vitriolic. Ha, we know that pissant."

Wilson laughed. "He's such a child."

"Anyway, a 4.4 average with eighteen reviews is a good start," I said. "We'll improve our game, polish some things. That average will only get brighter from here."

How I hoped that was true. And I certainly needed the money. Worry over my aunt had returned. Her medical bills had arrived, due upon receipt. As she recuperated, her injuries kept her homebound. But without some new sort of rehab, or something she had never tried, in time she would relapse. The endless cycle, ad infinitum.

As I pored over more Yelp reviews, I remembered that Noelle had neither called nor texted me back that day as to the pregnancy test results. Nine hours had passed with no reply. Again, as if someone up there enjoyed seeing me twist in the wind.

And then, almost as if on cue, Noelle's text appeared.

Three pregnancy tests, and all negative. And her period had arrived.

We're free were her last words. What did she exactly mean?

Damn. I had not tried to get her pregnant, but I felt part of myself hoping. Then again, what an ill-timed desire. First, Noelle did not want it. Besides, despite all my recent thoughts of starting a family, at last I learned I wanted my own dream restaurant more. At least at that point in my life. My decades-old vision was calling, and that already brought enough chaos. Through the fog of that chaos, along with my line, I had a mission to complete, a conquest launched from our kitchen.

I was approaching the salamander oven when someone squeezed my arm. Brooke. "Chef, can you show me how to do your garnish with the daikon and kiwi? I tried but my anxiety the last few days wrecks me in the end and I mess it all up. Don't know what's gotten into me."

"You're feeling more anxious than before?" I said.

"Much more," she said. "It's the soft opening, then the festival, then the grand opening, and now us just taking in more volume. I want to relax through cooking."

"Let me show you one way I relax," I said, "almost through a sort of Zen meditation in the kitchen. It's what you mentioned, creating an elegant arrangement through a garnish."

The server Cameron swung into the kitchen and announced, "Chef, I just seated a couple on six. Morrie and Greta. They asked to see you."

I spun away from Brooke as if in a trance and marched into the dining room.

Morrie and Greta sat at the bussed four-top, shopping bags resting beside their chairs. Even their eyes were hungry.

"I was hoping to see you both before you left town," I said. "Introduce you to some other dishes."

"You got your wish," Morrie said. "Sorry I'm hitting lunch hour so late. Or past it, by the hours posted on your door window. Can we still get service?"

"Absolutely, Morrie, Greta," I said.

"Thank you. And so," Morrie said, "that sampling the other day really pulled me in. No, beyond that—it was borderline celestial."

"Perfect. I hope to bring you to the heavens today," I said, and glanced at Greta. "But you caught me a bit off guard. I'll have to improvise, whip up something vegan."

"Oh, it's fine," Greta said with a wave. "I'm used to it here; I just tag along. I'm still full from breakfast, anyway. I'm accompanying Mr. Gourmand here. Since the festival, he's raved about your food, I might add."

"Really? So honored," I said, feeling suddenly bashful. "I'll let you peruse today's menu. A few new dishes. You're in good hands with your server Cameron. I'll head to the kitchen but will be back in a bit."

JaJuan was the first I spotted, watching us from his vantage point in the service area. I recalled Breton's words from days before and cleared my throat. What a frightening prediction. Was I heading for a grand disappointment, an utter defeat? Even through some set-up?

"JaJuan, a question," I began, drawing up close to him. That same lighthearted look from a man who seemed perpetually entertained, as if attuned to any humor around him.

"What has Breton said to you lately? Surely he's contacted you. Miserable soul."

JaJuan pulled himself from his relaxed slouch and straightened his back as a grin spread across his face. So, I had guessed right.

"He did call me a few days ago, Chef. Made a little overture, to be honest. Hinted he could make it worth my while if I..."

I felt myself lowering my chin, watching his eyes in anticipation. A few seconds passed. I wished I could pull the words out of him like a string.

"If I—if I conducted a little sabotage," JaJuan said. "Of our food at the festival. I hung up when he spoke the words. Sorry, didn't so much as make a peep 'bout it. Didn't want no drama."

Shock had me frozen where I stood. My read on what our old classmate had become had long been correct.

"I mean," JaJuan said, "we already got enough stress as it is, you and me. 'Specially, you know, Wilson."

JaJuan smiled, and I followed suit, remembering Wilson's perpetually wracked nerves.

"Thanks for your honesty, JaJuan. Thank you for your loyalty, old friend."

"Was actually thinkin' of tellin' you," JaJuan said. "After he talked trash at the festival. Then tried to cause a ruckus in here last night. You don't gotta worry 'bout me doin' anything like that, Laurent. It's against my code. But not his. Miserable soul, you right."

"I appreciate that, JaJuan. I'll always be, and you'll always be—a peasant to him. But in this kitchen, you're a duke. You're one of my top knights. And this line is a family."

That last line might have been hyperbole, as I recalled Etienne and his attitude, but the rest was true.

We walked into the kitchen. Someone tapped the bell behind us. Cameron.

"Chef. Can we make half orders? Your friend Morrie's calling for..." He glanced down at his notepad. "A half order of the Kor-ajun Pork Spare Ribs, a half order of the Szechuan Shrimp Creole and Lo Mein, a half order of the Mekong Cassoulet, finished off by one dessert of the Cognac Lassi. The gentleman wants the dessert and everything served all at once."

"Absolutely," I said. "Crew, get them whatever they want. And try your best. Consider them one step below Michelin Guide critics. Let me put it this way: The better you do on this, the better job opportunities you might have soon in this operation."

"Well then!" Etienne declared with a smirk. "The best is what you'll get. 'Cause I can't be a line cook too much longer."

I chuckled and said, "I see advancement in your near future, Cajun Cannon."

Etienne made no retort, or even a reply. Forming a skeptical expression, he began to rearrange his *mise*.

This time, I ensured I hovered above all stations. This one had to go off with no missteps. When it was time to put up the dessert kulhar and three dishes under the heating lights, I brought Pham with me for their delivery.

"Today is almost unprecedented," Morrie said as we arranged the dishes on the linen tablecloth. "Greta's suspending her veganism for this meal alone. She's only done that twice before in the Big Easy."

"Arnaud's and Brennan's," Greta said. "Because Morrie got me half-drunk, at both. But as for today, you've piqued my interest."

"I am truly honored," I said. "Those are the three half-portions you ordered, and the dessert. But—how about partaking in Crescent's first full-menu chef's tasting? A degustation, or our version of a Japanese *omakase*. There are other dishes not yet on your table."

Morrie shook his head. "Oh, you don't have to do that. After these, I will have tasted what, seven-odd dishes and two desserts of yours? A good chunk of your menu."

"Great, then," I said. "And Cameron will get you some spare plates. He'll be out shortly."

I dithered in the kitchen for twenty minutes, pacing like a nervous father in a hospital's waiting room, counting down the minutes to see his newborn child. The line spoke between themselves, but I did not follow their conversation. From all Ben had described, Morrie was an A-level player in the New York food world. What a great contact to call, a few years after

Crescent truly took flight.

At last, Cameron appeared and beckoned. I broke for the dining room, leaving Cameron and the line behind.

Morrie slapped his outstretched hand, palm down, atop the table. "My final analysis after sampling seven mains and two desserts over two days—is that you're everything my nephew Ben said you were."

"Why—why thank you, Morrie."

"A world-class, original talent," Morrie said. "Perhaps even a genius. Surely you were a wunderkind, as a boy. But you're limited here, son. Hemmed in. You need exposure. The world needs to see what I see."

All at once, I found myself elated, stunned, and captivated. I thought of commenting, but decided not to interrupt this man I had respected from the start.

"Look, Laurent, I live in the greatest city around. A great city of the world. The sister city of Paris, London, Rome. I'm proposing you come up to New York City and join forces with me. I'll fund a larger venue. Bigger kitchen, bigger staff. I'll bankroll everything. Hell, bring some of your line up there. You're packing more raw, native talent than the other chefs I've evaluated this trip."

I was nearly beyond words. I had not expected Morrie to propose something for the immediate future. Shyness overcame me, and then something else. Guilt. I was dazzled by a new venture that involved me abandoning Wilson.

"Morrie—you're too kind. And your proposition's tempting. At times I envision working in the Big Apple. But that's for my next step, after I build Crescent into a success."

"But it is a success. And it's recognized. Look at your two awards the other day. You can hand this baby off to your sous chef. Your most trusted lieutenant. I'll even help with your move."

Pham really did have the cooking prowess to run Crescent's kitchen. Too many in the industry underestimated his abilities, and his capacity to assert himself when need be.

"Laurent," Greta said. "Morrie really believes in you, to extend this offer. You have a lovely operation here. But this is a golden opportunity to get to that highest stratum of running a few restaurants as a celebrated executive chef. By getting into the business side of it, beyond the kitchen walls. You'd just be getting there sooner."

"She's right," Morrie said. "Hey, and if moving and resettling costs are an issue, I can loan you a few thousand, get your personal things moved up, get you settled into a studio apartment in Astoria or something. Just outside of Manhattan and Brooklyn. Just mull it over, son. I can give you three weeks."

I was overcome. One of my oldest dreams: a restaurant in New York City, perhaps the paragon of American food scenes. I strained to not lose control of my emotions.

"Of course I'll think it over, Morrie, Greta. Thank you," was all I could reply. "Thank you."

I looked up and across the dining room. Pham, JaJuan, and Etienne watched from the kitchen's edge. Wilson had at last emerged, standing in the hallway to his office like a battle-scarred sentinel. He stared our way, his expression quizzical. Surely he wondered what was said. Or had he heard every word?

My gut tightened into a ball, and I thought I felt a sweat break out on my back, imagining Wilson's shock and fear if he had caught this exchange.

Back in the kitchen, something had changed. With the orders no longer trickling in, much of my line stood idle, saying little or nothing. Almost none looked my way. As if they harbored some secret.

"All okay? Is it something I said?" My words sounded jocular in my ears. But no one laughed.

"Not said, but did, Chef," Etienne said, for once calling me the title all the others used.

"Let me hear it," I said.

"Your little peach blossom here came to you for guidance, advice," he said, placing his back against the stove and forcing a concerned and sensitive tone. "You came to her aid, then abandoned her to chase personal glory for the last hour with those bigwigs out there. Who strolled in late."

After all of Etienne's bullying of Brooke and Roosevelt, and his insolence to once again criticize his chef. But deep in my core, I felt this time he was right.

CHAPTER 20

—

Another post-grand opening dinner service drew toward its close, and the steady inflow of diners at last showed signs of abating.

The buzz from the grand opening and both that silver medal and the Best New Restaurant Award at Warehouse Fest had amplified Crescent's name through the grapevine all around town. For nearly each day, Crescent saw more and more covers. At times, the line and I found ourselves almost underwater.

"*Cállate, pendejo*," I heard Osvaldo shout. His dishwashing machine's cycle complete, he yanked open its cover, steam hitting his face, then pulled out the tray of plates. He pointed at a smirking Etienne.

Brooke's face was flushed red with humiliation.

"*Vete de aquí*," Osvaldo growled, still pointing at Etienne. "You leave her alone, *puto*."

"Cut it out, Etienne," Pham said. "Man, you're sick."

"Mr. Big Man Etienne, you and your teasing, taunting," she said, shaking her head.

"Etienne!" I shouted. "Hey, I've warned you before. Do you listen?"

Brooke watched me with gratitude, and again, that something else. The way Noelle once looked at me, in our first days together, and again as she eyed me during our grand opening.

Someone whistled at the pass-through behind me. Wilson.

"Laurent, WWL called," he said with delight. "They want to interview you, Pham, and me later this week for a feature piece. This place is about to get even busier. We probably need to hire more. At least one head. My gut's telling me maybe even two."

"Yeah," Etienne said across the kitchen, sneering. "My gut was correct earlier, 'bout makin' one more hire, right? But then we got JaJuan."

He laughed, a derisive cackle. Then he turned toward me, and Wilson.

"Hey, WWL wants to interview Pham. Why not me, too?" Etienne said. He was pushing Wilson and me, testing our boundaries.

"Because he's part of my life story, Etienne," I said. "Pham and I worked together in kitchens before this, and he was my first hire at Crescent. And we grew up together."

"Yeah, whatever," he said in a half-sigh, half-groan.

"I heard what you just said about me," JaJuan called out from his station. "You real funny. Yeah, maybe if you put in the time and earn your stripes here, you'll be part of an interview. Rather than expect it's handed to you. We were all blessed with an opportunity here."

"Why don't you shut that fat mouth," Etienne said.

"Wait, you sayin' I'm the one with the fat mouth?" JaJuan said. "Wanna take a poll, in this kitchen?"

Laughter erupted in various places around me. Even Wilson was laughing.

"Let's all settle down, team," I said. "Emphasis on that last word, team. We are all on the same team. Soon I'll make sure we are interviewed as a team."

"Haha, you almost sound like you're makin' music, Chef," JaJuan said.

I chuckled, then turned toward my kitchen's greatest headache.

"Etienne," I said, "the insults and bullying stop now. Or you know what'll happen."

He looked up and seized me with those fierce eyes, yet

remained silent, as if waiting.

I hesitated, then opted to finish. "At that point," I said, "your last check will be in the mail."

No "Yes, Chef" as my other line cooks would have said. No "Yes, sir" or "I understand." Just silence, and that glaring.

"Just keep trying to stare down your boss, pal. Smart move," I said. He smiled and shook his head, then continued fileting beef at his station. Not the best man for a chef to trust with a kitchen blade, either. Then the thought surfaced: after finding JaJuan uncooperative, had Breton won over Etienne? Had they conspired against me, Wilson, and my line?

Why had my mind been open to Etienne? I'd denied my instinct. Sheer foolishness. Naïveté.

"You tell me what you said to Brooke," I said, jabbing my index finger at him like a dagger.

"Guy should apologize for callin' Brooke names," JaJuan said. "Snaggletooth, and what's the pretty blonde singer with the crooked teeth? Yeah, Jewel. Etienne calls her Jewel."

I clenched my teeth, feeling as if one would crack.

Brooke was staring down at her clogs, as if awaiting my reaction.

"Shame on you, Etienne," I said. "One more insult, from now on, and you're finished here."

Silence was his only reply, as he stood removing the last vestiges of fat from the beef.

"Just remember, Etienne, I've believed in you all along," I said, and forced myself to walk into the service area.

I scanned the dining room. Ian McNulty, arguably the most prominent food writer in the city, sat on twelve. I always wanted to spend time with the man, one of the most intriguing New Orleanians. But one of my rules as a chef was to never socialize at length with food writers.

The president of Tulane, whose name slipped my mind, was seated on ten with three others. I must force myself to connect with my customers, to make the rounds across the floor. Press palms, make conversation.

A flash of anxiety gave way to a swell of pride. In my city, I had arrived—rather, almost.

CHAPTER 21

I loved Tuesdays. The one full day of the week Crescent closed. I made it a point never to plan anything for that day. Ms. Mary Anne Crowley—my mother—knew this and had invited me for lunch. For once I slept late, Noelle there at my side until she snuck out of my apartment to start her day, leaving me sleeping there for hours more.

When I pulled up at Mom's house in Mid-City, I remembered the important matter I'd meant to address. Hopefully that Tuesday, she would be less prickly when I broached the subject.

I entered with my key. I made sure I jingled my keychain and shut the door with a firm shove so she would not be startled. In the kitchen, Mom stood at the counter, peeling pears, her light auburn hair gathered into a shoulder-length ponytail.

"Pot roast?" I said.

She wiped her hands on a cloth and turned completely to face me, her chin turned ever so slightly upwards, her hands now on her hips, looking every bit of the formidable older Irish lady she was. She opened her arms wide, taking a step toward me.

"Hello, Jacques Pépin. Hope you're hungry." Her light blue eyes squinted, fixing onto mine as she flashed a broad smile.

"I was. But now after smelling this, I'm ravenous."

"Ha, good. What's new? I knew you were coming, so I cooked for four."

"I think I know what you've made. It could be three different dishes."

She smiled, squeezing me hard in one of her usual hugs, then pecked me on the cheek.

"It's been so long since I cooked it, you forgot that aroma," she said.

Mom lifted the lid on the wide pot, turned her head, and grinned.

"Now look at that, son," she said in the most confident declaration. "Remember this?"

I leaned over and peered down into the pot. My heart leapt inside my chest. It was a meal Mom once served on special occasions, but not since I was a boy: *bruciuluni*. Though some would call it *brucioloni* or *braccialoni*, *braciole* or *braciolona*, or even *farsumagro*. A Sicilian roast, stuffed with breadcrumbs, cheese, garlic, spinach, and herbs—and at times pancetta or prosciutto—and rolled into wheels, then braised and simmered in spaghetti sauce laced with white wine. As a teenager, Mom had learned to prepare this dish from a Sicilian friend, long since dead.

My father always mentioned, when we ate this, that the dish dated from the thirteenth century when the House of Anjou ruled Sicily.

I was poised to ask about him, after many months of not mentioning him to her, when she cleared her throat. She had returned to slicing and peeling pears, surely part of dessert.

"See, Laurent, instead of Creole-Asian fusion, you could just offer the traditional Italian and French dishes you learned at home. Not Creole, not Cajun, not fusion. True French and true Sicilian, Italian. So easy. You'd be a knockout."

Why couldn't it just be a relaxing meal, a mother and son catching up?

"Mom, many places here do that quite well. Just not French and Italian on the same menu. But still. Mom, I'm following my vision. We discussed this many times before."

"I did think it was worth another try," she said with a smile. Yet her eyes were weary. She was spent. She had tried to persuade me so many times. Like Mémère and all the others. Of course, they doubted the New Orleans dining public would go for my preferred form of cooking. Part of it was that to Mom's taste, and Mémère's, it was something eccentric, perhaps even bizarre. It also seemed they feared I was denying my French heritage, and my family's culinary traditions.

"What you ate at opening night," I said, "wasn't that a knockout?"

"It was great," Mom said, but in her eyes I could see she wasn't being completely forthright.

My heart stung. I cleared my throat. "In doing what I do, in fulfilling my dream, I can never please you. Even more, I will always frustrate you. Am I wrong?"

"Haven't I supported you, though?" Mom said, her eyes wounded within her quivering face. "Honored you? I did attend your opening night for a reason."

"That is true. Look, forget that. I really want to ask you some questions," I said, then hesitated, anticipating her reaction, "about Dad."

She continued working the pears with her knife as a sour, almost disdainful expression formed on her face.

"Ahhh, Laurent. Just leave the door shut, son. The door was shut long ago. Twenty-seven years ago, Laurent. You don't need to open the door. And don't disturb the dead."

"Don't disturb the dead? Mom, who are you, Marie Laveau the Voodoo Queen? I'm asking about my only father in the world. A person I was very close to."

She turned to me, her light blue eyes narrowing. Eyes that could be cold. Eyes that were always piercing. Eyes that always saw into my innermost depths.

"You always seem to want to ask me about the past, Laurent. Especially that part of the past."

There was something in her expression that was off. Something forced, a mask pulled down over something uncomfortable.

Then she lifted the knife and resumed her work on the pears. I stared down at my shoes.

Mom gasped, dropping her knife onto the counter, then gripped her left hand with her right.

"Mom?" I said, leaning over her. "Did you cut—"

"I'm fine!" she said, annoyed.

"Let's rush to the bathroom," I shouted. "Your first aid kit—still there in the cabinet?"

"Just wait here, son," she said, then marched across the kitchen and into the hallway in a jerking, halting motion.

I followed just a step behind, my heart racing, into the bathroom.

I washed out the cut at the faucet and sat her down on the closed toilet seat. For one fleeting moment, it was like I was a boy of eight again, when I had knelt and comforted my mother as I caught her weeping alone after some argument with my father.

"It's not a pretty cut, but won't need stitches," I said, almost in a whisper. "Mom, everything all right? You never cut yourself—you did seem so tense. Thinking of Dad caused this?"

She swung her gaze from her hand to the shower curtain behind me, then focused it upward, straight into my eyes.

"Look, son. You always did what you wanted. I've warned you, many times over. You will always say and do what you want. Like your father. And I have come to accept that."

I stood stunned as she lifted her gaze past me, up toward the ceiling, her eyes reminding me of some suffering saint—the name of whom I'd forgotten—painted by El Greco. Mom's pain at the memory of my father was undeniable. But I'd come too far to turn back, or let go.

"I was his son, Mother," I said. "Plus, he and I were close. Don't I have a right to inquire about him?"

She released a long sigh, shaking her light auburn bangs from her face. "Mémère mentioned you've been asking about him. What is it you want to know, son?"

"Several things," I said. "Where's that first aid kit?"

Mom gestured toward the cabinet under the sink. I squatted, then removed the bottle of hydrogen peroxide and fished one of the larger Band-Aids out of the box, cleansed her wound at the sink, and applied the bandage.

"Let's head to the table," I said, then followed her. We took our seats.

"Mom, you remember Dad died at forty. These last few months, the closer I get to my own fortieth birthday, I keep thinking more of him. And dreaming more of him."

She remained silent, gazing at the ceiling.

"Not only did he die at forty," I said. "He was a chef for many years. But gave it up near the end. I keep wanting to make him proud. And to finish what he couldn't. To do what he didn't."

"Laurent, I've always felt your dad's Vietnamese friend out in Village De L'Est knew more of the story. But I never asked him. Even when the man called to check up on me after the funeral."

"Ong Ngoai?" I said.

"Yes. Remember, I just shared a table with him at your new place's opening night. I never asked him because I was so angry with your father after he died. After all Claude put you and me through in his last years, and then came his suicide. He quit. Can't prove it, and no one could, but—"

"I agree, Mom. I don't think he was murdered. Not by that Rodney—"

"I just don't buy that. Claude took out one big fat life insurance policy on himself a couple months before the—incident. You've heard this. That's how I was able to keep us afloat, and help you apprentice unpaid in those European kitchens, and attend culinary school after NOCCA. Before the well ran dry. That's when our struggle got worse. You and I and Mémère."

"Why would Ong Ngoai know something?" I said.

"He and your dad were close. He was a friend to your dad when he was stationed in Saigon. Something like a father figure, too. And he knew things about your dad no one else did. I could see they shared this uncanny kind of—telepathy. Ha, yeah, Ong Ngoai."

Mom sighed, then said, "That's what your father taught you to call the man. I was ticked at first because that term means maternal grandfather. Your dad thought it was just nice that you called him that, that he would stand in for my own father. Who had shunned us because of your dad, and me remaining with him. But like many things with Claude, I learned to just put up with it."

"Sounds like that's what many had to do," I said. "Like Mémère did."

"Yes. And now it's your Aunt LaFaye," she said, her eyes narrowing with disdain. I felt guilty, just witnessing her expression. "She's the one we all had to endure, ever since Claude left."

I heard her words but was thinking of Ong Ngoai, and my schedule for the next week. I loved the man, but besides inviting him to Crescent's grand opening, it had been years since I'd seen him. I needed to visit with him, even if it was only to pay my respects.

"I suggest you go visit Ong Ngoai," she said, though I had resolved moments before to do so. "Follow the truth, son, wherever it leads. Just be ready for whatever you uncover."

A chill shot down my spine and across the back of my shoulders.

"Maybe it'll bring you peace, Laurent. I've found my peace."

CHAPTER 22

Later that afternoon, I found myself in the French Quarter, for it was one of those not-common yet not-rare days when Jim and I were both off work. I had invited him on one of our jaunts, but this time for a different reason. I wanted his opinion on Morrie's offer and a potential move to the Northeast, from a friend who had done the same.

Under a melancholy sky with its gray swirling clouds, Jim and I strolled down Royal, past its art galleries, cafés, and shops. I remembered Royal was closed each day to traffic from eleven in the morning to four in the afternoon, providing a corridor where various buskers and street artists could perform. A world apart from Bourbon Street, a mere block to the north, with its barkers, sign-holders, pickpockets, and inebriated revelers.

On the slate sidewalk, four teen boys played a clarinet, trumpet, trombone, and tuba. Further on, two other teen boys tap danced, a cardboard box of coins and cash at their feet.

We passed them, walking a minute longer, until Jim paused in front of the four-story, light-cream-colored brick building. He smiled at the structure with half-closed eyes as if in nirvana.

"Another worthy stop in the Quarter. Touristed but not a tourist trap," Jim said as a porter dressed in livery opened the door. "Thank you, sir. After you, Laurent."

As we breezed into the lobby of the Hotel Monteleone, Jim said, "If you're literary in the slightest, this place has a history worth mentioning."

Jim pointed at the floor. "Look at this marble, Laurent. And at those antique grandfather clocks. One of the oldest and prettiest hotel lobbies in the city, obviously from the Gilded Age, very Victorian. But that's not why we're here."

"I know why we're here, Jim," I said, and chuckled at my own deadpan delivery.

We hooked right into a room beyond the lobby. In the center of the long hotel bar of tables and cushioned red seats stood that curiosity I'd last seen as a man of twenty-three. An illuminated carousel about twenty feet in diameter, ringed by seats on pedestals. Two bartenders stood in its center. Just as I remembered, the carousel was turning, ever so slightly, like a rotating planet.

Jim lurched forward, as giddy over our destination as if he were a child. I took my seat beside him. The elevated chairs were almost full, mostly with tourists. A few laughing and chattering college students, Tulane frat boys according to some of their sweatshirts, occupied the seats to Jim's flank. The two mixologists in formal attire readied cocktails at a brisk pace. Jim groaned. As his face lowered toward the bartop, I noted an expression somewhere between shame and embarrassment. One of the bartenders turned and approached: an attractive woman somewhere in her late thirties, notepad in hand. On her face was a strange expression: amused, uncomfortable, yet emitting a sense of warmth.

"If it isn't James Scoresby. How the hell are you, Jim?"

"Sierra!" Jim said, now facing her. "Good to see you again. We're just cuttin' loose on our day off. Meet my pal Laurent."

She nodded at me and smiled. "Nice to meet you."

"I didn't know you were over here," Jim said. "You're no longer at One Eyed Jack's?"

She smiled, cocked her head at a slant, and eyed Jim with skepticism. "Would you have come here if you knew I was working the bar, Jim? My last day at One Eyed Jack's was back in on the third. It was time, though. So, can I start you gentlemen off with some adult beverages?"

"Don't twist my arm," Jim said. "What do you say, L?"

"A Vieux Carré, please," I said.

"Good choice. It was invented here," Jim said. "Sierra, I'll take a Ramos gin fizz."

Sierra vanished around the carousel's turning central column.

"I can't go wrong with a century-old cocktail invented by a bartender who was a preacher," Jim said. He then whispered in my ear, "Sierra and I were a bit intimate a few months ago. I'd curtailed my old ways. But I'd quaffed quite a few drinks, and I succumbed."

"Old habits die hard with you," I said. "But you weren't always like that, a man about town. From what you told me."

"I became that way after I returned from Boston, about eight years ago," Jim said. "A way to avoid tackling trauma from tragedies I experienced, to divert myself. Or so a therapist told me."

Sierra reappeared, and, without making eye contact, set the cocktails before us. With a parched expression, sucking her lips into her mouth with the utmost grimness, she whipped back around the column.

I smiled at Jim as he closed his eyes and shook his head.

"We should move out after this," I said and laughed.

"Copy that," Jim said, and smiled. "But—after we soak up our drinks, and this legendary place. You know, Faulkner, Hemingway, Tennessee Williams, Truman Capote all loved to stay here. Oldest family-owned hotel in New Orleans. Has a great musical history as well. Louis Prima played here many times, over in that section."

"I've meant to stop in here again," I said. "But haven't since I was in C-school."

Jim resumed his verbal tour of our surroundings, but the thoughts on my own habits that had been knocking, then pounding at the door of my mind, at last broke in.

Jim was studying my face, his eyebrows raised. He had asked me something, but I had not caught it.

"Perhaps I should not be drinking," I said.

Jim's mildly curious expression morphed into one of befuddlement.

"Life's been rocky," I said. "Bitter, and unpredictable. For years Mémère and my mother both advised me against it. They said, after suffering such losses, that I shouldn't do anything that might increase the pain. That I was too much like my dad, that I'd fall into his habits."

"Well, you are a chef. So, you must be like an elite soldier in the field. Operating on little sleep. Drink will destroy what little sleep you get."

"But it's my release, Jim, besides fine food. And some food goes best with fine wine."

"Laurent, their point is valid. Your mother, your grandmother," Jim said. "I should have advised you the same. I'm sorry. But you can't give what you don't have. One true adage. You know, there is a sickness that pervades most drinking establishments. Centered even more on the bartender than the bar patrons. Or, rather, the regulars."

"How that?" I said.

"Every bar's got its most loyal regulars," Jim said, "barflies, people worse off than us. There almost daily, who drink to some degree of excess, who are in reality bad alcoholics. These bartenders serve them, even encourage them to order more. Even after they know these customers are intoxicated. All in the name of money. Many barflies are lonely people, even loners. Even if they're surrounded by people who love them. They also come to feel a connection to the bartender, or to be in a group's guaranteed company. That's why they don't do it cheaper and just drink at home."

"This is true," I said.

"And to these bartenders, Laurent, they'll divulge matters of the heart, like one would do with a psychotherapist. And many of these bartenders, not all but many, the face they present to these people is false, contrived. Many can't stand those barflies. They tolerate them, put on an act for the money. All while the alcoholics sit there for hours, damaging their organs and their minds and spirits. Disgusting in many ways, if you ask me. You'll often see a bartender continue to ask the drunkard if he wants another drink, right when he's close to finishing the latest one. And when the person pays and is finally leaving, the bartenders will often say, several times, 'Are you okay to drive? Are you sure you can drive?!'"

Jim laughed. "I mean, what the hell do you think, *garcon?*"

"Then Jim, why do you continue to patronize such establishments?" I felt a tinge of shame, as my voice sounded irritated and condescending in my ears.

"Because I was lost in it before, Laurent. For a couple years. And now I am again," Jim said with both certitude and gravity.

There was an awkward silence. I regretted prodding Jim on his habit and his knowledge of its surrounding culture, until he exposed his open wound. And I did not want to speak further of my own struggle in that same realm. I would switch the subject.

"We all have our proclivities, I suppose," I said in a near-mumble. "Or most of us. Mine are cheffing, food, neglected or underappreciated restaurants, ironically booze, complex and beautiful women, rainy weather—"

"A born artist. Of the kitchen!" Jim said. "And a proud native son of N'awlins."

"I am, but the question is, will I stay?" The question emerged before I could measure my words. "And for how long?"

Jim stared, a smirk playing on one side of his mouth. That stare melted and his eyes became warm and accepting, along with something else. I caught the sadness in his face, and remembered that this man was, in fact, one of my best friends.

"Jim, it is a little—complicated. I received an offer that's had my mind really churning."

I took a deep sip, and then a deep breath.

"Let me start with this, Jim. Early in my career, I went across the pond for several months to enrich my knowledge and skills. But also to be away from it all, the madness, the violence, the tragedy and destruction of this city. I *know* you understand. You left for New England, nine years ago. The hurricane."

"True," Jim said. "But your situation's different."

"But hear me out. I've just wanted to lay low in the Warehouse District, while visiting Mémère and my family. Away from what's rotting my old neighborhood and this city from the inside out. You've got an epidemic of young men murdering not just each other but women, the elderly, even children. My old neighborhood isn't worthy of me or Mémère, though I still love the Channel and its people in many ways. Never felt like an insider in Mid-City. Definitely not when we lived Uptown when I was very young. Today I don't feel that accepted in New Orleans, period. Except for tourists, academics, hipsters and the young, people here aren't taking to my menu quite like I thought they would. They're proving Noelle and Mémère and Aunt LaFaye right."

"Really?" Jim said, squinting with disbelief.

"Jim, I've found success—but with a limited target market. I'm critically acclaimed but haven't won over the average Joe restaurant-goer in New Orleans. That's eluded me."

"Who cares about gratifying the hoi polloi's dining preferences," Jim said. "You don't run a po-boy shop, or a fast-food joint, Laurent."

"You've got a point there," I said. "So, the other day I met Morrie, Ben's wealthy uncle, in town from New York. Sampled a good bit of my menu, at the Warehouse District Restaurant Festival and then later at Crescent. He extended a verbal offer to fill the chef's spot in this New York restaurant he's planning to open. Did Noelle tell you? Or Ben?"

"No, actually. But that's something to consider, Laurent. That's a great market for your style of cooking. You won't be the first in that city, or the twentieth. But you can still love New Orleans from a distance. Like a man can love a woman from a distance. In New York, you could still help your family and home city from afar. All you've got to do is to keep pushing."

"That's a thought," I said.

"And if you join Ben's uncle, y'all could open more restaurants down here. If you can, later."

Jim leaned back in his chair and stared out the window. The rush of tourists flowed by, coursing over the slate and asphalt like a slow but steady stream.

"You could rebuild your life in New York," Jim continued. "In a larger, more cosmopolitan city. A metropolis. Where even I've contemplated reinventing my life. The hub where so many have. If you pull it off, you could have the best of both worlds. And you'd be building your résumé."

"That's if everything works out," I said. "Ah, I'm torn."

"Laurent, I assume Noelle would move with you?" Jim said. "I'm thinking the opportunities for her music there are almost as good as in L.A."

"I haven't gotten that far," I said, "in proposing that to her. I will, if I get closer to taking Morrie up on his offer. He wants me to decide in the next week or so. I'm feeling squeezed."

"Wait. Wilson Turner doesn't know about that offer, does he?"

"No. At least he hasn't dropped any clue."

Jim moaned as if a headache was coming on.

"And Jim, as for Noelle, you already know she's brought up her moving to L.A. several times. I'd lie if I said we're not on shaky ground. Not sure how this will all end."

"Yeah, Laurent, and this dilemma with Wilson—that's a big one."

"Truly," I said.

"Laurent, if you didn't leave his restaurant in good hands, you'd break his scarred heart. And this whole venture would just be one big tease for him. Wilson rolled the dice on you. You can't desert him. My read on what you've told me of your dad, as a chef in your position, he wouldn't desert Wilson, either. I bet that would've been against his code."

We fell silent, but the Tulane frat boys grew louder.

I was surprised he brought up my dad so casually. I wondered if he knew what had been on my mind those last several weeks.

"We should vacate this place," Jim said. "Grab a few morsels after this delicious poison. I know just what will do the trick."

Jim pulled some bills from his wallet and placed them on the bar. "This one's my treat. Hey, ever heard the bartenders can only leave the carousel by sliding *over* the bartop? Gotta love that."

We went for the lobby, and again the doorman opened the door for us. The afternoon breeze hit us with its February chill, almost like a playful slap to our faces. But the sounds of saxophones, trumpets, and other brass returned, and those classic French Quarter scents I loved: baked French bread, roux, boiled seafood, fried beignets, minus the acrid stench of vomit.

"Yes, I like your idea," I said. "Some morsels would be great right about now."

"Hey, you inspired a passage I wrote yesterday," Jim said, pulling his smartphone from his pocket. "Let me find it."

"Let's hear it, Jimbo."

Jim said, "'And no matter how far you traveled, you would relive that same feeling whenever your nostrils would catch those aromas that were so like restaurants in New Orleans. Always some scent of life lived to its limit, of the promise of a day or night when the senses could be sated in the most elegant but exciting manner.'"

"Stunning," I said. "Love that."

We strolled eastward on Royal until the sign for St. Louis Street appeared ahead. On our right behind a tall black wrought-iron fence loomed the marble courthouse, stately in its Victorian grandeur, that housed the Louisiana Supreme Court. Jim veered right on St. Louis and soon the renowned stucco corner building came into view.

"You know I've done The Napoleon House," I said.

"Ha, I'd be concerned if you hadn't," Jim said. "It merits another visit. Even a hundredth visit. An eternal gem, that is certain."

"I can agree to that," I said. "I like their muffuletta. And Pimm's Cup."

Knowing my friend as I did, I could see why Jim selected this place, I thought, as we approached the worn old wooden doors. The mere fact that the imprisoned Napoleon Bonaparte, if the British had chosen the offer of a different destination, would have been confined in this building—that would be enough for the Armstrong Lofts' top history buff to never stay away.

Jim opened the door and motioned for me to enter. Inside, the place buzzed like a packed hive, with so many seated in booths and at tables and at the lone mirror-backed bar across the large dining room. Even the courtyard's tables beyond were full.

We had made it just a few feet inside when a loud pop sounded out in the street, somewhere close, followed by another pop, and another. Then two more. It was almost as if a firework show had begun. And then a woman screamed.

Another sound emerged: Shoes slapping hard onto the slate sidewalk just outside in some desperate sprint.

I shuddered as I stared through the windows of the closed door. Seconds passed, but they seemed like minutes. At last, a lone figure shot by, straining to move as fast as possible in his tracksuit while gripping a pistol and a plastic bag, his face completely obscured by a ski mask.

A reflex sent me jerking right and spinning back behind the wall. Jim was already there beside me, matching my position: a shrugging crouch, sitting on the ankles.

"Say, looks like you've done this before, Jim," I said, then looked down at my hands, wrists. They were shaking in an involuntary reflex.

"Good Lord, man," Jim said. "It never ends. I feel sick."

The chatter around us grew louder, as the eyes of all around us fixed on the door and the front windows.

"Ahh, no matter—just a typical Sunday afternoon in New Orleans," Jim said. "Not even twilight and the bullets are flyin'."

I sighed. "Wow. This happened a couple blocks from the cop station and the courthouse. Let's wait a minute. Then let's get far away from this spot."

"Agreed," Jim said, as he swept his gaze back and forth across the dining room, and what we could see beyond of the rectangular courtyard with its second-floor wooden balcony rail. I could feel the charm of the dining room's centuries-old stucco walls, crossed with cracks and patches of exposed bricks. And then there were the small framed paintings here and there. Surely this was one of the oldest buildings in the country housing a dining establishment. It was unfortunate that our visit was ruined.

"Shootings, and news of shootings. Guess we better disappear," Jim said, and we rose and headed out of the door.

"Come on," I said. "Let's sprint south to the river. Just a few blocks."

I could hear shouting down the street in the direction that the man had run. And then silence.

I soon saw Jim lagged behind, so our sprint became a jog.

"You're gonna put me in my grave," Jim said, winded. "Guess I should finally start exercising. But good call. Few more minutes here, police will look for eyewitnesses."

"Broad daylight, and in a frequented area," I said. "We're seeing more of this."

We moved farther down St. Louis toward the river. As Decatur Street emerged, Jim slowed to a fast march.

"Laurent, let's just give it a fast walk, will ya? River's right there. And it's not like we're being chased. We're home free. Normally I'm more of the anxious one."

"Point taken," I said, slowing. "I want to live to at least make my big decision."

"Laurent, really. This city's been in decline, in a state of urban decay for almost seventy years. Do you ever—like me—contemplate how very dangerous this city is? We forget it due to conditioning. But you risk robbery and death every time you go out walking in many areas. Local media downplays it. Many of our hipsters never bring it up. 'Oh, New Orleans is just amazing, through and through!' They'll always disregard it or push back, should you broach the subject."

"Well then," I said, "why do you still live here?"

"I've just learned to make peace with the way New Orleans is," Jim said, pointing back over his shoulder at the blood-shed we'd just evaded. "I spent much time missing this place, years ago in Boston, and before that, in California, and Spain. It always inspired me. In all its decadence, sensuality, fatalism, escapism, the past and the present cohabitating. And what did Justin Lundgren write about this city? 'It's a fragile and extraordinary patch of land that has served as the cradle of American architecture, food and music.' Like I say, it's the Fertile Crescent. Not to be confused with your fertile, produc-tive restaurant by that name."

Jim grinned, cleared his throat, and continued, "Now, in my years away, I missed my family, but I also missed what makes this city unique and inspiring. A city mostly below sea-level, and sinking, due to generations of groundwater pump-ing. A city decades after its peak. As Owen Brennan once put it: 'New Orleans, the boomtown that never booms.' But even if the city's troubled—it's still worth inhabiting, for certain people. Especially for artists. And I'm willing to take responsibility for my fate, should I prove to ultimately be a statistic."

"If you're in the wrong place at the wrong time," I said.

"Yes, Laurent. I just wish the city could be even halfway cured. There's a chance in ten, twenty years, hardly one of its seventeen wards will be walkable, drivable, even livable. Relatively speaking. Maybe it's doomed. Still, there's a lot of pull here for now. New Orleans pulls me in."

"I feel you," I said. But true it was. For I felt much the same about our birth city and would probably feel the same if I left New Orleans again.

Yet my struggle over place was unique. Or, at least, different from Jim's. The question continued to present itself: Was New Orleans too close-minded, too traditional, to appreciate my vision? My city often did have a "the past is safer than the future" mindset. But Jim was also right—if I stayed, I could be killed before achieving any vision, whereas I could live to an advanced age in Morrie's city, with a very sophisticated eating public.

But I recalled the words of Anthony Bourdain, that New Orleans is the culinary capital of America. And it was a city where, to my benefit, its inhabitants of all races and religions and social strata were enamored with food. Where they don't eat to live, but live to eat. Where people dine at the table, while they discuss past meals and muse and even obsess about future ones.

"Truly, it was an unlikely city," Jim said. "The sliver by the river. You know what some call the land in NOLA up against the river—that's just high enough to not flood. What, eleven feet above sea level or so? The French saw this whole swamp and called it *La Flotant* or The Floating Marsh. And the Brits dubbed it The Wet Grave. Bienville's engineers urged him not to build a settlement here. But this city survived for centuries, and it wove a spell on me. And so many others. This strange city, with the largest pumping system in the world."

We drew within feet of Decatur. The massive parking lot against the levee and river appeared. We hooked left, approaching Jax Brewery on our right. Just beyond, the Steamboat Natchez was moored against the dock, though its massive wheel churned in the water. Steam snaked upward from the dual stacks, while a lone corpulent figure played the organ on its top deck.

"I'll be," Jim said, pointing at the man's silhouette, "if it isn't the notorious Ignatius Reilly. He's still around."

"Good one, Jimbo. Gotta love those literary allusions."

Eastward we continued down Decatur. Jackson Square emerged on our left, flanked on each side by the red brick façades and black wrought-iron balconies of the nearly three-hundred-year-old Pontalba Apartments.

"Ah," Jim said, "I love those Pontalba buildings. Oldest apartment buildings in the U.S."

Pigeons strutted and fluttered on the slate surrounding Jackson Square's wrought-iron fence, amongst the fortune tellers, clairvoyants, tarot card readers, and the painters and portraitists at their easels and the tables where they sold their creations. The mule-drawn tour carriages had lined up nearby.

Beside the equestrian statue in the square's center, a photographer snapped photos of a wedding party. Just beyond, near the entrance of St. Louis Cathedral, a quartet played a tuba, snare drum, trumpet, and violin.

"Now, this is the New Orleans afternoon I hoped for," Jim said. "But we should change it up a bit. Not our usual Frenchman Street Art Market. Or live music at the Blue Nile or Café Negril."

"Why, what are you thinking?" I said. "How about a little Old Algiers Point?"

"That is *exactly* what I was thinking," Jim said. "We could turn back and head west to Canal, then take the ferry over.

You can finish explaining your dilemma. Before New Orleans interrupted."

As we trekked toward the ferry, I detailed Morrie's offer, then laid out the benefits and drawbacks of both options. I added I was unsure if Noelle would accompany me to New York.

Indeed, the ghost of Noelle loomed over the entire situation, when that is not how I ever wanted to think of her. I remembered our after-hours dinner date in Crescent. I could never part with her, of my own will. Tears welled in my eyes, clouding my vision. Though she doubted it at times, my love for her still burned bright.

Jim paid our fares and, this time, unlike all other times, he said nothing. No sudden thoughts, no historical vignettes. Just intermittent nods, his fingertips massaging his chin in contemplation.

On the lower deck we stood, grasping the rail at the stern, watching the gulls swooping and soaring over the brown coffeelike waves of the Mississippi. Every few minutes one would dive into the waves and spear the water with its beak, angling for fish. The Central Business District to our left, and the Vieux Carré to our far right, with its cathedral's façade and spire and the bustling rectangular hub of the Café du Monde, and the riverboats docked near Woldenberg Park—all receded into the distance as the ferry neared the river's south shore.

I ensured my eyes avoided my far left: the Crescent City Connection, the old GNO Bridge.

We strolled along the deck until we came to a section of rail at the bow.

"The New York option," Jim at last said, "involves more risk. You're an ingenious chef, but the Big Apple—that's a lot of competition. I believe your initial instinct was right. Hone your skills, test out your vision in the New Orleans market for a few years, then take up Morrie on his offer."

"I've honed my skills here for two decades, Jim. The offer

might not be there at that point."

"But there will be others, I'm sure, Laurent."

From his position with both hands resting atop the rail, Jim gazed at the Algiers shore nearing us. A silent minute passed.

"Pondering your watering holes on the southern shore?" I said.

I bet I was correct. The Old Point Bar in all its divey glory, teeming with Algiers townies. Then would come the Crown and Anchor, that English pub selling crisps and room-temperature drafts of ale.

"We must have some strange brotherly ESP," Jim said, laughing. "More like twins have. I spent the first eight years of my life in Algiers. Place has declined since then. The Point's still nice, though. Or have I told you this before? I don't repeat myself, do I?"

Jim winked, and continued, "Anyway, Laurent. You're not in such a bad position. Consider your options, and at least you've got options."

"At least we'll have a good time tonight," I said.

"We're in the right city for that," Jim said, smiling. "Remember Sherwood Anderson. He wrote in 1922, 'New Orleans shows enjoyment of life, sense of leisure, and a background of joy in life with which to refresh the tired spirits.' That's what today's about. *Savoir vivre*. Refreshing the tired spirits, right?"

Just past Jim's shoulder, a small gull, perhaps a fledgling, rose from the waves and took flight over the choppy brown waves. Though I was no longer a fledgling, I envisioned my own impending journey, out of my own nest and farther north.

But would it ever come to be? And if so, when?

CHAPTER 23

I t was five in the morning when my phone buzzed. Wilson. It had to come after the afternoon and night I put all work and preparations aside and lived the Jim Scoresby life. I lifted my phone to my ear.

"I hope you're sitting—even better, laying down for this one," the breathy voice said, all cigarettes and sky-high blood pressure. Wilson sounded as anxious as I'd ever heard. Had he learned of Morrie's offer? Had something happened with Breton?

"We lost JaJuan. He—"

"Breton stole him back?"

There was a pause.

"No, damn it. Laurent, listen. JaJuan's down with the flu. He called me and his voice even sounds like a monster's."

"Oh Lord," I moaned.

"We're more than one short now," Wilson said. "JaJuan was like one and a half, or two."

"Very true," I said.

"Yeah, but that ain't all, Laurent. Etienne smells blood in the water. He heard JaJuan will no doubt be out a few days, so he got here early, issued us an ultimatum. Wants to negotiate a promotion to sous. He's pretty antsy now. As if he wasn't already."

"Figures. He's in the kitchen now?"

"No, he's sitting in the dining room. I'm trying to simmer down, here at my desk."

"I'll be there shortly," I said, and hung up. My stomach felt as if it were twisting within me.

When I arrived, Etienne was in plain clothes, drinking coffee with Wilson at table nine.

They gazed my way with solemn faces.

"That's too bad about JaJuan," Etienne said. "Sounds like he'll be out a good while. When business is booming."

"I'm sure you're all torn up about him," I said, sitting down at the table. "Wilson informed me you'd like to chat."

I paused, watching the eyes. There was something behind them I could not identify.

"Here early to discuss a promotion, right?" I said.

Etienne hummed in assent, with the slightest nod.

I said, "I was hoping to discuss this with our fearless leader in private a bit, first."

A foot tapped underneath the table. Probably Etienne's. He said, "Wilson says we can't afford it yet. And that Pham's still the sous for the near future. That set in stone?"

"It's true we're stretched thin for the time being, as to the pay increase part," I said. "Pham will still be sous chef. But maybe there could be two people alternating in the same role and—"

"Come on, man. Two in that role? It usually doesn't work; you and I know. 'Specially on a line like this."

"This is a lot to chew on, Etienne," I said. "Especially right after hearing JaJuan's out."

"That's what I told him," Wilson said.

"This is what I can offer," I said, weighing my finances. Etienne watched me, dead silent.

"Etienne, I can offer you, if Wilson's okay with this, a promotion to co-sous chef. I'll carve out an extra two hundred bucks per week out of my own salary, to add to yours."

"No can do, bud," he shot back. "You know I got more skill than any of 'em on that line. I admitted in my interview I expected a promotion sooner rather than later. Now it's later. Yeah, and how many weeks in? I'll have to walk."

"Wilson?" I said.

"I can't lose Etienne," he said. "I'll give you one hundred a week from my salary. So, you'll get three hundred more a week total. Laurent's really my partner in this. That was our original agreement. That he's my partner and Pham is sous. He'd rather lose his left hand than lose Pham."

They both looked my way.

"Correct," I said. "Sorry, Etienne. But this isn't a bad offer for now. We only got started several weeks ago."

"No deal. I could've made this place so much better," Etienne said. "As sous, but especially if I ran the joint. As chef."

"Wow, there it is," I said, astounded, but my suspicions vindicated. "It's been there all along. You have respect for my vision, and dishes and their presentations all flow from the chef's vision. But you never respected my abilities, or position."

He sighed, crossing his arms and leaning back in his chair. "I admit it: I know I could lead this crew better."

I said, "There are no boundaries on our menus here, and that makes it a special place. But there are in the kitchen. That's what makes it like any other functioning kitchen: It's got a chain of command. Otherwise? Chaos. That's what you never bought into, Etienne."

"Okay, Laurent, I'm sure we'll see each other around. Please mail me my last check," Etienne said and placed a black plastic bag on the table. I could see his kitchen whites inside. He turned and walked out of the door, without so much as a handshake.

Etienne never did position himself as a gentleman. And the line was short two heads.

It felt like the ceiling had collapsed onto me, like I was suffocating. I told myself to breathe deeply.

"Call the rest of the line," Wilson said, slapping the table-top with both hands. "This place is closed for the day."

CHAPTER 24

As I rolled eastward on I-10, past the French Quarter on my right, then past the Ninth Ward, then into New Orleans East, I realized how curious a sight I might provide to the Vietnamese passersby of Village De L'Est: a rusty old American car with a flat-cap-sporting white driver.

It was time, though. For years I'd wanted to visit my father's best friend, a great man I had always loved. Ong Ngoai still lived in that neighborhood, one of the largest Vietnamese communities in the nation. I'd resolved at that lunch at Mom's to visit him again. To get closer to the truth about my father, and to pay my respects to his best friend, before he was gone. On a lesser scale, to get Ong Ngoai's advice on my recurring self-doubt, with Etienne gone forever and JaJuan out sick. But to see this living treasure, I must endure his son and his son's wife, whom I was raised to address with affection as Uncle Minh and Aunt Tu. As a boy, and later as a young man, I was close with them. But recent years saw them make dismissive comments of my advancements using Vietnamese elements. Pham also knew them and told me he learned that, once they'd tasted my cooking at Crescent's grand opening, they were incensed at my distortion, my corruption of Vietnamese cuisine. This went along with their abject horror that evening ten years before, when I had brought my barbecued pulled pork pho for their dinner feast during Tét.

The unease in my belly over seeing Uncle Minh and Aunt Tu continued its rise until every clicking turn signal, every squeak and creak of my old beater sounded in my ears like a horn blaring. I laughed inwardly at the thought: So, this is what Wilson's nerves felt like. My work-free late morning had morphed into something almost as stressful as the grand opening at Crescent.

I passed the Vietnamese mall with its sprawling parking lot. The Buddhist monk still sat outside of the entrance in his bright orange robe, near the carts displaying bamboo plants and various curios fashioned with jade and fake gold, such as miniature Buddhas, crucifixes, and photo frames. Behind the monk stretched the row of bakeries, coffee and tea houses, and restaurants with flatscreens showing Vietnamese music videos. I turned left into Ong Ngoai's neighborhood. I cruised past the well-maintained lawns and small but well-kept ranch houses often fronted by Marian statues, stone crucifixes, and Buddhas.

I love the street names, I thought: Saigon, Vanchu, My Viet Drive.

I knew it to be the most vulnerable land in the city. Low, like Metairie and Lakeview. But bordered on three sides by water. Village De L'Est withstood a ten-foot-plus storm surge during Katrina yet rebounded. But it was a steep climb. Many families relied on churches like Mary Queen of Vietnam and Our Lady of Lavang for support and shelter. And FEMA gave preference to individuals and those in shelters, not communities. So many got no help. Truly, a red-tape nightmare.

I rolled down the window, allowing the cool air to waft through the car.

One of my favorite features of Village De L'Est was that many residents practiced advanced urban agriculture, both inside their homes and in their gardens. Much of the vegetables produced were sold there at outdoor farmers' markets every week, the most famous featured every Saturday morning on Alcee Fortier Boulevard. At that time, throughout the years, I was preparing my kitchen for service. But I remembered my father taking me a few times as a boy. The market was a carbon copy of what one would see in Vietnam, he'd told me. It opened so early—even at five AM—as to beat the heat during the long summers. It would mostly sell out by eight AM. Dad had said that Saturday morning market was really the most social venue in Village De L'Est, far more than its churches, restaurants, or bars.

I turned down another street. I loved how many of the houses were painted in such vibrant colors: blue, pink, and green. Dad claimed this tradition originated in Old Saigon.

Tremé's houses had a lot of those same colors, I recalled. Tangerine, maroon, violet, light blue, magenta, and canary-yellow buildings—a tradition carried over from the Caribbean and, before that, West Africa.

As I approached the compact red brick ranch house, its glass storm door encased in door-high metal bars, my nostrils caught the aroma I knew from my earliest years visiting Ong Ngoai: what I always imagined was pure South Vietnam.

I pressed the doorbell, though my deepest instinct told me conflict awaited.

Prepare to step into another world, I remembered.

The door opened. Standing there was Uncle Minh in a navy-blue long-sleeved silk shirt and black pants. His large, squarish head lowered and rose in a nod. His face, at first expressionless, broadened into a grin, revealing his gold-capped upper incisor.

"Welcome," he said, blinking rapidly as he ushered me inside. I stepped forward.

Despite his smiling eyes and grin, Uncle Minh then pursed his lips with what seemed like annoyance.

"I'm taking off my shoes, no worries," I said. "It's good form."

Uncle Minh hesitated as I stood there in the short foyer, pulling off my shoes. I glanced down at his diminutive, slippered feet, encased in thin black socks.

"So come in, come in," he said.

We walked past the family photos, framed on the walls of the foyer. I recalled that somewhere amongst them hung a photo of my father, overseas in his Army fatigues. But what always struck me was an amusing oddity, an incongruity: Aunt Tu's crucifixes and Marian icons being mere feet away from Uncle Minh's bronze statue of a seated Buddha.

I was not inside the house for more than a few minutes when the temptation grew too strong. I excused myself to Uncle Minh, Aunt Tu, and their daughter Mai in the kitchen and left out of the back door, heading down the flower-lined paved walkway toward the mother-in-law suite out back. Or, rather, the grandfather quarters, for that is where Ong Ngoai lived out the rest of his days and nights in seclusion after he had lost his wife to cancer, and later retired. As the years passed, and I got to know Uncle Minh and Aunt Tu better, I came to understand his need to carve out some space between himself and the family. Alone with his thoughts, and memories, with his green and black tea and his own special blend of Japanese tobacco. Even a short meeting with the most intriguing and mysterious living member of that family would be sure to serve as a salve to my bruised spirit. And perhaps an illumination as to the truth.

Yes, my old Ong Ngoai, born Truong Anh Thành, who besides young Mai was the one soul in his family who had complete confidence in my talents. The man who still dearly loved and remembered my dead father, and held his memory in great affection, even reverence.

I drew near to the door covered with a silk banner of the yellow dragon, that symbol of old Vietnam, and delivered five raps in my habitual rhythm, just so Ong Ngoai would know it was me.

The door opened after half a minute. The smell of tea poured out of the crack and that face emerged with its thin white mustache and goatee, the eyes smiling just an inch below mine. The edge of his mouth was turned upward in a playful grin, matching the youthful thickness of his hair.

"Ong Ngoai," I said, hearing the excitement in my voice. *Ong Ngoai. Maternal grandfather.*

"*Nha ao thuat!*" he shot back his nickname for me with glee. *Magician.* Since I was ten or eleven, he had called me a magician in the kitchen. He always had my deep respect, but he was not like many of the other Vietnamese elders of his generation: He did not expect the young to bow slightly before him, to avoid staring into his eyes.

"Now come in," Ong Ngoai said, switching to English and waving me inside. Nothing had changed within since my last visit, a few years before. There was the statue of Buddha in faux gold, but I knew Ong Ngoai was not simply a Buddhist. Like many Vietnamese in America, he adhered to *Tam Giao*, or the "triple religion" of Buddhism, Confucianism, and Daoism.

There again were the same homemade shelves filled with books and a couple of stacks of New Orleans East newspapers printed in Vietnamese, and then, not quite kitsch because it was befitting a retired professional fisherman: the small nets and the old bamboo fishing pole from the mother country mounted on the wall just underneath and parallel with the ceiling. The heritage flag still hung on another wall—the old flag of South Vietnam with its three red horizontal stripes on a yellow background. Just above this was the old framed black and white photo of Ong Ngoai's late wife.

"Sit down, *Nha ao thuat*. Some green tea?"

"No thanks," I said, lowering myself onto the old couch, the springs creaking beneath me.

I stared at the large, framed photograph of Ha Long Bay, with its magnificent limestone karsts rising in glory from the blue ocean, their rocky faces carpeted in places with lush green vegetation. Both Ong Ngoai and my father had told me it was the most sublime sight in all of Vietnam. Dad said it resembled some Greek islands, and the island of Capri in Italy.

"I really enjoyed eating at your new restaurant. How has that been?" said Ong Ngoai, snapping me from my daydream. "How are things?"

"The restaurant—it's been good. I foresee great things ahead."

"But how is your head?" he said with a slight smile, pointing at his forehead.

"That's a different matter. Been wrestling inside with a few things."

"Talk to me," he said, raising his teacup to his lips.

"I've always been able to talk to you. And you've always listened. Recently I made that big move. Thanks for accepting my invite to my grand opening, and I'm glad you enjoyed your meal. You experienced it: what I call true world fusion. Cajun and Creole and traditional Southern food fused with various cuisines from the East. Vietnam, Thailand, China, Persia, India. I've had some accolades and support, but some setbacks, some discouragement and disregard from people I expected to be pleased. And sometimes I wavered. Kind of teetered at the edge. Sometimes when I get disregarded by someone I really like and respect, and even love, it just knocks the wind out of me. Family, friends, the woman in my life, at various times."

"But this is all normal," he said. "You are undergoing what all champions have endured. From your great basketball stars to your greatest musicians and writers, painters. Chefs, too. The ones we all know about—they are there because they did not need the blessing of others. That approval—it was insignificant. The champions succeeded because they couldn't be deterred, or held down."

"I think I follow," I said.

"That's who you are, Laurent. Americans think they are the only ones who fought and left Vietnam, but the Portuguese did, and the French did. And the Chinese did—twice. Even in 1979, not that long ago. The Vietnamese couldn't be deterred. And that is why you will succeed, and your name will be known one hundred years from now. I sensed this when you were a boy."

"Ah, thank you, truly," I said. "I'm overcome."

"Don't be."

"Ong Ngoai, there's my next struggle. No one mentions my father anymore, in the family. Unless I ask. No one reveres him. Except you and me. It really weighs me down. My mother won't even put up one of his photos." I shook my head. "Glad it's been so many years since she and I lived together. Hey, now I appreciate why you live out here in your own separate quarters."

He looked at me with a mischievous smile. "Come out with me to the back patio."

"Even further from the main house? I see your logic," I said with a laugh.

Ong Ngoai smiled and led me across the main room and out of the sliding glass door. He motioned toward one of the two chairs as he stood in the doorway. "I'll be right back. Kiseru?"

"Of course," I said, knowing the old ritual.

I scanned the vacant lot before me, and chuckled as I always did at the sight. Despite that he had no ownership of that lot, Ong Ngoai had taken it upon himself to plant a yew tree and several rosebushes there to enhance his viewing pleasure. He later added to the garden with a few tobacco plants. He wished he could add certain tropical fruit trees, mangroves, and palms that he knew from South Vietnam, to remind him of his *que huong*, or homeland, but it was a lush garden, nonetheless.

He had so much time on his hands here anyway. He was retired, and it wasn't like he was driving anywhere. Like many elderly Vietnamese in the city, he had no driver's license, and relied on younger relatives for transport. Though he had a license for three decades, at one point he had let it expire, without a renewal.

Ong Ngoai returned a couple of minutes later with a tray bearing two Japanese kiseru smoking pipes, one an antique and the other a newer one, their bowls packed with the hair-like kizami tobacco, imported from Japan and difficult to find in America. He had first enjoyed kizami as a young man in the 1950s, during the Vietnamese war with the French. He lit my bowl, and then his own, and I drew into my mouth puffs of the rich, flavorful smoke.

"Look around you, Laurent. And think of your new restaurant, your achievements and your freedoms. Your friendships. That all was possible because—and we both are here because—because of your father. My friend, and he was my friend before he brought me here. That's it. If he hadn't stopped in my shop in Saigon to buy cigarettes, and other times for other things, my wife and I and my son Minh never would have made it out of Saigon. He got us into one of those last Hueys. The military helicopters, remember? April 29, 1975. Six thousand American troops evacuated that month, and took so many of us with them. We were part of the 120,000 refugees who escaped that week. Well, part of the 118,000 or so. Two thousand died when the Viet Cong blew apart many of those helicopters, the planes and boats taking off with so many of us stuffed inside."

I remembered the vivid images Dad had painted for me with words alone, as I asked him from time to time about that evacuation, which occurred when I was around one year old. How he had arranged to leave to get Ong Ngoai and his wife and son from one of the long lines inside the military terminal, then helped them into the square, gaping hole of the Huey, before he, too, leapt inside. Soon they were transported on an aircraft carrier, and later sheltered at Clark Air Base in the Philippines before the long flights to Eglin Air Force Base in the Florida panhandle.

"And Laurent, we were lucky because we were not part of those later waves of refugees that escaped in the years after. The Boat People, as they were called. Up to 200,000 died en route, in the South China Sea. Storms, pirates, faulty boats, overcrowding. Pirates would steal food and water and clothes, even their women and, at times, their children. Thai, Indonesian, Filipino freighters would help the Boat People but often had to pass them by. We did not have to endure any of this, *Nha ao thuat*. Because of your father. And he fast-tracked it because he found us sponsors in New Orleans. Back then, refugees needed a sponsor to get asylum.

"Then," he continued, "having finished his tour in the Army, your father helped me settle here in Village De L'Est. He helped me set up a fishing business, which led to the best four decades of my life. I would gladly die for that man fifty, a hundred times, over and over again. Despite what is said or not said about him. Now how's that?"

I was overcome. I struggled to speak, but found that I could not.

In my imagination, my father was there in his army green fatigues and black combat boots, the strapping young sergeant striding with an upbeat gait down a bustling Saigon street, turning into the shop where Ong Ngoai and his wife sold all matter of sundries, from cigarettes and soap to hanging bundles of dried milkfish and dried yellow-striped bass. Just as Dad had relayed that first moment to me: my father strolling up to the counter and Ong Ngoai looking up from his newspaper at him for the first time, greeting him with a grin. The random meeting that changed everything for Ong Ngoai's family.

After a few moments I was poised to speak. "That was beautiful, Ong Ngoai," I said, my words trickling out soft but steady.

"No, he was beautiful. Flawed and making missteps all could see. But a noble heart. And a strong mind."

"Thank you, Ong Ngoai. Thank you for all of this." I felt my heartbeat quicken. I was so close. Just that one remaining matter.

"Ong Ngoai, a question. It may make you uncomfortable. Bringing back painful memories. Don't you believe Dad took his own life? If so, why?"

"I see. Now, Laurent, there is something else."

"Yes?" I said, searching his face. He did seem uneasy. I could not wait another moment. "Tell me, Ong Ngoai. Tell me everything."

"It is a secret I've held inside for decades. And now I am in my early eighties. And you are well into manhood. I cannot die with this secret. You deserve to know."

Finally.

"He killed himself, didn't he?" I said.

"Claude did not die in a work accident on the *Cầu Con Cò*. What my people here call it. The Pelican Bridge. And no, he was not murdered, thrown from the bridge. Claude took his own life."

I drew in a quick breath. I did not know: Was I relieved, or disappointed?

"I've always suspected that," I said. "But Mom won't discuss it. And Mémère has no real answers. And my grandmother only started talking when I pried and pried. She said it was an accident. But—how do you know for certain?"

Ong Ngoai rose and led me back inside to one of his bookshelves. He squinted at the volumes, then pulled out two very thick hardbacks and set them on the ground. His arm disappeared into the new cavity, into the back of the bookshelf, and produced a leatherbound folder. We returned to our rear patio chairs and he opened it, then, with solemnity and both palms facing upward, handed me the folder. A one-page letter lay in its center, backed by a manila envelope. I recognized the letter's handwriting in an instant, that flawless, elegant cursive from another era, with the unusual letters *t* and *f*.

"A suicide note?" I said. "How did you get this?"

"It arrived in my mailbox one day after his death. In that legal manila envelope right behind that letter there. He must have mailed it to me the morning of his death. No one knows of this document, except me. And now you. Other than me, you are the only person who will know with certainty Claude took his life. Everyone else suspects various things. I never said anything because his family already viewed the man as a failure. I felt only I was left to defend him."

"Mind if I read this now?" I said.

"No, please do."

"Thành—

This is it. I cannot hold on any longer. My spirit has been crushed more by the years since I returned from 'Nam. The last several years of my life have been nothing but continuous humiliations and failings, struggles without end. I have tried. I fought hard. No more. I realized I am also worth more to my wife and son, mother and sister, dead than alive. Now, isn't that something? I really appreciate your friendship, all these years, and I really hope to see you in some next life. A better life. Please share this note with my boy one day when he is both a man and can handle it. Thanks for everything.

—Claude Ladnier
October 12, 1987"

"So that's what he did, after all," I said. It seemed like a dam was about to rupture within me, that I was on the verge of crumpling to the floor in a torrent of tears. But I stared at Ong Ngoai's face and the fortitude I saw there helped me keep my composure.

"I'll keep this secret. But my assumptions are confirmed," I said. "Dad planned it. His crew was doing repairs on one of the upper beams of that new span of the Crescent City Connection. He ensured he wasn't in his harness and 'fell' off the truss. Plummeted about three hundred sixty-five feet because he fell from one of the higher beams. From that high up, hitting the Mississippi must have been not like hitting water, but more like rock."

"Yes," Ong Ngoai said, looking down with a grim expression.

"I've had many dreams about this," I said.

"I have too, *Nha ao thuat*."

"Really?"

"Oh yes."

"Ong Ngoai, I've always wondered what he thought during that fall toward the river. Was he fearful? At peace? Was he imagining my mother, grandmother, you, me?"

"That we will never know," Ong Ngoai said. "So, I suspected there might have been a life insurance payout. But I didn't ask. I didn't want to know. I did ask your mother several times if I could help in any way. Money, cooked meals, anything. She always said your family was doing fine."

"There was a life insurance payout," I said. "In fact, my mom talked about that recently. That's how we stayed afloat for several years. And how I attended culinary school after NOCCA. And it helped me apprentice in Europe."

The thought was chilling: Would I fail in achieving my culinary vision, as my father had failed in his? If I did not reform my ways, and live healthier, would I meet the same end as my father, dead before my time?

I must succeed in realizing my vision. After all the sacrifices of my father, for that reason alone, I must succeed.

"Lauuuureeent?" a voice called from the main house. Aunt Tu. Dinner was surely ready.

"Coming, Ong Ngoai?" I said.

"You go. I'll come by in a few hours, scavenge something. They know I don't join most of their meals."

"Are you okay here, Ong Ngoai? Are they treating you well?" I studied his face for clues.

"They are, yes."

He did look and sound convincing. I stood, leaned over, and embraced him as he sat in his chair. His shirt smelled strongly of that kizami. "Thank you for all of this, Ong Ngoai.

For the truth, and your kind words. I needed it. I'll see you again."

I headed for the main house, replaying all of Ong Ngoai's words in my mind as I stared down at the paved path.

Alone. I must be alone. To release my emotions in my car, and, once within the confines of my apartment, numb them with drink. But for the moment I had to push those thoughts of my father's confirmed suicide out of my head. I must show respect and thanks to Uncle Minh and Aunt Tu for the dinner they had prepared, and offered. And then I would politely decline.

Once inside, I checked to ensure the leatherbound folder was still fastened shut and wedged under my arm.

I let my eyes crawl over the dining room walls as Aunt Tu and Mai placed the large, steaming bowls of pho on the table settings. This could be a dining room in some house in Vietnam—with its decorations of Vietnamese calligraphy, its large color photos of a Mekong Delta rice farming scene, a Buddhist temple, and some stone ruins of a Buddha statue I had never seen. Some decorations from the Tết celebration remained, though the season had ended weeks before.

"Laurent, I hope you enjoy it," Aunt Tu said, her cautious expression softening into a smile. That lovely face was as delicate and tiny as her build as she stood in a pink silk dress. I remembered she stood at four feet, eleven inches. "Minh's barbecued pork spareribs. And my brisket and eye round pho, with Minh's banh mi."

I imagined the ginger and star anise on my tongue.

"And mountains of rice, of course," Aunt Tu said.

"And *ca phe sua da* to finish it off," Uncle Minh said.

One of my favorites: strong Vietnamese iced coffee with condensed milk.

"And we have that steamed banana, mango, and sweet rice dessert you love," Uncle Minh said.

I drew in a deep breath as Aunt Tu filled the glasses

with cold soda chanh, that refreshing but not widely known Vietnamese mixture of lime juice, soda water, and sugar that I'd intended to offer on Crescent's menu.

Their daughter Mai was smiling at me, her twenty-year-old face illuminated with excitement and the innocence within her soul. I smiled back at her smoky eye makeup, her long straight bangs over one eye and her black choker and faded black My Chemical Romance T-shirt. Mai was so determined to remain caring, and just as determined to stay emo, though it was already several years past its heyday. I liked that she was obstinate in inhabiting her own world, holding fast to her unique tastes. In that sense, she reminded me of Jim.

It was so difficult—I so wished I could stay.

"Now I hate to say this," I said, "but I can't join you for what I know would be a delicious meal. Feeling very drained. I'm actually starting to feel sick."

Then my headache began to throb, full force.

Guilt surfaced within me. Uncle Minh had indeed appeared at Crescent's grand opening. He had also hosted me and cooked for me throughout my youth, and even when I was a teen and in my early twenties had given me *li xi*, or lucky money, in one of the red envelopes every late winter for Tết, in this same room. And he did not have to.

"I understand, Laurent," Uncle Minh said. "You seem stressed after talking with my father. And you do look like you're feeling sick. Everything good?"

"Just talking about my father," I said.

Uncle Minh looked down at his feet, a grimness, and discomfort, overtaking his face.

"I appreciate your support at my grand opening," I said. "I love you all. We will see each other soon. I promise."

Mai was watching me again. In those eyes I discerned a flash of approval, even admiration.

"Thank you, Laurent," Aunt Tu said. "Yes, soon."

My fatigue and anguish began to grow and most of what

I heard were isolated words, fragments of sentences. I longed for the privacy of my apartment.

"I am so sorry," I said. "But I'm just so tired. Can't fall asleep on the road," I said. "I love y'all, you know."

I embraced them where they sat, one after the other, then turned and walked down the corridor lined with framed photos. For a moment, I caught Claude Ladnier's face among them, standing beside a middle-aged Ong Ngoai.

I threw on my shoes, squeezed the leather folder under my arm, and unlocked the door, stepping out into the cold night. When I shut myself inside my car and placed the folder on the passenger seat, I burst into a paroxysm of tears.

"Dad—Dad—Daaad?!" I cried. Could he hear me?

I was rolling west on I-10 back toward the Lofts when the call came in.

"You sittin' down for this one, Laurent?" Wilson said in a halting, breathy cadence.

"Oh Lord, again?" I half said, half shouted into the phone.

"Ease up, Laurent. You're driving. Call when you park. Got some rather unsavory news."

"I can take it, Wilson. Just tell me."

"Laurent, one of our ovens is out. We knew she was old, but you thought she had a little more life left in her. And the other one is alive, but much worse off than days ago. We're hosed if we can't get a replacement—as in tomorrow."

"Which oven? The salamander oven or—"

"No, man. The combi oven. Tried to use it for my lunch. Discovered the thing's kaput. The other combi is failing fast."

I felt my world crashing again. The floor model combination ovens, complete with their own broilers, spacious and expensive high-volume models from those bygone days over a decade ago, when The Cayenne Club enjoyed far more covers. I had known they were old, but took for granted how they still functioned well after so many years and figured they would last at least one more.

"Wilson—you're sure it's gone for good?"

"Laurent, I just got the technician to check 'em out. One's spent and the other's failing. Will go out any day."

"Ah, kill me now," I said. "Well, we don't need a floor model one. Or one with a broiler. We can get an electric one, but it needs good capacity. At least we won't have that big gas bill. Can we score an electrical one from some restaurant that's being liquidated?"

"None are available. Nothing used. I checked. And waiting will take too long."

"How's your credit, Wilson?"

"It's shot, too. Kaput."

"That's two of us. How much is an electrical combi retailing for?"

"Just under ten grand, for the capacity we need. But I'm tapped out."

Ten? We were finished. Done. I wanted to scream, there as I drove, until my voice gave out. But I couldn't speak. Even a word.

"Laurent? Say something."

"That's a lot of money, Wilson. But let me go. Let me think."

I felt my brow break into a sweat. Setbacks and more setbacks. What was God saying? What was my father trying to say? Morrie's offer was still open.

"And something else, Laurent. Please, man. Please don't leave me. I'm taking the lion's share of the risk here. Not because of your concept, which is great. It's that a great chef can be hired away from the owner at any minute. This would put me in a real pickle. Please, stick with me, Laurent."

"Stop worrying, Wilson," I said as my own anxiety spiked, along with my guilt. Wilson must have had some great intuition. "Just let me think. That ten grand's somewhere."

"All right, Laurent. But we better think fast." And the line went dead.

CHAPTER 25

L ater that evening, Noelle and I lay atop my bedsheets, the sweat on our nude bodies drying.

"There are so many things in your apartment I've never asked you about," she said.

"Huh?" I said.

"We've already talked about your framed heroes there," she said, pointing toward my framed portraits and photos of Carême, Georges Auguste Escoffier, Julia Child, André Soltner, Paul Bocuse, Alain Ducasse, Eric Ripert, Daniel Boulud, and Anthony Bourdain.

"But tell me about that," she said, pointing at one of my most prized possessions, framed and preserved behind glass. "What's that spoon, Laurent?"

"That's a wooden ladle from France. Seventeenth century. That's when cooking really became an art form, in the West. With that whole culture of the kitchen—the *restaurant, chef, sous chef, chef de cuisine, garde manger*, the *tournant* cook, the *saucier*, who does the *sauté* work, the *pâtissier*, the *stagiaire*, the *entrée* and *dessert*, your workstation is your *mise-en-place*, or *mise*. There's a reason those are all French terms."

"That's cool, Laurent. And where did you acquire that?"

"Remember when I was backpacking in Europe? So many years back. Just out of culinary school, cooking in various kitchens. Mainly southern France, Italy. Bought that in a flea market in Nîmes, and they didn't know what they had there. I didn't at the time either. Now it's one of my most prized possessions. Next to my grandparents' cooking handkerchiefs.

Got this piece even appraised by an expert. Well, two."

I rose from the bed and crossed the room, pointing toward an item on the wall I'd forgotten.

"Same with that serving fork over here, from a Florentine flea market. It's three centuries older than the man managing the market thought it was. An antiques dealer in Milan and one in Paris dated it to the sixteenth century. It will never leave my wall. Wherever I live. You know, Italian cuisine's often deemed the mother cuisine of Europe. Some disagree."

I was standing below the framed fork, gesturing to it and shooting looks back at Noelle to track if she was following. She seemed amused. Perhaps I seemed like an excited child, showing his winning class project to his mother after school.

But she also seemed preoccupied, and she turned and gazed at the red roses I'd brought and placed in the vase on my nightstand. I waved at her as I lingered in her peripheral vision, trying my best to lure back her attention. Her pupils were dilated within the blue-gray of her corneas.

"Noelle, you there? You're staring at your roses."

"Why don't you lay back down, baby?" she said. "I wanna talk."

I lowered myself onto the side of the bed, sitting against her thigh.

"Oh—okay?" I said as I felt my heart drop. Something was coming.

It seemed like she was struggling to speak. Looking back, I suppose she was forcing it out of her heart, and through her throat, before she could reconsider.

"Laurent, I love you. But I've got bad news, news it hurts to share. Listen, I'm heading to L.A. Tomorrow."

Her words had caught me naked. "What? As in, recording an album, or—or moving?"

She paused. "Yes, baby. It'll just be so much easier for me

to be around the movers and shakers who can sign me. And promote me. As fantastic as New Orleans can be, come on, we both know it's got limitations. Remember what we talked about at The Maple Leaf? Of course, you're welcome to follow me out there. We'd be a great team. You could cook out there. But—I know you have your own project here with Wilson, and Pham, and Crescent. And you dream of New York. And working with that Morrie guy."

I nodded, but "Ah damn," was all I could keep saying. Over and over. Staring ahead with my knees now drawn up against my chest, like a child stunned by some horrible domestic scene he'd just witnessed.

It felt as if I were under attack, even ambushed, and by the one I had held closest to me. And so, she had finally done it. The big move to La La Land. An intimation, a threat, a mere dream no longer.

I recalled those two mysterious last words from her text announcing the pregnancy tests showed negative. *We're free.* Now I could see their true meaning.

We both knew it was a gut punch. But was I being understanding? What did I expect Noelle to do, just disappear without saying goodbye?

"I'm welcome to follow you out there? You don't really want me to, Noelle. Do you?"

I squinted, watching her eyes. She paused. She really was avoiding any answer.

"Well, Laurent..."

I felt crushed, vanquished through and through, more than I ever had. I was being dumped, utterly cut loose. Her silence had answered my question.

"Noelle, does any of this have to do with our age difference? Thirteen years?"

"Absolutely not, Laurent."

"Noelle, so was this to get our one last time in the sack? And to be able to remember my room and my stuff one last time, or something?"

Another pause, even longer. I sat in disbelief. It had all transpired in mere seconds.

"Laurent, you should take Morrie up on his offer while you can. Passing up on that for New Orleans and Wilson Turner is a *big* risk. Listen, I'm gonna miss you, Laurent. I'm gonna miss so much about you."

I looked down, then found I could not raise my eyes from the bed. Something had ruptured, had broken forever, somewhere within me, like some brutal stroke within my soul.

"We—we—would have made a great team," I said at last. In my own ears, I sounded so vulnerable, so fragile, and I hated that.

It was as much pain as I could bear. Soon she would be on the West Coast. And we would have to forget each other—if we could.

"I've got to leave, Laurent. New Orleans fulltime no longer fits into my life, my plans. I've gotta be free. Anyway, my flight's tomorrow. I'm spending the night at my mom's in Gentilly."

I released a moan and rubbed my palms down my cheeks. "Uhhhhhnnn. I've got to be free, she says."

"I'm sorry, Laurent," she said as she threw on her clothes.

"Noelle, I thought you wanted to be together. We can do it all together. Based here. And we can travel. As your career grows, you can tour."

She said nothing.

"Noelle, soon I'll hit it big. I'll own three restaurants. At least two. Most likely in different cities."

"You sure 'bout that?"

Her words seared into my ears like a red-hot poker. I turned, astounded, and judging by her face she half-regretted her words. But those words came from somewhere.

"Hey, thanks for the vote of confidence, Noelle."

I sat in silence for a moment. She did not respond.

"Listen, Noelle, there are many people who have much more faith in me. Not the first time you've said something like this."

She leaned over and kissed my mouth. But my lips did not move or respond in the slightest. It was as if she had already died, as if it was instead her ghost kissing me, and I could neither see nor feel her. She pulled her face back, looking into my eyes for a clue. I no longer wanted her. No longer could I endure her feeble support, her doubt, her disregard.

"I heard what you said, Noelle," I said. "Look, it's best that you leave this room."

She erupted from the bed and went for the door, opening it and closing it gently behind her.

My spirit within contorted with agony. But I could deaden it all with that unopened bottle of Lagavulin 18-Year-Old in my cabinet. I stood, locked the door, and approached the cupboard.

CHAPTER 26

T he next night I lay alone and still hungover in my bed, in the dark stillness of my studio apartment, but still felt the vise around me tightening further. Jim had replied he lacked the money, but there was something he could sell, though it would take him weeks. Even Ben replied he would be too tapped out from renting in L.A., where he was already scouting apartments online, and had even submitted one application with a deposit. I knew there was but one round left in my chamber. It would be painful, frightening, but inescapable. I had progressed too far in my dreams to not try, out of pride. I grabbed my phone and checked my savings account. Though it was really the cash portion of my retirement account. I would at last break one of my rules and access it.

And so, Wilson and I had survived. Or rather, we were reborn. I had lost Noelle, my pride, and perhaps a few years off my lifespan from stress, but that night had transformed my agony to catharsis. Despite the cool air, I found myself sweating into my bedsheets. My eyes welled up from both gratitude and relief of it all having ended. The uncertainty of her leaving me was over. And in my moment of need I found the funds for the oven replacement. And JaJuan had recovered from the flu. I envisioned Crescent's next service, with some tweaks to my menu. My excitement grew such that I could not shut my mind down to sleep. Minutes passed, then hours.

Three o'clock in the morning came and still I had been unable to find sleep. At least I had avoided that odd dream of the live oak branches moving above. It was even harder to sleep knowing Noelle had departed the Armstrong Lofts, and my life, forever. That was the most painful wound.

I did understand why she would at last move to Los Angeles for the career opportunities. I even understood why she didn't disclose her decision, and mention her flight, until the night before. I would have tried to stop her. That would have made it harder on everyone: me trying to thwart the inevitable.

What further augmented my agony: Noelle revealed in that last exchange that she doubted me until the end. Even if I went in with Morrie, she believed my rise would be minimal, at best. That moment in that last conversation played many times in my memory.

"Noelle, soon I'll hit it big. I'll own three restaurants. At least two. Most likely in different cities."

"You sure 'bout that?"

I forced my mind yet again away from Noelle. As I lay there, cooking concepts kept coming seemingly out of the divine ether into my imagination. I needed to get them down on paper. But was not my trusty pocket Moleskine journal still in my cubbyhole at work, with its candid journal entries about Noelle, Morrie, and my line? Sweat broke out on the nape of my neck. But then I realized I'd brought the journal home. It was stowed in the back pocket of my pants, discarded in the corner.

I rose and went for the pile of dirty clothes in the corner, pulled the journal from my pants pocket, then opened my window and stood there in the darkness, breathing the cool late February air through my nostrils. It was my favorite time of day, those few hours when the city snored in slumber, except for the ever-buzzing French Quarter with its tourists, conventioneers, and honeymooners.

Nothing stirred—it was just me alone with my thoughts. I sat again on my bed, switched on my bedside lamp, and scribbled away into my journal.

My phone buzzed on my nightstand. Wilson. And this time, when I answered, he was screaming.

"It's on fire, Laurent! Someone must have done this."

"Crescent?" I gasped, sitting up in my bed.

"Arson, Laurent! It's gotta be!"

I felt so lightheaded I nearly fainted, and grasped the edge of my mattress to steady myself.

When my old car roared onto St. Joseph Street, I spotted the flash of flames and caught the scent of smoke. I told myself it was just a minor kitchen fire. No, it could not be—but it was. Crescent was aflame. Surely not from a kitchen fire, and nothing electrical. Looking back, it was almost as if I felt that if I reached it several minutes earlier, I could have stopped the culprit and reversed the flames. And saved my dream from its destruction. But it was to no avail.

When I drew within a hundred feet of it, slammed on my brakes, and erupted from my car, I had already relinquished hope. As I ran toward Wilson, standing like a ghost in the middle of the street, his pale and weeping face illuminated by the conflagration, I could see my dream dying through the broken glass of the front door. The dining room was an inferno, its walls and ceiling covered in yellow and orange licks of flame. Smoke billowed through the Venetian blinds, darkening the white-painted brick façade. I imagined the innermost core of hell—my hell had arrived, after all.

I did not join Wilson in weeping, but instead screamed with the most all-consuming rage and despair, my arms thrown over my head in abandon.

The culprit must have just fled. I imagined Breton's BMW rolling, then speeding down the street, its sleek black color barely revealed by the gibbous moon's light.

Truly, I thought, the mystery arsonist was much like what Ong Ngoai would call a *phong*. A bad wind or ill wind. A supernatural spirit that can infect and sicken. And it had attacked me and destroyed my dream.

Fire truck sirens blared in the distance, along with what sounded like police sirens. But I could not remain a moment longer. It was already torture.

"Wilson, I can't—I can't stay. I've got to go," I said, shaking my head as I neared him. "It's gone, anyway. I can't see it burn any longer."

"It's—it's okay, Laurent," Wilson said, exhaustion throttling his voice. "I'm waiting here. The fire department's coming. I'm prayin' they're quick."

I ran back to my car, then drove off in a slow roll at first. After turning the corner, I gunned the car down an empty side street. With one hand gripping the wheel, I fished my phone from my pocket and turned it off. How I longed to drive off some pier, into the Gulf. Noelle was gone forever. Crescent was gone. My decades-long dream of bringing fusion mainstream in my hometown was gone. My beloved kitchen line was gone. My battered confidence seemed to be gone. I would lack the drive to rebuild Crescent, and I did not have the heart to abandon Wilson for Morrie. Truly, I had almost reached my bottom. There was but one place I felt I should go at that moment. It was calling me, drawing my core toward it like an incalculably powerful magnetic force.

Almost no one was on the road at that hour, on the streets or the Crescent City Connection, the old GNO Bridge. In less than fifteen minutes I reached the West Bank, in Gretna, and I turned back toward New Orleans. I pulled over and parked on the shoulder of the bridge's eastbound span, at the point before the shoulder disappeared and only four one-way lanes crossed the river. I locked the car behind me and departed on foot, holding close to the side barrier, marching at a brisk pace for another ten minutes until I was there. That very spot on that eastbound span where my father had fallen to his death from one of the steel beams two hundred feet above me. Leaning over the side, I could discern the dancing wavelets, which I knew to be one hundred and seventy feet below.

I had never pulled together the courage to come on foot to the place where it happened. But there I was. I would end my suffering just as he had. In my last moments, I would be sober and lucid, as he was. Leaping from the edge would be my way to draw close to him again. And if God would be merciful, my father would welcome me into the next life.

A car slowed as it neared, then slowed further. Its front passenger-side window descended.

"What are you doing? You okay, sir?" a man said.

It was just like New Orleans, after all, where strangers always spoke to each other.

"I'm fine, sir," I said. "Just going for a walk while it's quiet."

"But you're gonna get hit," he said.

"That would be ideal."

"What?"

"Sir," I said, "please let me take my walk in peace."

Off he drove into the night.

Once the car disappeared altogether, I stepped up onto the concrete barrier, holding fast to the vertical steel beam with my right arm. The Central Business District, then the French Quarter and Marigny farther beyond, were there in the distance. I could see why my father chose this spot—he no doubt loved that in his final minutes, he could see the city one last time.

If I just let go of the beam and stepped forward, I would plunge like a rock.

Yet I could not do it. I could not carry it through. Within me there still lived one lone glowing ember of desire. That fighting spirit, to make my beautiful dream reality once again. But this time—to see its full flowering. I must rebuild Crescent, and decline Morrie's offer.

I drew in a deep breath and jumped. Not forward, but backward, the soles of my shoes slapping in unison onto the pavement of the bridge. I looked around into the darkness as the cold wind whipped about my head, tousling my hair and whizzing and whistling in my ears. I shook my head and trudged back across the bridge to my car. No, I could never tell anyone of that moment.

As I drove to the Lofts, I hungered for sleep, to escape for scant few hours what I knew to be my harsh new reality. The aftermath of that fiery debacle would prove a long parade of inequities and humiliations. Breton, Gerard, Minnesota, Etienne would rejoice. I would lack the funds to pay my bills and rent. I would even be evicted. Unless I compromised my standards and took the first cooking job I could land.

Fatigue gripped me further, and when my head at last sank into my pillow, my thoughts returned to Crescent. Perhaps I should let go, I thought. Release my old vision into the ether and consign myself to cheffing in another traditional restaurant. Or even cashing in: I could helm the kitchen of one of the nicer hotels downtown. I had always avoided hotel kitchens, but I knew the money would be better than I'd ever seen, and I could help Mémère, Mom, and Aunt LaFaye immensely. But a hotel kitchen, with the high pay numbing my ambitions to sleep? Bourdain had written that was his greatest career mistake.

The darkest thought followed: Why was I obligated to keep helping them? I'd helped them with money for decades. How long would this continue? The youngest generation needed to try to make its way unimpeded. At least eventually.

After a night of earth-trembling shocks, even my own thoughts stunned me. What transpired that night on the bridge—that was not the real me, just a fleeting inner tantrum. But was I not poised to jump hundreds of feet to my death? I forced myself to draw in long, profound breaths, hold them for several seconds, and exhale. My eyelids grew heavier and soon I was able to release, at last finding the blessing of sleep.

In my first dream, that same image revisited me: I was looking upward into the cloudless blue, gliding under the overarching live oak branches dripping with Mardi Gras beads of every color.

But then came my next dream. I stood in the street, again watching the restaurant burn. Outrage swelled within me as I buried my face in my hands. In an instant I found myself alone, standing at the edge of the Crescent City Connection's eastbound span. The dark tongues and plumes of smoke billowed into the orange sky, under the full moon. I knew the smoke was from Crescent. Grabbing the short barrier, I prepared to lift myself onto it, and then to jump. Yet I sensed a presence at my back and turned.

My father stood, observing the column of smoke. He was around my age, the age when he had passed. His age on that last morning that I'd seen him. He was dressed in his construction uniform, holding his hardhat at his side.

Dad turned and looked into my eyes. Somehow I could see the thin veins in the whites of his eyes. His face was serene, confident as his shoulders stretched wide.

"You're considering ending it all, son," he said, "but trust me, it would be the greatest mistake."

"I know you took your life, Dad."

"Well done, finding Rodney. And asking your Ong Ngoai for the truth," he said in the calmest tone, not diverting his eyes from mine. "And protecting our family."

"Why did you do it, Dad? The depression? All the humiliations, the failed restaurant dreams? For our insurance payout? Do you regret it?"

He did not move in the slightest, not his face nor his limbs. Just that same enigmatic stare. Then the nostrils began to flare, and his eyes started to moisten, with rapid blinks.

"I loved you so much, son. And your mama. I loved my sister and mother so very much."

He seemed like he wanted to say more, and even embrace me. But I woke there in my bed, my heart in a stampede. The damp sheets clung to my shoulders and chest. Was it not late morning, or midday? Light had found its way around the edges of the Venetian blinds in my two windows.

I lay there for what must have been a half-hour, until five knocks shook me from my inertia. I knew that rhythm. It was our mutual signal.

Throwing the sheets from my body, I hobbled toward the door. A blister had broken out on my left heel. All that random walking in the wee hours on cantilever bridges.

As I crossed the hardwood floor, I spotted my image in my mirror, propped against the brick wall. My shoulders slumped, almost as if they were two once-strong beams at the point of collapse. It was a look of crushing defeat. This was not like waking on other mornings: I could feel my pride and hope almost completely decimated.

I unlocked my door and pulled it open. In the hall, Jim stood, with Pham beside him. Their dour faces brightened with hope and relief, then turned solemn.

"L, I know about the restaurant," Jim said. "Pham here called me. I'm—I'm sorry."

Pham said, "I couldn't reach you, Laurent. Your phone's turned off. You never do that."

"I needed to shut it all out for a while," I said. "Guard my sanity. Pham, I knew Wilson would update you all, for now."

"Wilson did. He texted the whole line way before dawn about the fire," Pham said.

"Yeah, the fire," I said. "Lovely surprise, huh? God knows there's some story behind that."

Pham said, "The police are investigating. Wilson already filed the insurance claim. Insurance conducts their own investigation."

"I just want to ask one question and then let's just drop the subject for a while," I said. "The fire take everything? Was anything salvaged?"

Pham's eyes succumbed to their characteristic gesture, as they fell floorward, toward his feet. He held his stare there, as if studying their shape.

"Our kitchen's a total loss. Wilson's apartment on the third floor isn't bad but the vacant second floor saw a lot of damage. Fire and water both. Good thing is, Wilson's office might've been smoked out, but no water or fire got inside. So, we didn't lose any of the line's W-2s, I-9s, the pay and tax information, all that. And Wilson kept hard copies of everything in his file cabinet. Him being old-fashioned was a blessing."

I sighed in relief.

"And the dining room didn't get completely torched," Pham said. "It'll have to be gutted, renovated. But that's it."

"I should be thankful, after all," I said, turning toward my coffee machine. "Wanna come in, gents? I'll brew coffee."

"Nah," Jim said, watching me with an expression of solemn sympathy. "I'm taking y'all somewhere. My treat. Will take your minds off all this."

Pham turned to Jim.

"Summon your appetite," Jim said. "Time for lunch at August. John Besh's place. Pham, I don't think you've ever been."

"Now that is an idea," I said. "I haven't been there in years."

"It's a crime we never went there together," Jim said. "But we need to hurry, beat some of the lunch service rush. Ha, a term I learned from my man L."

"But that's a great idea for another day, Jim," I said. "Why don't y'all just come in?"

They entered, Jim closing the door behind them, and they seated themselves on my couch while I began to prepare coffee.

"So, Laurent, seriously," Jim said. "Sounds like arson. They just haven't caught the culprit."

I said, "Could be that bastard Luc Bret—"

"I'm thinking no," Jim said. "Don't know who the hell it is, but I doubt it's Breton."

I said, "Jim, he could've paid someone to do this. Distract and demoralize me."

"That he did, whoever he is," Pham said. "But he won't succeed. We can rebuild."

Despite what I had decided on the bridge, I could feel myself wavering.

"I'm rebuilding, all right. Might be in the Warehouse District. But maybe on an island called Manhattan. Or in Brooklyn, or Astoria. Not sure there will be any more Dirty Coast for me."

"No, Laurent, don't," Jim said. "You and Pham had this city within your grasp."

"We did, didn't we?" I said with a wistful laugh. Jim was not speaking in jest. "I tell you WWL had scheduled to interview Wilson and Pham and me in a few days? It was all going my way. Then JaJuan was out with the flu. Then I went broke, putting a new transmission in Mémère's jalopy. Then I lost my biggest oven in my kitchen, had to raid my retirement fund. Then I lost Noelle. Then I lost Crescent. Now I'll lose my whole line. Well, I'll always have Pham."

"You'll always have Pham, and me," Jim said. "You could teach my sorry ass to cook! Ha, joking."

Pham said, "You know Brooke and Roosevelt will rejoin us. And probably JaJuan."

"Brooke, Roosevelt, JaJuan?" I said. "They'll be locked in by some other kitchen within days. And Wilson? He'll grab that insurance check, get the repairs done, then bow out. Retire somewhere east of here, on the Gulf Coast. Probably doesn't have the juice to fight his way out of this."

"Maybe not. Even so, Laurent," Jim said, "other restaurateurs will be jonesing to hire you."

"Like good Mr. Morrie Hesser?" I said.

"Yes," Jim said. "Players in New Orleans, too. If you choose to dig in and stay, that is."

I remained silent, and after several moments, nodded.

"You're right, Jim. I have options. I can take heart in that. Well, whatever happens," I said, slapping a hand onto his shoulder, "you are family."

"I agree, Laurent," Jim said. "And thanks."

"Here's a thought," I said, scouring the ceiling as if for the truth. "Our mystery arsonist might be Etienne, not Breton. The other one with the burn tattoo."

"Your sauté cook who just quit because you wouldn't give him Pham's spot?" Jim said. "Possible, but unlikely. This saboteur could've been after you before you ever interviewed Etienne. Could go by the nickname Minnesota. Forget about him?"

"I guess that *is* a possibility," I said.

My phone buzzed in my pocket. Morrie. I had to answer the call.

"Hello, Morrie, how are you?"

"Ben told me about Crescent. I'm sorry. Are you rebuilding? Or coming my way?"

I remembered Jim's words to me, mere minutes before.

"I just—I just need a few more days. How about a week? I'm getting closer to knowing."

"Very well, son. Call me soon." The line went dead.

CHAPTER 27

T hat next day, despair drove me to seek solace in that one thing besides food adventures and cooking that always calmed my nerves. I found myself on a barstool. My mother found me there, too.

"Son?" said my mother's voice as the line opened up. "Where are you? What are you doing?"

"I'm seated in a place," I said, turning up the volume on my phone, leaving out that I was in Pal's Lounge, one of my old Mid-City haunts, which I'd dubbed a maximum-security dive, as the bartender had to buzz the door for you to enter or depart. "Just relaxing, Mom. Clearing my head."

"Another bar? Can you go where it's quiet?" she said, her voice revealing an odd frailty I had not heard in her. "I've got something important to discuss."

I waved at the bartender, Cole, to buzz the door so I could step outside to talk. Upon reaching the entrance, the door buzzed and clicked, and I opened it into the cool night.

"Mom?" I said into the phone as I stood on the sidewalk, beside the royal blue façade of the neighborhood dive fronted by a triad of palm trees. "What is it?"

"I'm worried about you. After you lost Noelle, and the restaurant. I called to apologize, son. About the things I've said about your father. And avoiding—avoiding any talk about him. And I am sorry for doubting your dreams."

"Thank you, Mom. Maybe I should come by, and we can talk."

"Not today, Laurent. I can tell you've been drinking. Just come see me soon."

"I love you, Mom. I'll see you tomorrow morning."

"Love you, too, Laurent. Hey, take it easy on that drink. Don't fall into the bottle again. Just go to your apartment and get some sleep, okay?"

"I'll be there tomorrow morning, Mom. I love you."

When I hung up, I saw my father's face, and I knew that my return to the Armstrong Lofts would be greatly delayed, that the highest stratum of my thinking was no longer in control, and that there was still much steam to blow off, still much pain and worry that needed deadening.

Back inside, I waved at the bartender, who turned toward me at the end of the bar.

"Hey, Cole," I formed the words with my lips in silence. My Sazerac was done.

He held up a finger for a moment, and continued listening to a patron. I could feel my craving build, and my irritation. After all the money I'd spent in that place. After all the generous tips I'd given the man.

At last Cole approached, his head drooping from one side to the other with its pomaded rockabilly hairstyle and his feet brushing forward in a lazy gait. His eyes opened and closed in languid blinks. "Another Sazerac, Laurent?"

"I better downshift to beer. I'll take an Abita Amber draft. Frosty schooner glass, if I could."

"You look drained," he said, working the tap. "And kinda on edge. What's happenin', boss?"

"I lost Noelle. My girlfriend. She'd warned me she might relocate to California." I could not mention the suicide note. "Then—you heard what happened with my new restaurant."

"What? I didn't hear."

I sighed, then said, "Don't worry about it. Too painful to describe."

"Ah, I'm sorry, Laurent. This one's on the house."

"I appreciate you, Cole. But I'm not fishing for a free beer. This is how you get paid."

"Nah," Cole said, setting the frosty schooner down on the bartop. "I insist. Besides, you listen to all my lady troubles. This is different. From all you've shared with me over the last couple years, I know you loved her."

Lady troubles, Cole had said. As I sipped the beer, I began to long for comfort in a warm embrace, and much more, with one of my lady friends from the years before I met Noelle. Meredith lived just a block away, and Kaitlyn just a bit farther, but I could not call them. I had not spoken to them in years. Even more, I had evolved to share that same viewpoint Jim had described, that time at the Carousel Bar. That building desire to be a father, and husband—these women would remember I had expressed this, but moved on, and I did not want to again disappoint them. It would be better to leave those wild, steamy nights in the past. I must keep my lust and that desire for solace within. I had gotten just old enough and accrued just enough wisdom. I knew better. At least when I wasn't very drunk.

As I sat on the barstool and sipped my beer, my thoughts returned to that day at age five when my father had sat me atop his shoulders and strolled around the neighborhood park. Then there was that time several years later, as my father lay in his bed, hungover on his day off. Mom was washing the dishes in the kitchen.

"Don't listen to your mama," my father whispered to me. "You choose your own career. I know you live for cooking. You'll be a great chef one day."

I felt myself smiling there on my barstool, recalling Dad's expression. I shook my head, recalling hope lighting up his eyes, more than just a glimmer.

I stared down into the beer within my frosty schooner and sensed in my mouth its magnetic pull. My father and I, burdened with the same curse, but in different forms. I recalled that summer day at the beach in Destin, while my mother was out shopping, and a rip current caught Dad and a twelve-year-old me about sixty feet off the seashore. I sensed something drawing us apart, how I drifted away from him in an arc until my father's large hand found my forearm and yanked me toward him. Then I sensed an alien force, monstrous and even incomprehensible in its power, tugging us farther out to sea along the surface, while my father fought with desperation to free us from its grip while aiming shoreward. For one long moment it seemed he would fail, but he did not scream for help and seemed to fight the current with even greater ferocity, before he opted to swim parallel to the shore. At last, the current weakened and stopped pulling us seaward and we swam at an angle toward the bright white dunes, my father at times towing me by the arm. We reached the shore, near exhaustion, but not before a great wave crashed behind us and billowed beneath us like the rising cloud of an explosion, delivering a closing reminder of the sheer power of the sea. Truly, that is how that vice was within our blood, and somehow another rip current had claimed my father in the end, defeating him first within his mind.

The buzz of the door sounded behind me. A cluster of voices followed, one of them vaguely familiar. To my right, three men were seating themselves at a round table against the wall.

One of them I did not recognize, but two I certainly did: Wade and Breton. No surprise—it was just another of God's twisted cosmic jokes, to put this snake in my proximity. Of all the city's countless bars, and it had to be this one. Mere days after I lost Noelle, confirmed Dad's suicide, then lost Crescent. What did God want? A brawl? Some false truce or some bogus armistice of peace?

Since the fire, I had wanted to find Breton, to feel him out, to see if I could sense his culpability. But not there, not then, while I was caught in my cups.

I swung my gaze to the mirrored back panel of the bar above the rows of liquor bottles. But it was no matter.

"Hey, you there in the sharp blazer."

I turned back to them.

"Don't just glare at me," Breton said. "Come and join us for a libation."

Something told me to just leave, but I headed toward them, schooner in hand. Perhaps I would have my answer, as to the fire.

"Laurent! Pull up a chair," Wade said. I didn't want to insult the man, as he had given me that catering job in January. But Breton sat with him, and I could not lower myself into the remaining seat.

"No thanks, heading out soon," I said.

"I'm sorry, Laurent," Wade said. "I heard about the fire."

"Yeah, I guess I'm sorry, too," Breton said. "We all know I didn't want Crescent to get *too* successful. But I didn't want it to burst into flames."

I squinted, peering down into his eyes from where I stood not even four feet away. I had to admit—he did not appear to be lying.

"Guess you don't want to join us. Who wants to drink alone, in public?" Breton said.

"Well now," Wade said. "This might be how he comes up with ideas for his menus."

"There's more than a drop of truth in that," I said.

"I've seen your writer friend doing the same," Wade said. "Drinking alone in various watering holes."

"That's right, you're friends with that novelist," Breton said. "Something Scoresby. Hmm, Scoresby—why is he named after a bottom-shelf Scotch? Is that a pseudonym?"

"Here we go," I said. "Breton, you found your last name off a box of arguably bland water crackers. You know the one. Better yet, with the name Luc, you were named after some

Parisian chef you can't equal."

"Oooohh," Wade said as Breton just stared at me. "You were asking for that, Luc. Simmer down on that belligerence."

"That's the only way to deal with a bully," I said. "Bash him square in the beak."

"You're one strange bird," Breton said, rising to his feet. The third man followed suit, and Wade joined them with a pained expression.

"Annoying upstart, Laurent Ladnier," Breton said. "The fusion maestro of New Orleans, as some fools say."

I said, "You mean the guy you tried to sabotage at a dinner party of Mr. Connaughton here? And I refused to get revenge on you. Even let you eat in Crescent. Only asked you to leave when you caused another scene. Why can't you and I coexist in the food world? We both work in completely different cuisines. There's no harm there. Why be such a hater?"

"I tell Luc the same," Wade said, shaking his head. "Luc's just so stubborn, and proud. But he'll come around."

"Why not just be secure in where you stand?" I said. "You have the traditional scene cornered. And I play in a completely different species of cooking. No threat there, right?"

Breton paused. "But being a successful chef involves preparing food that is delicious. Ladnier, you miss that mark by far. You play too much with ingredients. You get carried away. You're a snob of the plate."

"At least I'm an imaginative snob," I said. "And many find my cooking delicious."

"Look, you're intelligent. I discern this," Breton said, "but your food's too intellectual, too daring, with unlikely combinations of ingredients. Their combination is even jarring. It's not harmonious. It's aesthetically pleasing cuisine, true. It's pleasing to the mind and eye, and not as much to the belly."

I said, "That's subjective, Breton. Your palate is surely more traditional. South Louisiana, European. Am I wrong? Or is it that you want all attention on yourself, like some prima donna actress?"

"I am a great chef in the cuisine I work in, yes," Breton said. "But you're still an overhyped hack, probably still broke, and your fifteen minutes of fame already came and went. I know you well, Ladnier. Or I know you enough."

"You'll know a little more about me soon, Luc," I said with a smile. "It will bother you."

"How so?" he said.

I turned and headed for the bar, where I placed my half-full schooner. I pulled the cash from my wallet and placed it in front of Cole, who was now free.

"Until next time, Cole. Thanks. I appreciate you."

"Hope things turn for the better, brother," Cole said, studying my face as if he saw something broken, or off.

Once outside, I opted to leave my car parked out of caution and set out on foot at a brisk pace down the street. I hoped to leave that uncomfortable encounter far behind me. Minutes later, I allowed my pace to slow. I knew that I'd soon be seated at another nearby bartop. And probably another one, after that, further on my route back to the Lofts, via taxi or foot. No doubt my last stop would be a few hundred feet from my apartment, at the Corporation Bar. Once my fuse was lit, it would take hours for me to finish heating up, and to at last cool down.

But this night was different. It was almost as if my whole wounded spirit was aflame. Like a chemical fire, a white-hot inferno burning wildly out of control. However it would end, I knew it would be a night like no other.

CHAPTER 28

Morning light brought me back, streaming on my face, and, as if seeking to pry into my closed eyes, jerked me from the dream of a five-year-old me on the shoulders of my father in the park.

Soreness throbbed in my back from where I'd been sleeping against the shop front.

I recalled my taxi ride over to the French Quarter, for a night like that invited a crescendo of diversion and the liquid numbing of psychic and emotional pain. Those following stops in the Dragon's Den with its barely illuminated Gothic mystique, then Sylvain, Erin Rose, and The Kerry Irish Pub. My long detour through the Quarter ended with a cab ride over to the Warehouse District for Vic's Kangaroo Café and then that final stop in the Rusty Nail. I recalled that conversation, perhaps slurred on my part, with the bartender Wesley, then my hitting on the young actress, who soon had her hand in mine as we sat out on the back patio. But then I had forgotten her name, not once but twice, and she pulled away in disgust and vanished. Back at the bar, Wesley chatted and joked with me, but then soon cut me off. I could barely recall setting off on my final walk.

The shame hit me, then humor at the utter failure of my inebriated self with the half-inebriated actress, then shame once more. This was swept away when the tidal wave of reality crashed upon me: Noelle, and Crescent, were gone.

I glanced at my wristwatch. 7:13 AM. My mother was probably already texting me. But then I recalled my phone was dead, my car parked in Mid-City, and somehow I'd left my keys on the bartop in the Rusty Nail. Yes, the reason for my wandering through the Warehouse District streets. I could not let myself into my apartment, nor could I knock on Jim's door, waking up the entire floor in my sloppy state. And so, I had crashed far away from the Lofts against the façade of a building.

My head throbbed hard. An old friend's words returned to me: Drunkenness is stealing from tomorrow to enhance today. Something like that.

My beleaguered body cried out for sleep, water, caffeine, nicotine, but notably, no longer for alcohol. It was no longer solely my spirit that felt beaten down, vanquished. It was my body as well.

I blinked my eyes open. A car door was opening nearby.

An older Black lady, well dressed and with her chin poised with a stately air, was carrying a large metal container up to the entrance beside me. Encircling her neck was a royal blue scarf, and I remembered my favorite handkerchief from my grandparents, lost for so many weeks.

I heard the grunt in my throat, and realized I would be quite a sight.

"Long night?" she said.

I noticed that, while she did not seem to struggle, she was advancing her red flats one after the other on the asphalt with caution.

"Unfortunately, yes. Want some help with that, ma'am?" I said.

"I might take you up on that, sir."

I stood and dusted my jeans and blazer off with my palms. "I've had many nights like this. But my first night ever sleeping off booze outdoors. Thank God it's not too cold. Or May already."

"Good point. I'm Dr. Joanna Chennault-Humphrey," she said, smiling, as she waited for me to walk over. "But call me Joanna. What's your name?"

"Laurent Ladnier. Nice to meet you, Joanna."

She handed me the tray. A familiar scent.

"Gumbo. For the charity inside that door," she said. She unlocked the door with her key, then led me through a corridor and into an empty kitchen.

"Did you cook this, Joanna?"

"I did," she said, motioning for me to set down the tray on the stovetop. We headed back outside.

"That's great. So did you enjoy cooking this?"

She raised her eyebrows at my question, but her answer came in a reflective tone. "I like cooking. But I love cooking when I can see it going to people who will really enjoy it. To nourish them and make them happy. Or less unhappy."

"That's a great reason," I said. "Many years ago, that used to be why I'd cook."

How simple and pure and brilliant a reason, I thought. Maybe that should be my credo, when I next found myself at the helm of a kitchen line. And to not be consumed with being the greatest. Or forging something completely novel.

I recalled my motivation in the kitchen from my adolescence and early manhood: to bring human souls together, to aid them in building or even forging relationships, through a great sensory experience. Somewhere along the journey, I'd forsaken that. But could I not regain it?

Even at that moment, I could feel something shift inside of me.

I looked again at her face. There was a quiet serenity and a strength there, and somehow I sensed hers was the tale of a life that was hard, but lived to the point of triumph.

"Think you could bring the other two trays in?" Joanna said, as we stood outside.

"Yes, ma'am," I said. As I exited the building after carrying in the last tray, the thought arrived.

"So what charity is this here, Joanna, you were mentioning?"

"Well, it's an organization. A charity, and a lifestyle. Have you heard of N.A.?"

"I can't say I have."

"Narcotics Anonymous. Think of it as the less popular sibling of Alcoholics Anonymous."

"Oh," I said. "That's great you help them with the cooking."

"I have time; I retired from medicine. But I also chair some of the Alcoholics Anonymous meetings nearby. I'm in recovery myself, in A.A. Almost four years of sobriety."

"Wonderful, Joanna. Congratulations."

The light switched on inside me. Aunt LaFaye...

"Could you help my aunt? Please, Joanna. She's wrestled with crack for years, tried rehab a handful of times. But it wasn't N.A., and it never stuck. But I can tell she'd like you. Respect you. Would probably listen to you. I think that program might turn her around."

"Absolutely, Laurent. I'll introduce her to a sponsor. If she wants it, wills it. Sticks with it."

I felt my worries about Aunt LaFaye dissipating, as if spirited away by some breeze.

Even more, I was so happy I almost wept, but I still felt unwashed in my clothes. And it was cold. I was cold. I had to get moving—somewhere.

At least I still had my wallet. I opened it; all its contents remained. I needed to find breakfast, and some accommodating waiter or barista to recharge my phone. It would be several hours before Wesley opened the Rusty Nail and I could recover my keys, then get to my car, then clean up at the Lofts. And then I would head back to Mid-City. Had I failed my mother?

I had failed her. And myself.

Truly, substances were like a cruel spirit that had destroyed my father and sought to annihilate his only sister and his only son.

"Wanna go grab a cup of coffee, and maybe a bite?" Joanna said. I grinned, thankful for her suggestion. It was as if she could read my mind.

CHAPTER 29

M y watch struck five in the afternoon the following day and they had all made it to the tables inside Rue de la Course coffee house, every last one of my shattered line, all save Etienne, who was gone forever. I felt dazed as Wilson handed them their last paychecks in sealed envelopes. Truly, the mood was dour, even funereal. The questions came fast, and with great frequency. Would we ever reopen? If so, when, and where? And with the same concept?

I endured the barrage of inquiries, seated there at the head of the table, my arms folded across my chest as I stared down into my water. Wilson was seated at the other head.

"Tell me, team," I said, "what is it that you would like to see, to do?"

I studied their faces, awaiting their responses. What if I could not fulfill the wishes they expressed? I remembered Morrie's fading offer. If I would accept it, I must tell the line here and now. Sweat broke free on the nape of my neck. Though seated, I felt dizzy.

The ever-reserved Osvaldo smiled at me, a wise, grandfatherly grin. I knew his opinion, without even having to ask.

"Rebuild and get back right where we left off," Brooke said. Once again, those eyes riveted on mine, yet softening by the second. "You're a brilliant chef, Laurent. A great one, even. All that vision, this concept, you aren't just going to let that die, right?"

Something colossal moved within me, like the sudden shift of a tectonic plate. Brooke truly was the one woman who believed in my skills, vision, and project in equal measure. As if by reflex, I wanted to gratify her wish.

"Absolutely," JaJuan said. "Same building. Same menu. Same line. But no Etienne. No no no." As we laughed, he smiled and added, "And let's pretend this fire never happened."

"I concur," Roosevelt said. "Return to where we were and what we were doing. We had momentum. Let's get it back."

"Pham?" I said, turning to my right. We smiled at each other in unison.

"You know, as if by telepathy," Brooke said, staring into me. Again, that look of attraction.

"Of course," I said, smiling inside at her expression.

"There's only one problem," Roosevelt said. "We can't hang on forever, out of work. There's a pastry chef opening at The Windsor Court Hotel. Still, Crescent is where I want to be. When do you think renovations will be done? When will we have a replacement for—the jerk?"

"The adjuster just came out not long ago," Wilson said. "But Roosevelt, this is New Orleans. No telling how long until the check arrives. And until the contractors are done. That's the challenge. The scouting, interviewing for the open rec? Laurent and I can do that in a few days."

Wilson's eyes found mine.

"All in all, my guess?" he said. "In sixty days we will be operational again."

"But sixty days of hell it will be," I said, the words seeming to erupt out of me. "For Wilson and me. The rebuild."

Wilson turned to the line, and said, "Look, friends—hold, just hold on. Can you all somehow hold on?"

Roosevelt and Brooke stared back at Wilson with a blank expression. JaJuan stared down at the table, as Pham nodded at me with a wink.

"Now, Wilson," I said, "they're going to have to find some work in the meantime."

After a pause, Wilson nodded.

"Did you ever discover the cause of the fire?" Roosevelt said. "If it's too private, please don't bother answering."

I felt my heart launch into a gallop. Had Wilson learned this from the investigators? He had said nothing.

"I learned yesterday," Wilson said. "Laurent and I thought it was arson. But the insurance investigators found otherwise. Fire started in one of those two old broiler ovens, the one that was still operational. I know we were closed, but I was still using that one to make some of my lunches."

There was a stir around the table. Expletives, gasps, muttering.

Good God. One of the two combi ovens both Wilson and Etienne urged me to get replaced? I'd disregarded their advice, arguing they had more life in them. Wilson had honored my wish, that we direct those funds toward advertising.

Shame overcame me. My arrogance had cost me my dream, and Wilson's business, and our income and that of my line. Because I always knew better.

I lifted my gaze from the table. Wilson was eyeing me with a look not of accusation, resentment, or judgment, but of deep sadness. In an instant, it made me love him more.

But I was too stunned and saddened to speak. As Wilson and our line went their separate ways, I walked to my car parked on North Carrolton. My phone buzzed in my pocket.

Let me guess. Jim? Mémère? Mom?

But it was Morrie. As if he'd been listening to my conversation with my kitchen line.

"Hello Morrie," I said, cradling the phone against my ear.

"Yes! How is my young friend Chef Ladnier? I'm so sorry—my nephew's still updating me on you from the West Coast. That fire..."

"I'm still so in shock," I said. "Wilson says the insurance check's coming soon. Then the repairs, renovations begin."

"Laurent, I know I'm applying some pressure this time. I hate doing that. I'd told you weeks ago that I'd give you as long as I could. But I'm gonna need that decision now."

"My apologies that it's taken me so long to decide, Morrie," I said. "It was so much for me to weigh. Hard to focus with this new chaos."

"Understandable for the circumstances, Laurent. Now first, hear me out. If you pass on the New York route, I'll be disappointed, but with no hard feelings. I'll respect your choice. There's another investment I'm looking into as a backup— something completely unrelated to food or cooking. But I would prefer working with you. It really is a bit of—a leap of faith, but I believe in you. I know you have the chops and the talent to hit it big here. Now it's far more cutthroat than what you've seen down there, but you can take the hits. This would fast-track you to where I think you'll end up, regardless. You know I love your town. But the international exposure we'll probably get—it would dwarf anything you'd have in the Big Easy. So—what have you decided?"

The pregnant pause. It was Morrie's final sales pitch. Damn, he was good. My heart picked up pace.

Drawing in a deep breath, I turned back toward a now-languid North Carrollton Avenue and envisioned the streets of Manhattan and Brooklyn teeming with pedestrians in the summer sun, some buzzing into and out of restaurants and cafés.

I exhaled through my nose and paused a moment more, then another, my thoughts firing in a frenzy.

Was it wind I heard? No, it was Morrie breathing into his phone. He was waiting.

I cleared my throat. I recalled my original dream as a chef, and then remembered the faces of my line and the faith they had just expressed in my skills, and concept. I saw Wilson's eyes, the fragility within them, and the words then welled up fast within me.

"I can't, Morrie. I can't, my friend. I'd love to come up,

in time. But first I have to re-start Crescent. Complete my mission."

"Understood. But keep in touch," he said, his voice deflated, yet warm. "Deal?"

"Of course, Morrie," I said. He hung up as I stood there in silence.

I detested hurting, even disappointing, this kind man who so believed in me. Sadness gave way to pain as I recalled Morrie losing his son in that mysterious tragedy.

The phone buzzed. Was it Morrie again?

I smiled at the caller ID, the muscles in my neck and jaw relaxing.

"Dr. Joanna, how are you?" The words were warm and upbeat, even jubilant, in my ears.

Joanna cleared her throat. "Doing great, Laurent. Hey, I had this idea for you."

"Uh oh," I said, then chuckled.

"It's an idea all right," Joanna said, "but it's also a challenge."

"Am I not now challenged enough?" I said, then laughed. "Give me another. In seriousness, I bet you have a great idea."

"It will help get you outside of yourself, Laurent. While you work on your next move as a chef. You'd forget the competitive food scene for a while, and focus on others. These people need help."

Joanna did have an intriguing concept.

"I'm interested. What is it?"

Joanna chuckled. "There's an N.A. meeting this coming weekend and I remembered your auntie you wanted to bring. For hopefully her first meeting of so many."

"Joanna, I'm there. I'll bring her. She's healed enough to leave the house, and she's been bugging me to take her out. A little unsteady on her feet, but I'll help."

"So glad to hear that, Laurent. And there's something else I thought of. Before I cruise over to the Lodge today. Where

N.A. and A.A. are, not that location where we first met. Be my sidekick today in my kitchen? I'm bringing gumbo and jambalaya. And you can meet Harlan, my husband. You two will get along. And your aunt can join, hang out with us a couple hours?"

I laughed—honored, tickled, and surprised. It had been many years since I was a sous chef.

"Joanna, we're there," I said, the words shooting from my mouth in a hearty declaration. "Wouldn't miss it. I'll call Aunt LaFaye now."

"Beautiful," Joanna said. "I'll text you my address."

It was but an hour and fifteen minutes later and I found myself part of a unique project, along with my showered and well-dressed Aunt LaFaye, in the kitchen of Dr. Joanna Chennault-Humphrey's Uptown home.

"Cut me some of that celery, Laurent, if you will," Joanna said, both exciting and humbling me in equal measure. My sous chef days were so far behind.

"About two cups, segments this thick." She showed me with her thumb and index finger.

"And LaFaye," Joanna said, "Can you hand me those onions on the counter? I'll get us all in tears in a second. And we haven't even made it to the Lodge yet."

Joanna laughed as she took the onions from my smiling aunt. It was easy to love her, and her husband. A slightly built retired teacher with soft, warm, and twinkling eyes, at first glance many years older than Joanna, Harlan Humphrey stood at the island, smiling as he sipped a mug of tea.

"Joanna's got you enlisted in her latest mission," he said. "She's so serious about her gumbo, and jambalaya. She gets in this certain headspace, and I can't distract her from it."

"It's where I find peace," Joanna said. "And enjoyment."

"I can definitely relate to that," I said.

"So, I was telling Harlan about the fire in your restaurant," Joanna said. "I didn't know you were the chef at Crescent until well into our conversation that day we met. Harlan and I'd planned to get over there one night for dinner."

I felt my cheeks flush. If only I had heeded Wilson's call and changed out those two old broiler ovens.

"Ah, I'm sorry about what happened, Laurent," Harlan said. "Will you rebuild?"

"I am," I said.

"So," Joanna said, "while we're on that topic of rebuilding. LaFaye, I hope you find today's N.A. meeting helpful. If you do and want to commit, I'll pick you up at your house about thirty minutes before each meeting. It'll do wonders—if you stick with it."

"For sure, count me in," Aunt LaFaye said. "I want to get it right this time. Sober, for good. I got nothing else to lose."

"I'm so happy to hear that," Joanna said.

"It really has done wonders for Joanna," Harlan said, "Well, A.A. has, these last four years."

"Ms. Adams, God sure pulled you out of it, all at the eleventh hour," Joanna said. "He does have some sort of rhyme and reason behind things. We just have to discover, and make reality of, what it is."

I smiled as I cut the celery. What a great new friend and connection I'd found.

"Guess you never expected to be a sous chef again," Joanna said, with a mischievous chuckle.

"True, but this is for all the best reasons," I said, laughing.

"It's a huge help for me," she said. "And it'll be good for you. God has an interesting way of tearing us down sometimes. So He can rebuild us. Stronger, and better."

"Like a muscle, I suppose," I said.

"Exactly," Joanna said. "Now how about we team up on that roux? But first, chop me some of the andouille links. Into medallions."

Our buzzing about the kitchen continued until hours later, Joanna pulled her SUV into the parking lot. She led Aunt LaFaye and me toward the Lodge. Joanna carried the large pot of rice, and I carried the large pot of gumbo. In my next trip, I staggered with the deep pot of jambalaya past the crowd of people smoking cigarettes and cigars outside the entrance. Once inside, my eyes wandered around the packed foyer and lobby, studying the motley assortment of humanity under the dark wooden rafters. The aroma of hot coffee and fresh donuts wafted through the air as I brought the pot into the kitchenette. There were plenty of heads with snow-white hair, more than a few with very young faces, probably just a few years after teendom, and plenty in between.

There was something *extreme* about a great many of them. Many of the young women and men were as tattooed as could be, several of them with more than a few piercings, even facial piercings. Many spoke far too loudly or far too quietly. Some seemed outright standoffish, and some acted as if they were campaigning for political office, trying to shake as many hands as possible.

Joanna placed her arm around Aunt LaFaye's shoulder, and motioned to the main meeting room. Inside the open doors, people were taking their seats. The thick, dark wooden beams of the ceiling and the cedar walls called to mind some old ski lodge. Glass wall-mounted cases displayed trophies and hardback volumes I could not identify.

Joanna turned back to me. "Laurent, I'm taking LaFaye into her open N.A. meeting. I strongly advise you to attend that A.A. one there. That's an open meeting in that room to your right."

"Me?" I whispered.

Joanna smiled, then nodded, her eyebrows raised.

"A.A.?" I said.

She nodded once more, and I understood.

"Remember how I first met you. Right? We'll meet you outside here, after," Joanna said, and proceeded with my aunt into the large meeting room.

Inside my meeting, at the edge of the group sat a slender white man in Dickies clothes, staring into his lap with red eyes and a quivering face—he was not sick, but weeping.

A stocky white man in his late fifties, with an aquiline nose and square jaw, sat behind a small table, squinting with a stern glare into the room. He wore a Postal Service cap, but beside his table's small stack of books was a black motorcycle helmet. Even so, he exuded the aura of a senior military officer.

"All right, folks," he said, clearing his throat. "The seven PM meeting of the under-one-year Alcoholics Anonymous group is starting. My name is Peter, and this is an open meeting. I'm serving as your chair today. Please kindly open your Big Book to page 142."

He began to read the passage in a resolute, gravelly voice, but I did not listen. My mind wanted to drift, and I allowed it. Didn't this seem like an extreme move, in itself? Me at an A.A. meeting? But I held on—this was interesting, after all. And what did I have to lose?

Once Peter invited attendees to comment on the passage or to offer their shares, or short testimonies, I began to notice, and feel, something else. Each share revealed a raw vulnerability, an honest, unadulterated self-examination I had never heard in public. It was as if each speaker sat inside a confessional but held nothing back, at times shedding tears, and we were their silent confessors, their priests or ministers. Many speakers revealed a deep spirituality I expected to hear at a religious retreat, or in a seminary.

I felt an affection, even a strong one, for these wounded but courageous people. To admit they had a great vice, and disease, and to combat it publicly and within a disciplined regimen, and then to strive to save others with the same affliction.

That feeling of affection gave way to one of kinship with those around me. I let my shoulder blades rest against the back of my chair and I exhaled, remembering my new friend.

Had this been part of Joanna's plan? I smiled at the stealth, and wisdom, of her strategy.

CHAPTER 30

That following evening, as Jim, Pham, and I departed the Prytania Theatre after the film, I felt that long day's full weight of fatigue pulling me down. Yet some of my days after losing Noelle and Crescent were better than others, and it had been one of those better days.

Despite the burden of this new reality of my shattered business, and my shattered future with Noelle—the glow of hope warmed me as I remembered my sobriety and that of my aunt's, and envisioned Crescent in several months on reopening night. Jim repeated that the single-screen cinema behind us had just celebrated its centennial that year, that in *A Confederacy of Dunces*, John Kennedy Toole had set a great scene in the place, but my mind continued to drift.

Was it just that simple, that with the insurance check now cashed, all Wilson and I needed to do was select the contractors?

"Where to now?" Pham said.

"Jim, can you run me by that gas station down on Tchoup?" I said. "Need to get some bottled water to hold me over for the night."

"No beer, wine, or Scotch?" Jim said. "I forgot about your new regimen. Bravo. Let's go."

We headed south on Jefferson and, once Jim parked his truck near the gas station's entrance, I jumped out.

"Be right back," I said and closed the door.

Once I faced the glass door, it flew open. Two teenagers

burst out, one grasping a small canvas sack. Wasn't the other holding a pistol?

I heard one pop, then two, as I was jerked in a violent arc backward and groundward onto the pavement.

Pain seared through my chest like the thrust of some scalding poker, thin but swift.

More pops sounded as I heard Jim's voice, unlike I'd ever heard it before, "Get down! Get down, damn it!"

I was lying on my stomach when I felt the next thud chased by sharp pain, this time searing and cold all at once, in the meat under my left armpit. How could this be? Why was someone trying to snuff me out, eliminating an eyewitness?

Shots followed, deeper and louder, coming from a few feet away. I glanced upward to an unexpected sight. Jim had drawn a pistol and was firing away.

I heard a car door open, an engine start, and a car backing up and screeching away.

"Get the hell out of here!" Jim screamed. "Call the cops, Pham. He got Laurent!"

Jim was kneeling beside me, his eyes molding into an expression of pity as they searched me. Pham was crouching beside him.

"Where are you hit, Laurent?" Pham said.

I gestured to my armpit, then toward my chest. It burned like some internal fire, just inside my ribcage. The pain grew so sharp I somehow let go and felt this sudden liquid warmth all down my groin and legs. I had urinated on myself.

"Can you move your legs?" Jim said.

Oh God—it could not be—that would mean I would never chef again.

I tried, and felt each leg move beneath me. "Yeah, both of 'em."

"Thank God you're not paralyzed," Jim said. "No waiting for ambulances in New Orleans. Let's get him in the truck bed. I'm driving him to Ochsner."

"Seriously? Are you sure?" Pham said.

"It's just a quarter-mile up St. Charles, Pham," Jim said.

My fatigue was growing. Bleeding out, no doubt, from my chest wound. An arm scooped beneath the backs of my legs and another below my chest.

No, I could not let death come so soon.

"Let's turn him over," Pham said. "Let's get him in the truck bed."

My body turned and in a moment I was in the air, four strong arms and plodding steps moving me further from the spot where I caught the sight of my blood pooling onto the concrete.

I felt my back against the truck bed and Pham and Jim pulled me farther into it. A blanket of warmth covered my chest, but I realized it was my own blood. Jim and Pham squatted beside me.

"Pham, stay here in back with him, please. Whatever you do, don't let him pass out. Apply pressure on these two wounds with your open hands."

"I will, but hurry," Pham said. "You can't wreck."

As the tailgate slammed shut and the truck bed vibrated below my back, I watched Pham's silently weeping face as he unfastened my neckerchief, pressed it with his palm hard against my chest wound, and held it there while pressing on my other wound with his other hand. I had never seen him cry before. My loyal friend, more like a brother, steadfast from the start.

My gaze wandered upwards past Pham as I felt the truck roll backwards, turn, and hurtle forward with great speed. Pham almost toppled backwards from his crouch. He swore, then knelt with both knees onto the truck bed while still applying pressure to my two wounds. Mere moments later, I noticed them above me. *Quercus virginiana*, as Jim would say. The live oak branches drifting past, many dripping with Mardi Gras beads of many colors, as the cloudless blue sky revealed itself every few seconds. It was a fast-forward of that exact image from that recurring dream. My dream from so many nights in the last few months.

It seemed preordained: being shot in a robbery, then hauled away in a truck bed down St. Charles. But I never saw what followed in all those dreams. Is that why nothing ever followed the image of the branches, except taking flight? Because I must slip into the oblivion of death?

I fought with all my might to keep my eyes open, recalling Jim's warning. My body jolted—another New Orleans pothole—but at least it woke me up a bit. I felt it: These were my last moments alive. If only I could live just long enough to re-start Crescent. My ill luck—it had won. My culinary dreams were snuffed out. I would not be there to morally support Aunt LaFaye, Pham and Jim, to thank Wilson, Morrie and Ben, or to help Aunt LaFaye, Mom and Mémère. Cold, dark Death had thwarted me. Its victory was complete.

I closed my eyes, and that is when I saw it. For a fleeting moment I was gazing down at my body, with Pham trying his best to press both of my wounds as the truck bumped and swerved around vehicles. Then came what I recognized from one of my dreams. I was soaring free over my city, perhaps a thousand feet in the air. Except this time, my path over the city was somewhat different. I first saw the Uptown mansions below, bisected by St. Charles with its grassy neutral ground and line of moving streetcars.

I soared southeast over the Irish Channel. Somehow I could see—or I was allowed to see—Mémère at her kitchen table reading her Bible, and Aunt LaFaye gazing out of the window with her hands on her hips, as if she sensed something was wrong. Then I moved eastward over the Warehouse District and saw the corner building holding the remains of Crescent. I swung northward past the old cotton mill-turned-condominiums and corporate high rises and glided low over the Creole cottages and shotgun houses of Mid-City. Mom was seated in her recliner, thinking about her bills. For a moment, I felt my father's memory enter her mind. I did not linger there, but instead was carried southeast over the Tremé. There was Willie Mae's Scotch House; there was Dookie Chase. Both had lines of eager diners outside their doors. I glided south over the French Quarter, right over Royal Street with its revelers and tap dancers, jazz quartets and mimes.

For the first time I could gaze down into the Quarter's hidden courtyards with their moss-covered bricks and French doors, and somehow I now knew the plants within: banana trees, sweet olives, moss-covered brick, jasmine, magnolias, camellias, gardenias.

Farther east I soared, over the Marigny and the Bywater. There was Vaughn's on the corner. For a moment I could see through the roof. Wilson was the lone soul seated at the bar, drinking a glass of whiskey. I could feel how much he missed his wife. I could feel how much he still believed in our dream. Yet I also felt the sheer weight of his despair—nearly suicidal—within me, as if it were my own. Was this what the dead could feel, sense?

My flight continued over the Ninth Ward, with some of its roofs covered by solar panels, and yet there were so many lots where once-flooded houses had been razed. I passed over Arabi and then the grassy field and earthworks of the Chalmette Battlefield and north into New Orleans East, over its small ranch homes and shotgun houses. In moments, Village De L'Est was below, and I passed right over Uncle Minh's house. He and Aunt Tu and Ong Ngoai were digging with spades in the backyard vegetable garden. I could feel Ong Ngoai's pain and loneliness, worse than I ever imagined, enflamed by his haunting memories of Vietnam.

Something changed. I was still flying but enclosed within something. Somehow I knew it was a Huey, and, startled, I looked about. It was packed with Vietnamese civilians and a few American servicemen in green battle fatigues and helmets. Was this *the* helicopter? I turned to my left. Kneeling while bracing himself against the riveted metal wall near the open square door was my father. His fresh-faced youth was the first thing I noted—he was exactly twenty-eight, just as in many of the war photos. And he was watching me. His eyes brimmed with love and pride—but pride in *me*, as a middle-aged Ong Ngoai and his wife huddled beside me. What more could Dad be telling me with that look? Where were we going—to America? I turned and saw Uncle Minh, a mere teen, squatting on the metal floor to my right. Through the open square door, I spotted another Huey alongside us, a couple hundred feet away. In a flash, it exploded into a fireball.

"Hang on! Hang on, hard!" Dad yelled, then repeated the same in French for Ong Ngoai and his wife to tell the others. And then like a rocket we picked up speed, heading out over the dark blue waves, minute after minute, as the riveted metal cabin shook and groaned as if about to come apart. My vision faded to black. Nothingness. Had I perished? Was this the end?

I found myself in St. Louis Cemetery No. 1, yet this was an actual memory. I was but a boy of twelve, and my cousin Champy was sixteen. That overcast afternoon, he had persuaded me to accompany him, and, once there, led me through the rows of white and gray crypts. But it was not the famous crypt of Marie Laveau—the voodoo queen and hairdresser to the wealthy—that Champy sought. He stopped before one that was much taller, wider, and deeper than Laveau's and most of the others. It was one of the few broken into that had yet to be secured, repaired. I waited as Champy activated his flashlight and disappeared past the corroded metal door that was bent near the edge and slightly pried ajar.

As I stood eyeing the dark aperture, I caught in my nose a musty, pungent smell I had never experienced. Like something spoiled, but worse.

"Here it is, cuz," he said, reappearing at last and pulling the door open further. "Already been inside yesterday. Follow me in. Thieves been all through here pretty good. Wait 'til you see what's inside."

"No, no, I can't."

But my protest was futile. Champy grabbed my forearm and tugged me toward the door as my sneakers lost their grip. I began to slide on the pavement, still wet from the rain, toward the opening. I gasped, and then screamed with terror as if I were being pulled from the familiar light of living into the gaping dark maw of death, and the unknown.

CHAPTER 31

Mine was a spiritual experience, if anything, that close brush with death. The floating above my body in the bumping and jerking truck bed as Pham pressed down on my wounds. The soaring above my city, seeing my loved ones where they stood at that moment, fully feeling what they felt. My rocketlike flight over the water. Seeing these two beautiful twins—a boy and a girl—accompanying this thick-set, salt-and-pepper version of me in polyester kitchen whites. The children looked around as we strolled across the Brooklyn Bridge on a barely warm but bright autumn day. Between me and the children was a woman in striking indigo Birkenstock sandals. Her ponytail of gray and blonde hair reached midway down her back. I could not see her face.

Then I heard my mother singing the comical Irish song she used to sing to me as a boy, then Mémère beckoning me back from sleep, singing at my bedside that French hymn her grandmother used to sing to her.

But it was a welcome return, back to the world. When with all my will I began to blink, I had somehow moments before seen Aunt LaFaye weeping in the hallway, there into Mémère's shoulder. Somehow I had hovered near the ceiling of a surgery room down the hall, where a team of nurses and a doctor were fighting to bring a young child back to life. Somehow, without a shadow of a doubt, I knew he had been hit by a delivery truck.

The next realm was a strange and unpredictable place, and

I was not ready for it.

At last, I blinked my eyes open. Nurses were trickling out of the door. To my immediate right, a man in a white lab coat grinned down at me. Peering up at an awkward angle from my bed, all I discerned with my still-blurred vision were large, warm blue eyes and a set of very white teeth.

"I'm Dr. Keith Fontenot. Well done, sir," he said. "You pulled yourself through. Now the body's healing begins. I've heard of your cooking. I want you to respond well to rehab so you can be back in your kitchen in a few months. And I can stop in and eat. Now, some good folks you might recognize are here to see you."

Before I knew it, Mémère and Mom, Aunt LaFaye, Ong Ngoai, Uncle Minh, and Aunt Tu were assembled at my bedside. Mom was hugging Mémère and Aunt LaFaye, and as they pressed themselves together as if to form one body, I caught Aunt LaFaye's muffled weeping and Mémère's reassuring tone. A voice born of eight decades of wisdom from living, and the confidence that comes from deep faith.

It was the first time I'd seen all of the elders gathered since my father's funeral in October 1987. And here in a hospital, no less. I recalled what Ong Ngoai once told me, that upon settling in America, at first Viet families avoided entering American hospitals. They associated white—the color of much of the walls and the medical garb—with death, sorrow, mourning.

Mom stepped forward and clutched my hand. On the other side of my bed, Mémère approached and grabbed my other hand. Something squeezed my right ankle. Standing beside Aunt LaFaye, Ong Ngoai smiled, nodding as if vindicated in some way.

"*Nha ao thuat*," he said in a soft voice. His old nickname for me again—*magician*.

"I'm here, Laurent," Mom said. "I'm here now. And—and—I'm sorry. Sorry for everything, and anything."

"I am sorry, too, Laurent," Uncle Minh said as he stood a few feet behind Mom, beside Aunt Tu.

"I love you, Uncle Minh," I said. "Love all of you."

"I knew you'd be back," Mémère said. "Just knew it in my bones."

"Me, too," Aunt Tu said.

"I didn't. Sorry, Laurent," Aunt LaFaye said through tears.

"Grandson, your aunt's been shaken up good by this news," Mémère said. "But like I said, I knew you'd be fine."

"Why? How?" was all I could say in reply.

"You got too much cookin' to do," Mémère said with a gentle laugh. "Makin' us all proud."

"Yes, Laurent," Mom said. "We are all proud."

"Your dad is proud," Mémère said. "He loved you so much. He would love that you check on me so. And help me and your aunt and mama."

"And that you saved me," Aunt LaFaye said.

"So true," Mémère said. "And you know somethin'?"

"What's that?" I said.

"He would've been at your grand opening," Mémère said. "Well, he was there."

"He'd be happy to see Wilson and our crew," I said. "He'd be impressed by Crescent. Before I lost the place. And my line."

"But the menu was all from you," Mémère said. "Cookin' was overseen by you. You can hire new people. This is still New Orleans."

"Wilson and Pham will stick with me," I said. "If I must hire the others, I will."

"Glad you're not givin' up," Mémère said. "It would crush your friend Wilson. He's out there in the hall. He's lookin' fragile, a walkin' mess already. I'm thinkin' y'all's place is his last hoorah."

"So, we're going down the hall for now, Laurent," Mom said. "So your friends can visit. Then you better get more rest."

They filed out of the room. A familiar face rounded the

corner, then drew near to my side.

"We're so proud of you, Big L," Pham said, his sweatshirt stained with my blood. "Ready for our next adventure. We can do *anything*."

"I love you, brother," I said, smiling.

"I love you, too, Laurent," Pham said. "I did try to keep you alive. As hard as I could. And Jim got us here like he was racing in the Daytona 500."

There was a knock at the door.

Wilson plodded in, his steps sounding tired and mournful as they fell onto the floor. I strained, trying to study his face. The image that came to mind was a child's face, the first moment he had heard his sibling was never coming home, but instead bound for an early grave.

Whether from pure soul or soul mixed with whiskey, tears sparkled in his bloodshot eyes. Within them I was surprised to see an uncharacteristic vulnerability, even something—to use Mémère's term—fragile. The eyes were of a man asphyxiating, as if choking on something mid-throat. There, at the opposite side of my bed from Pham, Wilson started to weep.

"Pham called. I was a couple glasses in, down at Vaughn's," Wilson said. "A friend was nearby, got me here in minutes. There's no place I'd rather be right now—than here."

"You are my friend, Wilson," I said. "Truly."

"I love you more than you can imagine, Laurent," Wilson said. "You turned my life around. You trusted me. You believed in me. I trusted, believed in you. And your dream. This goes beyond the business side of it all. There's a real friendship there."

"I don't doubt you, brother," I said, feeling my own face contort to fight tears. "I feel the same."

Wilson said, "Laurent, beautiful thing is—because of you I don't want to die anymore. I want to live. And do many things."

"Rest up, L," Pham said. "Hey, JaJuan and Brooke and

Roosevelt called. Even Russell Ledoux. They're outside waiting to see you. With Jim and a couple I hadn't met, Joanna and Harlan. It's like a Laurent Ladnier reunion out there."

"We'll be just outside, if you need us," Wilson said as they departed, Pham following a few steps behind due to his clubfoot.

Seconds passed, then minutes. As I lay half-asleep in the hospital bed, the shadows moving in the fog of my imagination began to take clearer form and solidify into matter. Into two restaurants. Wilson, Pham, and I would relaunch Crescent. After a year, maybe two or three, Wilson could have Pham as his lieutenant over Crescent and, if Morrie could still finance it, I could launch and chef at a New York operation. Later, Morrie and I could hire or promote a chef to act in my stead in New York, and after that venture gained stability, I could return to New Orleans. Yes, this would be spectacular. Even so, Crescent reaching its full potential would be enough for me.

My heavy eyelids began to war against me, and I felt sleep return like a warm blanket, heavier by the second. I was near the point of release, of yielding to it entirely—as I had done in the truck bed—when I sensed a presence in the room.

No, please, I thought—no more visions of my dead father in a fleeing Huey. Nothing more to put shock into my system. At the foot of my bed, something stirred, then softly chuckled. Was it Jim, playing a prank?

"*Nha ao thuat.*" The whispered words wafted over my bed like a breeze.

"Ong Ngoai! Ong Ngoai!" I said, fighting to open my eyes. Just beyond my feet he stood, dressed in a bulky coat. After all, every Louisiana winter and early spring was cold to my Ong Ngoai. He was unscrewing something—a thermos.

"I have something for you," Ong Ngoai said. "Something to lift your spirits." He stepped along the side of the bed and drew even with my shoulder.

"Not sake or whiskey, right?" I said.

"Haha, no. *Ca phe trung*," he said. "Remember? Your favorite, as a child. It was your occasional treat."

With mildly tremorous hands, he lifted the thermos to my lips. I was thankful my bed was still set at a slight recline. I shut my eyes. The sweet coffee, warm and rich with condensed milk and raw egg yolk, trickled into my mouth without spillage. I imagined myself as a boy, when Ong Ngoai would often join my father and mother on Christmas Day.

Ong Ngoai pulled back the thermos and paused, looking down at me with anticipation.

"That was wonderful," I said. "It does take me back. I'll take a little more."

I swallowed a few more mouthfuls and nodded. "That's great, enough for me. Thank you so much for thinking of this, Ong Ngoai."

He drank deep from the thermos and then set it down at his feet.

"That is not all," he said with another chuckle and reached inside his breast pocket of his baggy coat. He produced one of his antique kiseru pipes.

I laughed. "Another reason you wore that big coat. I know where you're going with this."

"Just a reminder to heal soon. So you can enjoy such pleasures again on the outside. Outside, in the world again. You will be a great chef again, in a great restaurant. Because you have *tran can cu*."

I remembered the term, a combination of hard work, patience, and the drive to succeed.

"And you have so many more things to accomplish. Your family and I prepared you for it. *An man tra dao—An qua nho ke trong cay*."

How did those two proverbs go again? If one receives a plum, one must return a peach. The following was: When eating a fruit, think of the person who planted the tree. Ha, Ong Ngoai was trying everything, even responsibility and a bit of guilt, to ensure I made it out alive. And that kiseru pipe—I sensed it was another way to motivate me, but more original.

"Ong Ngoai, you intend to pack that bowl and light it up here?"

I studied the face before me, its mischievous smile crackling the weathered skin even further with a crosshatch network of wrinkles. In a way I could see the adolescent within, perhaps my favorite part of the man, a spirit that had not become cynical or tamed in all of eighty-four years. Something told me this was another trait my father had loved.

"If you wanted, we would," he said. "I brought my pouch of kizami. But you can at least imagine you were puffing it again."

"Ong Ngoai, I bet you were hoping there was a window we could crack."

"Of course, that would be wonderful."

"I don't want security booting you out of the building. Then you might not be able to visit for—as long as I'm here."

"It might be worth it," he said with that same grin. "I'd see you when you were released."

I laughed. "You're one of a kind. Such a great mentor and friend. I love you, Ong Ngoai."

I placed the metal stem in my mouth and puffed through the kiseru's empty chamber, imagining I drew real smoke. I handed him the pipe and he stowed it in his breast pocket.

"And you can see I love you, *Nha ao thuat*," he said. "You can see we all do. Now you should rest."

As the door shut, I realized Ong Ngoai had achieved his intention. My spirit rose within me. I was reminded of what I had missed in my travels abroad, what so many of my friends and some of my family represented. That whimsical, hedonic spirit of New Orleans breathing all day and night on the other side of that hospital wall.

CHAPTER 32

L ate morning found me seated in Crescent's dining room, gazing through its newly painted window frame at the street outside. The rays of the late summer sun already beat down with near full intensity, and I was glad to be waiting in the air-conditioning. Running my palms across the side of my chest, I drew in a deep breath. My months of both healing and helping Wilson oversee Crescent's reconstruction were complete. And it was my fortieth birthday. It was apparent, neither Wilson nor anyone on my old line knew. And my friends had forgotten.

Yet I had made it to the last hurdle. I had fought to survive my brush with death, and the city had fought for me: Erik Brauer forgiving those few months of rent during my convalescence, Noelle, Jim, and Ben crowdfunding from their wide networks to help restore Crescent and extinguish my medical bills. Uncle Minh had comped Mémère's grocery and energy bills while I convalesced. And again, I had cast my gamble with the city of my birth, with my community, to stay and fight until Crescent was thriving for at least a couple of years. Now to rebuild my long-dispersed kitchen line. I'd texted and left voicemails for my old staff the day before, with no response.

"Think anyone's gonna show?" Wilson said from the table nearest my back, as he pored over his accounting files.

"At least Pham's a commit," I said. "There will always be Pham. My right arm."

"Our line was shattered," Wilson said. "Tellin' you, they're all settled in at their new gigs."

"One or two are bound to show," I said. "But I get it. Tomorrow I'll put out an ad."

Forty-five minutes passed. My cell dinged in my pocket. A text from Roosevelt, who I hadn't seen since he'd visited me months before in the hospital:

can't ditch my gig at the Grill Room in the Windsor Court
they love me here
sorry L you'll always be my friend
glad u stayed in town comin' to visit y'all soon

The Grill Room in the Windsor Court? Well done, Roosevelt. No doubt his desserts proved a smashing hit at its Sunday brunch.

My spirit sank within me. My dessert virtuoso was gone.

"Roosevelt texted," I said. "Can't pull away from his new job at the Windsor Court."

"No doubt he likes the money there," Wilson said. "But Rosie and I are cut from the same cloth. So, he'll have a heart attack there. But first he'll really shine at that busy Sunday brunch. Nothing I can do now, bud. Might as well just sit here as I sip my whiskey sour. But don't let me tempt you. If I could quit, I would."

I turned as he shuffled over to my table. The sight and smell of the cocktail would not make me succumb. Though one drink would help me forget the spots in the kitchen I had to fill. Two or three drinks would help me forget—for a time—what I had imagined ten thousand times, the last minutes of Claude Ladnier. A thought that would never leave me. But I knew full well a drink would derail me, in the long term, and my focus. While beginning a cycle.

The door squeaked open. Ramón, the star of Bacchanal's outdoor kitchen.

"Laurent?" he said.

"Come on in, Ramón. Great to see you," I said.

"And you, too. Man, you survived hell. The fires of hell torching this place, and then being shot. Heard all about it from Russ Ledoux."

"Yes, the experience wasn't exactly enjoyable," I said. "You still over at Bacchanal?"

"Yes and no. Russell and Chris Rudge and me had a great talk. Explained my interest in innovative types of cooking. That I want to move to more of a 'white tablecloth' venue. They understand. You can call either one of 'em. They encouraged me to check in here. They know it's my top choice. I actually swung by here yesterday, but no one was here."

"Russell visited me in the hospital. Heard about that, Ramón? Terrific human being. Anyway, I've enjoyed your cooking many times, so no demo needed. Ha, were you scared I was going to try to hire you as a *stagiaire*? An unpaid intern, like they have in Europe?"

He smiled.

"You're hired, Ramón. If you're good with working six days a week. Thirty-six hundred bucks a month. Pham's my sous chef, but you'd be close behind, somewhere on the line."

"I'm in," Ramón said with a single clap. "I'm so in."

"Perfect," I said. "Show up Monday morning at eight, ready to get your hands dirty. I think I have just the kitchen whites to fit you. Or I can order you some."

"I'll even be a little early," he said, a blissful smile on his face. "I'm excited."

"I like that. I am, as well, Ramón. And I know Wilson here is, too. He's the owner of this place. But lets me hire my team."

Wilson leaned forward and gave a firm shake of Ramón's hand.

"If he likes you, then I like you," Wilson said. "By the way, put your digits into my phone."

Wilson handed his smartphone to Ramón, who input his number.

"Go rest up now, Ramón," I said. "I'll be calling Russell,

and Chris Rudge, to thank them."

"Understood, and thanks," Ramón said with a wave and crossed the dining room and exited through the door.

Wilson raised his eyebrows with a giddy expression and said, "Now your crew is three, including you. Rebuilding the old empire. You told him show up Monday at eight. You got your old confidence back. That we'll have a line by then."

I said nothing, just resumed my gaze through the front window.

Wilson plodded over to the bar area and began to perform his frequent ritual. A knock sounded behind me. I turned, and the door opened.

Was I hallucinating? Who would have expected Luc Breton, in this place and at this hour?

Adrenaline rushed through my veins as I reeled back in shock, then stood.

"I know I've been banned here, understandably. Let's chat for a minute?"

I bristled inside, but looked closer.

Odd, but his expression seemed to carry a sort of gentle contrition. The eyes were soft and fell toward the floor between us. I'd seen that look in those weighed down by depression, and in others after some personal defeat. After their spirit had been, at least in part, broken.

I felt my resistance melt within me. Something in Breton had turned.

"I'm okay with it," I said. "You, Wilson?"

"Sure," Wilson said. "I'm assuming you'll be more civil this time. Pull up a seat."

Breton sat, and Wilson and I along with him.

"I've been meaning to apologize. I've been a monster to so many people, including you gentlemen. The more I've thought about this place burning and struggling to return, well—I wanted to give my apology and to put my money where my mouth is."

He leaned back in his chair and, reaching into his pocket, produced his wallet.

"I bet at one point," Breton said, "you suspected I torched this place. I could understand that. I wanted to be the best. And I wanted JaJuan back on my staff. But I didn't want you destroyed, man. So Wilson, here's a check written to your LLC. I knew the name, did my research. Please accept this. And this move comes from me. Connaughton didn't put me up to this. That wise ol' angel on my shoulder."

I could not speak, and Wilson did not, either.

Breton chuckled, shaking his head. "Anyway, men, we'll bury the hatchet. I will ply my trade, and you can ply yours. We can coexist in this little food scene."

Wilson took the check, held it in front of his eyes, and said, "You don't have to do this, Luc. Is this check already canceled? Ha. But if you insist, I'll accept. Laurent?"

Wilson handed me the check. Five thousand dollars?

I reached across the table and shook Luc's hand. His grip was neither firm nor soft.

"What a *beau geste*. This is one great gesture, Luc," I said. "We are both doing great things. Food is supposed to be a celebration, right? So, we can celebrate each other and each other's creations. Maybe one day we can grab lunch together somewhere."

Though I meant them, my words sounded odd in my ears. But it was an odd day.

"Agreed," he said. "Good idea."

I thought Breton would stand, and head for the door, but instead he just sat there.

"What's on your mind?" I said.

Breton paused, and cocked his head to the side, in a pensive manner. "I'll share, then. That time in Gerard's dining room, when I complained to his son—you looked deflated, almost humiliated. As if you were weighed down by guilt. I think you realized you probably shouldn't have tested out your ideas on the public without getting permission from your employer. Am I right?"

"Gerard wouldn't have allowed it," I said.

"His son led you around the floor like you were his chastised pupil," Luc said. "It was all there in your eyes. Even though what came out of your mouth was all confidence. Then at Crescent's grand opening, when you threw me out, you seemed artificially inflated. Like you were puffing yourself up, just acting the part of bravado. But I guess you were getting your sea legs on that night with the sheer quality of your cooking, as everyone could tell by the media reaction. The last time I saw you, back at Pal's Lounge, that doesn't count. You and I were both a little drunk. I get it, you were trying to forget the fire. And I was being an ass. And now, look at you—you're a different person."

"Yeah?" I said.

"Poised. With a calm, a peace. Like you've struggled and seen defeat before, even experienced a sort of death, but survived. And ultimately triumphed. You learned that all the greats, if they fight long enough, will taste defeat, here and there. And they can lose everything at any moment. But still they hope, believe they'll succeed. So that's what I see. Well done."

"Wow, Luc," I said. "I'm honored by your words. And I see a new man in you, too. We are dynamic people, right?"

"We are," he said.

"If I might ask," I said, "what provoked the change of heart?"

"It started with hearing of the fire. And not too long after, that you were almost murdered. Eventually that news about your shooting reached me. That it seemed like someone had you and Wilson ruined. I realized you were right about us working in totally different realms of cooking. That we can coexist."

"That's so true," I said, nodding.

"That got me halfway to my new mindset," Luc said. "Then my wife hit her limit. So, I started reconsidering things. She said if I didn't basically get a personality transplant, she was leaving. That cut deep. 'Cause I always loved her. We argued a lot, but I never hit her, never cheated on her."

He paused, looking up at the ceiling as if studying a crack, or a vent, as his eyes started to water. But he cleared his throat and stared down at his hands on the table.

"Yeah, I'm feeling it now," he said. "That guilt that hits me a few times a year. The worst guilt always came after I lashed out from jealousy or frustration in either sabotage or some violent act. Acts so shameful it seemed I was possessed by—some sinister spirit. Though that would negate my responsibility. I knew all these acts—they sprang from this—white-hot cauldron of envy and rivalry in my heart."

His words were astounding, not just for their candor and the introspection they revealed, but for their beauty. And then he continued.

"And it was just so easy for me to mistreat my underlings. Who I knew deep down, due to a combination of fear and true professionalism, never truly slacked off. I'd chosen some of the best in town and molded them further. Like JaJuan. You believe I resented him, but I secretly came to respect him."

"Really?" I said.

"Because he fought for himself and got away from me. He knew his worth."

"I appreciate you, Luc," I said. "I appreciate your honesty. And you were the first person really to notify me of my arrogance. I was bent on achieving glory over the sheer love of cooking I'd always had from the start. I just didn't see it."

"Ladnier, I've been the most arrogant, but thanks. Hey, I'll tell you a dirty little secret. I know a handful of souls in this city who are better chefs than I. You are one. I always thought I could just outwork the bastards. Ha. Or if need be, I'd try to thwart them somehow. Like at Wade's party. Sabotage, some plot, whatever. Many of the greats break the rules. And cheat, at times. I learned this in my years at CIA."

I recalled Luc had attended the Culinary Institute of America, in Hyde Park, New York. My top choice post-NOCCA, but I lacked the funds. And I had to stay close, to help Mom, Mémère, and Aunt LaFaye.

"Anyway, playing dirty," Luc continued, "I preferred winning over just *feeling* I was the best."

Uncanny—he and I shared a few realizations. I was in awe. Breton—my dark doppelganger.

"Still, there are chefs here whose stature can only be equaled," Breton said. "And I cannot *really* surpass them. Paul Prudhomme, John Besh. Emeril Lagasse, Susan Spicer, Donald Link."

Breton chuckled. "Yeah, and Susan might be one the few mentally healthy chefs in the city."

"Quite possibly," I said, smiling.

"I did a lot of looking inward," Breton said, "and a lot of contemplating life, after my wife's ultimatum. I learned what I think you already know: An artist should play clean and just strive to be their personal best, and the best is always subjective. And the artist better have fun along the way. Because life's hard. Unfair. And it's so short. Maybe this helps you understand me more?"

I struggled to reach within and produce the words.

"It—it does," I said. "There's a lot of wisdom there, Luc. I appreciate you."

"We both do," Wilson said.

"Good. I'm grateful for that," Breton said. "One more thing."

He reached into his pants pocket and produced my missing royal blue handkerchief. My favorite from my grandparents. He slid it on the table toward me and I grabbed it.

I could barely speak, but mumbled, "How—did you—"

"I snagged it from Wade's countertop right before you

rushed in and caught me about to habanero-sauce your creation. I was gonna wear it to your opening night around my own neck just to screw with you. But I forgot. Rest assured that sick prank was from the old me."

"Thank you for this," I said.

"Why do you wear those neckerchiefs everywhere, by the way?" he said.

"Ah," I said, smiling. "Long story. Maybe one day I'll divulge."

He rose, and Wilson and I rose along with him.

"Well, I should run back to my own kitchen," Breton said. "Glad I got to see y'all. The hatchet is buried. Six feet under."

"Ha, indeed it is," I said, still stunned. If I could forgive him, remembering how much I'd focused on my culinary dreams over Noelle, I could forgive myself. And if I could forgive myself, I could forgive Luc.

"Thank you, sir, and have a good one," Wilson said, as Luc shook our hands and disappeared through the door.

In silence we sat, staring at the door, then at each other, as I contemplated all the day's oddities and surprises. We began to speak of Luc, of the next festival closing in, of our new hires we'd have to scout.

"Well, how about it?" Wilson said. "We don't have to build out the kitchen much from what we have now. You and Pham, our core. And Ramón. Three."

"We only need three more," I said. "I bet you're running to the bank this afternoon to cash that, right?"

"Your bet's correct," Wilson said with a laugh, and headed toward his office.

Minutes later, a familiar silhouette filled the glass of the front door, which then opened. Wilson had surrendered too soon.

Brooke stepped forward, shutting the door behind her, and stopped at the hostess's podium.

"So, what's with all the yellow roses?"

She motioned to the table along the wall.

I drew in a profound breath.

"Oh, those. Yellow roses, signifying friendship. Remember my ex, Noelle? Now out in L.A.? She sent me those. After crowdfunding so much to save me, my grandmother and this place, this dream. Noelle will always be a great friend."

"Wow, wonderful. And I always liked her fabulous voice," she said, then continued forward and embraced me.

"God, I was hoping I'd see you," I said, allowing my head to fall onto her shoulder, catching the scent of sage fused with eucalyptus. Classic Brooke. Incense, with some organic body lotion, was my guess.

"I was hoping I'd see *you*, handsome. No offense, Laurent, but you look so much better than you did in that hospital bed. Anywho, I'm in. I wouldn't miss this chance for the world. To finish what we all started in that kitchen."

"I wouldn't miss it either," I said, shaking my head. Brooke was lovely. More than I'd ever noticed before. I took a deep breath—she was giving me that look. Those large hazel eyes brimmed with both adoration and desire. Or was this just in my head? But she had uttered the word *handsome*.

But I could not cross that line if she was to work in my kitchen. My eyes drifted floorward. I felt deflated. It could have been wondrous, Brooke and I together. And then I spotted them: those striking indigo Birkenstocks from my hospital vision I'd never shared with a single soul. The graying blonde walking beside me and our children as we crossed the Brooklyn Bridge.

It was the first time I'd seen Brooke wearing any footwear besides kitchen clogs or faded black Converse Chuck Taylors.

I remembered what Mémère often said: *Amazing things are about to unfold, and God loves us.*

Brooke was returning to my kitchen line. I considered my code, still unbroken after all this time. But was not Oscar

Wilde correct, that rules were meant for breaking?

"I'm taking you to dinner soon, Brooke. Just us. A surprise venue."

"Oh?" she said. "That would be very nice. I've been hoping for that."

She embraced me and then pulled backward, smiling upward into my face. This was sublime.

"I've got to get going somewhere, but when should I be here? For work?"

"Monday at eight. At least for a test run. We'll have at least four, including me. But I'll call you before that. Remember, dinner?"

She giggled and headed for the door. "I'll look for that call."

And once again it was just Wilson and me. We sat talking for what seemed like an hour about tweaks to the menu and decor, and how far we'd come since that chance first meeting in early January. The light through the blinds began to dim. Dusk was approaching. An odd day, but a great one. It wasn't the worst footing—we were still down, but rising, and my crazy kitchen would see its resurgence. We were already at four. I needed one more on my line, though I could really use two. I knew I would get them soon.

"Say, Laurent," Wilson said. "Could you do me a favor? My back's been killing me, so I can't do it, but can you head back to my office and bring those boxes of wine from the back room and stack them in my office? There are about ten of them. Long story, I know."

"Well, sure," I said, befuddled. "You gonna start downing all that wine in your office in coming days?"

I laughed, but he just stared at the table. "Not that. But long story, like I said."

I was carrying them, one by one, to the office, and stacking them against the wall when I heard Wilson plodding around in the dining room. I was on the fourth box when I heard him open the front door, perhaps to pop a smoke out-side. I hauled in the fifth, then the sixth, and the seventh. Into the office I walked with the eighth when I heard foot-steps, a sort of gasp, and a muffled laugh. I headed out of the office and down the hall as I collided with my hunch as to Wilson's scheme. Grinning, I shook my head. I was indeed blessed, beyond measure.

"Surprise!" The word erupted in a volley from the beaming faces spread out among the tables.

"Happy biiiirthdaaaay too youuuu," they started to sing.

Mémère, Mom, and Aunt LaFaye stood near the yellow roses.

Aunt LaFaye produced a faint smile but seemed on the verge of tears. It was as if she, suddenly weary, had paused for breath in her sprint through the last few months. She looked vulnerable, even defenseless, as she lowered her gaze, but I knew better. This was Aunt LaFaye reborn and triumphant: completing all twelve Narcotics Anonymous steps at break-neck speed and even bringing two women into the program as their sponsor.

My gaze shifted to Mémère, just as her eyes caught mine. A nostalgia marked her tender smile, as if she were in reverie.

Ong Ngoai, Uncle Minh, Aunt Tu, and Mai clustered mere feet away. Pham stood beside Wilson, JaJuan, Brooke, Osvaldo, Roosevelt, and Jim.

I stood immobile, basking in the glow from their broad smiles and fervent singing. Roosevelt approached me and leaned down toward my ear. "Brooke tells me she'll be here Monday at eight. I'll be here at seven. I was just joking about staying onboard at the Windsor Court, silly."

"You scored a *pâtissier* spot at the Windsor Court and you're giving that up for us?"

"Clearly," he said.

"I love you, Roosevelt!" I shouted, grabbing him in a tight embrace, then tried to lift him upward—to no avail. I felt the strain in my back and stopped.

Roosevelt squeezed me back, then JaJuan joined in.

"Big L, now I can quit temping," JaJuan said. "All those temp jobs, and none in kitchens. I'm here Monday morning."

"Amazing!" I shouted. "Can this be real?"

"It is," Pham said, then screamed, "We did it, L!"

With wet eyes, he swept in for a hug, followed by Jim, Brooke, and Osvaldo.

Ong Ngoai was waiting just beside me for his turn. I turned and leaned down, and as I held Ong Ngoai about the shoulders, I sensed my father's presence somewhere nearby.

But where was Wilson? I grinned as the old funk music burst from his stereo, flowing all around us.

Forty was not exactly unsavory, after all. I sensed forty-one would hold even greater triumph, and joy.

ACKNOWLEDGMENTS

Many thanks to Jenny Wall, Sandra Wall, Tiffany Yates Martin, Jack Kaulfus, Gracie Meadows, Alex Kale, Ronaldo Alves, Felipe Betim, Mario Major, Chris Beale, Dakota Reed, Chef Kevin "The Twang Man" Ayestas, Chef Michael Gulotta of Maypop (and MoPho), Tom Gilliland of Fonda San Miguel, Jennifer Costello of The Bonneville, Argyle Wolf-Knapp of Commander's Palace, Benjamin at The Rusty Nail, Kris Adkins, Addie Hauber, and Kasey Pierce of Barley Swine, Doug West of Vino Vino, Freddy Lee of Michi Ramen, Chef Iliana De la Vega of El Naranjo, Evelynn Martinsen of Tommy's Cuisine, Chef Blakely Kymen and Steve Wood of Marcello's, Tyler Nguyen, Britta Jensen, and Becka Oliver.

ABOUT THE AUTHOR

A New Orleans native, **CHADWICK WALL** is the author of three novels: *Water Lessons* (2014), *The Second Cortez* (2018), which was named finalist in the 2018 Red City Review Book Awards for General Fiction, and now *The Fertile Crescent* (2025). He has written for *The Baton Rouge Advocate*, *The Times-Picayune/The New Orleans Advocate*, and Austin.com. A resident of Austin for a decade, he now lives in the greater Houston area with his wife and two sons.